A Summer in Brighton

Jann Rowland & Lelia Eye

One Good Sonnet Publishing

A SUMMER IN BRIGHTON

Copyright © 2014 Jann Rowland & Lelia Eye

Published by One Good Sonnet Publishing

ISBN: 0992000084
ISBN-13: 978-0992000080

Dedicated to our spouses and children,
the inspiration for our perspiration.

ACKNOWLEDGEMENTS

An effort to write is always for naught
Unless there is someone to write for.
So thanks to our family for helping allot
Time for us to slave evermore
Even through the long nights —
None of it matters without you in sight.

"The first week of their return was soon gone. The second began. It was the last of the regiment's stay in Meryton, and all the young ladies in the neighbourhood were drooping apace. The dejection was almost universal. The elder Miss Bennets alone were still able to eat, drink, and sleep, and pursue the usual course of their employments. Very frequently were they reproached for this insensibility by Kitty and Lydia, whose own misery was extreme, and who could not comprehend such hard-heartedness in any of the family."

Pride and Prejudice, *Chapter 41*

Chapter I

While Lydia and Kitty continued to bemoan their fates, speaking incessantly about redcoats, Brighton, their father's intractability, and anything else which crossed their minds, Elizabeth looked upon the situation they were facing with a philosophical turn of mind. The regiment was leaving—and with it, Mr. Wickham—and she welcomed the return of the peace and quiet they had enjoyed before the militia had so completely upset the balance of their lives. It was, therefore, a surprise to be invited to Brighton herself.

Since the previous winter, Elizabeth had made the acquaintance of the new wife of the colonel of the regiment. Mrs. Forster was a woman only a little younger than Elizabeth, and in her, Elizabeth found a bright and enthusiastic young lady who looked up to her in the manner of an elder sister. Their first few meetings had resulted in several interesting tête-à-têtes, allowing a confidence to grow between them which had become a most delightful friendship. And though Lydia had apparently attempted to ingratiate herself with the young woman while Elizabeth had been away in Kent, Elizabeth had resumed her friendship with Harriet upon her return as if they had never parted.

Still, close though they had become, Elizabeth had not expected an invitation to stay with Harriet in Brighton, and for a time, she had thought of refusing despite her desire to continue her acquaintance with her new friend. She *had* just returned from one extended trip, after all, and while the tranquility of Brighton was alluring, she also felt a strong desire to avoid Mr. Wickham.

However, her subsequent discussions with Mrs. Forster convinced her to accept the invitation. The woman was a sensible companion, after all, and regardless of Lydia's fanciful imaginings of never-ending balls and parties, Elizabeth knew that she would not necessarily be required to be in the company of the officers with excessive regularity. Besides, the opportunity to visit new locales and meet new people was too enticing to pass up. Though she hated to acknowledge it—even to herself—Elizabeth was also aware that the ability to avoid the trip to the North Country with her aunt and uncle was a motivation which weighed upon her mind.

Now, it must not be said that she wished to shun her relatives, for nothing could be further from the truth. No, it was the fact that due to important business on Mr. Gardiner's part cutting short the length of their northern tour, they would be spending time in *his* county and staying very close to Pemberley itself! Given the unpleasant scene at Hunsford and the way she had misjudged Mr. Darcy, Elizabeth was eager to avoid any further meeting with him until she had settled her own feelings. She did not think it *likely* that she would meet him, for surely Derbyshire was a large county, but Brighton appeared to be a much safer option.

The reaction of her family upon hearing the news was predictable, with the loudest opinion being voiced by her youngest sister.

"But Mama, it is so unfair!" exclaimed Lydia the evening the invitation came to light. "Lizzy gets all the amusement, and the rest of us have none! *She* went to Kent. *She* has been invited to Brighton! I am Mrs. Forster's friend and have as much right to be invited as she does. Why can I not go?"

Lydia's petulant whine was echoed by her sister Kitty, who sported an identical expression of frustration upon her face.

"Shall I point out the fact that Mrs. Forster has not invited you?" queried Elizabeth.

"Oh, hush child," snapped Mrs. Bennet. "Lydia merely speaks the truth; *you* have had more than your fair share of amusement. I believe we should send Lydia in your place."

"And how do you propose to do that, Mrs. Bennet?" interrupted the voice of her husband. "For Lydia has not been invited, and Lizzy has, though I must own that I am loath to part with my Lizzy again so soon after her return." This last he said with a smile at Elizabeth, which she returned with equal affection.

"I am sure Mrs. Forster will be vastly pleased to modify the invitation for our Lydia," said Mrs. Bennet. "She is so close to our youngest after all."

Elizabeth knew Mrs. Bennet to be overstating the level of friendship subsisting between Lydia and Mrs. Forster, if her words were not indeed an outright falsehood. Harriet had told her in confidence that she considered Lydia to be a shameless flirt, and Elizabeth suspected that regardless of her mother's schemes and whether or not Elizabeth was ultimately allowed to spend the summer in Brighton, no such invitation would be extended to Lydia.

This new proposal by the Bennet matron was not agreeable to one of her other daughters.

"But Mama!" protested Kitty. "*I* am as close to Harriet as Lydia, and I have even more right to go, as I am *two years older!*"

"Nonsense, Kitty!" cried Mrs. Bennet. "I am sure you cannot truly appreciate a trip to Brighton, as you are not nearly so handsome as Lydia nor so agreeable in company. I should think it would be better for you to join your aunt and uncle on their trip to the North Country. Yes, that would do very well indeed. You, Kitty, should go with your aunt and uncle, while Lydia should go to Brighton!"

"Mrs. Bennet, that will be enough," said Mr. Bennet quite firmly. "You will not impose upon either the Forsters or the Gardiners in such a manner."

"But Mr. Bennet—"

"No, Mrs. Bennet, I have heard enough!" said her husband, rising from the dinner table. "There will be no further discussion of this matter. If Elizabeth so desires, she shall accompany the Forsters to Brighton, and if the Gardiners wish to take one of our other daughters, then they shall choose which one."

Mr. Bennet then left the room, surprising them all. Rarely had he raised his voice in the past; he was generally more disposed to laugh at his wife's excesses than to be angered by them. Something in his wife's manner—whether it was her insistence on challenging him or the impropriety of her plans—had apparently touched a nerve.

With a huff and a glare at Elizabeth, Mrs. Bennet threw down her napkin and stalked from the room in high dudgeon. After a moment, Lydia followed her mother's example, but not before leaving a parting shot directed at her elder sister:

"You are very selfish, Lizzy, to be keeping such amusements to yourself. It is not as if *you* could attract anyone other than Mr. Collins to be your husband."

And with that, she flounced off. The sound of her stomping up the stairs and a louder noise of the door slamming as she entered her room echoed back down to the parlor in her wake.

"I do not know what shall be done with Lydia," commented Mary. Her voice contained the familiar superior quality she used when she was trying make a point. "As the great Dr. Fordyce has said, 'Remember how tender a thing a woman's reputation is, how hard to preserve, and when lost how impossible to recover; how frail many, and how dangerous most, of the gifts you have received; and what shame has often been occasioned by abusing them!' I am truly afraid that Lydia, in her shameless flirting and insistence on exposing herself in every forum, shall lose that which is most precious."

Mary then continued to eat her dinner, unconcerned and seemingly forgetting the words which she had just spoken. And Elizabeth, though by now her middle sister's tone of voice and overly self-righteous words caused to her to almost automatically roll her eyes, could only agree with what had been said. Lydia required a firm hand to check her behavior, lest she expose the entire family to the severest of censure.

"Lizzy," began Kitty hesitantly, "I . . . I wish to apologize for my behavior."

Elizabeth stared at her, wondering if this were truly Kitty she was seeing before her.

"I should not have spoken so," continued the girl, visibly screwing up her courage. "I should not follow Lydia as I do, but it is difficult. Mama and Papa have no time to spare for me, and you and Jane are so much older and immersed in your own concerns. I know I should not behave in such a manner, but Lydia *can* be great fun, and I *do* so enjoy spending time with a sister."

In a moment of clarity, Elizabeth suddenly understood Kitty. Mary was usually considered to be the forgotten Bennet sister, and much was made of her lack of beauty and her ability to moralize with little provocation. But Kitty was every bit as forgotten as Mary. It could not be easy living in Lydia's ebullient shadow, especially since Kitty rarely received any notice from her parents.

Clearly, Elizabeth had been remiss in her conduct, particularly where it concerned her younger sisters. Kitty was starved for attention, and Mary was made to feel inferior to the rest of the family. They both could use some guidance from their elder sisters, for they would certainly not receive it from their parents. Neither Kitty nor Mary was beyond assistance, as she feared Lydia was rapidly becoming.

She shared a glance with Jane — who had clearly come to the same conclusion — and turned her attention back to Kitty, who was staring down at her plate, her cheeks flushed with embarrassment.

"I thank you for your apology, Kitty, but I believe I owe one to you as well."

Kitty's eyes rose to meet Elizabeth's, marking her surprise, and Elizabeth could also feel Mary's expressionless gaze upon her.

"In fact, I believe I owe both you and Mary an apology. I have not given either of you the guidance of an older sister as I should have. I have been as remiss as Mama and Papa, and for that, I apologize. Perhaps I should not have agreed to this trip. Perhaps I should — "

"No, Lizzy," cut in Jane. "You should go to Brighton. I know you enjoy spending time with Mrs. Forster." The look in Jane's eyes made Elizabeth wonder if her sister knew something of her desire to avoid seeing Mr. Darcy. "Maybe our aunt and uncle will take either Mary or Kitty with them. I shall remain here. Perhaps I can reason with Lydia."

Elizabeth looked at her sister. She knew the Gardiners would enjoy having Jane with them, but it was true that at least one sensible sister should remain with the Bennet daughters who did not go. It seemed particularly important now that Elizabeth and Jane had realized the need to give Mary and Kitty guidance.

After what had happened with Mr. Bingley, it might be beneficial for Jane to leave Hertfordshire once more. Yet Elizabeth wondered if Jane still held on to the vain hope that Mr. Bingley would return and that all would be well. She knew otherwise, but she could not bear to hurt her sister by imparting her knowledge of Mr. Darcy's interference. If Jane were to learn the truth, it would only bring pain. Should Jane somehow be reunited with Bingley, however, then he could tell her the whole of it. But if he was not to return, then there was no good to be found in divulging the secret.

As for the possibility that Jane would be able to curb Lydia's behavior, well, Elizabeth doubted that there would be any success on that front. But Jane could certainly provide support to Mary and Kitty. Perhaps it was not too late to extract Kitty from Lydia's yoke, and perhaps Mary could move from moralizing to holding slightly more lively conversation. Elizabeth and Jane had shared confidences to the exclusion of their younger sisters, and that needed to be remedied.

It could be that the parting was indeed necessary. Elizabeth smiled at her sisters. "Very well. I shall go to Brighton. But I am not going for the chance to pursue men in red coats. I fancy I have seen enough of their kind for a lifetime."

"You must tell us all about it when you return, Lizzy!" said Kitty eagerly. "I understand the sea bathing there is splendid!"

"I shall tell you all about it, Kitty, provided that you mind Jane while I am gone and try not to follow Lydia when she misbehaves."

"If Mama convinces Papa to let Lydia go to Brighton, do you think she will let me go, too?"

Elizabeth raised an eyebrow. "I am fairly certain Papa has already made his final decision on that subject, Kitty."

Kitty sighed, looking downcast. "I wish I had been invited to Brighton."

"You have enough time for adventures yet," said Elizabeth gently. "In a few years, I am certain we shall be begging to hear tales of your travels."

Kitty smiled. "Thank you, Lizzy."

Elizabeth turned slightly. "Mary, I was playing the pianoforte, and I seem to be having great difficulty with the fingering of a run. Would you perhaps be able to assist me?"

Mary hesitated. Perhaps Elizabeth was not being subtle in the least, but at last Mary agreed that she would be pleased to help her sister with the instrument.

Jane smiled warmly and caught Elizabeth's eye. Elizabeth smiled back at her.

Their actions were belated, to be sure, but at last they were working to improve the situation with their younger sisters.

The trip to Brighton was affirmed to Harriet Forster, and Elizabeth began to ready herself for her upcoming departure. She was not allowed to do so in complete peace, however.

Considering Lydia's love of redcoats, Elizabeth was not surprised that Mrs. Bennet invited several of the officers to dine at Longbourn, but she was less than pleased to learn that Mr. Wickham was among them. She had read Mr. Darcy's letter so many times that his accusations toward the officer had become almost tangible to her, and she was agitated at the thought of being in the same room with Mr. Wickham. She should have been more aware of the impropriety of Mr. Wickham's leveling harsh accusations at Mr. Darcy to such a new acquaintance as she had been. Mr. Wickham had fed on her prejudices, and that did not sit well with her.

Upon first seeing her at the dinner, Mr. Wickham smiled at

Elizabeth, but he was not able to speak with her until the party had gathered in the drawing room after the meal.

"Miss Bennet," said he when at last he had managed to reach her.

"Mr. Wickham," returned she.

"I trust you are well?"

"Indeed, I am."

"You certainly appear well," said he softly. He was gazing at her with a gleam in his eyes and a slight smile on his lips.

Feeling uncomfortable with the way he was looking at her, she endeavored to change the subject. "I am still tired due to my journey back to Hertfordshire, but I am certain I will be recovering soon. I feel I must mention, however, that I saw some mutual acquaintances of ours in Kent. Both Mr. Darcy and his cousin Colonel Fitzwilliam spent three weeks at Rosings. I assume you are acquainted with Colonel Fitzwilliam?"

The surprise—and perhaps displeasure—on his face was easy to mark, but he quickly recovered himself and gave her a smile. "Why, yes, I have met Colonel Fitzwilliam many times before. He has always struck me as a fine gentleman. Do you agree, Miss Bennet?"

Her own smile was one of genuine affection as she thought of the man. "Yes, I do. Colonel Fitzwilliam seems to be a very honorable fellow, and he is a fine conversation partner."

"He is certainly amiable," said Mr. Wickham in agreement. "I believe he is a much more pleasant conversation partner than his cousin. Did you see Mr. Darcy often while you were in Kent?"

"I saw him nearly every day. My cousin, Mr. Collins, is his aunt's parson, and she was generous enough to extend several invitations for us to visit Rosings."

"That must have been unpleasant to see Darcy so frequently."

"Not at all," said Elizabeth. "In furthering my acquaintance with him, I have discovered that he is not actually unpleasant at all."

"Surely we speak not of the same Mr. Darcy!" cried Mr. Wickham in surprise. Then, lowering his voice, he added: "Has he changed his foul countenance to one that is actually pleasant to look upon? I dare not hope he has changed quite so drastically."

"He is still taciturn, but I would certainly not call his countenance 'foul,'" said Elizabeth, her tone somewhat reproachful. "He has been kind enough to me, and I dare say I do not dislike meeting with him."

"Kind?" echoed Mr. Wickham. He seemed surprised, but his expression soon became almost thoughtful. "Well, if he is indeed improving himself, then I am glad of that. His pride might not be so easily wiped away, however. I fear it has been part of his character for far too long."

Elizabeth stared at him for a few seconds. There had been something strange about the thoughtfulness of his expression. Was he merely considering whether Mr. Darcy truly could have changed? Or had something else captured his interest?

"Mr. Wickham," said a voice near them.

Startled at the sudden intrusion, Elizabeth turned to find Harriet Forster standing near them. The sight of her brought Elizabeth a sense of relief, and she could not help but regard her warmly.

"Are you trying to steal away my dear friend for the evening?" asked Harriet.

Mr. Wickham smiled at her. "Can I be blamed if I wish to have Miss Bennet to myself?"

"Well, do not worry, Mr. Wickham. She will be traveling to Brighton with me as my companion, so you shall see plenty of her in the future."

Such a statement made Elizabeth fight to hide a grimace, but Harriet did not know that Elizabeth was planning to avoid the officers as much as possible during her trip to Brighton. But even had she not heard such unfavorable accounts of Mr. Wickham, she would still have felt irked at the man's attempts to renew his attentions to her when he had not long before transferred his affections from her to another woman for primarily pecuniary reasons.

Mr. Wickham, looking pleased at Harriet's revelation, said: "You will be going to Brighton? That is good news indeed."

"I have heard much of the circulating libraries there," said Elizabeth, "and I am eager to see them for myself."

"Well, I hope they live up to your expectations," said Mr. Wickham. "I know your love of books."

"I hope you will not be reading the whole time," teased Harriet. "You must spend at least *some* time walking alongside the sea with me!"

Elizabeth smiled and told her friend: "You know I cannot turn down the chance to look upon the beauties of nature."

"Yes, indeed," said Mr. Wickham, "Miss Bennet is the greatest walker I have ever seen."

"The Good Lord gave us two legs and two eyes, and I intend to use them both to the fullest."

"Well, He also gave you a mouth," said Harriet playfully, "and I shall expect you to use yours to entertain me with your delightful conversation."

"Only if you promise to use your ears. Sometimes you are so caught up in your thoughts that you do not listen to a word I say!"

"How unkind!" cried Harriet. But she was beaming with good humor. "I hang on your every word!"

"Your wit enthralls all your listeners," said Mr. Wickham. "Surely you are aware of this, Miss Bennet?"

Elizabeth raised an eyebrow. "Suddenly, everyone seems keen on stoking my vanity. You must beware what might happen — I may attain such an opinion of myself as to render me most disagreeable and conceited. I do not believe you should all favor me as well then."

"Nonsense, Elizabeth," contradicted Harriet. "I do not doubt it is beyond your power to appear anything other than lovely and agreeable."

"I concur," murmured Mr. Wickham. He appeared to be easy and friendly in company, but Elizabeth fancied she could see something in his eyes which prevented her from feeling completely comfortable. Perhaps she should not have made light of his opinion of Mr. Darcy after all.

"Be that as it may, I fear I must steal my dear friend away from you, Mr. Wickham," said Harriet.

"Of course, Mrs. Forster," replied the man with an extravagant bow.

Elizabeth was led away by her friend, but she could not help but be aware of the uncomfortable sensation of Mr. Wickham's eyes following her.

The final days before Elizabeth's departure passed in a largely uneventful manner. Elizabeth, reflecting that packing her trunk for an extended journey was not nearly as agreeable as the journey itself, nevertheless threw herself into her preparations, acutely aware of the fact that she had only recently been overseeing the unpacking of her belongings.

Life at Longbourn continued to be somewhat strained, with an atmosphere of discord present anytime Elizabeth was in the room with Mrs. Bennet or Lydia. Her father kept to his bookroom with a greater frequency than usual, while her mother continually complained of his hard-heartedness and determination to ruin them all by not taking them to Brighton for the summer. The constant cacophony that this behavior caused undoubtedly contributed to Mr. Bennet's aversion to any sort of company.

When Mrs. Bennet was not protesting her inability to persuade her husband to change his mind about a family trip to Brighton, she was berating Elizabeth for selfishly ruining Lydia's happiness. As for Lydia herself, she was as incensed as her mother over Elizabeth's good fortune, and while she complained just as loud and long as Mrs. Bennet, she added more to the tense atmosphere of the home by directing dark looks whenever she felt Elizabeth was not looking (and often even when she was). Lydia's mood took a turn for the worse when word came from Cheapside that the Gardiners were quite willing to take one of the other girls with them on a tour of Derbyshire now that Elizabeth had another engagement. Jane and Mary were to stay home at Longbourn and watch the Gardiner children, so it came down to Kitty or Lydia. And since Lydia had, unbeknownst to her, been removed from consideration by previous arrangement between the eldest sisters and the Gardiners, an invitation arrived for Kitty to accompany them.

After *that* piece of news had been imparted to the youngest Bennet sister, her fury had known no bounds, and the inhabitants of Longbourn were allowed no respite from her loud accusations, her bitter wailings, and her unending complaints over the unfairness of it all. Elizabeth knew that Lydia had no interest in the tour—for Lydia had deemed it "dreary" and "a tedious affair"—but was angry solely because Kitty was being allowed an amusement that she herself was denied. Such was the selfish nature of the youngest Bennet daughter.

It had finally taken the emergence of Mr. Bennet from his bookroom—no doubt due to the fact that Lydia was interrupting his solitary time with his books—to reassert control over the wayward girl. When his demands for her immediate cessation of her tantrum had no effect, Lydia was sent to her room and instructed to remain there until she could behave as a young lady rather than a spoiled child. It had taken her more than a full day to emerge, and even after she had done so, her sullen expressions of reproach and her injured air ensured that she remained quiet for much longer. All her family bore her silence quite well indeed.

As for her other sisters, though it was early in their tutelage concerning the proper behavior of young ladies, the manner in which Kitty and Mary appeared to grow and the way in which they listened and obeyed their elder sisters heartened both Elizabeth and Jane. Though the two girls still had a long road ahead of them, their transformation had begun.

The last few days in Hertfordshire were also a time for Elizabeth to be out and in company, for there were many farewell gatherings for militia hosted by the families of the area, and invariably, the Bennets were invited to these parties. And though the opportunity to be in the company of good friends was welcome after her recent visit to Kent, a part of Elizabeth wished to stay home and spend time with her family in order to fortify herself for the coming separation, which she knew would be of several months' duration.

She *was* able to see Mrs. Forster several times, and she was happy that they continued to interact with one another in a manner which could only be deemed intimate. She truly was anticipating the next several months in Harriet's company, and some part of her was impatient to be gone.

As for the officers, although there were definitely good men among them—Lieutenant Denny, for instance, was particularly well-liked in Meryton—she was, for the most part, indifferent to them.

Of course, these feelings of indifference did not include Mr. Wickham, who caused a large number of emotions to well up within her all by himself. Elizabeth was aware of her prior preference, and although she had conquered such a sentiment some time previously, she could not help but remember their long conversations and his intelligent manner of speaking and gentlemanlike conduct. And while she did not for one moment discount Mr. Darcy's narrative of what had passed between them, a part of her longed for the simpler days when she had hated the one man and liked the other. She did hope, however, that though Wickham had behaved in an infamous manner toward Darcy in the past, he was now on the road to repentance and a repudiation of his former lifestyle. If only he had not imposed upon her with his falsehoods regarding Mr. Darcy, then she might have been able to believe it!

Her ill feelings toward Mr. Wickham only seemed supported by the fact that since her return from Kent—and incidentally, Mary King's sudden removal from Meryton—his attention appeared to be once again firmly fixed upon her, as if he believed her empty-headed enough to forget that he had abandoned his admiration of her for the money of another. More than once, she was left gnashing her teeth in frustration and almost reconsidering her decision to subject herself to several more months during which she would be in close proximity to the regiment of which he was a member.

Chapter II

*F*inally, the day arrived when Elizabeth was to begin her journey to Brighton. The morning dawned as fine as any she had yet seen, and while she stowed the last few items in her reticule, she reflected on the great pleasure of traveling on such a beautiful day, even if the journey were certain to be long and tedious.

When all had been made ready, she stepped from the house and, seeing her trunk already secured to the back of the carriage, turned to bid farewell to her family.

Lydia had declined to make an appearance — which did not surprise Elizabeth in the slightest — but Mrs. Bennet was waiting for her, if somewhat unwillingly. Elizabeth was well aware that her mother would have eschewed her leave-taking if it had been possible, but Mr. Bennet had exerted control over his wife, insisting that she be present. Mrs. Bennet's absence would undoubtedly have led to gossip, so although she did not say a word and glared at Elizabeth with an injured air, Elizabeth was glad to see her. The farewells of her other sisters and her father more than made up for the lack of any well wishes from her mother.

"I shall miss you, Lizzy," said a teary-eyed Jane, even as she engulfed Elizabeth in a fierce embrace. "We have had so little time together these past months, as one — or both — of us has been almost constantly absent from Longbourn. Please keep a record of your adventures in Brighton, so that you may give me a full accounting upon your return."

"I will, Jane," whispered Elizabeth, returning her sister's hug with equal fervor. "I shall miss you, too, and I promise to write as often as I can."

Kitty and Mary said farewell in a much more sedate manner, yet though they were not as effusive in their comments, Elizabeth could sense that they would miss her. She certainly had not felt any such thing when she had left for Kent, and she was able to revel in the changed feelings which subsisted between herself and her younger sisters.

Mr. Bennet was perhaps the hardest farewell, for Elizabeth knew that her father not only doted upon her, but also counted on her to be his intellectual partner and his source of sanity in the house where his wife and youngest daughter were by far the most vocal and silliest of its inhabitants.

"Off again, are we, Lizzy?" said he with an understated melancholy present in his voice. "I am glad that you take so much comfort in flittering from here to there, seeking after amusement. I hope you think on me from time to time, stuck in this house with talk of lace and finery and with a bevy of the Gardiners' children about to descend upon me."

"Papa, I should think you know that I am not such an uncaring daughter as you speak of," said Elizabeth with a fond smile. "You know very well that I shall be glad for Harriet's company and could not disappoint her when she invited me."

"Indeed, you could not," agreed Mr. Bennet. "You appear to have become quite the popular girl, for the number of invitations you have garnered in such a short time is impressive indeed."

Elizabeth smiled warmly at him. "I shall miss talking to you, Papa."

"Not as much as *I* shall miss *your* company, I can assure you. *You* will be able to escape the constant complaints and loud moans of your youngest sister, whereas I shall experience no such good fortune. Perhaps I should accompany you to Brighton, Lizzy. I am certain I could find a way to entertain myself there."

"Now, Papa, we both know you would not be content away from your own library. Why, wherever would you go to escape the society of others without it?"

He chuckled and nodded. "Quite right, Lizzy. I am afraid I am much too attached to my book-room to leave it behind. As a sanctuary, it has done me well, though I might like it better if it also shut out the voices which are often raised in a high pitch throughout the house." His eyes moved to look at the carriage. The horses were shifting in place, eager to be off. "Are you certain you have packed enough feminine frivolities for your trip? I expect you to return from Brighton with at least one suitor in tow, so you will have need of them."

"Papa!" exclaimed Elizabeth.

"No, I am serious, Lizzy," said he, the teasing look in his eyes belying his words. "You have already made the acquaintance of the officers, and you will be familiar company to them in Brighton. Familiar company is always appreciated, and pleasant familiar company is appreciated in particular. Why, I should not be surprised if you came back with a handful of suitors at your back clamoring for your hand."

"I have no plans to search for a husband, Papa," said Elizabeth firmly. In fact, she wanted to *escape* the thought of marriage for a time, as it made her remember, with no small measure of guilt, the letter she had received in which Mr. Darcy explained his actions regarding Mr. Wickham. "I wish merely to relax."

"Well, we shall see," said he with a chuckle. "I know how young women enjoy being crossed in love from time to time."

Elizabeth shook her head, though she smiled affectionately at her father. "Goodbye, Papa."

"Goodbye, Lizzy," returned Mr. Bennet. "You must not forget to write. You know your wit acts a balm for your old father."

After a few more words of farewell, Mr. Bennet helped his daughter into the carriage. Harriet Forster was waiting inside, not wanting to intrude upon the intimacy of Elizabeth's parting. Colonel Forster was to travel with his men, so Harriet and Elizabeth would travel without him. When Harriet saw Elizabeth entering the carriage, she smiled brightly.

"Take good care of my Lizzy," said Mr. Bennet to Harriet. Though his tone was light, there was a sort of solemn sadness in his gaze. He really did hate parting with Elizabeth.

"I have the feeling *she* shall be the one taking care of me," returned Harriet good-naturedly.

Mr. Bennet let out a bark of laughter. "I suppose I shall not be surprised if that turns out to be the case. My Lizzy is very clever, after all." He dipped his head a little. "Well, you had best go, then."

When the carriage jerked forward at the horses' pull, Elizabeth leaned her head out the window. Unabashedly, she waved farewell to her sisters and her father. The girls waved back, and she could hear

Jane's cry: "Goodbye, Lizzy!"

Elizabeth smiled as the carriage moved forward. She was glad Lydia had not wanted to see her off, as she would have ruined this tender parting. It was much more pleasant without her.

As the figures faded into the distance, Elizabeth brought her head back inside the carriage. It felt as if she had only just arrived back at Longbourn. She hated to be leaving again so soon, but she knew she would enjoy herself.

Harriet smiled at her. "I am glad you agreed to be my companion."

Elizabeth returned a smile of her own, setting her reticule on the seat beside her. "As am I. I suspect we shall be very content spending time with one another."

"We certainly shall! I enjoy my husband's company very much, but he is often busy with the officers, and there are certain subjects which men simply do not understand."

"Men are hopeless when it comes to reticules and ribbons," said Elizabeth. "The composition of a proper dinner also seems to elude them."

"Imagine what a dinner should be like were a man to determine what the menu should be!" cried Harriet. "Why, there would be nothing but meat piled upon the table, to say nothing of the fact that everyone would be soused by the end of the meal!"

"Ah, but we would be hopeless when it came to military maneuvers," said Elizabeth, "so I suppose we all have our strengths."

Harriet tilted her head. "You do not believe I could order officers to do my will, Lizzy?"

Laughing, Elizabeth told her: "Well, I suppose you could, Harriet, but if there were an actual battle, you might be out of your element."

"I suppose I shall let my husband maintain his position then," said Harriet with the heavy sigh of sacrifice.

"At least you have a husband who dotes upon you," said Elizabeth, smiling. "I am at times convinced I shall die an old maid."

"Surely not, Lizzy!" cried Harriet. "I have seen more than one man look favorably upon you, and I know you shall soon find a husband. For instance, Mr. Wickham—"

"I do not believe Mr. Wickham and I are compatible," broke in Elizabeth. "I suspect I shall not find a husband among the officers."

"Mr. Denny is a kind man."

"A 'kind boy,' more like," countered Elizabeth. "But I suppose you are right. He is certainly pleasant enough in company. Perhaps I should not be averse to his paying attentions to me. He is handsome, and being youthful is not a negative quality. How soon do you suppose we might arrange a wedding?"

"*Lizzy*," said Harriet, laughing.

"Oh, you are quite right! I completely forgot. I must first be proposed to before I can plan a wedding. How do you suppose I might induce him to propose at the earliest opportunity?"

Still chuckling, Harriet replied: "Perhaps my husband can drop hints that Mr. Denny should marry."

"Ah, but can Mr. Denny catch them? I think mayhap we should provide him with a bucket."

"Or perhaps a net. They must certainly be large hints if we intend for Mr. Denny to recognize them."

"And where might we have the wedding? I might not mind an elopement. Perhaps I might even propose to him. I should have to be coy about it. Mayhap I should inquire as to whether he would like to travel to Gretna Green with me."

Harriet began laughing harder than before. "Ah, Lizzy! Here is another reminder as to why I am so delighted that you shall be my companion. Not even my husband can make me laugh as you do. I am surprised you are not married yet."

"It is not for want of offers," said Elizabeth to her friend. "For I have turned down *two* marriage proposals."

"Two!" cried Harriet. "Whatever do you mean?"

Despite their intimacy, Elizabeth had not told Harriet of either proposal. But though she was going to Brighton in large part to avoid being even remotely near Mr. Darcy, she knew she would have the man frequently on her mind, and she felt it would be beneficial to be able to speak to someone about him. Harriet was no replacement for Jane, but she was a good friend, and she would keep what Elizabeth said in confidence. "I had the pleasure of turning down my cousin Mr. Collins in November, and I rejected a proposal from Mr. Darcy last month."

"Mr. Darcy!" cried Harriet. "Surely you do not mean the wealthy man too proud for Hertfordshire society?"

"I am afraid I do mean that very man. He was so certain of the success of his application for my hand that I am afraid I disappointed him very much."

"I am surprised that you could refuse such a suitor, Elizabeth. With the entail on your father's estate, I should have thought you would feel pressured to accept an offer from someone whose finances are in such an enviable state."

"Considering how ill-made his proposal was, I do not believe you would blame me had you been there to hear it. It consisted primarily of his detailing at length the inferiority of my connections and his struggle to fight against the affection which had come over him."

Harriet stared at her, surprise written all over her features. "This was the content of his proposal?"

"Indeed. I refuse to begin a life with a man after an insult such as that."

Harriet shook her head in wonder. "I dare say you must have hurt his pride very much when you refused him if he expected to be accepted after *that* sort of a proposal."

"You are fortunate to be wed to such a man as Colonel Forster. I am afraid that I appear to attract the very sort of men who could do nothing but make me unhappy."

"Perhaps we shall find you a nice man in Brighton," said Harriet gently.

"You have forgotten, my friend — I am to be married to Mr. Denny!"

"Oh! How could I forget? Perhaps we should write to your mother this instant so she may begin wedding preparations."

"Ah, my dear Harriet, but remember — I shall be eloping! There will be no need for preparations, wedding breakfasts, or anything of the sort. And I dare say my father shall be very thankful to me indeed, for he shall not have to endure my mother's unending effusions as she shows me off to all the neighbors — and that is not to mention the fact that he shall not have to endure all the planning and the conversations about wedding dresses and my trousseau! Indeed, now that I think upon it, I believe a trip to Gretna is the only manner in which I should wish to marry, as I doubt *my own* ability to withstand my mother's enthusiasm!"

"Your mother is very . . . fervent about such things," replied Harriet, her diplomatic way of speaking inciting a responding laugh from Elizabeth. "But the joy of having a daughter safely married to a man —"

"*Boy!*" interjected Elizabeth.

Both ladies collapsed in fits of giggles which they were simply unable to master for some time. Finally, however, they were composed enough to return to their banter, with Harriet being the first to speak.

"*Boy!*" echoed Harriet in a perfect imitation of Elizabeth. "As I was saying, before *someone* forgot her manners and interrupted me, your mother's delight at having you safely paired off with someone of the *opposite sex* would no doubt be a balm to her injured feelings. I dare say she would forgive you for not allowing her to indulge in a frenzy of wedding preparations the moment your handsome beau stepped out of the carriage."

"I believe she would," said Elizabeth. "In fact, I should think that Mr. Denny would not even need to be handsome to win her approval. The only requirements he would need to meet are being male and having a pulse."

"Elizabeth, you are too cruel!"

"Perhaps," said Elizabeth. "However, I assure you that my exaggerations do not stretch the truth a great deal where my mother is concerned. Perhaps the only thing I have left out is the possession of a fortune, though that lack may be forgiven if the man is handsome enough."

"Well, I am sure you know your mother better than I," said Harriet. "But what of your sisters? What would they think?"

Elizabeth made a great show of mulling it over, though the tittering beside her spoke volumes as to the effect she was having on Harriet.

"Jane would be happy for me without a doubt," said Elizabeth finally. "She would think me somewhat imprudent, perhaps, but if she believes me to be content, then she will make no objection. And I suppose Mary and Kitty would profess their happiness for me, though Kitty would demand an accounting and make all the appropriate sighs when I told her how romantic my secret marriage was, while Mary would undoubtedly find it necessary to moralize on the subject and chide me for the fact that I could have ruined my reputation with such an escapade.

"Lydia, however, would never forgive me, not only for being married before her, but also for marrying one of her favorite officers, when the first opportunity should *rightly* have belonged to *her*."

A rolling of the eyes accompanied Harriet's laugh, and Elizabeth, who was well aware of her friend's opinion of her youngest sister, could only commiserate.

"Your youngest sister is most certainly a menace!" cried Harriet. "After you left for Kent, she attached herself to me like a leech, claiming to all who would listen that we were the closest of friends. I declare that nothing I did or said could deter her. Jane, dear girl that she is, attempted to intervene, but Lydia would not listen. Even your father did nothing; rather, he seemed content to watch her and laugh at her behavior."

Elizabeth sighed. "Unfortunately, my father finds far too much amusement in the antics of my youngest sisters to ever check their behavior. Jane and I have tried to rein them in, but my mother allows—

and even encourages! — their excesses, and as we are their elder sisters rather than their parents, there is little we can truly do. I shudder to think of the trouble in which Lydia would have found herself if you had invited *her* instead of me."

Harriet's shudder was somewhat embellished, but it did possess some sincerity. "Of *that* you have little to fear, Elizabeth. Perhaps I should be silent, Lydia being your sister, but three minutes in her company is too much, let alone *three months!*"

A grimace was Elizabeth's only response; she was all too aware of how trying Lydia could be. A melancholy descended upon her as she thought of her youngest sister. Sooner or later, if Lydia was not checked, she would undoubtedly find herself in a situation which could not only be disastrous to herself, but which could also be damaging to the family's reputation. Short of begging Mr. Bennet to take an interest in their welfare or lock Lydia in her room for the rest of her life, Elizabeth was not certain what was to be done.

"Come now, Elizabeth. We did not undertake this journey to fret over the actions of your youngest sister."

Elizabeth smiled at her friend, grateful to be pulled out of her gloomy thoughts. "Indeed, we did not. I shall not be a very good guest if I continue to brood over Lydia's behavior."

"Exactly! Now, I absolutely forbid you to think of your sister — at least in my presence — for the rest of our time together. You must think of happier things, such as the time we shall spend in one another's company, the confidences we will share, and perhaps the charming young *boy* you will wed at the end of it all!"

Laughter once again rang out from the carriage, and the two women embraced each other, Elizabeth feeling thankful she had such a wonderful friend who could pull her from her darker thoughts. Though she had been somewhat anxious about leaving her home again so soon after returning, she was now eager to spend time with Harriet. They would, she did not doubt, experience much pleasure in the other's company.

Their journey to Brighton passed by uneventfully, and after stopping in London for the night at the Gardiners' home, the two travelers once again set out on the road to Brighton, arriving late on the second day. The sun shone down on the city, bathing it in the redness of its late afternoon rays as they rode through. By this time, both young women were eager to alight from the carriage and move into the comfort promised by the house which had been rented by the colonel.

At length, they pulled up in front of the residence and entered, their eager eyes taking in the details of what would become their home for the next few months at least. Elizabeth would have to leave eventually, of course, but Harriet would be staying there until the regiment was once again ordered to its next destination.

The house was not overly large, but it was clean and comfortable, and if it was not in the most fashionable district of Brighton, it was not a hovel in a squalid slum either. There were several bedrooms, enough for visitors to stay the night if necessary; sitting rooms for the ladies; a gaming room, complete with a billiards table for the colonel; and a dining room with space for almost a dozen diners, which would be essential, as the colonel could be expected to dine with his officers at least a few times a week.

The thought of such dinners brought a slight frown to Elizabeth's face. Undoubtedly, Mr. Wickham would be one of those officers on occasion, and Elizabeth truly did not wish to be in the man's presence any more than absolutely necessary.

But there was nothing she could do. The man *was* an officer in the colonel's regiment, and though Elizabeth would have liked to avoid him completely, she could hardly ask the colonel to ban one of his men from his table without a very good reason. And short of breaking Mr. Darcy's confidence there was nothing to be done, as she could not make unproven accusations about him. She would simply have to elude the man as much as she could and be civil when evasion was not possible.

Elizabeth's room was down the hall from the master suite that Harriet would share with her husband. It was bright and airy and decorated in the muted blues and greens of which she was so fond. Her trunk was sitting at the end of the bed, and the maid was already unpacking her dresses industriously.

After looking around the room for a few more minutes, Elizabeth set about arranging her personal effects, which had been somewhat haphazardly set upon the vanity. When she had finished, she enlisted the maid's assistance in exchanging her travel clothes for a light-yellow summer dress. Then, content with her appearance, she made her way below stairs. She could already feel the difference in the climate of the city. The air was heavier, and it was warmer than it had been in Hertfordshire, yet she did not think it would take long to become accustomed to the change.

As the house was not large, she was able to find her way down to the eastern-facing sitting-room with little trouble. She intended to wait there for Harriet—if indeed the other woman had not already arrived—and then eat supper. Elizabeth was not precisely hungry after her long journey, yet she knew she had better partake of a light repast at the very least.

It was in the midst of her thoughts of their journey that she entered the sitting room, inattentive to her surroundings. A few moments therefore elapsed before she realized she was not alone. In fact, if the man waiting in the room had not risen to his feet and opened his mouth, she might very well have remained ignorant of his presence.

"Good day, Miss Bennet."

Startled, Elizabeth jumped slightly. Why was *he* already present in Brighton?

"Mr. Wickham!" cried she in surprise. She quickly regained her composure and stared at Mr. Wickham with a hint of annoyance. "What a . . . surprise to see you here. Is the regiment not traveling with Colonel Forster?"

His answering smile was the essence of the man: cheerful, yet with a certain underlying counterfeit charm which he exuded from every pore. And he seemed to take no notice of—or else he completely ignored—the lack of enthusiasm his presence engendered. She was not certain when she had started to notice this mask which he put up for the world, but she almost wondered if the realization had begun even before she had heard Mr. Darcy's account of his character in Kent.

"I volunteered to be part of the advance company preparing the location for the regiment's arrival," said he. His smile became somewhat self-deprecating, but something about his frank and appraising gaze made Elizabeth uncomfortable. "I know it was perhaps impetuous of me, but the thought of waiting in Hertfordshire while a certain lady went on ahead to Brighton was more than I could bear."

He clearly expected Elizabeth to blush and thank him for his flattery, but at that moment, all Elizabeth could think of was the displeasure she felt at his presence and the evidence of his continued attentions to her.

"You could not bear the thought of being parted from me?" said she, a raised eyebrow showing her skepticism.

Mr. Wickham apparently missed her tone. "I could not. I was away from you far too long as it was during your sojourn to Kent. I found myself unequal to the prospect of even a few days longer without being in your company."

"If you recall, our separation has been of a much longer duration, Mr. Wickham."

Her statement appeared to perplex him. "I am not certain I understand your meaning, Miss Bennet."

"Come now, Mr. Wickham. Surely your memory cannot be that deficient. You must recall that during the three months complete before my departure, you were rarely seen at Longbourn—or at any other gathering in Meryton, for that matter—and I only saw you once a few days before I left for Kent."

The reminder of his previous activities and especially the reference to his pursuit of Mary King set Mr. Wickham to squirming, and he looked away from Elizabeth, his discomfort clear. It was time to twist the dagger a little and let him know she did not appreciate his continued flattery or his professions of undying regard.

"In fact," said she, with an exaggerated show of contemplation, "I seem to remember the distance between us occurred about the time that Mary King was revealed to have suddenly acquired an inheritance of *ten thousand pounds*."

By now, Mr. Wickham's face was flushed, and he was alternating between looking at her with wonder and endeavoring to look anywhere *but* at her. Confident she had him exactly where she wanted him, Elizabeth continued:

"I believe I should inform you, Mr. Wickham, that my financial situation is no better now than it was before you went on your fortune-hunting expedition, nor is it likely to change any time in the future.

"In addition," continued she with a little more steel in her voice, "I should inform you that I am not one of those foolish empty-headed girls whom you normally favor with your attentions; I am not blind to your other activities, I am not impressed by your attempts at flattery, and your manners have little effect on me.

"Now, I am perfectly willing to behave in a congenial manner and treat you the same as any other acquaintance, but in order for us to avoid descending into acrimony, I will require you to remember these facts. You must also remember that I have more in my head than a bit of fluff."

The poor man—if he could be termed as such—was by now thoroughly embarrassed. Whether it was because he had been called out or because his plans had been disrupted, Elizabeth could not say, but if it gained her a respite from his attentions, then it was well worth it. She did not wish to spend her entire time in Brighton fending off an overly amorous Mr. Wickham.

"Are we clear, sir?"

Though the officer appeared not to know where to look or how to act, he murmured that he understood and sat down upon the sofa he had been occupying when she entered.

It was at that moment that Harriet entered the room. She stopped, startled to see Mr. Wickham sitting there, and looked questioningly at Elizabeth. It could not be said that Harriet was slow of thought or incapable of observation, as her raised eyebrow conveyed volumes to Elizabeth. Clearly, Harriet expected an explanation at the earliest opportunity, and Elizabeth, though not of a mind to protect Mr. Wickham in any way, was not entirely certain what she should tell her friend of her negative feelings toward the gentleman.

A small shake of Elizabeth's head was all Harriet needed to take the hint, and she instead welcomed Mr. Wickham and asked him if he would be staying for dinner.

"I am afraid not," was Mr. Wickham's reply. He stood in haste, and his manner suggested he wanted nothing more than to be gone from the place as soon as could be. "My purpose in coming here was to inquire after your health and comfort and to ensure you had arrived quite safely. Now that I see all is well, I shall depart forthwith, as I still have much to do to prepare for the regiment's arrival."

He bowed to them and quit the room, and though Elizabeth could tell he was not *precisely* hurrying, he did not tarry either.

Harriet looked at Elizabeth, her eyes dancing with amusement.

"What did you say to poor Mr. Wickham, Elizabeth?" demanded Harriet. "I swear I have never seen a man so glad to leave a room in which you were present during the entire time I have known you."

Elizabeth managed to smile in return, but she was still trying to decide what to tell Harriet. Some of her knowledge of the man must be kept secret; while she was certain Harriet would believe her implicitly, Elizabeth also knew her friend would feel obliged to approach her husband about her intelligence if she knew the full story. Yet without Mr. Darcy's testimony, the colonel would be able to do nothing. Furthermore, the information would put him in the position of having his trust for his officer compromised without any real prospect of ever having those suspicions verified. If Mr. Wickham were to fall back into his old ways in the regiment, Elizabeth was certain he would eventually be found out by other means, so it would do her no good to besmirch his reputation without proof.

However, it did seem wise to tell her friend some of her reasons, so Elizabeth said:

"I merely clarified a few things with Mr. Wickham."

"Such as?"

Elizabeth shrugged. "I told him that I did not appreciate his flattery."

"But you always enjoyed speaking with him before, Elizabeth."

"Yes, I did," said Elizabeth. "And there are times when I still consider him to be pleasant in company. But Mr. Wickham appears to be under the misconception that he can continue his attentions to me as he did when he first arrived in Hertfordshire, ignoring the fact that he spent many months in between pursuing Mary King and her ten thousand pounds."

Harriet's answering reply was serious, and she gazed at Elizabeth with a penetrating eye. "That reeks of jealousy, Elizabeth."

"Call it what you will," replied Elizabeth with an open display of nonchalance, "but Mr. Wickham has a habit of making himself agreeable to members of our sex, and I wished him to know that I am not taken in by his good manners and overly cheerful disposition. He is an acquaintance, but no more. At times he gives the appearance of toying with a lady, as a cat may toy with a mouse. I will not be his chosen mouse."

The pointed words seemed to have an effect upon her friend, as Harriet relaxed and seated herself on one of the chairs. "Good for you, Elizabeth. Mr. Wickham indeed has a reputation in the regiment of making himself agreeable to *all* the ladies, and I know his interest in you has not gone unremarked. It is well that you wish to keep a distance from him."

"Believe me, Harriet, I wish for nothing more," was Elizabeth's fervent reply.

"In that case, let us speak no more of Mr. Wickham," said Harriet.

Elizabeth smiled, immediately grateful for her friend's perception, tact, and ability to redirect a conversation.

"I believe we should eat a light dinner and retire early tonight. But what say you to taking in some of the sights of the city tomorrow? Given your love of the outdoors, I am convinced that two days cooped up in a moving carriage has left you with a desire to be out and about, and while a city such as Brighton cannot likely provide the clean air to which you are accustomed, I should think that any relief would be profoundly welcome."

Elizabeth chuckled. "You know me too well, Harriet. Your scheme sounds delightful, and I am very much looking forward to sampling the circulating libraries, as I have said."

"Now, Elizabeth," said Harriet with mock-firmness, "I am well acquainted with your love of books and your ability to engross yourself within the pages of one for a great deal of time, but I will not have you subjecting me to hours more in the confines of a small room."

The two friends laughed heartily together, and Elizabeth, donning a suitably chastened expression, assured her friend that she had no intention of spending endless hours with a book on the morrow.

"In fact," said she, "I am very much anticipating the sights of Brighton. In particular, I cannot wait to see the famed beaches of Brighton and visit the variety of shops."

"Now, *that* is closer to *my* tastes, Elizabeth," said Harriet with a laugh. "A trip to the nearest shopping district will more than suit my needs, and a clear day along the beach should be refreshing and agreeable."

"In that case, my dear Harriet, I suggest we do as you say and retire early tonight so we may partake of such delights on the morrow."

And that was what they did. The small supper which had been ordered was ready soon thereafter. Then, once they had finished, they spent some time in the sitting room conversing in their usual lively way—which was, of course, one of the things Elizabeth most enjoyed doing with her friend—before they both sought their beds in anticipation of the following day.

Chapter III

*T*he next morning, the friends arose early, and they eagerly set about preparing for the day's activities and their expedition into town. The morning was crisp and clear and promised to be even warmer than the previous day, prompting Elizabeth to wonder what it would be like once full summer descended over the city. Surely they would be in for some most uncomfortable weather if this were to continue.

Once their morning routines had been completed and they had impatiently eaten their fill of the breakfast which had been laid out for them, the two ladies set out into the city, eager to see the sights which had made Brighton famous.

It was perhaps a quirk of the location of the townhouse which had been let for their comfort, but the district in which they found themselves was within walking distance of most of the attractions they had discussed the previous evening. The bulk of the military presence in or around Brighton was situated to the west of the city, and Elizabeth and Harriet had discovered the previous evening that if they stood close to the window of the second story sitting room at the very front of the house, they could see down the street which led out of town to the west and could just make out the rows and rows of tents of the encamped regiments in the distance. Harriet was pleased that the colonel was so close to his men's encampment, yet Elizabeth privately wished for more distance between herself and Mr. Wickham.

The two women also, through some questioning of the servants, discovered that there was a shopping district situated little more than a ten-minute walk to the north of the townhouse. Furthermore, the beach was about fifteen minutes in the other direction, and there was a theater nearby, not to mention other entertainments such as museums and art galleries.

They decided to visit the shopping district first, and with their escort—a large burly footman who had been assigned to their protection while they were out in the town—they left the house in search of amusement and possibly the purchase of a few trinkets.

As they walked through the city, they chatted about inconsequential things, gazed about them with interest in their surroundings, and stopped every so often to more closely observe something which interested one or the other.

Elizabeth had only been to one other city during the course of her life, and though perhaps Brighton was similar to London in essentials, it was very different in feel. The London she had always known was crowded and often dirty, and it possessed very little in the way of beauty, with the possible exception of the tower and the few city parks and other specifically preserved locations which she had visited. Unfortunately, the unsavory aspects of London grew even more objectionable in the summer, as an unpleasant miasma often would hang over it for weeks, and disease and the unpleasant odor of sewage tended to run rampant through the city.

In Brighton, though the problems the capital experienced were also present, they were obviously to be found on a much lower scale. When Elizabeth had been in London two days previously, the summer heat was already making the city feel unclean, whereas Brighton was still very pleasant. Brighton was also much more open than London—the houses were not as cramped, there were trees clad with fresh green leaves that blew prettily in the breeze, and the parks seemed to be much more open and well cared for than those she had seen near Gracechurch Street.

In addition, though it could simply be the area in which they were staying, Elizabeth felt that the problem of crime which was widespread in London was also not as much of a problem in Brighton. Obviously, the benefits of a city on a smaller scale could outweigh the advantages London had in its availability of amusements, though Elizabeth could not truthfully claim to have experienced much of higher society during her stays at the Gardiners' home.

The shopping district in which they found themselves could best be termed as "quaint." There were many shops proclaiming their wares, and the ladies were able to browse to their heart's content. Though they purchased little, they saw much and were impressed with what they came across.

They took luncheon in a small café to the side of the main shopping thoroughfare, both savoring the taste of the delicate fish they had agreed upon trying and enjoying their tea in the shade of the umbrella positioned over their table. Elizabeth could not remember the last time she had had such a charming outing; usually, her shopping trips to Meryton were rendered somewhat unpleasant due to Lydia's boisterousness and Mrs. Bennet's demands for lace and other finery.

Finally, when Elizabeth and Harriet had spent all the time they desired in the shopping district, they wandered back in the direction of the house, only to bypass it completely and make for the beaches under the ever-watchful eye of the faithful footman.

Her first glimpse of the ocean caused Elizabeth to catch her breath. She would not have believed that so much water existed *anywhere* in the world. The peaceful sound of the waves crashing upon the shore and the great vision of the white spray of the surf captured her interest, and she wished for a moment she could throw propriety to the wind, taking off her shoes and running with abandon through the foaming water. Before the endless waves, the white beaches stretched off as far as the eye could see, the sands glowing and twinkling in the afternoon sun like a sheet comprised of millions of tiny diamonds. Elizabeth was unable to do anything but gaze at it in wonder.

"Elizabeth, look!"

Her friend's voice pulled her from her amazement, and Elizabeth gazed in the direction Harriet had pointed. Off in the distance at various points stood great contraptions on wheels—like large wagons with tents on the seaward side—sitting along the beach at the edge of the water.

Laughing with delight, Elizabeth exclaimed: "Those must be the bathing machines of which we have heard so much!"

"I believe we simply must try that," said Harriet, her own eyes sparkling with delight.

They stood looking at the devices for several moments, noting the eager patrons who approached to use them.

They watched the activity down at the coast for quite some time as they meandered along the path which ran parallel. There was so much to see that Elizabeth thought she could hardly take it all in.

They had been walking for a while when Elizabeth turned to speak to Harriet. To her great surprise, however, she came to an abrupt stop against a hard and unyielding surface. She lost her balance and hit the ground, the air leaving her chest in a sudden rush. She sat there for a moment, stunned, before two sets of masculine arms reached down to help her up. As she was pulled to her feet, she was able to see who the arms belonged to—the stern footman and an embarrassed Mr. Denny.

"Miss B-Bennet," stuttered the red-faced Denny, "are you well?"

"Yes," managed Elizabeth in a small voice, still feeling sore from her unexpected contact with the ground. Taking in a shallow breath, she struggled to compose herself. She told him as levelly as she could: "I think it shall take more than a mere fall to put me out of sorts, Mr. Denny."

But the young man did not seem reassured in the slightest, which was likely because she still seemed shaken. "Please accept my heartfelt apologies, Miss Bennet. I should not have stopped in front of you as I did. It was very foolish of me."

Elizabeth tilted her head. "Seeing as you did no lasting damage to my person, Mr. Denny, perhaps I can find it in my heart to forgive you." But he still seemed so anxious and anticipatory that Elizabeth gave him a gentle smile and said: "I was jesting, Mr. Denny. There is nothing to forgive. This was a mere accident, and I hold no ill will toward you. You need not worry about my well-being, as I am perfectly fine."

He stared at her for a moment, obviously trying to determine the veracity of her statement. Finally, a relieved smile tugged upward at the corners of his mouth. "I am glad to hear that, Miss Bennet."

Harriet, who had been standing by and looking somewhat amused, said at last: "I am surprised to see you here, Mr. Denny. I thought it would be at least a few more days before we came across you."

He colored a little and cleared his throat, appearing uncomfortable. "Wickham convinced me to be part of the group making preparations for everyone's arrival. We have been rather busy, and I saw an opportunity to escape for a little while, so I did. I must confess I was eager to see something of Brighton before all the other officers arrive. There is quite a lot happening in the city, and I wanted a glimpse of it."

Elizabeth allowed herself a small smile of satisfaction. Sneaking off to avoid duties sounded very much like a boy indeed, and it was difficult to keep from saying as much to Harriet.

"I cannot fault you for wanting to see more of such a city as this," said Harriet. "After all, Elizabeth and I have been engaged in that very activity for most of the day. Brighton is charming, is it not, Mr. Denny?"

"Indeed," replied he. "But I am afraid I have tarried here too long." He gave them a small bow and said: "Mrs. Forster, Miss Bennet." And then he took his leave, still looking a little anxious.

Elizabeth and Harriet stared after him for a few seconds, watching as he hurried away. Elizabeth wondered if he thought Harriet would tell Colonel Forster about his absence. If so, he was worrying over nothing. Though boyish, Denny was of a good sort, and Harriet would want to do nothing that might lead to his being punished.

"Are you certain you are well, Miss Bennet?"

The two women turned in surprise to the footman, Woodston, whose blank expression and emotionless tone conveyed nothing of the concern which his words seemed to indicate was the purpose for his application. Yet he *was* looking straight at Elizabeth, so the statement did not appear to be a mere formality.

"Yes, I am, thank you," replied she with a gentle smile.

The footman gave a slight nod but said nothing more. The burly man rarely spoke, so it always came as a surprise when he did. Elizabeth suspected there was a kind man hidden underneath that stony exterior, but she doubted she would ever see more than a glimpse of him. Yet she and Harriet would be exploring what Brighton had to offer quite frequently, so perhaps there would be time enough for her to determine some of Woodston's true nature. Colonel Forster believed him a good man, but Elizabeth knew little beyond that.

They began walking again, their eyes settling once more on the coast. Harriet, with speed and obvious eagerness, moved closer to Elizabeth in order to speak more intimately with her. Then, in the softest of voices, so Woodston would not hear, she teased: "I think the man who is set to be your future husband may be feeling a certain partiality toward you already, Elizabeth! This is indeed good news! Perhaps your elopement is not far off! Maybe you should start deciding what you shall wear to Gretna Green."

"I do not believe the *boy* we just saw felt anything more upon seeing me than embarrassment at having made me crumple into an undignified lump on this lovely path," replied Elizabeth. "Poor Mr. Denny! He really did seem distraught."

Harriet could not help but let out a giggle. "Would *you* be composed after having made your future spouse take a painful tumble?"

"I fancy that *I* would have been paying enough attention to the path that I would not have allowed anything of the sort happen!" said Elizabeth playfully, speaking a little louder than she had intended. Her cheeks turning slightly pink at the realization of her volume, she glanced back at Woodston, who did not appear interested in their conversation in the slightest.

"Come!" said Harriet. "He was apologetic, was he not?"

Would that Mr. Wickham had learned some of his friend's humility, thought Elizabeth to herself wryly. Out loud, she murmured to her friend: "He certainly was. I suppose I must own that such would be a fine quality to have in a husband. After all, a man must always apologize when he feels he has committed a wrong."

Her mind flicked uncomfortably toward Mr. Darcy's letter — though filled with pride, there had been somewhat of an apology mixed up in it — and she nearly grimaced. It was difficult to think of that letter without also feeling humiliated over how she had acted toward the man who had written it.

Trying to forget the piece of correspondence, which she had actually brought with her to Brighton against her better judgment, she continued: "But I do wonder what Mr. Denny and I shall live on. His salary must only be enough to support himself. Must we feast on love? Assuming, of course, that love should ever spring up between us."

"That is where my husband comes in, Elizabeth," said Harriet with mock-seriousness. "I am certain he could assist a fine young man like Mr. Denny with advancing to a better position in the militia."

"No, I am afraid it is best that Colonel Forster refrain from such actions. I do not believe *boys* should be placed any higher than Mr. Denny is at present. Perhaps I shall wait five years and see if he is of marriageable material then. They say half a decade can do wonders to a boy's maturity."

Harriet narrowed her eyes a little. Elizabeth looked away slightly, suspecting she had accidentally let slip the extent of her present dissatisfaction with men. Sometimes, she forgot how perceptive Harriet could be.

"Elizabeth, surely you do not wish to wait that long to marry," said Harriet slowly. She almost looked worried.

Though a part of Elizabeth balked at the idea that she should ever marry any man at all, she knew that it would be the best option for a young woman in her position. With the entail stipulating that Longbourn would devolve to her cousin, her mother's fears that the Bennet females would be cast out upon Mr. Bennet's death might very well come to pass. Mr. Collins certainly held no particularly positive feelings toward Elizabeth since she had rejected his proposal.

But Elizabeth preferred not to think such dismal thoughts, and so she returned lightly: "I am not certain I wish to marry at all. My sister Jane shall soon find a fine husband with a nice little estate. Perhaps I shall live with her. I am sure she can find a small room for me. If I am fortunate, it shall overlook a garden!"

"Ah, Elizabeth! Sometimes it is difficult to know when you are jesting and when you are serious!" cried Harriet.

Elizabeth smiled, her eyes glinting in amusement. "I shall give you a hint as to how you can determine the difference: I am never serious."

Harriet burst out into a peal of laughter. "Now, Elizabeth, we both know that is not true. But I shall not press the issue any more. If you wish to feign perpetual playfulness, then I shall allow it! Now, let us plan our itinerary for the week. There are still plenty of parks to walk in and visits to make to museums and art galleries, and we must of course prepare ourselves to experience the wonder of those bathing machines!"

"Indeed!" replied Elizabeth. "I am not certain we have ever done anything in our lives as adventurous as this shall turn out to be!"

"I agree wholeheartedly! We must shop tomorrow for bathing outfits. Though it may not be as adventurous as you make it out to be, I do fancy a sea bath shall, at the very least, be the highlight of our time in Brighton!"

"I think the mere sight of the sea has been an especially enjoyable part of my visit here, but it certainly will be nicer to move closer to it. But perhaps I should not tell my mother about it. She shall already be lamenting my departure and proclaiming how much good would come to her from a soak in the waters of Brighton. If I wrote of it to her, I am certain my father would never forgive me!"

"Then we shall keep the pleasure a secret from her," said Harriet. "But I doubt I shall be able to contain my excitement in front of my husband."

"And I would not wish you to do so," said Elizabeth with a smile. "After all, you must prevail upon him to provide you with funds for our venture to find bathing outfits. You would not like it if he should wish you to use your money sparingly."

"Definitely not!" cried Harriet. "Especially if I decide I wish to have an outfit with lots of ruffles!"

"Oh, yes, you cannot forget the ruffles! To do so would be a tragedy indeed!"

Chapter IV

*I*t did not take long for Colonel Forster and his men to get well settled in Brighton. The advance company did a thorough job, and Elizabeth did not hear the men make any complaints about their arrangements.

Colonel Forster seemed especially glad that Harriet and Elizabeth were pleased with the townhouse, and he was even more pleased to take in the small changes his wife had already made to their temporary home.

"If you had despised the house, I should have had to search the city for something more suitable," said he jovially. "I am glad to hear that is not the case!"

While Elizabeth doubted that such would have truly happened—townhouses as well suited to his purpose as this one were probably not in abundance—it was obvious he did dote on his wife, and Elizabeth was grateful for that. Harriet deserved a kind husband, and Colonel Forster played the part admirably.

Unfortunately for Elizabeth, dinners with the officers soon began, and she found herself dining with Mr. Wickham far earlier than she had anticipated. Fortunately, however, she managed to ensure she was seated near Mr. Denny rather than Mr. Wickham. This development was a source of amusement, primarily because she kept seeing Harriet look toward Mr. Denny and then toward her with a secretive smile that made Elizabeth fight to hide a smirk.

Though Elizabeth did not have to sit near Mr. Wickham at dinner, she was not fortunate enough to be spared his company in the drawing-room after the meal. When he first drew close to her, she could do little more than stare at him in wonder, shocked at the audacity he was exhibiting in approaching her. If he was willing to talk to her again, then he must have mustered up an abundance of courage since their last conversation. What sort of game was he playing? Did he believe she was merely being coy, or did he want to prove himself an annoyance due to some sense of hurt pride? Elizabeth was not sure of the reason; she knew only that it mystified her.

"Miss Bennet," said Mr. Wickham formally in greeting. There was no trace of apprehension in his features; instead, there was only the easy confidence and appearance of amiability which had so enthralled the populace of Hertfordshire. "I trust you have found Brighton to your tastes?"

"I certainly have," replied Elizabeth. "It is a lovely city."

"There are many enticing pleasures for young women such as yourself," said he. "Have you and Mrs. Forster already begun frequenting the circulating libraries?"

"I still maintain a fondness for books," said Elizabeth carefully, uncertain of the reason for his interest. There was a certain something in his smile that worried her, and she shifted in place uncomfortably.

"I am glad to hear you have not changed in essentials, Miss Bennet," said Mr. Wickham in a low voice. He smiled at her, and she could not help but take a step backward in reflex. There was something almost predatory in his gaze. She felt suddenly like a fish facing the gaping maw of a giant shark.

"Mr. Wickham," began Elizabeth somewhat shakily, not certain what she was going to say, but knowing she had to regain control of the situation somehow. She knew he could do nothing improper in the Forsters' townhouse, yet that knowledge could not quell the feeling of danger pressing in on her.

"Miss Bennet," said a voice suddenly.

Relief washing over her, she turned to look upon her savior. Standing before her was Mr. Denny, and she was not certain she had ever felt so glad to see someone in her life. She almost could have embraced him.

"Mr. Denny," returned she, managing somehow to maintain her composure and speak in a steady voice. She did not know how Mr.

Wickham had managed to so utterly disarm her, but she did not want it to ever happen again. The next time she was in a drawing-room with Mr. Wickham, she would to try to ensure that she did not leave Harriet's side.

The expression was so fleeting that Elizabeth almost missed the dark look Wickham directed at the newcomer. It was enough, however, to rouse a hint of curiosity in her despite the discomfort she had experienced moments before.

"Did you find dinner to your liking?" asked Elizabeth, keeping her eyes trained on Mr. Denny, though she kept Mr. Wickham in her peripheral vision.

"Mrs. Forster keeps a very fine table," said Mr. Denny pleasantly.

Perhaps Elizabeth should have felt pleased at his statement—she had, after all, helped Harriet choose the courses for the night's meal—but instead, she could only think of how desperately she wanted Mr. Wickham to leave.

Mr. Denny turned toward the other man, who was standing nearby stiffly, and asked: "Do you not agree?" There almost seemed to be a hard edge to his voice, though Elizabeth could not quite be certain.

Mr. Wickham's expression was practically a glower as he stared back at the other officer. In a barely audible murmur, he allowed that the food had been very good. Elizabeth gazed at them, wondering if there had been some point of contention between the two young men. Before, they had been great friends—after all, Mr. Wickham had only been able to don a red coat due to Mr. Denny's influence—but now it seemed as if speaking five words to each other was almost painful.

The two men stared at one another for a few moments before Mr. Wickham finally took his leave to approach a nearby group of three officers. She wanted to ask Mr. Denny what had happened between them, but propriety dictated that she hold her tongue. Despite all her jests with Harriet, she did not actually know Mr. Denny that well. She certainly did not know him well enough to ask for the details of a dispute. Mr. Wickham might have been willing to air his grievances with Mr. Darcy—false though they may have been—to someone with whom she barely had any sort of acquaintance to speak of, but she doubted his former friend would be quite so eager.

"I take it you and Mrs. Forster enjoyed exploring Brighton?" said Mr. Denny suddenly.

"Yes," replied Elizabeth with a smile. "I am fond of walking, and I must say we have done quite a lot of that since arriving."

He looked at her, his gaze searching. "You were never alone, were you, Miss Bennet?"

"No," said she, wondering at his question. "The footman you saw remained with us the entire time. There is no need for concern, Mr. Denny. I am certain that he is strong enough to fight off a whole battalion of ne'er-do-wells."

He gave her a slight smile, though he still seemed a bit agitated. "Well, you must be certain not to go anywhere in Brighton without him, Miss Bennet. The city is a dangerous place for young women. Please promise me you will be careful."

"Do not worry, Mr. Denny. I shall indeed be careful," said Elizabeth softly, a frown creasing her forehead. He truly was puzzling her, and she began to wonder if he truly was interested in her as Harriet had suggested. "But I dare say I cannot take the footman bathing with me."

He laughed. "Of course not, Miss Bennet. But the beach designated for female usage shall not have any men on it, so I suspect you shall be safe enough in such a case." He glanced away. "Pardon me for my boldness, Miss Bennet, but you are still unattached, are you not? I had thought Mr. Darcy seemed keenly interested in you, and you have recently returned from Kent, where I understand his aunt lives."

Elizabeth stared at him in shock. Such an application *was* an impertinence, but of even more concern was the thought that Mr. Denny was more perceptive than she had given him credit. To the best of her knowledge, the only indication Mr. Darcy had given of his partiality for her during his time in Hertfordshire was their single dance at Netherfield; after all, even Elizabeth herself had missed his admiration! The idea that Mr. Denny could know something of the matter was surprising indeed!

She knew her astonishment must have shown clearly on her face, yet Mr. Denny, though he still had a slight nervousness in his manner, continued to gaze at her, waiting for her answer.

"I assure you, Mr. Denny, that I am completely unattached," said Elizabeth finally.

"In fact," continued she, feigning an incredulity which was not entirely invented, "I could wonder where you obtained such a ridiculous notion. Mr. Darcy is a very proud and exacting sort of man. I do not doubt that I place well below his expected level of suitability, not only in the amount of my fortune, but also in the breadth and importance of my connections. Both of those considerations must be of great significance to a man of his consequence."

"Forgive me for overstepping myself, Miss Bennet," replied Mr. Denny, his manner earnest. "It seemed obvious to me after he invited you to dance at Netherfield. He appeared to have no interest in dancing with anyone else."

"I believe you read too much into Mr. Darcy's actions, Mr. Denny. Certainly, I am acceptable to Mr. Darcy as a conversation partner, for we are interested in some of the same subjects and reading material, but for you to step from that to admiration on the basis of a single dance might be presuming a little too much." She said this last lightly, so as not to offend him, and then she continued:

"Now, I simply must declare in the most animated fashion that though I do not deny that I was sometimes in Mr. Darcy's company when I was in Kent, there was never any sort of formal understanding between myself and Mr. Darcy. I am not engaged, sir."

A bright smile lit up the officer's face. "In that case, perhaps my conjectures were incorrect. I suppose that his disinterest is a matter of great relief to you, Miss Bennet, knowing as I do your opinion of the gentleman."

"Oh, I was forced to acknowledge that Mr. Darcy is not so very bad once I began to understand his character better, and I cannot but own that any desires expressed on his part to pursue a relationship beyond a mere acquaintance with me would be somewhat flattering. He has many advantages in his favor, after all."

Elizabeth paused deliberately, her words designed to provoke Mr. Denny into revealing more of his motives. In this endeavor, however, she was destined to be disappointed, as her companion merely smiled.

"I dare say you are correct, Miss Bennet. And though I do not know the man beyond the little interaction I have had with him in Hertfordshire, I shall have to trust your judgment when you say that he is not the betrayer you formerly believed him to be."

"You refer to Mr. Wickham's story of his mistreatment at the hands of the gentleman?" asked Elizabeth.

"Among other things. Wickham has been particularly vocal about Mr. Darcy's treatment of him, certainly. I also know Darcy has been accused of being overly prideful and above his company in Meryton. But though I had suspected an admiration on Mr. Darcy's part due to his actions last autumn, I had wondered if *you* had had a change of heart on the matter."

Elizabeth was not certain what to say. Mr. Denny appeared to have some inclination of Mr. Darcy's former admiration for her and had even gone so far as to question whether she continued in her distaste for the man. She knew not what she should reveal to him. There were certain subjects — such as Miss Darcy's experiences with Mr.

Wickham—which were clearly off limits, but she wondered whether she could safely hint at Mr. Wickham's duplicity with regard to Mr. Darcy's treatment of him. Furthermore, there was the issue of Mr. Wickham's propensity to descend deeply into debt and then leave when the situation became intolerable.

Though Elizabeth was not comfortable in discussing such subjects in detail with a young man whom she did not, after all, know well, she immediately determined that Mr. Wickham's debts of honor might very well extend to his fellow officers, and if nothing else, Mr. Denny should be warned about the kind of man he truly was.

"I *have* had somewhat of a change of heart, Mr. Denny," said Elizabeth. "As I alluded to before, a closer acquaintance with Mr. Darcy does allow a greater understanding of him, and with that understanding, I cannot find it in myself to dislike him to the extent I did before.

"And as for Mr. Wickham's dealings with Mr. Darcy," continued she, choosing her words carefully for truthfulness while ensuring she did not give too much away, "I have come to the understanding that much as there are two sides to any coin, so there are two interpretations to the dealings between the two gentlemen. Though I would not accuse either of overt falsehoods, I have learned that when looked at from a certain point of view, Mr. Darcy's actions in the matter of Mr. Wickham are not at all the gross betrayal that we have heard them to be. In fact, I also heard something else of Mr. Wickham which suggests that despite his cheerful and engaging manner, he is not necessarily well thought of in some of the places he has visited in the past."

"Indeed?" was the reply. Mr. Denny appeared to be extremely interested in Elizabeth's words, causing her to wonder if she had said too much.

"I must warn you, Mr. Denny," said she, "that I have no personal complaints to make of Mr. Wickham. In my own experience with him, he has always seemed amiable, though I will own that I do find his manner a little too familiar. I am merely stating that my own experience since the autumn suggests that I may have made an error in listening to one side of the story without any thought as to what the other party might say in response. It would behoove us all to take great care in pronouncing judgment upon others when we do not have all the facts. Or perhaps more importantly, we should refrain from taking sides in a dispute when only one of the principles has shared his version of the grievance with us."

"You are correct, of course, Miss Bennet," said Mr. Denny with a smile. "You have hit the point quite admirably, but I must note that if what you say is true, then it casts Wickham's assertions in quite a different light. If he is capable of misrepresenting Mr. Darcy in such a manner, then I might wonder of what else he is capable."

"And that question I cannot answer," replied Elizabeth, content with the direction in which the conversation had taken. "The only way you or I shall come to a satisfactory answer is to observe the man in question and come to our own conclusions."

"Then that is what we both must do."

A sudden playfulness came over Elizabeth, and she smiled coyly at the young man. "I might wonder to what end these questions can possibly tend, Mr. Denny," said she. "You asked me about Mr. Darcy's intentions and whether I have an attachment to him, yet I cannot help but wonder if you have some other purpose in mind for your inquiries."

A sudden blush suffused Mr. Denny's features as Denny the boy made his abrupt reappearance. "I . . . Well, you see . . . You . . ." stammered he, looking anywhere but at his conversation partner.

Elizabeth stared at him, wondering yet again whether Harriet's jesting words about Mr. Denny's admiration for her were indeed correct. Could he be this boyish about the matter if he were *not* interested in her?

Though he appeared acutely embarrassed, Mr. Denny squared his shoulders and looked Elizabeth in the eye. "I find you very charming and an excellent conversationalist, Miss Bennet. For anything else, I think we shall just have to see what happens."

"I am sure we shall," replied Elizabeth with a calmness she did not feel. Mr. Denny's words could have several interpretations, and though she still was not convinced of his admiration, she could not completely discount it either. This would undoubtedly take more study of the young man in question before she could come to a conclusion.

Their conversation continued on for several more moments before Elizabeth was called away to attend her hostess. Mr. Denny bowed over her hand and professed himself happy with the opportunity to speak with her again, citing a hope that it would be repeated many times in the future before he went away.

Elizabeth was about to make her way to Harriet's side when she caught sight of Mr. Wickham. The man was scowling darkly at Mr. Denny, his expression one that she did not think she had ever witnessed upon his face previously. All that changed in an instant when his features transformed back into the disarming smile he usually wore as he looked at Elizabeth. His slight bow and wide smile were no doubt intended to charm her, but she thought she could detect a hint of insolence and over-familiarity. Though there were many people in the room, she found herself grateful to be in close proximity with her friend again.

The next few days found the ladies falling into a routine. In Brighton, there were, of course, many amusements to maintain the interest of all persuasions, yet the two women had already explored the city to such an extent that they were able to more carefully make good use of their time in planning outings to walk along the beach, to visit the better museums and art galleries, and to explore the circulating libraries which so captured Elizabeth's eye. During the evening, there were plenty of dinners to hold or attend, and they were invited to more than one assembly. And when the limitless attractions were added to Colonel Forster's familiarity with the region—for he had a few well-placed friends in Brighton—the result was that his wife and her companion were kept quite busy indeed.

Elizabeth and Harriet visited the men's camp occasionally, but the officers present there were frequently flirting with women or playing at cards, and the camp utterly lacked the glory Lydia had complained so loudly she would be missing. The possibility that Mr. Wickham might be found at the camp also made Elizabeth anxious about visiting it. As a result, Harriet requested to see the officers at their camp far less often than she might have done had she been a different sort of woman.

Fortunately, Harriet was nothing like Lydia and had no more interest in flirting with the officers or matching Elizabeth with one than she was in locking herself into a small room and doing nothing but painting screens all day. She was not as learned as Elizabeth was, not feeling anything that approached her friend's love of books, but she was intelligent enough in her own right, and she recognized there was no need to do something that would make neither her nor Elizabeth especially happy. So the two young women merely made the number of visits to the camp as might be expected of Colonel Forster's wife, and they spent the rest of their time in more agreeable pursuits, pleasing their eyes by viewing colors other than the attention-catching scarlet.

They were not always out and about, however. Elizabeth made certain to dedicate a small part of her day to letters. She did not always finish a letter before she ceased writing in order to leave the townhouse with Harriet, but she did nonetheless write diligently. After all, she wished to provide her three eldest sisters and her dear aunt Gardiner with an account of some of her more delightful explorations of the city's many attractions. She also wanted to provide her father with some witticisms that might brighten his days, which must have been dismal indeed due to Lydia and Mrs. Bennet, who were, no doubt, still bemoaning their inability to partake in Brighton's sea bathing.

But Elizabeth's letters were not merely her way of detailing what had happened to her or entertaining her father. Rather, she found the receipt of letters from her sisters to be much more interesting and rewarding than her own written communications. While Jane was unable to rein in Lydia with any success, she kept Elizabeth informed of the progress that had been made with regard to Kitty and Mary, and Elizabeth looked forward to reading Jane's glowing reports, though soon it would be necessary to rely on her dear aunt for news on Kitty since she would be touring Derbyshire in Elizabeth's place.

Though Jane was her primary source for information on Mary and Kitty, Elizabeth found the letters from the two young girls to be enlightening in their own fashion. Mary's letters used to be filled with several lines of moralizing and references to Fordyce's sermons; now, however, there had been a definite decrease in the appearance of such subjects, and Mary was slowly revealing herself to have interests of which Elizabeth had been utterly unaware. She had no doubt that Mary was opening up in large part due to Jane's kind influence and not to Elizabeth's own letters. Still, it pleased her to see the changes being wrought.

Kitty's letters were also exhibiting signs of change. Once, the young girl's letters were as messy and full of frivolities as Lydia's. Now, however, she was making an obvious effort to be neat—Elizabeth thought perhaps she detected a few of Jane's beautifully embellished curves in Kitty's careful script—and she talked about more than ribbons and her youngest sister's doings. Not once did Kitty bemoan the lack of redcoats in Hertfordshire, and that in and of itself was enough to make Elizabeth very happy indeed. Kitty even made some surprisingly insightful comments about literature. She had inquired of Jane to learn some of Elizabeth's favorites, and upon reading them, Kitty had learned there were pleasures to be found within the pages of a good book. Kitty still mentioned the occasional pretty bonnet, but it was less in order to compare it with what Lydia possessed and more in order to express an appreciation which she appeared to believe her sister might share.

Elizabeth had not yet received a letter from her father, though that was not unusual, as he generally made for a poor correspondent. She knew from Jane, however, that he was often to be found among his books, though with a greater frequency than normal.

She had received one long letter from Lydia that was sloppily written—with blotches of ink and large angry strokes everywhere—and frankly not even worth replying to. In essence, it was a long complaint about how Lydia was far more deserving of the trip to Brighton than Elizabeth was. The accusatory letter only slightly irked Elizabeth. Instead of focusing on the letter's negativity, she thought more of how she could not be thankful enough that Lydia had not been allowed to come to Brighton. Being known in Meryton, her behavior was well known to most, and really only those such as Mr. Darcy who were new acquaintances found it to be jarring.

At the thought of Mr. Darcy Elizabeth grimaced. He had been completely accurate with his estimation of her family's poor behavior, and it had unfortunately matched some of her own thoughts on the subject. His letter's compliment to her and Jane—backhanded though it may have seemed, as he had told her that she and Jane were remarkable for having conducted themselves admirably in spite of the poor behavior of their relations—was not enough to wipe away her shame. Though she loved her father dearly, even he had failed to conduct himself properly all of the time, as Mr. Darcy had seen fit to point out. Indeed, she knew her father should have been the one to curb the improprieties of his youngest daughters; it was not a duty that belonged to Elizabeth and Jane.

She stared down at her hands, having barely begun a letter to Jane. Her thoughts were now on the letter from Mr. Darcy, which she had read so many times that it must have been burned in her skull. The truth of his words continued to pain her; perhaps it would always be so.

A part of her still wanted to doubt Mr. Darcy's accusations and reject them as gross falsehoods, that she might feel better about the insults she had thrown at him. Yet even if he had not told her to apply to Colonel Fitzwilliam for confirmation of the truth, she knew she could not truly doubt the veracity of what Mr. Darcy had said, particularly in light of Mr. Wickham's recent behavior. There *did* seem to be some sort of depravity present in Mr. Wickham that could not be wiped away. And if Elizabeth had judged both him and Mr. Darcy so poorly, then how was she ever to trust her judgment of another man?

And if she could never trust her judgment of a man, could she ever bring herself to marry one?

With a sigh and a slight shake of her head, she began writing again, the lines coming out cheery and not at all reflective of her state of mind. As her pen wrote, her mind continued to wander.

She wished she could speak to Jane about all this, but she would not want to worry her sister. Considering Jane's continued low spirits due to Mr. Bingley's disappearance from Hertfordshire, Elizabeth knew Jane's feelings were delicate enough without something adding to her stress. And as for Harriet, well, Elizabeth did not feel it was her place to express such thoughts to her, as it would be difficult to tell of some of the more important parts of her thought processes without betraying Mr. Darcy's confidence. No, she would simply have to continue on without the support of a confidante with whom to share her thoughts.

At least she had learned something recently. She would have to be very cautious indeed when it came to dealing with Mr. Wickham. That was one lesson she had taken to heart.

Chapter V

While exploring the social scene of Brighton, Elizabeth made several new acquaintances. But the most interesting of her new acquaintances by far was Mrs. Blanche Wade.

France was the country of Blanche's birth, but she had lived in England so long that she had only enough of a trace of a French accent to make her seem charming. Any more of an accent, and she might have seemed a little *too* foreign.

Her husband—who was now deceased—had been a very wealthy Englishman and landowner who had acceded to all her whims and let her do whatever she desired. Since what she had desired for years was to make an impact on the social scene in Brighton, that was what she had set about accomplishing, and she had done so in an admirable fashion.

Blanche had a certain charisma that was seldom to be found. Part of her success in Brighton was due to that charisma, yet there were other qualities that were just as important, if not more so. There was the air of mysteriousness she cultivated at her home, which was filled with exotic objects, and in her person, which was always adorned with enchanting dresses; her status as a wealthy widow and thus a potential wife; her lavish parties, which were always discussed for months afterward; and her uncanny ability to read people. It was perhaps this last quality which unified all the others into a cohesive whole that made her one of the most spoken of ladies in the upper tiers of Brighton society.

Blanche always realized when a man was a fool, but even more importantly, she knew when that man was a useful fool or a useless fool. She could handle all manner of personages to her satisfaction — and to theirs, as they rarely realized they were being manipulated — and she treated socialization almost as if it were an art and she were a careful sculptor. While the widow's actions did not always appear to make sense to an outsider, Elizabeth was certain that there was usually a greater logic working of which most people remained blissfully unaware.

There was no doubt in Elizabeth's mind that Blanche was a woman of great intellect, and even though the widow occasionally feigned far less intelligence than what she actually possessed, it was always for the sake of pleasing others. While she enjoyed power, she did not demand subservience and make those around her miserable. Rather, Blanche aimed to please almost everybody. And as a result of her efforts toward this goal, she pleased herself. Brighton was certainly fortunate that she had not put her skills and wealth to a more nefarious use.

Many people speculated as to whether she would remarry, and this was talk that would have pleased Blanche, were they to mention it in her presence. Many believed that a wealthy widow still of childbearing age — and lacking heirs — needed to remarry, and of course, the ones who were loudest of all in proclaiming this belief were the single men who were desirous of making such wealth their own through marriage.

Occasionally, Blanche would take a young woman under her wing and assist her in navigating the social scene of Brighton. Frequently, this led to the young woman's marrying a very well-to-do man, though it also meant more than that, for Blanche, who was as skilled a sketcher of character as Elizabeth had ever seen, was also able to match personalities between a man and woman. That meant her protégée ended up with a very happy life indeed. So far, however, she had shown no signs that she was truly interested in marrying any of the supplicants for her hand.

Shortly after meeting Blanche Wade, Elizabeth was accepted into the older woman's bosom. It had taken neither woman long to take the measure of the other; Elizabeth quickly recognized that Blanche was smarter than anyone else realized, and Blanche saw that Elizabeth was neither insipid nor stupid and had no desire to feign being either. They recognized each other as intellectual equals, and that was something to which Blanche was not entirely accustomed.

Though Elizabeth refused to be coddled (as she suspected the woman's previous protégées had allowed), Blanche nonetheless warmed to her since Elizabeth at least allowed her to rule in all matters Brighton. It was partially because of this woman that neither Elizabeth nor Harriet (the latter of whom was accepted along with Elizabeth by sheer virtue of their close companionship) had yet bathed in the sea despite its closeness and easy accessibility. Blanche—for she insisted that Elizabeth and Harriet call her by her first name—said that they needed to wait until the perfect day before they undertook such a venture.

It seemed almost as if that "perfect day" would never come, but at last it arrived.

Elizabeth and Harriet prepared for their outing amid a flurry of clothes and questions, which reminded Elizabeth of many a day spent at Longbourn with her sisters as they all struggled to get ready in time for some event. At last, however, they were prepared with all the items Blanche had deemed essential, and they enlisted Woodston as their escort to their destination, though the footman could not, of course, actually step onto the women's beach. Blanche had particularly admonished them that they should ensure the trusty footman accompanied them, and she had instructed them as to the proper location where he should wait for their return, how they should pack their possessions, how long they should stay in the water, and how they needed to handle a whole host of other things which she believed necessary for the successful completion of their endeavor.

In a way, Elizabeth, though she liked the woman immensely, was able to draw comparisons between her and another lady of her acquaintance whom she most certainly did *not* like. Lady Catherine de Bourgh and Blanche were both similar in that they greatly enjoyed being of use to others and expounding upon their knowledge of the world. But where Lady Catherine was overbearing and sanctimonious about her superior knowledge of virtually *anything*, Blanche was bright and sunny and always eager to help, and if her ways appeared to be somewhat officious, her cheerfulness was nonetheless comforting and spoke to the fact that she clearly meant well.

Perhaps Elizabeth was able to bear the woman's bossiness *because* she had been subjected to Lady Catherine, but unfortunately for Harriet, her own opinion of the lady was *not* tempered by an experience with Mr. Darcy's aunt. Harriet, indeed, found Blanche's manners and nature difficult to endure at times, and though Elizabeth believed that her friend truly did like the older woman, she made her displeasure known whenever Blanche had managed to rile her about something.

"'You must stay in the water no longer than thirty minutes,'" said Harriet, mimicking Blanche's authoritative tone. "Indeed, Elizabeth, I do not believe I have ever had the misfortune to meet such an utterly meddlesome woman."

Elizabeth gazed at her friend with an upturned eyebrow, and soon both ladies stopped and giggled.

"Oh," said Harriet, "I have heard all of your stories about Lady Catherine and the way she loves to direct the lives of everyone within her reach, but I simply cannot imagine anyone more interfering than Blanche Wade. The woman is truly beyond belief in her estimation of her own abilities and cleverness."

"And for all that, you like her indeed!"

Harriet scowled, but her heart was not in it, and before long, she was tentatively smiling along with Elizabeth. "Oh, very well. I will own that I do like Blanche, though sometimes she vexes me greatly."

"Take care, Harriet!" said Elizabeth with a laugh. "If you persist in speaking in such a manner, I shall be forced to declare that you sound uncommonly like my mother!"

"Heaven forbid!" cried Harriet, slapping Elizabeth playfully on the shoulder.

It was mid-morning by the time the two ladies had finally set out on their adventure. Elizabeth was happy to learn that Blanche's insistence that they wait for the perfect conditions was proven well founded. The weather that day as they set out was warm and held the promise of being almost uncomfortably hot as the day progressed, and Elizabeth knew she would be thankful for such when she entered the chilly water.

Their arrival on the beach was accomplished as they were reaching the peak of their anticipation, and after expressing their gratitude to Woodston, the ladies departed from his company, assuring him that they would return directly to his protection after visiting the bathing machines they had engaged for their excursion. The young man bowed in their direction, and the ladies hurried off, their excitement building to heretofore unseen levels.

The beaches of Brighton lay before them, and here and there dotting the sand sat the odd-looking yet welcome bathing machines, which were essentially small square compartments on four wheels. For each machine, stairs led up to a door on the landward side, while jutting out over the water on the seaward side was a canvas awning which extended a little more than the length of the wooden compartment. Though they were somewhat awkward in their overall design, Elizabeth, uncomfortably aware of the appearance of a typical *bathing costume*, was grateful for the privacy which they offered.

Elizabeth and Harriet made their way across the sands to the two machines they had hired, noting as they approached that all the attendants on the beach were, indeed, women as well—the prohibition against men even setting foot on the beach was apparently strictly enforced.

After a brief conversation with the two attendants and an exchange of money, Elizabeth gave her friend a farewell hug and then ascended the steps to the small room in which she would change. It was lit by a single lantern and was bare of any ornaments, and it had benches lining both sides of the wagon, between which was a narrow aisle leading from the landward door to the seaward.

Thankful she was wearing a simple gown which would be easy to manage without assistance, Elizabeth began disrobing, only to receive a bit of a start when the machine suddenly lurched and began to move back. She suspected her fitness due to her penchant for walking long distances was the only thing that helped her avoid being deposited upon the floor.

As abruptly as it began, the contraption stopped, and a moment later, Elizabeth heard a sharp knock on the door leading out under the awning, signaling that her dipper was ready to assist with Elizabeth's descent into the sea. Taking a deep breath, Elizabeth removed the last of her clothes and opened the door.

The light under the awning was muted, yet it was still abundant enough to see clearly. To the side of the stairs, standing on the sea floor, stood a woman whom Elizabeth assumed was her dipper. The woman was older—likely her mother's age—and though she was somewhat large and was not what could be termed "handsome," her face was set in a broad smile, and she appeared amiable.

She introduced herself as Millie, and then she invited Elizabeth to come down into the water, responding with a smile when Elizabeth returned the favor of the introduction.

"Do not be embarrassed, my dear," said Millie when she noticed Elizabeth's hesitation. "I have been employed thus for nigh on ten years now. There is very little in the way of young ladies' attributes I have not seen. Now, come. The water is fine today, and I dare say it will do you good. It always does."

Taking courage from the woman's tone, Elizabeth smiled gratefully and took a step down into the water, only to withdraw her foot with a hiss of discomfort. The water was exceedingly cold!

Millie chuckled. "Your reaction tells me that this is your first time sea bathing, my dear. Once you are in the water and become accustomed to how it feels, you will not be uncomfortable."

Drawing on all her fortitude, Elizabeth stepped down into the water and allowed Millie to hold her as she lay back and floated upon the gently undulating waves. It was a most enjoyable experience, and the soothing tones of her dipper, coupled with the feeling of weightlessness while bobbing on top of the water, was relaxing to Elizabeth, and she nearly fell asleep in Millie's arms. When Elizabeth attempted to apologize most profusely for her inattention, Millie simply chuckled and told her that it was a common occurrence. In fact, she much preferred a pleasant young woman such as Elizabeth to many young ladies who were often demanding and never satisfied.

Elizabeth found her experience completely to her taste and spent the time alternately rolling upon the waves and standing on the seafloor, marveling at the feeling of the sand between her bare toes. Millie's company was also enjoyable, for she took pleasure in relating anecdotes about her experiences, imparting some of the information she knew of the area, and telling of the delights to be found on the seabed.

Unfortunately, as with all good things, this one had to come to an end. Thanking Millie for a most enjoyable time, Elizabeth ascended into the square room and soon found herself dressed and sharing the story of her experience with her friend, who had also loved her time under the awning.

"Is it not the most amazing thing, Elizabeth?" cried Harriet as Elizabeth emerged from the wagon. It turned out that Harriet had finished her own sea bathing experience only a few minutes before Elizabeth had herself.

"It is indeed, Harriet," replied Elizabeth with delighted sincerity.

"Then we simply must do it again."

"Agreed! I believe I am free again tomorrow morning," said Elizabeth with a laugh.

"But we cannot do it again so soon," said her friend. "After all, according to Blanche, 'one cannot partake in such pleasures to excess, or the activity shall lose its novelty.'"

The words were spoken in such an apt imitation of their imperious friend that Elizabeth was forced to laugh gaily. "Indeed, we must not!

However, I think I am quite willing to risk the lady's wrath in order to experience such a wonder far sooner than she would advise. If you are agreeable, of course."

"You know I am, Elizabeth," replied Harriet, taking Elizabeth's arm and steering her toward the entrance to the beach. "I suggest we wait until next week, and then we shall visit this marvelous place yet again."

Their plans set, the two young ladies walked toward the location where they had left Woodston when they arrived, talking gaily, laughing, and completely enjoying themselves. Sea bathing had turned out to be an experience that neither would soon forget, and both ladies were in the highest of spirits.

They were nearing the entrance to the ladies' beach when Elizabeth saw a flash of red ahead. She froze in indecision before rushing forward and off the beach. Behind her, she heard Harriet crying out after her: "Elizabeth! Where are you going?"

Unable to help her curiosity, she continued on, increasing her speed.

But the beach-seeking crowd was too thick and the distance between her and the red-clothed form too large, and she lost the person in her sights. Sighing, she slowed to a stop, gazing off in the direction where the figure had disappeared. It was too late to get close enough to determine the man's identity.

Still, though she could not be sure, she was almost certain the person had been Mr. Wickham. And she was also convinced that the man — whoever it was — had been staring at her.

Perhaps her mind was tricking her. Perhaps it was just another officer, such as Mr. Denny. Or maybe it had merely been someone in red who had briefly been looking at someone behind her.

Yet though she tried to rationalize it, she was almost certain the man had been Mr. Wickham. And if it *was* him, had he specifically sought her out, only to change his mind, or had it been a coincidence that he was near the women's beach?

She did not know. But regardless of the reasons for Mr. Wickham's appearance — if it *was* really him, of course — she did not like it.

"Elizabeth," said a voice at her side. "Why did you run off like that?"

She turned to Harriet. "I am sorry," muttered she, pulling her mind away from what had just happened. "I thought I saw someone."

Harriet gave her a puzzled look, but Elizabeth simply smiled and said lightly: "Shall we find Woodston, then? The poor man is probably scaring passersby with his imposing figure."

Harriet chuckled. "You are correct. His is a form that sends rabid dogs away howling like frightened puppies. Perhaps we should take pity on those near him and fetch him to ourselves."

The two women walked away, laughing about Woodston and then chatting about their experiences in the sea. But though she had had a pleasant time, Elizabeth could not wipe away the sense of unease that had been created by her accidental spotting of that man who had looked very much like Mr. Wickham.

The next day, Elizabeth and Harriet reported to Blanche on their sea bathing trip. The wealthy widow insisted upon hearing every detail, and since they were in the privacy of her drawing-room, with no servants to overhear their conversation, she even went so far as to say: "It is very freeing, is it not, being loose in the sea without the encumbrances of clothing? It is as if one is taking a bath as nature intended."

Elizabeth and Harriet exchanged an uncomfortable look. Considering the newness of their acquaintance, Blanche's words were quite bold, yet even as there was something disconcerting about her boldness, so was there something refreshing in it. After all, Blanche had made certain they were utterly prepared for what they were to experience while bathing in the sea, and both women were quite grateful for that. And though there always seemed to be something which Blanche knew and the bulk of the world did not, both Elizabeth and Harriet realized that the woman would not hesitate to tell them anything she believed they truly needed to know.

"Some people desire to view their trips to the sea as bracing, as if the main purpose is scouring the imperfections from their bodies," said Blanche, "yet I find that a trip to the sea is most enjoyable when the weather is fine. It makes it seem as if the sea is not quite so cold."

"It certainly was shocking when I first touched the water," said Elizabeth in agreement. "Had the day been windy, I should have been quite terrified to actually venture into the sea."

"There have been some terrible squalls out there," said Blanche with a tone of worldly wisdom, "or so I have heard, at least."

Elizabeth noticed Harriet seemed to be trying to suppress a snort, so she ventured: "My dipper was very kind."

"They usually are," said Blanche. "An unpleasant dipper does not attract many customers, as the activity is already a sensitive one. Am I correct in assuming you wish to go back again?"

"You know you are," said Elizabeth with a smile. "Anyone who dislikes sea bathing either hates nature or hates the sea. One who hates either can probably not be a good friend of mine."

"Oh, Elizabeth," said Harriet, shaking her head, "I am certain you would not shun anyone simply because they detest water!"

"Well, I certainly shall not embrace them either! If they detest water, then they probably detest bathing—"

"And their odor would most likely drive all polite company away," finished Blanche for her. "I must say, Elizabeth, your conversation does delight me."

"It is not so easy to craft such witticisms," said Elizabeth. "There is a fine line to tread between insulting and playful. There are some that consider me quite impertinent."

"Well, I am certain I should find those people boring indeed!" replied Blanche. "I had much rather be amused than pleased. In the former, there is laughter; in the latter, there are only smiles."

Elizabeth nodded. "But there are some people who prefer to neither smile nor laugh. With such people, you can either ignore them or attempt to breach the barrier of their dourness."

"And which do you prefer to do, Elizabeth?" asked Harriet.

Elizabeth's thoughts jumped immediately to Mr. Darcy. She had attempted to ignore him, yet she had evidently broken through his taciturnity despite herself. At least, she had led him to make a proposal, even if that proposal were not particularly pleasing. Suddenly, she felt almost like laughing. If she had agreed to marry him, would he have scowled at their wedding? While teasing him, she had seen a lighter side to him which she had initially thought could not exist. Yet she was not certain she had seen him give her a genuine smile—a smile that held the love which his mouth had professed but his face had seemed to deny. If she had seen such a smile, would her heart have softened toward him, or would the words of his proposal have merely seemed even more repulsive?

Pulling her thoughts back to her friend's question, embarrassed to have been thinking about Mr. Darcy yet again, Elizabeth answered firmly: "I should prefer to ignore such a person. It is not my duty to make unhappy persons merry. I shall instead seek to make myself happy without heeding their unhappiness."

Blanche gave her a pensive look which made Elizabeth fear she had been silent in thought for too long. But Blanche only said in response: "We differ somewhat there, Elizabeth. I fear I sometimes attempt to make people happy when I had best leave well enough alone."

"Well, your placement in life is such that you can do what you wish," said Elizabeth lightly.

Blanche gave a small smile. "Yes. I need not expend my energies in search of a husband. A widow certainly has greater freedom in our society than a woman who has never been married. It is a respectable enough position. Perhaps you should marry a wealthy old man, Elizabeth."

Elizabeth laughed. "I am not so desperate as to need to marry someone I expect shall die within a few years."

"Are you certain?" said Blanche, a teasing glitter in her eyes. "I think I know a few men who are well past their prime and would find your company to be very pleasant indeed."

"I thank you for your benevolence, but I do not mind being unmarried. After all, it means I am able to serve as a companion to my dear Harriet."

"And I should certainly be sad if my friend were taken away from me," said Harriet with a smile. "I might then have to accept the companionship of someone more interested in bonnets than witty conversation."

"Perhaps I am merely skilled at hiding my love of bonnets," teased Elizabeth. "Perhaps I secretly obsess over the right ribbons and fabrics and colors. The face we put on for the world does not always match the expression we carry inside."

"Do you hide a great pain, Elizabeth?" Blanche's question was light, yet there appeared to be a seriousness in her eyes that made Elizabeth clench her fingers a little.

Was Elizabeth so transparent that Blanche could see how troubled Elizabeth felt about everything involving Mr. Darcy, Mr. Wickham, and Mr. Bingley? She had not yet told Blanche much about her life in Hertfordshire, but the woman was very perceptive. It was certainly possible that Blanche—who was very perceptive—would be able to see that Elizabeth, in spite of wanting to enjoy herself in Brighton and put the troubles of Hertfordshire and Kent behind her, was finding it difficult to utterly dismiss thoughts of missed chances and close calls.

Somehow, Elizabeth managed to stretch her mouth into a smile and answer: "I suspect we all have our pains, but I do not believe mine to be greater than anyone else's. My greatest pain at this moment is that I have not found one perfect seashell to take home to my father. I am afraid his desk shall have to go unadorned, and he shall be severely disappointed."

"There is still time yet to find that seashell," said Harriet. "We must go bathing in the sea again! I should be very happy to assist in your noble endeavor. We cannot have your father disappointed, after all, for want of a single shell."

The three ladies laughed together, and Elizabeth was grateful for close friends to pull her from her heavy thoughts and melancholy reflections.

Their visit soon ended, and the two younger ladies prepared to depart. While Harriet moved to one side to accept her gloves and parasol from one of the servants, Blanche stepped up to Elizabeth and spoke in a low voice:

"I shall not pester you for any accounts of your past which you do not wish to share, Elizabeth, and I understand every person's need for their own private affairs. But I believe you hold some measure of sorrow in your recent past, and I wish you to know that I am always available to provide counsel or a sympathetic ear, should you wish to discuss your troubles."

Elizabeth could barely keep her emotions in check. It was in *this* that Blanche was different from Lady Catherine. She could not imagine the great lady offering to allow a friend to unburden herself, no matter what the circumstances.

"I thank you, Blanche," replied Elizabeth with much feeling. "If I should feel such a need, I certainly shall speak with you."

Blanche smiled fondly and squeezed Elizabeth's hand. "You are a good girl, Elizabeth, and I desire for you to be happy. Any teasing aside, I am not certain one of the officers would be a good husband for you; most of them seem to be somewhat of a simple lot for an intelligent young lady such as yourself. I *am* sure, however, that there is someone out there who can keep up with you. I shall be vigilant and direct him toward you if I should happen to come across him."

"Then I cannot fail to meet him one day!" cried Elizabeth, laughing gaily.

Harriet turned toward them, raising an eyebrow in question, but Elizabeth shook her head. Then they said their final goodbyes to Blanche and departed from her house.

Chapter VI

$\mathscr{S}$ea bathing was not the only activity on their list, and although they were able to visit the beach several more times, the majority of Elizabeth's time with her friend was spent in other pursuits. They shopped, walked in the many parks and along the beautiful beaches, visited museums and art galleries, went to theaters and concerts, and participated in a vast array of activities.

Of course, they were also invited to many assemblies, and they were occasionally called on to entertain the officers of the regiment and attend gatherings with the members of other regiments.

It was a pattern remarked upon by Harriet that Elizabeth had two officers who paid attention to her above all others, namely Mr. Denny and Mr. Wickham. Yet though they both were interested in Elizabeth's doings and could often be found in her company, they did not do so in tandem, for their behavior soon proved that they had suffered a falling out in their friendship. Though Elizabeth had been given to know that their acquaintance prior to Mr. Wickham's joining the militia had been a slight one, the two men had given every appearance of camaraderie and had often been seen in company together while the regiment had been quartered in Meryton.

Since their arrival in Brighton, however, they seemed to be at odds. Very seldom were they seen speaking to each other, and though they took some care to conceal their disagreement from the colonel, Elizabeth witnessed many instances in which one or the other glared at his former friend when he thought he was not being observed.

Alarmingly, it appeared that the source of their disagreement was *her*.

She had nothing specific about which she could complain concerning either man, as neither had done anything improper. Lieutenant Denny was all that was agreeable, attentive, and pleasing, and he almost appeared to be courting her in his actions, though his words left much to be desired, as he did not impart the subtle hints one gives a person to whom one wishes to attach oneself. He often claimed the first dance in an assembly and would endeavor to sit next to her at dinner or claim her as a conversation or card partner when they were in company. Yet he did not speak words of admiration to her, kiss the back of her hand, or otherwise act in a manner which would suggest that he was trying to woo her. It was all very vexing, especially since Harriet, seeing the young officer's behavior, had taken to gently teasing Elizabeth over her conquest of the "boy" of her dreams.

Mr. Wickham, on the other hand, was more erratic in his behavior. He would often speak with her at great length, engaging her attention, sometimes long after it was polite to do so. Other times, he would stand apart from others, staring at her covertly or brooding over his drink. The only experience with which she could compare it was when she had been in Mr. Darcy's company the previous autumn. Mr. Darcy had frequently stared at her, and she had scarcely known what to do other than to ignore it. Wickham acted in much the same way— particularly when she was in Denny's company. The major difference was that Mr. Darcy's stare, though somewhat irritating, had never made her uncomfortable. Mr. Wickham's scrutiny, however, brought her to extreme levels of discomfort. The more time Elizabeth spent in his company, the more certain she became that what Mr. Darcy had informed her of Wickham's character was the absolute truth. She fancied that seeing Mr. Wickham in such a state, so contrary to the façade he presented to the world, was merely an instance of his true character shining forth.

Even more alarming was the impression that Mr. Wickham was watching her at unusual times. Ever since Mr. Denny had given her his oblique warning about never going out by herself, Elizabeth had endeavored to be very vigilant and observant of her surroundings, and several times since that day at the beach, she had thought she had seen Mr. Wickham out of the corner of her eye. Of course, when she turned to look, he was gone, leaving her wondering whether her eyes were playing tricks on her. She had not again gone running after him as she had that first day, but she found it to be increasingly difficult to feel at ease, even with the ever-reliable Woodston nearby.

Mr. Denny's reaction to Mr. Wickham, on the somewhat infrequent occasions where she was in the company of both men, was a little more difficult to gauge. While he was overtly cordial to Mr. Wickham and assiduously avoided him whenever possible, he did not appear to be precisely *angry* when she was with Mr. Wickham. He appeared anxious rather than angry and often took to pacing when she was engaged in speaking with his newfound nemesis.

Though she would have preferred Mr. Denny to be less attentive to her, he was at least a comfortable companion. He was intelligent and had read more than most of the officers—who were in general a rather obtuse lot—and was capable of holding an interesting conversation.

The genesis of the disagreement between the two men remained a mystery. Whether they had both stated their admiration for her and been upset that the other was interested or whether there was something else at play, Elizabeth could not be certain. What she *was* certain of was the fact that she was rapidly tiring of the games the two of them were playing and wished they would leave her in peace.

It was during a visit to the camp when Elizabeth's relationship with Mr. Wickham suddenly changed. She and Harriet had completed their tasks for the day and were socializing for a few minutes with the officers before they were to return to the city to prepare for an evening at the theater. Elizabeth had been speaking with Mr. Denny when he had been called away. Not a moment passed before she was approached by Mr. Wickham, who was sporting a serious expression.

"Good afternoon, Miss Bennet," said he. "It is a pleasure to see you here today."

Swallowing her distaste for the man, Elizabeth forced a smile to show on her face. "I thank you, Mr. Wickham."

"It is no trouble. As you are the particular friend of the wife of my commanding officer, it is my duty to see to your comfort and care."

"Indeed, Mr. Wickham, you do not need to concern yourself with me. I am well."

"On the contrary, Miss Bennet, it is my pleasure."

The repugnance of his salacious leer was not overlooked, though as usual it was hidden underneath his carefully constructed amiability.

"However, I should wish to clarify something of which we spoke previously, if you will allow me."

Perplexed, Elizabeth could only give her assent.

"When you first arrived in Brighton, you made some references to my association with Miss King, and I received the distinct impression you disapproved. I understand how it may have appeared to you at that time, but I should not wish you to have a mistaken impression of me or of my actions toward that young lady."

Elizabeth did not know to what Mr. Wickham was referring, nor did she particularly wish to know more about the extent of his relationship with Mary King. Even when she had first learned of Mr. Wickham's sudden involvement with the young woman upon Mary King's unexpected acquisition of a large sum of money, Elizabeth had realized that there had been no real love in her heart for the man, and she had expressed as much to her dear Aunt Gardiner. She had accepted the cessation of his attentions with a sort of mental shrug. It had been pleasing to her vanity to be the object of such a handsome man for a little while, yet the loss of it was nothing to incur heartache.

Now that he had—presumably—resumed his attentions to her, she was absolutely frustrated. She was frustrated with Mr. Wickham staring at her, frustrated with constantly looking over her shoulder, and frustrated with jumping at shadows in the belief that she had almost spotted him watching her yet again. The game of continual vigilance was not an enjoyable one, particularly when the one exercising said vigilance was normally playful and carefree, and it was making it difficult to take pleasure in her time in Brighton. While she was still able to enjoy herself with Harriet, she could not tell her friend of her suspicions, and so she was left constantly feeling there was something lurking in the background.

Whether Mr. Wickham was truly following her or not, he certainly appeared to hold some sort of interest in her. Yet surely he realized that he did not, at this point, have even the slightest chance of her accepting *any* sort of relationship with him, if that was indeed what he truly wanted—and since she was not well dowered and knew his habits required sums of money which she did not possess, she assumed that his purpose was either to reduce her to the level of slave to his petty attentions or to attempt to seduce her. She needed to find a way to make him understand the impossibility of his obtaining his desire, as the situation appeared to be quickly getting out of hand.

Taking in a deep breath and drawing on all the semblance of calm she could muster, she began: "I assure you, Mr. Wickham, you need not explain—"

"Please, Miss Bennet," interrupted Mr. Wickham. If he saw the irritated look in her eyes, he chose to ignore it and act the part of the wrongly accused man. "You *must* allow me to explain myself. When I was seen so frequently with Miss King those months ago, you must have wondered whether I was being utterly mercenary—"

"*Mr. Wickham,*" said she sharply, "as I was trying to say, there is *no need*—"

"I was not pursuing her to marry her," continued he, determined to make himself heard, "though I realize now that it must have seemed that way. Indeed, how could it have appeared otherwise? Yet it was more innocent than that. You see, Miss Bennet, I learned that the grandfather who had passed away and left her with her inheritance had been intimately acquainted with my father, whom you must realize I loved dearly. By becoming acquainted with her, I was merely hoping to learn more about my father, for she had heard many interesting tales about him. I was fascinated by what she told me, and perhaps that led me to act in ways I should not have. Unfortunately, she initially failed to realize that my motives were not her hand in marriage, and when I told her the truth, she left—"

"Mr. Wickham," cut in Elizabeth at last, her eyes flashing in anger, "do you really think I shall be taken in by such drivel?"

He looked surprised at her irascible response. Apparently, he had believed his charm—which had served him well in the past—would succeed in winning her over once again. But if he had thought that she would return to her previous preference without question, he was overestimating his abilities to a great degree. Now, every instance of his so-called charm only served to make her even more upset at having been fooled by such a man.

Mr. Wickham opened his mouth to say something—most likely to ask her what precisely she meant—but before he could say a word in response, she continued in a low voice: "I am not 'wondering' whether you were mercenary in your pursuit of the unfortunate Miss King; I am certain of it." His lips pressed together tightly, and in response, she hardened her tone, though she still managed to keep quiet so as not to be overheard by any eavesdroppers. "At one time, Mr. Wickham, I was willing to dismiss your pursuit of her as prudence, but now I know it as the fortune-hunting act that it was. I must warn you that I have been made aware of certain of your *improprieties* in the past, and for all I know, some of them have extended into the present. Regardless, I must tell you, Mr. Wickham, that we can never be anything more than mere acquaintances now that I know your true character."

He appeared irritated as he stared at her, his fists clenched at his sides and his eyes narrowed. "If Darcy—" began he, somewhat loudly.

"If Mr. Darcy told me *anything* about you," said Elizabeth quietly but firmly, trying with great effort to control her growing anger, "then you, of all people, should be aware that I am the sort of person who would carefully examine *all* the facts before accepting them. And I can assure you, *Mr. Wickham*, that I have been observing you and your behavior of late with a critical eye, and nothing I have seen has shown you to possess the kind of character which you would have the world attribute to you. I know now that your actions have always been tainted with impropriety. That I did not realize it before was the unfortunate result of my prejudice against Mr. Darcy." She stared at him with utter seriousness, making her voice as authoritative as she could. "And I would advise you to stop trying to feed me your despicable untruths. I shall never again heed anything you say, so it is useless to continue to try to impose upon me."

There was a long pause in which they stared at each other. In pointing out her awareness of his true nature, she might have surprised him, but he obviously was not about to run away like a dog with its tail between its legs. Evidently, he was willing to avoid Mr. Darcy's presence at a ball, but he was not willing to simply bow down to her.

Finally, though a large part of her wished it would be otherwise, he found his voice.

"Miss Bennet," said he, feigning an expression of pain which might have been enough to convince a bystander but which had no effect on Elizabeth herself, "it hurts me that you should hold such a low opinion of me after all the time we have spent together. I am sure that if you would but allow me a few moments to defend myself against these harsh accusations—"

It was all Elizabeth could do to keep from letting out a bark of laughter. The audacity and perseverance of the man knew no bounds! Did he actually believe he could persuade her to believe his lies over Mr. Darcy's truths?

"As I just told you, there can *never be* anything between us, Mr. Wickham," said she, steadily maintaining eye contact so that he could see she was speaking in earnest. "Attempting to persuade me to your way of thinking is folly. You must cease following me at once. I will not stand for it."

She carefully watched his face and saw a slight flicker. The reaction was not quite enough to confirm that he had actually been watching her, so she resolved to push harder.

"I do not know what you are talking about, Miss Bennet," said he, taking obvious care in his words. "I have not been following you. If you recall, you came to the camp today; as an officer, I fear this is my home at the moment."

But there was something too self-assured—too *oily*—about his reply that convinced Elizabeth of his insincerity. Yet still she had minor doubts—and so she determined to tell a small lie of her own. "Do not be coy with me, Mr. Wickham. I have seen you watching me. You think you have escaped my notice all this time, but you have not. You can deny it all you wish, but I know the truth. And I must insist that it stop."

There was a dangerous gleam in his eyes as he moved toward her, and she took a step backward without even thinking. She had the feeling that if they had been in an empty room rather than a wide open camp, he would have backed her up against a wall. She felt trapped, once more the prey, with Wickham as the predator.

"Step away from me, Mr. Wickham," said Elizabeth, trying to keep her voice from shaking. "It is not proper for you to be this close."

"Miss Bennet," said he, his voice low and sinister, "I might have expected this level of senselessness from your younger sisters, but I had thought that you were more discerning. Six weeks away from me in the company of *Mr. Darcy*, and suddenly you are a changed person who is intent upon denying the truth. Can you not see that Darcy has imposed himself upon you and turned you against me?"

"All I can see, Mr. Wickham, is a man who took distinct advantage of my dislike for another man and blatantly lied to induce me to believe him capable of unchristian behavior."

Mr. Wickham threw his arms up in the air, his frustration now emblazoned upon his face. "How can you believe his story over mine? How can you believe *him*, Mr. Fitzwilliam Darcy, who struts about as if he owns the world while sneering down upon the insects beneath him, to truly be above *me*?"

"I came to know him, Mr. Wickham," said Elizabeth. "Mr. Darcy explained a great many things to me regarding your connection with him. I know what the truth about what happened with respect to the *conditional* living, your debts in Lambton and Cambridge, and your attempted seduction of a fifteen-year-old girl."

The officer's eyes widened at this assertion, but Elizabeth was not finished. "And moreover, Mr. Wickham, Mr. Darcy offered the testimony of others to verify his actions, whereas you offered nothing but your charming smile and your affected manners as proof. Your tale was a pretty piece of fiction blended with truth, but with the whole story in hand and the information you left out filling in the blanks, it makes so much more sense. Do not attempt to tell me that Mr. Darcy's version is anything but the truth. I have taken the measure of you both, and I must say that there is much more merit in Mr. Darcy's words — and character — than in yours."

Shock and rage warred across Mr. Wickham's face, the expression so far from the congeniality he normally affected. His hands clenched and unclenched while he ground his teeth together, and the fury which now covered his face was quite intimidating, as she had never seen him wearing such an expression.

"You might as well give up this pretense," said he, his voice quietly dangerous.

"I know not of what you speak, Mr. Wickham," said Elizabeth. "I merely wish to be left alone."

"On the contrary, you know perfectly well of what I speak, Miss Bennet. You may think that the coquettish manner in which you undoubtedly accepted his pathetic attempts at pleasing you might succeed in drawing him to you, but I seriously doubt he will make you an offer. He has been tolerating the advances of young women seeking to marry him for his wealth for many years now. You will have to make your fortune with someone else."

This time, Elizabeth could not suppress her laughter at his assertion, greatly enjoying the unknown and unintended irony of his words. At the same time, she did not wish to confirm anything he said; she had no doubt that his hatred of Mr. Darcy was such that her life in Brighton could become even more uncomfortable if Mr. Wickham suspected that Mr. Darcy had made her an offer. She was not certain what he would do, but she could not put anything past him at this point.

"Your assertions are without foundation, and your opinions mean less than that of a gnat. If you have such an active imagination, perhaps you should retire from the militia and begin writing your own novels. Perhaps you could earn yourself enough money that you could gamble it all away yet again at a much slower pace."

His rage was now an almost physical entity, and he took another step forward with clenched fists. "Perhaps Darcy does actually have a real interest in you of sorts. You *are* a pretty thing. Perhaps his desires are . . . baser. In fact, if Darcy has sampled your wares, then I — "

"Miss Bennet!"

Elizabeth stepped to the side adroitly, immensely grateful to see the concerned countenance of Mr. Denny peering back at her. He was glancing back and forth between Elizabeth and Wickham, suspiciously sizing the other officer up while alternately watching her as if attempting to determine that she was unharmed.

"Are you well, madam?" asked he.

"Very well, I thank you," said Elizabeth, taking the opportunity to move further from Wickham.

"And why would she not be, Denny?" asked Mr. Wickham, his charming smile once again back in place. "Miss Bennet and I were merely discussing one of our mutual acquaintances from Hertfordshire, were we not?"

The man was audacious and very practiced in his role, Elizabeth had to own. "Among other things," said she. "And I really must insist that you importune me no further on the other subject of which we were speaking, Mr. Wickham. I have already stated my opinion and will not be moved from it."

Mr. Wickham's smile never wavered, though Elizabeth thought she could detect a dangerous glitter still there in his eyes, which were fixed upon her. The situation was escalating by the moment, and try as she might, Elizabeth did not know what she could do to persuade him to leave her be. She did not think she had enough information with which to approach the colonel, much to her chagrin. But it was becoming apparent that the colonel's protection might not be enough to safeguard her any longer if Mr. Wickham felt comfortable enough to speak to her in such a fashion out in the open where anyone might overhear.

"I would not dream of speaking to you further of the matter, Miss Bennet," replied he. "I believe that I have taken up enough of your time. I shall bid you farewell."

"Until we meet again," murmured he under his breath as he stalked off.

Elizabeth did not think Mr. Denny had heard him, though she knew what he had said. She heaved a sigh of relief as he left, wondering if it might not be time to depart from Brighton and return to her family. A little distance from Mr. Wickham would undoubtedly be *very* desirable at this particular time.

"Miss Bennet, are you well?"

Having forgotten her companion, Elizabeth started slightly and opened her eyes to look at the lieutenant in an almost wild manner. Chastising herself for her skittishness, she forced a smile upon her face and replied:

"Very well, Mr. Denny. I dare say that I have spent enough time out in the sun and should very much like to return to the house for some rest."

Looking concerned, Mr. Denny offered his arm. "Perhaps, then, I should escort you to Mrs. Forster's side so you may return as soon as may be."

"That would be very much appreciated, Mr. Denny."

They began walking, and as they progressed, Elizabeth took the opportunity to surreptitiously observe her companion. He appeared as if he wanted to say something further to her, but for whatever reason, he could not force the words out. She wondered what his motives were in regard to her for what seemed to be the thousandth time. However, no flash of inspiration burst into her mind. His motives — perhaps more than Mr. Wickham's — remained a mystery.

In short order, Elizabeth was conveyed back to the side of her friend, and as soon as she explained her desire to return to the house, the carriage was ordered and the ladies were on their way. The journey was accomplished largely in silence, and Elizabeth, concerned over Mr. Wickham's continued impositions, pondered his reactions to her words and the possible necessity of leaving Brighton and being forced to give dear Harriet some excuse for leaving early.

What a tangled web! lamented Elizabeth. It appeared that Brighton was not the restful adventure she had expected it to be.

Chapter VII

For the next few days, Elizabeth was exceedingly careful to avoid the company of Mr. Wickham, though her caution seemed unnecessary. It appeared as if Mr. Wickham had finally given up on his pursuit of her. She saw him infrequently, and though she did feel that uncomfortable sensation of being watched a few times, she decided that she was being slightly irrational in her fear, as she had yet to catch a glimpse of him. Mr. Wickham even turned down an invitation to dinner with the other officers at the colonel's house, claiming that he had duties to perform which he could not delay. Needless to say, Elizabeth was not upset over the loss of his society.

Mr. Denny, by contrast, was more in evidence than he had heretofore been. The manner of his attentions was similar to what it had been before, with the man attaching himself to Elizabeth without demonstrating any other overt displays of admiration. However, Elizabeth was grateful for his care and concern, whatever the reason could be. Her latest conversation with Mr. Wickham had put her even more on her guard, and she felt safer with Mr. Denny nearby.

The colonel and his men for the most part continued to be pleasant and attentive to her, and Elizabeth, after having taken a few days to put her latest argument with Mr. Wickham behind her, was beginning to enjoy herself once again.

On a night in which they were to attend a dinner at Blanche's house, Elizabeth sat in front of her vanity, waiting patiently while the maid put the last touches on her hair.

Harriet stood nearby, having already completed her own preparations for the evening. "I do always enjoy going to Blanche's home," said she. "She always has such mysterious objects on display that it is a wonder no one refers to her house as a museum. I heard she recently acquired something from India which we apparently must see without delay, and I must confess that I am not opposed to looking upon it."

"I always thought there was no better reason to go to a woman's house than to cast an eye on her possessions," teased Elizabeth. "I should wonder why we even visit most homes more than once a month. After all, except for our wealthy friend, most people take at least that long to acquire anything new and interesting. Few ever trouble themselves to amuse us *that* much!"

"If that is your opinion, then I dare say you find my home to be excruciatingly boring," replied Harriet good-naturedly. "I hardly ever venture to buy anything new beyond the occasional dress."

"I could never find a building with you in it to be dull!" cried Elizabeth. "You must know that, Harriet."

The maid finally completed her attentions, and Elizabeth thanked her and dismissed her. Looking at Harriet, Elizabeth said with much warmth: "After all, who should then be able to tease me about the boy always hanging about me?"

Harriet shook her head, mystified. "It is rather strange, is it not, how Mr. Denny only exhibits half the signs of a man in love?"

"Not every man expresses himself in the same fashion," commented Elizabeth thoughtfully. "But perhaps he is interested in me solely as a conversation partner and nothing more."

"Perhaps," echoed Harriet. She tilted her head, looking at her friend, and smiled. "You look lovely, Elizabeth."

"Thank you. But I think your new dress much more fetching than my old one."

"Well, I suppose we must agree to disagree!" said Harriet. "Are you nearly ready?"

"Yes. I suppose I am. Perhaps Blanche will see fit to compliment me on my necklace!"

Harriet laughed. "As fond as she is of jewelry, I am certain she shall not fail to notice that very thing!"

They left shortly thereafter while attempting to guess at the possible composition of Blanche Wade's guest list. For a time, Blanche had been somewhat subtly attempting to determine whether Elizabeth had any feelings toward the officers—perhaps out of interest to ensure that Elizabeth did not marry any of the men that Blanche believed to be of no great consequence—so Elizabeth supposed there was no reason to be surprised to find both Mr. Wickham and Mr. Denny at Blanche's dinner party along with a whole host of other officers from a number of regiments. Indeed, Elizabeth had found that part of Blanche's gift at reading people relied on seeing how they interacted with others, so it would only have been a matter of time before Blanche was able to put Elizabeth in the same room with at least one of the two men. But though Blanche might have chanced on what would likely be considered a veritable mine of intrigue by having both men present, Elizabeth was determined to make it difficult for Blanche to clearly read her relationships—or lack thereof—with the two officers. Unfortunately, her scheme did not work out as planned.

Upon first seeing Elizabeth, Blanche commented, to Harriet's vast amusement, on Elizabeth's necklace. Elizabeth managed to suppress a giggle and thanked her before proceeding further within her friend's home.

The dinner that night was slightly exotic—it would probably be talked about for some time unless an elopement or some other such scandal made the gossip rounds—and there were several pieces of art that could not fail to draw the eye. Elizabeth found the meal to be a pleasant surprise, and she was feeling somewhat proud of herself for having successfully avoided conversation with the two officers who were on her mind. In the drawing-room after dinner, however, her efforts ceased to have any effect.

It started with a comment from Harriet. "Elizabeth," said she quietly out of the corner of her mouth, "Mr. Wickham appears to be staring at you with an expression that is positively malevolent."

Elizabeth turned her head to look at the man and saw that his expression was unmatched by any he had worn previously. Something in his face changed a little as he saw her watching him, but he refused to tear his gaze away.

Uncomfortably, Elizabeth averted her eyes and murmured: "I am afraid Mr. Wickham and I have learned that we do not see eye-to-eye on many subjects." It was not exactly a lie, even if it did skirt around the issue.

Harriet stared at her, perhaps doubting the truth of her statement, but they were in a room full of people, so she said no more. Elizabeth thanked her silently. She felt guilty for keeping Harriet in the dark about so much, but she did not wish to pull Harriet into the tangled web that her life was becoming.

"If you will excuse me for a moment, I think compliments are in order for the meal," said Elizabeth lightly. She began to move toward Blanche, who smiled upon seeing her approach. Harriet remained behind to speak with a nearby lieutenant who had approached her.

But before Elizabeth reached Blanche, Mr. Wickham appeared in front of her. "Miss Bennet," said he by way of greeting.

"Mr. Wickham," replied she tightly. Having no desire to be drawn into conversation with him, she attempted to maneuver around him, but he stepped into her path.

"I suspected you would be here," said he darkly. "I heard that you had made a powerful friend."

Elizabeth's mouth tightened, and she resisted the urge to look at Blanche. "Mrs. Wade is indeed becoming a good friend of mine, but I must assure you, Mr. Wickham, that my interest in her rests solely on my estimation of her person, not on her power or wealth. Now, if you will excuse me—"

Mr. Wickham began to step in her way again, and then, suddenly, Mr. Denny was there.

"Miss Bennet," said Mr. Denny kindly, "I am fortunate to see you again so soon."

Elizabeth's relief was almost palpable. "And I am glad to see you." That was an understatement. He really did seem to be a blessing of sorts; in some ways, she felt he was her Woodston for social events. Granted, the two men had opposite personalities, but they both protected her from unsavory characters.

Mr. Denny's eyes flickered to the glowering Mr. Wickham and then back to Elizabeth. Somewhat awkwardly, he said: "Have you heard from your family recently? How is everything in Hertfordshire?"

"My sisters are well, so far as I know, and both my parents appear to be in good health."

"I am glad to hear it. I know I found your sisters to be most charming."

By this time, Mr. Wickham had apparently realized that his former friend was not going to leave him alone with Elizabeth, so he gave a stiff bow and excused himself with a mutter. Mr. Denny watched him go and spoke of something inconsequential, but Elizabeth was too busy watching the other man's departure to pay him much heed. The tightness and rage that filled his countenance disappeared when he reached the side of another officer, yet his eyes kept returning to seek her out.

She finally managed to extract herself from speaking with Mr. Denny, and she walked up to her wealthy friend, as she had intended to do initially. When Elizabeth approached, the woman with whom Blanche was speaking politely stepped aside and went to find another conversation partner.

Blanche looked at Elizabeth with a frown. "Are you well, Elizabeth?"

Elizabeth pasted a pleasant expression on her face. Something about the careful way Blanche was watching her indicated that Blanche had not missed a moment of what had just happened with the pair of officers. Yet Elizabeth was not about to try to answer any questions Blanche might have had — if, indeed, Blanche would have ventured to ask them — in a room filled with dinner guests.

"Of course, Blanche. I simply wanted to compliment you on your dinner party. I was hesitant to try the dishes at first, but I was very glad I did."

Even Elizabeth realized there was a certain characteristic vitality lacking in her statements. She was fighting against the urge to become very angry with Mr. Wickham, and it did not help her mood to realize that she would likely have to offer Blanche some sort of explanation for what had just transpired.

"I believe you think me a simpleton." Blanche's tone was stern, and she eyed Elizabeth with some disapproval. Yet she said nothing more for the moment — she glanced about, clearly examining the press of diners and the complete lack of privacy in the room, before turning her attention back to Elizabeth.

"There are far too many eyes to see and ears to hear our conversation at present, but do not think you have escaped an accounting. I shall expect you to attend me tomorrow morning during normal visiting hours, Elizabeth. As all other callers shall be barred from my home, we should have ample opportunity to speak of what has happened here tonight."

It was clear that Blanche's words were *not* a request, and although Elizabeth would have chosen otherwise, she could do nothing but acknowledge the instructions she had been given and promise that she would come to visit. Besides, a part of Elizabeth longed to be able to unburden herself of her secrets and fears and to obtain the compassion and understanding of another. Truly, there could be no better lady of her acquaintance from whom to accept advice about the rapidly deteriorating situation.

Blanche regarded her with an inscrutable expression before accepting Elizabeth's declaration to attend her, and the ladies made small talk for several more moments before parting. However, for Elizabeth, the night was essentially ruined. She could not speak with Blanche due to the other woman's distraction, and she was now more concerned than ever about Mr. Wickham's intentions. Wherever she moved, she could feel the weight of his gaze upon her, making her feel tense and discomposed.

Finally, after Elizabeth spent some time wandering the room lethargically and struggling through half-hearted attempts at conversation, Harriet noticed that something was wrong and arranged for the carriage to take them back to the house. Though Harriet pressed her, Elizabeth only said that she had a sudden headache and had been requested to visit Blanche on the morrow. Harriet snorted at the news of the imperious summons, but she said nothing further, though she continued to regard Elizabeth worriedly.

The following morning arrived much too soon for Elizabeth. She had spent the night deep in thought and had not slept well due to her restlessness, and now she was feeling discomposed and listless.

She did her best to appear her normal self at breakfast that morning, but she knew that Harriet could tell that something was wrong. Even the colonel, who was friendly and kind and hopelessly obtuse about such things, noticed her distraction. In a way, Elizabeth was happy to remove herself from the house that morning despite feeling guilty at the worry she was causing her hosts.

Soon, Elizabeth found herself in Blanche's sitting room, sipping tea while her friend peered at her over her own cup. They spoke of inconsequential things for some time while Blanche's countenance became more stern and forbidding. Finally, the woman lost all patience.

"Now, Elizabeth," said she, "I noticed something very strange happening in my house last night, and I dare say you cannot help but know just to what I refer. I believe you owe me an accounting of what happened."

Elizabeth truly wanted to relate everything she knew, but some small part of her still resisted as she struggled to keep Mr. Darcy's confidence while muddling through her problem on her own; as a result, her answer was affected and somewhat light-hearted:

"Oh, it was nothing of consequence, Blanche. It was just a simple disagreement with Mr. Wickham."

Blanche fixed her with a severe glare. "Whatever it was, Elizabeth, it was *not* a *simple disagreement*. Perhaps I should tell you what *I* saw last night."

With a meaningful frown, Blanche continued: "First, though you were successful in avoiding the gentleman during dinner, Mr. Wickham glared at you almost the entire evening. Then, after dinner, that glare did not soften—if anything, it became worse as time went on. When at last he approached, you became defensive and unhappy. Finally, upon spying you and Mr. Wickham together, young Mr. Denny, who was standing not five feet from me—*and* who had been watching you himself all evening—suddenly deserted his conversation partner with hardly a word to go galloping off to rescue you from his colleague. Mr. Wickham departed shortly thereafter, and his face was like a thundercloud until he reached someone else whom he felt he must impress and it changed to one of geniality. But his eyes, Elizabeth—his eyes continued to follow you for the rest of the evening."

Blanche paused to ensure the full extent of her understanding of the situation was made clear; then she began to speak once more. "I told you last night not to make the mistake of thinking me a simpleton, and I reiterate that directive now. There is something happening between you and the two young men, and as it appeared that something unpleasant was prevented by Mr. Denny from occurring in *my house*, I demand you tell me at once what is happening!"

Elizabeth was in tears by the end of Blanche's words, and though she felt miserable, she could not but own to herself that she *did* need someone in whom she could confide.

"Oh, Elizabeth," murmured Blanche, crossing the distance between them and enfolding Elizabeth in her embrace. "I do apologize, my dear. My demands were not, perhaps, made in the most tactful manner, and I have been aware of your distraction for some time, though it was only last night when I discovered its source."

"No, Blanche," said Elizabeth, pushing away from her hostess while favoring her with a watery smile. "You are, of course, quite right. It is better that I confide my troubles in you; if nothing else, it would bring me greater peace of mind."

Elizabeth fell silent and thought about the situation, attempting to determine the most efficient manner in which to impart her knowledge. Moreover, she needed to decide *what* to reveal about the things with which Mr. Darcy had entrusted her. Blanche, somewhat uncharacteristically, was silent as Elizabeth attempted to gather her thoughts for the tale.

"Recently, Mr. Wickham has been making me feel quite . . . uncomfortable," said Elizabeth at length.

"*That* I can see, child," said Blanche, a slight measure of amusement present in her voice. "Perchance you should start with the beginning of your acquaintance with the man?"

"Perchance," replied Elizabeth with a half-hearted chuckle. "I must first tell you, Blanche, that I believe that Mr. Wickham is not a respectable young man. I have heard tales of his bad conduct—charges of gambling, amassing debts, and participating in all sorts of other bad behavior have been laid at his door. And though I was, perhaps, hesitant to believe it at first, I am now convinced it is all true."

"And where did you gain this knowledge?"

"From a mutual acquaintance—a Mr. Darcy."

Blanche was silent for several moments before responding. "I have never met the gentleman, but I have heard it spoken that he has a great estate in the north—one can hardly read the newspapers without hearing the name 'Mr. Darcy.'"

Elizabeth laughed. "I believe we are speaking of the same man."

With that, Elizabeth began her tale. She spoke first of Mr. Darcy's arrival in the neighborhood, her initial dislike of the gentleman, and their interactions in society. After that, she imparted information concerning Mr. Wickham's arrival and subsequent defamation of Mr. Darcy's character and of how she had believed his assertions without thought of the impropriety of such statements. She then proceeded to lay out the subsequent knowledge she had gained from Mr. Darcy in Kent and to explain both Mr. Wickham's actions since she had arrived in Brighton and Mr. Denny's apparent intention to defend her.

Of course, she did not tell her friend everything. Any mention of Mr. Darcy's feelings for her and his botched proposal at Hunsford was assiduously avoided, as was any mention of Georgiana Darcy's near elopement. Everything else she detailed in full, and for justification of Darcy telling her of Wickham's conduct, she scrupled not to tell a slight untruth, insisting that Mr. Darcy had informed her due to her intelligence that one of her sisters was infatuated with Mr. Wickham.

When she was finished, Elizabeth regarded her friend with some anxiety, wondering what the perceptive woman had deduced from her account. She need not have worried, as Blanche immediately favored her with a kind smile and said:

"I suspect you have not told me everything of your dealings with either young man, Elizabeth. However, as the rest may be in confidence or perhaps not related to the situation, I shall not press you. We are all entitled to our own little secrets, are we not?"

"I suppose we are," replied Elizabeth with a laugh.

"Now, let us discuss this rationally. This Mr. Wickham is making life uncomfortable for you, yet you have said nothing to his commanding officer. Why?"

"In short, I have no proof. Mr. Darcy has not authorized to make his affairs with Wickham public. I hesitated to tell even you."

Blanche fixed her with a firm look. "But he is making life difficult for you, Elizabeth, particularly at a time when you should be enjoying yourself."

"But I *am* enjoying myself," said Elizabeth. "Harriet and I go out into Brighton frequently, and I enjoy her company—and yours!—and there is so much to see and do that I do not think we shall have time to accomplish a fraction of it. And I have even been sea bathing!"

"And I am happy that you are taking pleasure in your stay in Brighton, my friend. But Mr. Wickham seems intent on ruining it. Should you not at least tell the colonel about his actions and how they are making you uncomfortable?"

"I should prefer not to do so. I do not wish to cast aspersions on Mr. Wickham's character which I cannot prove. As long as I keep to the company of others and avoid being alone, I am safe from Mr. Wickham. There is no need to worry about me, Blanche. I can assure you that I have every intention to be cautious. No harm shall befall me."

Blanche studied Elizabeth for a moment. Elizabeth nearly squirmed under the scrutiny of that gaze—and the penetrating nature of it—but she forced herself to meet it. Her friend meant only the best for her.

Finally, Blanche spoke again, but she did so with a careful slowness that indicated her great reluctance. "Are you certain you do not wish to return home? It would save you from the need to exercise caution. I suspect the militia shall not return to Hertfordshire. You would be safe enough there, should you intend to return. And returning might be for the best."

Elizabeth shook her head adamantly, her mind already having been made up on this issue. She would not be chased away by nothing more than the glares of an unpleasant man! Mr. Wickham might be unscrupulous, but she did not fear him. He disturbed her, bothered her, made her uncomfortable, certainly. Despite all that, however, she did not believe she would come to any harm at his hands.

Accruing debts from activities such as gambling and eloping with a girl whose fortune interested him were all actions that did not recommend the man, but Elizabeth did not believe they indicated he had any interest in causing her harm. Though his pleasant façade might have masked a much less pleasant core, she did not believe Mr. Wickham to be so bad as to attempt anything with her, particularly if she did not give him the opportunity to do so.

"I am enjoying myself far too much here to be chased away," said Elizabeth firmly. "I will stay. I have thus far handled a little discomfort while in Mr. Wickham's presence, and I can certainly tolerate more on the few occasions I am forced to be in his company. Please, do not concern yourself with this."

Blanche gave a slow nod of acknowledgment, yet she seemed pensive; Elizabeth wanted to ask what her thoughts were, but since Blanche did not seem keen on revealing them, any such effort would likely be made in vain.

Finally, Blanche spoke again. "Have you told Harriet about any of this? She is with you more often than I am."

Elizabeth somehow refrained from flinching in guilt. She had told Harriet—and not Blanche—about Mr. Darcy's ill-made proposal, yet she had not had any sort of conversation with Harriet about Mr. Wickham's bad conduct. Harriet was *not* a simpleton, and she was aware that something was awry. Some sort of conversation was forthcoming on that front, and Elizabeth was still not certain what she was going to say.

"I know she has seen Mr. Wickham's dark looks toward me," said Elizabeth, staring down at the ground, "yet I have given her no reason for their cause. I do not want her to be tangled up in all this if it is to be avoided, but I fear it might be too late for that. Unfortunately, I do not know what to tell her about him."

"And you think that if you told her about Mr. Wickham's past conduct, then she would feel obligated to tell her husband," said Blanche, displaying her perceptiveness. "And that would defeat the purpose of your refraining from telling Colonel Forster about Mr. Wickham. You may not know what to tell Harriet, but you *do* intend to tell her something, do you not?"

"I am trying to induce her to believe his actions are the source of a disagreement between us," said Elizabeth, her eyes averted from Blanche's. "It is not entirely untrue. I have tried to tell him to leave me be, yet he persists in speaking to me and glaring at me from across the room. I can, of course, have no control over who sees that."

Blanche's brow furrowed in concern. "Elizabeth, I—"

"He is merely upset that his charm has failed him," interrupted Elizabeth. "It has opened so many doors in the past that he is shocked that one of those doors has closed. He must be upset that he can no longer appeal to my vanity since I have seen through his façade."

"Regardless of his reasons," said Blanche, "I should like to pay closer attention to this Mr. Wickham. He bears watching. I am certain of that."

Elizabeth gave her a small smile. "I suppose I should be grateful for your assistance," said she lightly. And she was. It was good to know that she had someone such as Blanche to look out for her, as Blanche was both perceptive and resourceful. Her curiosity might be a little bothersome at times, yet Blanche knew when not to push. One such proof of her discretion was her ability to rein in her curiosity short of learning the full truth about the past dealings of Mr. Darcy and Mr. Wickham.

"You need feel nothing of the sort!" cried Blanche. "I consider you a dear friend, Elizabeth, and friends must always watch out for one another. But you must be certain to tell me if anything untoward happens. I hold a small measure of power in this city, and it may be that I can do something to aid you. Yet I cannot help if I do not know what is occurring."

"If anything especially alarming does indeed happen," said Elizabeth, "then I should be thankful for whatever assistance you can provide. But I do not believe it shall come to that."

"Let us hope not," said Blanche softly.

"Now, let us talk of other things!" said Elizabeth, wanting to retreat from the subject of Mr. Wickham. That man had already taken up too much of her thoughts, and she wanted to enjoy a little of her time with Blanche. "I saw the way you were speaking with that young lieutenant—Mr. Folingworth, was it not?"

"That *boy?*" cried Blanche in surprise, her eyes wide. "Why, I am nearly old enough to be his mother, Elizabeth!"

Elizabeth did not bother hiding her smile. "Oh, I doubt that, Blanche. He *is* quite handsome—"

Blanche waved a dismissive hand. "Handsome in the way that a young pup is handsome, perhaps. I was merely examining him closely to see if he had left any of his buttons undone in his rush to get dressed! He did not seem to me to be the sort of boy who would notice such things!"

"I think your eyes were on his face and not his clothes," said

Elizabeth teasingly, and Blanche began to protest very loudly that such was not the case, offering forth several instances of his sloppy manner of dress. The mood was thereby lightened by Elizabeth's diversionary tactic, and they continued to speak in such a fashion, teasing each other—and protesting against said teasing—until Elizabeth finally left, feeling much better than she had the previous night.

When Elizabeth returned to the Forsters' townhouse, it did not take long for Harriet to sequester Elizabeth in the drawing-room, where she proceeded to ply her with probing questions.

The first question was, somewhat understandably, as follows: "Elizabeth, why did the great Blanche demand your presence?"

"Harriet!" said Elizabeth in admonishment, trying to fight against a smile.

"Well, she *does* believe she is great," said Harriet under her breath. She then gave a saccharine smile and with false reluctance continued: "What did our *dear* Blanche want?"

"She wanted to talk to me about the dinner party," said Elizabeth casually.

Then came the second question: "Was it about what happened with Mr. Wickham?"

So much for hoping there would be time to consider what to tell Harriet. It was tempting to tell an untruth, but Elizabeth could not force herself to do it. She would simply have to answer Harriet's queries slowly while planning how much to reveal and what to conceal.

Elizabeth nodded, careful to keep her face blank. "Yes."

"I assume Blanche noticed how he acted as well?"

Elizabeth was unable to suppress a sigh as she looked down at her hands. "She did."

"Elizabeth, I know you said there was some sort of disagreement between the two of you, yet there was such malice in his glares that it seems as though it extends beyond that." Harriet let loose a sigh of her own. "Is there something you are not telling me, Elizabeth? Is there something I need to know?"

Elizabeth smiled gratefully, aware she had been blessed with truly wonderful friends who cared for her a great deal. And though she would have preferred to evade an accounting of her relationship with Mr. Wickham, she could not possibly rationalize refusing to tell Harriet anything at all. Therefore, she decided it was best to reveal part of her trouble with the man.

"You are correct in your conjecture, Harriet," said Elizabeth. "Mr. Wickham seems to have developed something of a grudge toward me. I cannot be certain exactly what he holds against me, but I suspect it has something to do with the fact that I will not be taken in by him again."

"Taken in?" said Harriet. "Has Mr. Wickham misrepresented himself?"

Knowing she had to be careful to impart a reasonably plausible explanation while refraining from outright lying, Elizabeth spoke slowly and clearly, considering each word before it was spoken.

"You perhaps remember my initial interactions with Mr. Wickham?"

"Though we were not dear friends at the time, I do remember something of them."

"To be honest, Mr. Wickham charmed me immediately upon his arrival," said Elizabeth. "I was flattered at the attention he showed me and found him to be pleasant and handsome, with the best of manners and an extremely happy disposition.

"But then, if you recall, he learned of Miss King's inheritance, and he could not make himself agreeable enough to her. Of course, at the time, I put it down to prudence, but I have since come to recognize it for what it truly was—hatefully mercenary and of the most blatant of self-interest."

"Yes, I do remember that," said Harriet. "Not being a single woman and never having been affected by—or the recipient of—Mr. Wickham's charm, I had looked on the preference so many ladies showed him with a certain amusement."

"Indeed," said Elizabeth, her cheeks burning due to the knowledge that Harriet's perceptive statement could, with a certain amount of truth, apply to her as well. "When he pursued Miss King, I learned that my heart had been touched but little by his charm and flattery, and I was rather philosophical about the whole experience.

"However, upon my return to Hertfordshire, Mr. Wickham resumed his attentions as though he had never ceased them. It quickly became apparent he thought my vanity would be so gratified by the recommencement of his flattery that my former preference for him would be restored regardless of what had occurred in the interim. The first day after we arrived in Brighton, I immediately disabused him of that notion in a most forceful manner."

"Ah, so that was the content of your discussion," cried Harriet. "I had thought something of a rather peculiar nature had occurred between you."

"Indeed, that is exactly what happened," said Elizabeth. "Mr. Wickham was most surprised and displeased to learn of my newfound discernment, and he was frustrated at his inability to reclaim my partiality. I dare say that he has not often failed in the past, and it is vexing him greatly. I believe that is the genesis of our current difficulties."

Harriet appeared to consider Elizabeth's words for some moments before she once again questioned her friend: "But Elizabeth, I cannot imagine that Mr. Wickham would look upon you with such malevolence if he were merely unable to capture your attention as he previously had. There must be something more to his anger than hurt pride."

Elizabeth had been afraid of this. Harriet was far too perceptive for her own good, and it had been almost inevitable that she would sense that Elizabeth's explanation was insufficient to explain the lieutenant's behavior. Elizabeth was therefore forced to fall back on the other part of the story which she was willing to share with her friend, hoping that it would not be enough to prompt her to tell it to her husband.

In a moment of clarity, Elizabeth had to suppress a chuckle at what she was doing. She had two friends with whom she had shared diametrically opposite parts of the story—she had spoken of Mr. Wickham's bad conduct with Blanche, and she had told her true history with Mr. Darcy to Harriet. Elizabeth wished she could just share the entire story with both and be done with it.

"You are very perceptive, indeed, my friend," said she with a laugh. "Unfortunately, Mr. Wickham *does* have another offense to place at my feet it seems. You are of course aware of the considerable level of antipathy shared between Mr. Wickham and Mr. Darcy. In Kent, I was able to hear Mr. Darcy's accounting of their history, and while the generalities of their transactions together are identical, the particulars are quite different. Mr. Wickham now accuses me of listening—and giving credence to—scurrilous slander from Mr. Darcy and not believing *him* as I ought."

"But Elizabeth, if you know something of Mr. Wickham, then you must share it with me—my husband must know if there is some danger to the members of his regiment."

Elizabeth shook her head. "There is no danger to the regiment of which I am aware. And as Mr. Darcy has not given me leave to disclose his personal affairs, I am afraid I must decline to be more explicit. Suffice it to say that although Mr. Wickham can be very persuasive, you should not give credence to all of his assertions concerning Mr. Darcy. Mr. Darcy was blameless in the affair and was able to provide proof of his version of their history—Mr. Wickham's proof was merely his engaging manner and his pleasing smile."

"This is all very singular, Elizabeth," cried Harriet. "What could have induced the man to be so explicit with you, a woman who is wholly unconnected with him?"

Elizabeth's responding smile was impish. "But you are forgetting, Harriet—the man wished for me to be *wholly and intimately connected* with him!"

The two friends collapsed with mirth, and Harriet, always eager for a good laugh, slapped Elizabeth playfully on the shoulder. "Yes, but it was a connection which you did not desire in the least!"

"Too true, my friend. I rejected his proposal with much acrimony, to my chagrin. In the course of my rejection, I threw the matter of Mr. Wickham back in Mr. Darcy's face, and Mr. Darcy responded by laying his connection with Mr. Wickham before me in its entirety."

Silence once again reigned in the room as Harriet struggled to take in Elizabeth's intelligence. Elizabeth suddenly felt ashamed of herself—Harriet deserved to know, at the very least, that he was a liar and a womanizer. Elizabeth was unsure how far the man's past indiscretions had extended, but a woman as attractive as Harriet should have been warned to be on her guard as far as the silver-tongued snake was concerned. But Elizabeth had fallen into the same trap that Mr. Darcy had—she had neglected to inform those of her acquaintance of Mr. Wickham's bad conduct. Now, at least, she had remedied that in part, sharing with her friend what she could.

"Elizabeth, may I have your word that Mr. Wickham is not a danger to the regiment?" said she, fixing Elizabeth with an intense gaze.

"His indiscretions against Mr. Darcy are of a different kind than anything which may lead him to trouble here," said Elizabeth, reflecting that it was nothing more than the truth. "As for the rest, you should perhaps be careful for yourself when you interact with him and have your husband keep an eye on him to make certain he is not running up debts which he cannot pay. I would request, however, that you keep Mr. Darcy's name—and my own!— out of any explanation you feel you owe to your husband."

Harriet laughed. "I do not know quite how I shall be able to do that, but I shall do my best. Perhaps I should merely state that I have heard rumors of debts and thought that he should know—he will undoubtedly do the rest."

"I have every confidence in your ability to obfuscate, Harriet," replied Elizabeth playfully, which prompted a giggle in response from her friend.

"Very well. I shall speak with my husband and endeavor to keep an eye on our inestimable Mr. Wickham. I cannot have him chasing my dearest friend from my side before it is time for her to depart!"

"No, indeed!" A thought occurred to Elizabeth, and she allowed a sly smile to steal over her face. "You know, Blanche declared the exact same thing before I left her house this morning. I dare say you and Blanche are far more alike than I had previously thought."

"My dear Elizabeth!" cried Harriet, her disapproving frown belied by the upwardly twitching corners of her mouth. "I am most displeased that you would think me similar to such a meddling old woman!"

The two young women laughed at Harriet's description of their friend.

"She is not quite *that* bad, Harriet! Nor is she even that *old*!"

"No, indeed, Elizabeth. But I should prefer that you keep such observations to yourself. Blanche can be very helpful and amiable at times, but even you must recognize that she *can* be somewhat of a busybody."

"True. But she is also very pleasing. I am glad to have made her acquaintance."

Chapter VIII

$\mathcal{T}$he days following Elizabeth's confessions to her two friends were spent largely separate from the company of the officers. Harriet, sensitive to Elizabeth's apprehension where Mr. Wickham was concerned, adroitly scheduled activities such as sea bathing which precluded the presence of any male companionship save the stolid Mr. Woodston.

It was during an outing when another incident occurred that induced some worry and concern. Elizabeth and Harriet had decided to investigate a circulating library. It was somewhat crowded, but Elizabeth and Harriet derived pleasure from it rather than the reverse. Though Harriet was not as much a student of character as Elizabeth was, both women nonetheless enjoyed speculating on the personalities or relationships of strangers. They were debating what kind of unfortunate bird had loaned its feather to a woman's hat when Harriet suddenly moved close to Elizabeth, who was facing the opposite direction from her. Speaking slowly out of the corner of her mouth, Harriet murmured: "Is that Mr. Wickham?"

Elizabeth froze, surprised by her friend's words. Was it an absolute certainty that Mr. Wickham had followed her this time?

Trying not to make any sudden movements, Elizabeth turned to gaze at the entrance, where Harriet's eyes were still fixed. But the door was closing, and no one was in sight. Elizabeth looked back at Harriet, not certain if she should be relieved or disappointed at having missed the man's appearance.

Harriet frowned, looking agitated as she peered from her friend to the entrance. "He was there, Elizabeth! I am certain it was him! Do you believe he fled because he saw us?"

"Perhaps it was someone who looks like Mr. Wickham, or perhaps he did not notice us," said Elizabeth with a calmness she did not feel. In truth, she believed it *had* been Wickham, and that made her uneasy.

"Yes, perhaps he did not notice us," echoed Harriet, but she sounded unsure.

"Let us not concern ourselves about it," said Elizabeth firmly. She was beginning to detest every mention of the man's name, and at that moment, she was not certain she could bear talking about him any longer. "I think we should move on to the next item on our agenda. You have planned everything so precisely that I should hate to be late for anything!"

"Ah, Elizabeth!" said Harriet with a chuckle. "You do tease me so! But you are correct. We should continue to follow the day's itinerary." Harriet's love of planning was a constant source of amusement for them, and Elizabeth was often able to use it as a diversion from the less pleasant subject of Mr. Wickham. Harriet was clever enough that she likely recognized it as the diversion it was, but she was not forcefully assertive in the way that Blanche was, so Elizabeth knew that Harriet was generally willing to grant a reprieve from conversations that brought discomfort.

They became engaged in more pleasant activities, and Elizabeth was thus able to move past this near-encounter with Mr. Wickham and enjoy the rest of the afternoon with her friend. As the day was fine, they were soon caught up in pleasurable pursuits, though both were sad that they had not planned a bathing trip for that day, for the conditions were perfect.

Unfortunately, Mr. Wickham's presence was soon felt all too closely by Elizabeth at a public assembly. The situation was, perhaps, exacerbated by the fact that Mr. Denny was not present. Elizabeth knew he could not serve as her personal barrier against Wickham's malice all of the time, but Denny *had* managed to attend quite a few of the events at which she had seen her adversary.

It struck her suddenly as she once more studied her surroundings that she always searched for the two aforementioned men when attending assemblies of any sort in Brighton, for she felt it necessary to determine what situation she would be facing and how she needed to handle herself. If Denny was not present and Mr. Wickham *was*, then she needed to attempt to make herself scarce.

At this assembly, Mr. Wickham did not appear to see her at first, so she hurriedly endeavored to pull Harriet with her toward a crowd of people behind whom she could hide. The line of dancers already separated her from Mr. Wickham, yet she did not trust that alone to serve as cover from the man's eyes.

"Elizabeth?" said Harriet in confusion after her friend had stopped. Though Harriet had allowed Elizabeth to guide her to a new location, it was obvious she had failed to see Mr. Wickham. "Is there something wrong? Do you feel ill?"

"I was simply hoping to avoid Mr. Wickham," said Elizabeth with a grimace. Perhaps her actions were cowardly, but she was tired of facing the insufferable man!

Harriet frowned. "If you would prefer that we leave the assembly, Elizabeth—"

"No," said Elizabeth quickly. "We need not leave." She gave her companion a light smile. "Besides, do you not wish to see your *favorite Brighton friend* again?"

The corner of Harriet's lip quirked upward in amusement; she knew immediately of whom Elizabeth was speaking. "I am certain I will be able to see Blanche another time, Elizabeth. After all, she *does* live in Brighton."

Elizabeth raised an eyebrow. "Ah, but she may have details on that mysterious man from Germany of whom everyone has been speaking. Surely you would not deprive yourself of such valuable information? Perhaps he may even prove worthy of marrying dear Miss Araby?"

Harriet shook her head, obviously amused. "Ah, Elizabeth! I suppose it would indeed be a tragedy to fail to attain such intelligence. After all, what should we talk about if not the doings of others? And what should we do if not attempting to match every single woman with a single man?"

"Exactly," said Elizabeth brightly. "We should be very bored indeed without the aid of gossip and matchmaking to entertain us. Why, they serve as one of our most important forms of sustenance, coming only after air and perhaps food."

"I still have yet to find a proper man for you, Elizabeth," said Harriet with a slight pout.

"Well, perhaps I am simply not meant for a military man," said Elizabeth. "And as dear Mr. Denny is not here, perhaps we should focus on finding me a more dependable suitor. Perhaps the German man is wealthy and wishes to settle down in England!"

As Harriet laughed, Elizabeth smiled and tilted her head in greeting. The jovial Colonel Forster was walking toward them, beaming.

"Harriet!" cried he with pleasure. "And Miss Bennet! I had wondered where you wandered off to! Please tell me what secrets you are discussing so intently. I am always deeply interested in the conversation of young ladies such as yourselves, and you dare not deprive me of the content of your discussion. It would simply not be fair for me to be left out of such engaging communications."

"Ah, but if we should tell you, then they should not be secrets anymore," said Harriet fondly to her husband. "Surely you do not begrudge us our intrigue?"

"Never!" proclaimed Colonel Forster. "I wish only to be a part of it, my dear. But I shall not insist upon your compliance. I suppose women must be allowed to keep some secrets. And so long as you do not talk to me of ribbons or reticules, then I suppose I can remain satisfied."

He turned to regard Elizabeth with a warm expression. "Miss Bennet, I am surprised you are not out among the dancers. I am certain there is an officer or two around here who would rejoice should you favor them with a dance. You do not wish to disappoint them, do you? Surely at least one of them is handsome enough to catch your eye. I dare say we may find you a husband among my men yet!"

"Colonel Forster," said Elizabeth fondly, "you are beginning to sound like Sir William Lucas. Do not worry. There are plenty of women present to dance with your officers, who appear not to be feeling the loss of a dance partner, and I am quite content to observe the couples and rest my feet. The assemblies here are a little different from those in Hertfordshire, so I have entertainment enough in merely watching."

Colonel Forster smiled. "Well, Miss Bennet, if you are not inclined to dance, then I shall not try to persuade you. But I must make a request. Do you mind if I steal my wife away for the next set? I know you women have things to discuss, but perhaps you could spare her for a little while?"

Elizabeth inclined her head and told him warmly: "Far be it from me to separate you from my dear friend! Indeed, if you did not dance with her at least once, then I might think you a neglectful husband!"

"I should hope that would not happen!" cried he. "I am as fond of my dear Harriet now as I was the day I married her."

Elizabeth smiled. "And I do not doubt it. You are obviously a fine husband to Harriet — and above reproach."

"Well! I do not know if I am above reproach, but I do know my dear Harriet is."

"Ah," said Harriet, smiling broadly, "the two of you had best leave off this line of conversation. I dare say you shall make me blush."

Colonel Forster turned to look at Elizabeth. "Then, by all means, Miss Bennet, you and I should continue to talk in such a fashion. I must own that I am fond of Harriet's blushes."

Elizabeth laughed. "Spoken like a true doting husband!"

Harriet joined in with her laughter. "I suppose I am indeed a fortunate wife."

For several more minutes, they continued to talk in such a pleasant fashion. Finally, however, it was time for the next set.

"I am afraid you must excuse us, Miss Bennet," said Colonel Forster apologetically.

"By all means, go. And enjoy yourselves."

Colonel Forster gave a bow, and Harriet favored Elizabeth with a bright smile. They really did love each other, and for that, Elizabeth was glad; in a world where possessions were often valued above all else, Elizabeth was firmly of the opinion that nothing could match the importance of true marital felicity.

As Colonel Forster took Harriet away, Elizabeth turned slightly and saw Blanche approaching. Smiling at her friend, Elizabeth waited for her to come closer. Unfortunately, however, Mr. Wickham — whom she had not even realized was nearby — reached Elizabeth first.

"Miss Bennet," said he in a low voice.

Elizabeth stiffened upon seeing and hearing him. She did not understand why Mr. Wickham even feigned courtesy any longer — she had made her unhappiness with him more than clear, and he would have been better off leaving her alone and seeking out a woman actually willing to fall prey to his charms, though, of course, she would never wish such a fate on another of her sex.

After staring at him with a look she deemed sufficiently cold, Elizabeth offered in a stiff and unwelcoming tone: "Mr. Wickham."

"I was hoping you would dance a set with me." His voice was pleasant enough, but there was no mistaking the villainous glitter of those eyes.

What gall! Elizabeth could not understand the man. What possessed him to believe that he could make an application for her hand in a dance and expect it to be accepted? Did he take her for a fool or a coward? Did he believe persistence would finally enable him to take hold of her?

Fighting against her simmering anger, she forced herself to speak to him in a calm but soft voice. "Mr. Wickham, should you be the last man remaining in England, I would still not wish to dance with you. You have been nothing but rude and unappreciative of my feelings. Can you not content yourself with being in the same room as I am? Must you attempt to encourage me to do something which you must know can only be repugnant to me?"

"Repugnant?" replied he, almost in disbelief. It was apparently still difficult for him to recognize the failure of his charms.

"Yes," hissed Elizabeth, her wrath growing. "I may frankly say that you disgust me, Mr. Wickham. You are not a gentleman in any sense of the word. You are but a wolf in sheep's clothing, professing to be that which you are not."

His eyes narrowed in anger. "Miss Bennet," growled he, "you shall not speak to me so." His hand darted out and grabbed her arm with strong fingers.

She wrenched herself from his grasp. Then she glared at him as if her mere expression were enough to cause him to burst out into flames.

"Mr. Wickham," said she in a dangerously low voice, "if you touch me like that again, I shall ensure that you regret it. Or do you forget that my dear friend is the wife of your commanding officer? I am not without protection."

He stared back at her darkly. "Is that a threat, Miss Bennet?"

"A threat implies *probable* trouble," scoffed Elizabeth. "I can assure you that there *shall* most certainly be trouble should you venture to take me into your grasp again, Mr. Wickham. Do you understand what I am saying, or must I use smaller words?"

His eyes were mere slits. "I understand."

"Good," said she sharply. Then, drawing herself up to her full height, she shot him one last disdainful glare before sidestepping him and walking toward Blanche with her head held high and her back stiff.

As Mr. Wickham did not step in front of her, Elizabeth assumed he was letting her go without any trouble, but she dared not look behind her to give him any reason to believe she felt fear or doubt.

Though she had temporarily solved that problem—if only for the night—she was unfortunately walking straight up to another. The expression on Blanche's face was enough to tell Elizabeth that her friend had witnessed the entire episode. And Blanche was not the type to let something such as this pass without addressing it.

It did not take long for Blanche to speak: "Elizabeth—"

"Now is not the place," murmured Elizabeth, who was already hoping desperately that no one else had noticed the confrontation. Her blood was now rushing through her veins, and she felt weak. "Might we discuss it later?"

Blanche sighed but gave a reluctant nod. "I suppose we may."

Elizabeth made a morning visit to Blanche the next day. The rest of the assembly had been blissfully free of Mr. Wickham—save for her occasional glimpses of his angry eyes from across the room, which merely served to make her even angrier with him—yet at the end of the evening, Blanche had been certain to remind Elizabeth of their need to meet in order to discuss "a few pressing issues." Elizabeth had thus agreed to visit her the next morning, knowing there would be no sense in delaying the inevitable.

Fortunately, when Elizabeth mentioned the visit, Harriet did not seem to realize that the cause for it was Mr. Wickham. Rather, Harriet simply let Elizabeth go with the instruction to tell "that harpy" she sent her good wishes. Elizabeth had snorted a little at the epithet but had not bothered to admonish her friend. This time, Blanche and Elizabeth did not even bother starting with petty conversation topics in an attempt to transition into the reasons behind Elizabeth's visit. Rather, Blanche closed them both inside her drawing-room and said without preamble: "What happened last night?"

Fortunately, an answer did not require much thought, as there was not much to say. Elizabeth merely raised an eyebrow and said lightly: "I should think you would have seen what happened. Mr. Wickham grabbed my arm in hopes of forcing me to dance, and I disabused him of the notion that I would ever be interested in dancing with him."

"Elizabeth!" cried Blanche in consternation. "It is not nearly so simple as you make it out to be! Did he believe you had given him permission to dance with you, or did he presume to grab you without caring for your preference? I was frightened when I saw that, Elizabeth. I wished to come to your aid, but I was afraid he might become violent if I did so."

"Violent?" echoed Elizabeth skeptically. "I do not think it would have come to that." She believed Mr. Wickham to be a serpent without any real venom—a garden snake rather than an asp. He was capable of inducing worry and even a little fear, but he lacked the ability to hurt.

"But he took your arm forcibly, Elizabeth! Was it *with permission*?"

"I should think Mr. Wickham believes he can take anything he desires by sheer virtue of his looks and personality," said Elizabeth with some heat. "He asked me to dance, but there is no way he could have misinterpreted what I told him when I declined his entreaty."

Blanche appeared worried. "Are you not frightened of him, Elizabeth?"

"As of this moment, all I feel toward the man is anger! He has no right to importune me in this manner!"

"Elizabeth," said Blanche carefully, "this behavior is worrisome. Perhaps you should consider returning to Hertfordshire—"

Elizabeth shook her head adamantly. "No, Blanche. I refuse to cower before Mr. Wickham. I will not allow him to ruin my stay in Brighton. Do you not see, Blanche? This is exactly what Wickham wants. He has spent his whole life making himself agreeable with the use of his good looks and his pleasing manners, yet there is not a jot of substance to the man. Now that he cannot impress as he desires, using methods which have never before failed him, he has turned out to be nothing more than a common bully, and like a bully, he is a coward at heart. He wishes to intimidate me into fleeing from him so he may congratulate himself on his courage and ability to frighten defenseless young women.

"I will not allow myself to be intimidated by such a man! He has not the wherewithal to truly harm me, and I shall not give him the satisfaction he so obviously desires."

Blanche was silent, but her countenance bespoke her continued worry. Elizabeth was touched by her new friend's concern—truly, she was!—but she would be firm. Mr. Wickham could not be allowed to triumph over her. She came to Brighton to keep her good friend company, and that was what she would continue to do until it was time to return to her home.

"Elizabeth, I am not trying to drive you from Brighton," said Blanche. "You do understand this, do you not?"

"Indeed, I do, Blanche," replied Elizabeth. She reached out and gripped the older woman's hand, squeezing it affectionately. "I am touched and heartened by your concern, but I assure you that in this case it is unfounded. I shall be well, and even if by some miracle Mr. Wickham were to acquire a measure of courage, I never leave Harriet's house without an escort. In all other social situations, Mr. Wickham can hardly do anything to me while there are others in attendance."

"But Elizabeth, are you certain you are judging Mr. Wickham on the basis of your anger toward him, or are you completely dispassionate about this situation? I am far too fond of you to see you hurt by one such as Wickham."

"I am angry, Blanche. I do not deny it. Yet I do know that he has not a shred of courage to accompany his complete lack of moral uprightness. I *shall be* well, Blanche. Of that, you may be certain."

Blanche appeared as though she would have liked to gainsay Elizabeth's opinion, but she held her tongue. Whether she was convinced by what had been said or merely believed that Elizabeth would not be moved was uncertain, but Elizabeth was grateful for her friend's forbearance regardless. She truly enjoyed her time with Blanche and would prefer not to be angry with her, as would have been the case should the woman have persisted in pressing her case.

Elizabeth's relief was great when at last she stepped into the carriage for the return trip to the colonel's house. The matter of Mr. Wickham had been utterly decided in her mind, and she was ready to be done with the subject.

The scene at the Forsters' house was much different from the one which Elizabeth had left that morning. Though nothing physical appeared to have changed, there was an almost palpable air of suspense hanging over the townhouse, like the entire structure and everyone in it waited with bated breath for some significant event. Elizabeth was almost afraid to ask what had occurred.

She was not left to wonder for very long, as Harriet accosted her almost as soon as she walked through the door, ushering her into a small sitting room with scarcely a word. She rounded on Elizabeth the moment the door was closed and affixed her with a stern glare.

"Why did you not tell me of Mr. Wickham's actions last night?" demanded Harriet.

"I owe you an apology, Harriet," murmured Elizabeth, an immense feeling of contrition welling up within her. "You seemed as though you were completely unaware of what had passed, so I must confess I thought little of the matter and decided not to cause you worry by informing you."

Harriet threw her hands into the air in exasperation. "That is so like you, Elizabeth. You try to handle your disappointments and fears by yourself rather than impose upon others. Well, I would like you to know that I appreciate the opportunity to commiserate with you and share your burdens. We are *friends*, Elizabeth, and friends confide in and assist each other."

"I am indeed sorry, Harriet, for causing you to worry and feel neglected. You are quite right in scolding me. I should have mentioned it to you afterward, but everything to do with that scoundrel has me feeling so angry that I did not wish to speak of him any more than necessary."

"I suppose that is what you discussed with Blanche this morning," said Harriet with some disgust. "Should I be insulted that you deemed it necessary to seek her advice rather than my own?"

Elizabeth pulled her angry friend into a brief embrace before telling her earnestly: "I did not attempt to elevate her above you, so please have no concerns there. Blanche witnessed the whole episode, so I had no choice but to discuss it with her. She was not about to let it go without a fight, as I am certain you already understand."

"Well, I must warn you that our dear Blanche was not the only one who witnessed your altercation with Mr. Wickham."

Elizabeth paled in response. "I had been hoping it went largely unnoticed."

"I dare say it did. However, one important person did indeed witness the incident, and he was not amused by what he saw—quite the opposite, in fact."

"It was your husband, was it not?" said Elizabeth, a sinking feeling forming in the pit of her stomach.

"It was indeed, and I was quite unable to account for his behavior last night," said Harriet. "He became distant suddenly while we were dancing, and afterward, he began to ply me with questions about Mr. Wickham. I had spoken earlier of Mr. Wickham with my husband, in accordance with the agreement you and I had made, and I believe he had determined to take the news of Mr. Wickham's likely debts somewhat less than seriously, as his initial queries revealed nothing.

"However, Mr. Wickham's behavior and treatment of you last night—and the glares he has been directing toward you for weeks, which my husband has noticed at times—caused him some concern. He *is* responsible for your well-being, after all, while you are with us in Brighton, and he genuinely likes and respects you."

Elizabeth dreaded the question, but it needed to be asked. "And did he confront Wickham himself?"

Harriet's snort was unladylike, but it clearly indicated what she thought of Mr. Wickham. "Last night, my husband made it clear to Mr. Wickham that he was not to approach you under any circumstances and that he was to present himself this morning for further discussion on the matter.

"Yet when my husband arrived at camp this morning, Mr. Wickham did not appear as instructed. Needless to say, my husband was furious with Mr. Wickham and gave directions to the other officers that he was to be found and delivered immediately. Mr. Wickham finally arrived here at the house an hour ago and was bustled into the study. I must say that I had always considered Colonel Forster to be a mild-mannered man, but this morning, his voice literally rang throughout the house as he berated Mr. Wickham for his conduct, which was not becoming of an officer, much less a gentleman. He forbade Mr. Wickham from approaching you any further and threatened him with the stockade if Mr. Wickham ever demonstrated similar behavior while he was under my husband's command."

Elizabeth could hardly believe her ears. Grateful though she was that the colonel had granted her the protection from Mr. Wickham she desired, she dreaded what she would be forced to tell him of the previous evening and her knowledge of Mr. Wickham.

But would it be so bad now? Obviously, the colonel was more disposed to think of Mr. Wickham as being the villain that Elizabeth had come to know him as. But would she still not be forced to relay her knowledge without any proof? Even if the colonel might be disposed to thinking Mr. Wickham a dishonorable sort of man, he could really do nothing without some evidence of bad conduct.

She was certain Colonel Forster was a trustworthy man, but still she could not feel comfortable betraying Mr. Darcy's confidence in such a manner. She *had* done so with Blanche, but that was only because Elizabeth knew the other woman would not rest until she knew the truth.

Elizabeth looked at her friend. "Do you know what Mr. Wickham was doing this morning when he was to meet with your husband?"

Harriet's responding glare suggested she thought Elizabeth was being daft. "I do not, nor do I believe his story of taking a walk to clear his head. But given his seeming obsession with you, not to mention the fact that his appearance at the circulation library has now taken on a whole new meaning, I cannot help but conjecture that he was engaged in watching you."

"That may very well be true," said Elizabeth, worrying at her lip.

"Elizabeth, I appreciate your independence and your ability to take care of yourself. But I must tell you that Mr. Wickham's actions make me afraid for your safety. I seriously doubt I can prevail upon you to return to Hertfordshire—and I should not wish you to do so!—but I must ask you to allow us to assist you. Mr. Wickham's actions lead me to believe that he will harm you given the opportunity, and I would be devastated if anything were to happen to you. Please permit us to help you!"

"But you have," said Elizabeth with a smile upon her face. "You are truly the most wonderful friend, and your husband, no doubt, has forbidden Wickham from importuning me any further. From this time forward, I shall keep you in my confidence and ensure I am always in your company. You need not worry any longer."

Elizabeth embraced her friend once more, and the gesture was returned with the fervency with which it was offered. "I most heartily apologize for the worry I caused by not confiding in you last night. It was unconscionable, and I shall not do it again. However, you must understand that there are some confidences I am not able to betray despite the inducement. What I have told you thus far concerning Mr. Wickham will blacken his character sufficiently, I should think."

"You speak of Mr. Darcy's confidence, no doubt," said Harriet with an exasperated sigh.

Harriet waved Elizabeth off when she would have spoken. "No, Elizabeth, I do understand and shall not press you any further.

"But I *will hold you to your promise*," said she with a determined glare. "I expect you to confide in me in the future as you said you would. And do not think you have escaped the interview with my husband—he was most insistent that he speak to you after you returned."

Elizabeth groaned but bowed her head in acceptance. Three such interrogations in one day— it was almost too much to be borne!

The expected summons to the colonel's study came less than an hour later, and Harriet was proven correct. Colonel Forster was, indeed, a mild-mannered man, yet during their interview, he showed another side of himself; while he was calm and collected, he was focused and not a little angry with his officer. Elizabeth could see why the man held the rank he did—when it mattered, he was forceful and put up with not a hint of nonsense!

Elizabeth concentrated on repeating the specifics of the intelligence she had already imparted to Harriet, implying the existence of other information regarding Mr. Wickham's past which she could not share but believed without reservation to be true. The colonel, shrewd as he was, did not press her. He appeared, rather, to be content with what she was able to tell him and to focus on the issues of which he had already been made aware.

When the particulars of Mr. Wickham's actions had been relayed and discussed, the colonel leaned back in his chair and stared out the window, apparently lost in thought, allowing Elizabeth her own time to reflect upon what they had discussed.

The silence could not last, however, as eventually he turned his attention back to her and smiled. "Thank you for making me aware of this information, Miss Bennet. I appreciate your candor and your willingness to share at least a part of what you know of my officer. It cannot have been easy—nor could it have been easy to deal with the man—but you have my thanks and my admiration.

"Now, as for the specifics of the future of your stay here with us, I have instructed Mr. Wickham that he is not to approach you in any way during the rest of your time in Brighton. I would ask you to inform me should he break this embargo. If he speaks to you, stands near you, brushes past you, or even looks at you in the wrong manner from across the room, I wish to know of it. I am responsible for your well-being while you reside with us and have no wish to see you harmed by this man."

The colonel leaned forward and rested his elbows on the desk as he fixed her with his gaze. "I gave your father my personal assurance that I would keep you safe and return you to him when your time with us was complete, and I assure you that I take this promise very seriously. Can you promise to inform me if Mr. Wickham makes you feel uncomfortable again?"

"I shall, Colonel Forster," said Elizabeth. "I thank you for your care and concern."

The colonel regarded her for several moments before continuing, his easy manners and jovial demeanor belying the utter seriousness of his words and voice. "Miss Bennet, I know you are a sensible and intelligent young woman, and I want you to know I have the highest regard for you. I am very grateful for your unstinting friendship with my dearest Harriet, and I am happy to have you stay with us for as long as you and my wife wish to remain together."

Elizabeth assured him of the pleasure she continued to receive from her association with Harriet and thanked him for his hospitality. However, she was still curious as to Wickham's fate and the state of his finances, which, Mr. Darcy had assured her, were usually very bad once he had stayed in one place for very long.

When she voiced the question to the colonel, he grimaced and fixed her with a penetrating gaze. "Yes, Harriet spoke of the rumors of Mr. Wickham's debts, but they appear to be just that—rumors and nothing more. Can I assume you know more of this than I have been previously told?"

"I do, sir."

"And this is one of those confidences which you are unable to break?"

When Elizabeth confirmed this, the colonel let out a sigh and leaned back in his seat. "I was tempted to treat this all as an unsubstantiated report and let the matter rest. But I know that rumors often hold a grain of truth, and I therefore began to investigate his affairs here in Brighton. While I did discover some unpaid gaming debts and debts of honor among the officers, I have unearthed nothing of any debts with any merchants located in or around Brighton."

This revelation puzzled Elizabeth exceedingly. She had been certain that Wickham had been in Brighton long enough to have begun to amass at least a small amount of debt with the locals. For a moment, she was gripped with uncertainty. Could Mr. Darcy have misrepresented Mr. Wickham in at least that portion of his explanation?

But no—she could not believe Mr. Darcy capable of such deceptions. Of course, the irony of that thought nearly caused her to smile at herself; it was not so very long ago that she had felt certain that *Mr. Wickham* was equally blameless. But despite this, she had to believe Mr. Darcy. He had been proven to be the better of the two gentlemen and had offered to provide evidence of his claims, including the testimony of his cousin Colonel Fitzwilliam, of whom she thought quite highly. Mr. Darcy would not have done so had there been any possibility at all that his assertions would be proven incorrect. Mr. Wickham, on the other hand, offered no such assurances and had demanded her belief based on nothing more than his pretty manners and charming smiles.

"Can you not send to Meryton to discover whether he has left any unpaid debts there?" asked Elizabeth, rousing herself from her thoughts.

"Unfortunately, I can do nothing officially," said the colonel. "Since I have found nothing to support your claims here, to send to Meryton would be deemed an improper attack upon him. However, given his other activities in Brighton, I suppose he has not had time to descend into his usual proclivities."

"What do you mean?" asked Elizabeth.

He affixed her with a speculative eye. "Harriet informed me that she saw Mr. Wickham at the circulating library. Can I infer this is not the first time the man has followed you?"

Elizabeth blushed. "I believe it is not. Many times since I have been here, I have experienced the sensation of being watched, and I have on occasion caught a glimpse of a man I thought to be Mr. Wickham, but I could never be certain."

"Unfortunately, that fits with some other information I have concerning Wickham. He has been neglecting his duties since we arrived in Brighton—though I have certainly never been able to accuse him of being the most diligent of my officers—and I believe your suspicions regarding his spying on you to be the most reasonable explanation for how he has been occupying his time."

The thought brought a chill to Elizabeth's very center; suspecting Mr. Wickham's scrutiny was one thing, but being virtually certain of it was another! For the first time since she had arrived, she began to wonder exactly what depths Mr. Wickham was capable of descending to. She would have to be more on her guard than ever before.

"You may rest assured that Wickham will not be allowed to continue in his behavior," said Colonel Forster, his tone reassuring. "I have spoken with him and brought him to an understanding of what is expected of him while he is in my regiment. I dare say he will no longer have much time available to engage in clandestine surveillance of your person. And though I cannot bar him from my table outright at this time, I can ensure he is on duty more often than not on the nights when my officers are dining with us. Is this satisfactory?"

"Indeed, it is," replied Elizabeth with a grateful smile. "I thank you for taking such prodigious care of me, Colonel Forster."

The colonel's answering smile was fond. "You are a wonderful young woman, Miss Bennet, and I am glad to do what I can for you. Besides, Harriet would be devastated should anything happen that induced you to leave her side. Again, I wish you to know how pleased I am that you are continuing to provide companionship to my dear Harriet. I am afraid I cannot always give her as much of my attention as I would like."

Elizabeth smiled at him, so glad that her friend had this kind man as a husband. "I can assure you, Colonel Forster, that the pleasure is all mine. Your wife is very dear to me, too, and I should not wish to abandon her. I dare say we still have much of Brighton to explore yet!"

His deep chuckle resonated warmly through the room. "I am certain that you shall remedy that before long, Miss Bennet. After all, you cannot leave a corner of Brighton undiscovered! That would be a pity indeed!"

"It certainly would!"

"Now," said Colonel Forster, suddenly serious again, "I shall tell

Woodston specifically to be careful of Mr. Wickham. He is a rather quiet fellow and a great man, so you can rest assured that he shall not spread any gossip."

Elizabeth nodded. "With all of your assistance, I am certain no harm shall befall me."

Colonel Forster dipped his head. "I shall do everything in my power to ensure that is the case. Remember, however, Miss Bennet, that you must inform me the second there is any sort of new development, no matter how small."

Smiling, she told him: "I understand completely."

For a few minutes more, they talked of lighter matters. Finally, Elizabeth was dismissed with one more assurance from Colonel Forster that he would make certain she had nothing to worry about from Mr. Wickham.

She left his study feeling pleased despite her earlier apprehension at having to face another interrogation. She felt a burden suddenly lifted from her shoulders, though she had scarcely been aware she carried it. The situation with Mr. Wickham had apparently troubled her more than she had known. Now, there would be a luster to everything that had been lacking before.

To think—she would be seeing less of that despicable Wickham! It was exactly what she had needed to make her time at Brighton more enjoyable. She now had only to venture forth and take advantage of her newfound freedom from that wretched man.

With a smile, she provided the waiting Harriet with a summary of her discussion with Colonel Forster. She felt guilty that she had so strongly refrained from discussing Mr. Wickham with her friend before. Yet it really was difficult to speak of Wickham's ill doings without being able to list what they specifically were. Still, after her unkindness to Mr. Darcy, she felt she owed it to him to keep his confidence as best as she could. Perhaps she was not doing a splendid job of it, but she doubted he would ever have expected to find her in the state she was in.

She could not help but smile at the thought of it. How might Mr. Darcy have acted if he had known the troubles Mr. Wickham was inflicting upon her? Would he have been angry, indifferent, or pleased? No, she knew he would not have been pleased. And even if he was furious with her because of what she had said to him after his proposal, she knew he would not have been completely indifferent. Mr. Darcy was a good man, and a good man would never have been indifferent to the plight of another.

As the conversation between her and her friend moved from Mr. Wickham to a different subject, Elizabeth found her thoughts hovering on Mr. Darcy. Was she wise to have rejected the notion of going to Derbyshire? She might not have ever seen Mr. Darcy. Yet the possibility *had* existed, and she could not help but own to herself that it would have been nice to see him one last time for the purpose of determining whether he begrudged her the ill opinion she had held of him—an ill opinion fed by her wounded vanity and Mr. Wickham's lies.

She refused to allow the likes of Wickham to control any more of her life. She hated that she had once been a vessel for his lies, and she refused to be so any longer!

Chapter IX

$\mathcal{T}$he next few days were blissful for Elizabeth and well worth cherishing. Though initially it was difficult to rid herself of her habit of constantly looking about her to determine whether Mr. Wickham might be nearby, she soon became acclimated to the thought of a more relaxed state, and she was able to laugh and move about alongside Harriet with the attitude of a woman who had not a care in the world.

The two ladies expanded their exploration of the city, as if the changes with Mr. Wickham affected them both, and they enjoyed themselves more than they had before. They were all mirth and happiness, and even Colonel Forster remarked upon it.

Yet though Elizabeth felt lighter, soon something happened which utterly discomposed her. She was at a public assembly — walking and trying to look down at her right slipper, which was pinching a little at the toe — when she nearly ran into a man.

"P-please," stuttered she as she looked up, "my apolo —" She cut off in surprise, using every ounce of effort to keep her jaw from dropping. "Mr. Darcy!"

The man stood before her, tall and imposing, his eyes fixed upon her. "Miss Bennet," he replied in kind, and for a few seconds, he merely gazed at her. Finally, however, he seemed to collect himself and said with a slight bow: "What a pleasant surprise to see you here. I am fortunate indeed to meet with you."

Elizabeth could not help but stare at him for a few moments before she was able to bring herself to speak. She had had no idea she would be seeing Mr. Darcy this night, if ever again! She had avoided visiting Derbyshire in order to prevent even the slightest opportunity of seeing him there, and now here he was in Brighton, standing right in front of her! Her cheeks became hot at the memory of how they had last parted and how badly she had treated him. She felt he would be justified to be unhappy at the sight of her, yet he did not appear to be displaying any such negative emotion; he simply continued to gaze intently at her. If anything, he appeared almost . . . happy.

Elizabeth finally managed to find her voice. "I was not aware you would be in Brighton, Mr. Darcy." There was a hint of a question in her statement—why *was* he here? She would never have believed *Brighton* to be the sort of place he would visit for either business or pleasure. Of the former, there could not be much, and of the latter, well, she simply knew that he was not the type to pursue pleasure for pleasure's sake.

"I arrived very recently; it is not only women who enjoy the baths of Brighton," replied he shortly. He did not, she noticed, seem keen on giving an extended response to her implied question. "Have you been enjoying your stay?"

"Yes," said she with a nod. "I am here at Mrs. Forster's invitation, and I have been accompanying her about the city. We have enjoyed the sea baths, but there are also many other amusements. In a city such as this, it would be difficult indeed to find oneself wanting for activities to pursue. The circulating libraries alone are enough to entertain me for quite some time, though Mrs. Forster does not allow me to sit with my nose in a book for long."

There was a slight motion at the corners of his mouth which she was certain had almost been a smile. Then, he inquired casually: "Have you enjoyed the society of Brighton?"

"I know the officers, of course, from Hertfordshire," said Elizabeth. She considered mentioning the fact that Wickham was around, but Mr. Darcy must have surely realized that. Besides, to mention Mr. Wickham would also be to bring to Mr. Darcy's mind the lies the man had told, and she did not wish to do that. "But there are many kind people here. In particular, I have become close friends with a Mrs. Blanche Wade."

"Mrs. Wade?" echoed Mr. Darcy, tilting his head in interest, though there was something odd in his expression. "I have heard her name before."

"Her deceased husband left her quite a fortune, and she is well established among the upper members of Brighton society. I should not be surprised if you have heard of her."

"Her fame appears to have gone before her," was Darcy's dry reply. Elizabeth did not know to what Mr. Darcy was referring, but he did not leave her with much time to think on it. "Perhaps you would be so good as to introduce me to her during my stay."

"I am certain that can be arranged, Mr. Darcy."

The situation was awkward, and it was made even further so by the fact that neither Elizabeth nor Mr. Darcy knew where to direct the discussion. There seemed to be an embargo on every subject.

"Excuse me, Miss Bennet, but your family is all well, I trust?" said Mr. Darcy suddenly.

"Oh, yes, very well, I thank you."

"And all your sisters—are they still at home?"

Elizabeth thought this was a very strange question. To ask after her family was merely polite, but to ask after her sisters was odd, especially since he had never given any indication of wanting anything beyond mere acquaintance with any of them.

"My sisters are all at Longbourn but one," replied she. "My second youngest sister, Catherine, is traveling to Derbyshire with my aunt and uncle, and they intend to stay for a short while at Lambton, where my aunt spent some years of her youth."

Elizabeth laughed and continued in a teasing tone: "I am afraid they have invaded your very neighborhood, Mr. Darcy."

"I hardly think they could be called invaders," rejoined Mr. Darcy with a slight smile. Elizabeth could only reflect that if he had smiled more often when he had first come to Hertfordshire, she might have looked on him with something other than contempt. "I dare say your aunt will appreciate the ability to once again visit with acquaintances from her youth. Lambton is a delightful town."

"Yes, sir. I believe she was anticipating it keenly," said Elizabeth.

She paused for a moment, studying him, and then, determined to mirror his civility, she said: "Excuse me, Mr. Darcy, but is your family well?"

"Yes, indeed. I thank you for asking. I was recently in London with my sister, but she has since returned to Derbyshire to spend the summer months. And Lady Catherine and her daughter are much as they ever were, while Colonel Fitzwilliam is engaged in his duties as usual. In fact, as his duties often bring him to Brighton, I should not be surprised if we see him here at some time or another."

"It must be very agreeable to know that he was not sent into the fight against Napoleon."

"Yes, it is. I believe his mother — my aunt — is particularly grateful that he appears to be safe from such a dangerous post for at least the near future. He will join my sister and me at Pemberley later this summer, where we hope he will be able to stay a few weeks at least."

"I am certain that would be most welcome, indeed," murmured Elizabeth.

Unfortunately, one could only speak of acquaintances for so long before a conversation felt forced. Their avenues of conversing seemingly exhausted, they stood for some moments, each unsure as to what to say, and though the assembly hall was quite crowded and raucous, it seemed as if they were alone, and the silence between them was deafening.

She still did not understand how Mr. Darcy had come to be here of all places. She wondered whether their meeting was one which he had planned or one which had occurred completely by chance, incredible though that chance appeared. Furthermore, she wondered why he truly came to Brighton . . . and what he now thought of her.

But the man was an enigma — his countenance and his words were ever-cryptic and difficult to understand, giving her no indication as to his thoughts. This was a man in whom she had mistaken admiring looks for those meant to discover faults and criticize; it seemed hopeless that she would ever have enough insight into his character to gain even a modicum of understanding of him.

Suddenly, the silence between them became so oppressive to Elizabeth that she grasped at even the feeblest excuse at conversation. "I was surprised to see you here, sir. How long will you stay in the area?"

"I have not yet decided," replied Mr. Darcy. "I should hope to stay some weeks, as I have spent little time in Brighton, though I have heard much about it." Mr. Darcy paused, and a wry smile appeared on his face. "Originally, I had an engagement at Pemberley scheduled for the beginning of August, but since that has now been canceled, I find myself quite at my leisure. I believe that I shall stay for some weeks at the very least. And you? Do you mean to stay through the summer?"

"I am entirely at Mrs. Forster's disposal. I have been here since late May when the regiment departed Meryton, and I believe I shall likely stay until at least the end of the summer. However, there was no fixed limit upon the amount of time I was to spend with my dear friend, and should she ask me to extend my stay, I should likely be quite happy to do so."

"Miss Bennet, if you are not otherwise engaged, will you do me the honor of dancing the next set with me?"

While Elizabeth was shocked to have met Mr. Darcy in Brighton of all places, his application for her hand for a dance was especially astonishing. By all rights, this man should have avoided her as though she carried some deadly contagion, yet he spoke to her amiably, though perhaps not with perfect composure, and he had even asked her to dance! What could he mean by it?

He grew uncomfortable as she stared at him without making a reply. "You may refuse if you like," said he, his voice calm, though she was certain he was anything *but* composed on the inside. "If you wish it, I shall withdraw my application so that you may still dance with other men."

"Oh, that is not necessary, Mr. Darcy," said Elizabeth, attempting to ease his discomfiture. She saw in an instant that he had made the application impulsively, though what that said about his intentions, she was not entirely certain. "I would be happy to dance the next set with you, as I am not engaged for it."

"Are you certain, Miss Bennet?" asked he, fixing her with his intense stare. "Your silence suggested that my request was not welcome, and I would not wish to make you uncomfortable. I would gladly withdraw rather than make you feel so."

"Mr. Darcy," said Elizabeth. "I assure you that I am not discomfited in any way. I will be happy to allow you the dance you requested. I had merely not expected such an application—I had rather expected you to avoid me as much as possible after what happened the last time we met."

The intensity of his gaze never wavered, though he was silent for several moments, apparently trying to decide exactly how to respond. For a moment, Elizabeth dared to believe that he held her in the same regard as he had in Hunsford—he *had* spoken with her almost amiably and asked her to dance, after all. Then, reality asserted itself; he was, first and foremost, a gentleman, and one with a proud and illustrious heritage. He would naturally be very conscious of offering every civility with any of his acquaintances, even those who had refused an offer of marriage in an acrimonious manner.

"Miss Bennet, despite our shared history, I would like to believe that we can behave as respectful adults when in one another's company. In fact, I should very much like to approach our meeting here as a fortunate happenstance that shall allow me to make amends for the poor impression I gave when I first arrived in Hertfordshire. As you know, I was not at my best at the time, and though that is not intended to be an excuse, I should very much like to come to know you better and in a more agreeable manner than our initial interactions allowed. If that is pleasing to you, of course."

For perhaps the first time in the course of her acquaintance with Mr. Darcy, Elizabeth fancied she saw something else in him other than that titanic pride which had been so overwhelming a characteristic before. It did not help that the man was gazing at her hopefully, a slight smile gracing his face. Yes, she was now becoming very aware of the devastating effect this man could have upon members of the opposite sex if he only smiled more often.

Besides, what he had said was only sensible, after all. She had already allowed him finer qualities than she had previously been willing to acknowledge, and the thought of coming to know him in a setting where he could relax and allow his true self to come out was very appealing.

"I believe I should like that, Mr. Darcy," said she, feeling a hint of a blush upon her face. "Perhaps we can make an attempt at being friends without the misunderstandings of the past coming between us."

If she thought the half smile which had adorned his face previously to be devastating, it was nothing compared to when he broke out in a truly delighted smile at her declaration.

He said not another word, merely taking her hand and leading her to the dance floor, as the music for his promised set had begun. Out of the corner of her eye, Elizabeth saw Harriet watching nearby. Elizabeth was certain there was an expression of curiosity mixed with absolute amazement on her friend's face—just as she knew Harriet would be interrogating her quite mercilessly later—but she dared not look at her directly. Elizabeth was not entirely sure what she should be feeling, and there was a chance she would begin flushing uncontrollably if she caught Harriet's eye. It was better to concentrate on Mr. Darcy alone for the time being. It would be safer that way.

They assumed their positions—Elizabeth doing so with only the slightest sense of trepidation—and the set commenced.

There was something vitally different about this dance when compared to their first in Hertfordshire. Back then, conversation had seemed as if it would never come of its own accord, and she had finally forced Mr. Darcy to speak on the subject of dancing itself—and of how their status as dancers required them to say *something*, whether it simply be to remark on the number of couples or on the size of the room. His countenance then had been stern, and the conversation between them had been somewhat forced. He had not been disposed to speaking in the slightest, and she had wanted to induce him to do so only because she felt it would serve as a sort of punishment to him. It had not been a pleasant dance for a variety of reasons—not the least of which was her mention of Mr. Wickham's loss of Mr. Darcy's friendship—and Elizabeth could barely refrain from grimacing upon thinking about it.

Now, the way they danced together appeared subtly transformed. His mouth did not make a firm and unhappy line; rather, she thought she saw the traces of a smile tugging at it. And the touch of his hand, rather than being an inconvenience to be borne, was a curiosity to be sought after. No longer could she view him as cold and conceited and worthy only of contempt. Though it had been painful to be shown the error of her ways—and though she had tried so desperately to avoid seeing Mr. Darcy again—she had made it through the trials of her prejudice, and now that she was looking upon him, she realized that she was immensely glad to have been given the chance to be in his company once more. Whether she would continue to see him throughout his stay in Brighton remained to be seen. She was surprised, in fact, that he should have chosen to attend an assembly such as this alone, for she knew how much he disliked dancing with strangers. But perhaps the reason for it was something she would learn in time.

Yet as she stared across at him, trying once more to figure out the mystery that was Mr. Darcy, she found herself hoping—much to her surprise—that she *would* be able to see him again. And perhaps he hoped that as well; he had, after all, said he wished to approach their meeting "as a fortunate happenstance," and he had even said he hoped to come to know her better. Furthermore, he *had* indicated he wanted her to introduce him to Blanche, and that would only be possible were he and Elizabeth to see each other again.

Finally, Mr. Darcy said to her: "It has been some time since we last met."

Elizabeth suppressed a smile. If the taciturn Mr. Darcy was attempting to make conversation, then he must have been at least somewhat inclined to please her. Teasingly, she told him: "It has not been that long, Mr. Darcy. Do not say that you missed me. I am certain you have had far too much to capture your attention for you to spare me a second's thought."

He did not respond verbally; he merely gave her a half-smile which again affected her more than she cared to own to herself.

They continued to dance without much more conversation. Mr. Darcy did inquire as to precisely where she was staying, but they discussed little more than that. Elizabeth was too consumed by a myriad of confused thoughts to pay much heed to the fact that Mr. Darcy did not seem inclined toward conversation either.

Since she had left Kent, Elizabeth had imagined several times what it would be like to come across Mr. Darcy again. Never had she believed that it would happen in Brighton—and that he would request she dance with him! Perhaps that was what seemed so strange. She had been so taken aback by his request that he had mistaken her surprise for reluctance, if not distaste. She had already been unbalanced by the circumstance of their meeting in Brighton, and his application for her hand had merely exacerbated that. On first speaking to each other, it had been awkward, but rather than their meeting as two people between whom hard feelings existed, it had been more as if they were meeting as two repentant and embarrassed children in order to make amends for fits of pique.

Of course, there was little that was childish about Mr. Darcy's figure. His form was handsome, which she had always known, but the grimness of his countenance had always detracted from his natural beauty. Now, however, with just the slightest of smiles touching his face, it was as if he had transformed. She could not help but marvel at it.

When the set ended, Elizabeth smiled at him and received a brilliant smile in return.

"Thank you for allowing me this dance, Miss Bennet," said he softly.

"It was my pleasure, Mr. Darcy," replied she, trying to suppress the shiver that traveled down her spine at the sound of his voice. "You are a skilled dancer."

"All of my grace, if indeed there was any to be found, was simply a product of having such a fine partner." He turned his head slightly, an amused expression touching his face as he beheld something nearby. "I believe your friend wishes to speak to you." He gave a smooth bow of parting. "I will let you go to her. I look forward to seeing you again."

"And I you, Mr. Darcy," said Elizabeth with a curtsey. Her cheeks were warm. Had Mr. Darcy asked where she was staying so that he might call on her, or was she reading too much into his words? Ah, if only he was not so difficult to read!

He gave her one last smile before moving to walk away, and she watched him, almost in a daze. She still was not utterly certain that this was not a dream.

A few seconds later, Harriet was at her side, whispering furiously: *"Elizabeth, was that really Mr. Darcy?"*

"Yes, Harriet, it was," said Elizabeth calmly, as if seeing Mr. Darcy were an everyday occurrence. But inwardly, her heart was pounding at the memory of that last smile.

"I scarcely recognized him with such a pleasant expression on his face!" said Harriet, tugging Elizabeth to a more secluded area so they would not be overheard. "What did you say to him to make him smile so?"

Elizabeth shook her head, trying to clear it. She had indeed never seen him quite so happy. "I am not certain. I merely know that I was surprised to find him here. I had rather thought he might be in Derbyshire."

Harriet's answering grin was almost mischievous. "Do you think he is here because of you?"

"Do not be silly, Harriet," said Elizabeth dismissively. Though the thought had actually crossed her mind—briefly—she knew it could not be the case. "He had no way of knowing I would be in Brighton. I doubt he would have spoken to anyone in Hertfordshire about where I was, and I certainly did not realize before I left Kent that I would be coming to Brighton, so I did not say anything to him about such travel plans. I do not see how he could have found out."

"You do not believe he could have made inquiries in Hertfordshire?" persisted Harriet, determined to make a link between Elizabeth and the appearance of Mr. Darcy.

"I do not believe he would do that," said Elizabeth firmly. "I doubt he is on intimate enough terms with anyone in Hertfordshire to make any queries of the sort that you mention. He did not go there for the purpose of making new friends."

"But he once wished to make you his wife," said Harriet in a low voice. "Is it not possible that he came here with that aim in mind?"

"Mr. Darcy is not the type of man to pursue a woman from one city to another," said Elizabeth confidently. "His presence must be coincidental. I am sorry, Harriet, but I do not see any other explanation."

Begrudgingly, Harriet said: "Perhaps you are correct, Elizabeth. But think of poor Mr. Denny! He shall have some competition now—only Mr. Darcy is very much a man rather than a boy, so I fear Mr. Denny shall be the one to be disappointed!"

Shaking her head, Elizabeth somehow refrained from rolling her eyes in exasperation. "Any possibility for a future between Mr. Darcy and me is in the past, Harriet."

"Judging by the smile on his face, Elizabeth," said Harriet, "I should think you are quite wrong indeed!"

The next day, Elizabeth and Harriet visited Blanche during the usual morning hours. They were taken to the drawing-room, where they found Blanche wearing a headdress intricately decorated with feathers. Impressed, Elizabeth commented on it, and Harriet then inserted playfully: "Perhaps you ought to look into obtaining one yourself, Elizabeth! After all, Mr. Darcy might like it!"

"I doubt that, Harriet!" replied Elizabeth, her mirth almost overflowing. "After all, Miss Bingley was a great lover of feathers, if the outfits she wore while living at Netherfield were any indication, and I doubt Mr. Darcy ever looked twice at her, however much she might have wished he had!"

"Mr. Darcy?" echoed Blanche in confusion.

But Harriet was completely oblivious to Blanche's sudden bewilderment. "Yes, did Elizabeth not tell you? This previous autumn, we met a gentleman who was staying temporarily in Hertfordshire, a very rich and proud man named Mr. Darcy from Derbyshire."

Blanche's sharp gaze rested upon Elizabeth. "I believe the name of the gentleman has come up in conversation."

"Well, last night he appeared at the assembly without any warning. And you know what he did? He danced but one dance—with Elizabeth—before quitting the place entirely."

"Indeed?" said Blanche, one elegant eyebrow raised in Elizabeth's direction.

"It is nothing, really," said Elizabeth, directing a pointed glance in Harriet's direction. She was uncomfortable with the situation given the fact that she *had not* informed Blanche of her history with Mr. Darcy. She trusted Harriet with her secrets—truly, she did—but Harriet could not know how much Blanche had been told.

"Mr. Darcy is in Brighton for some relaxation and sea bathing," continued Elizabeth, "and he happened to be at the assembly last night. I was the only one there who was acquainted with the gentleman, and as Harriet is aware, Mr. Darcy is not particularly skilled at making new acquaintances and does not dance with women whom he does not know."

Harriet had apparently taken the hint, as she was now silent and watchful, a vaguely apprehensive expression on her face. Elizabeth, by contrast, was doing her best to appear nonchalant about the affair.

"And is Mr. Darcy not acquainted with Harriet?" asked Blanche.

"Mr. Darcy did not *see* Harriet," said Elizabeth. "I was the first one he met whom he knew."

Blanche peered at her suspiciously. "So Mr. Darcy gave no more explanation for his presence in Brighton other than a desire to partake in sea bathing?"

"I should think that Mr. Darcy does not feel he needs to justify his movements to me—or to anyone else, for that matter."

"I suppose he does not," murmured Blanche, "though I find it somewhat surprising that he would leave the assembly so quickly after having danced but one time."

Rather than encourage further speculation, Elizabeth took the opportunity to turn the conversation to other matters.

While her diversionary tactics seemed somewhat successful, Elizabeth continued to watch Blanche closely. The other woman gave the appearance of complacent amiability, but in truth, she contributed little to the conversation. This news of Mr. Darcy had done something to Blanche's equilibrium, but the reason for it escaped Elizabeth; Blanche had already told Elizabeth that she was not acquainted with Mr. Darcy, so Elizabeth was unsure how the man's arrival could affect Blanche.

Of course, Blanche could be attempting to determine the reason for the man's sudden appearance, perhaps considering the possible causes of Elizabeth's reticence to discuss her relationship with Mr. Darcy. Whatever she had guessed, Elizabeth was content to allow her to speculate—perhaps there would come a time when she could share with her friend the events of her connection with Mr. Darcy, but she preferred to remain silent for now.

After the appropriate time for a morning visit had passed, Harriet and Elizabeth departed to take in some more sights of the city. Blanche said farewell, giving them every indication that she would return their call in the next few days.

Little did Elizabeth know that she would be experiencing a very strange week after that visit. One welcome development was the fact that she saw very little of Mr. Wickham. The colonel, true to his word, was watching the man closely, making certain that he performed his duties as he ought, which left Wickham little enough time to be following Elizabeth throughout the streets of Brighton. And the one time the officers had been invited to dine with the colonel and the ladies, Wickham had been on duty and was unable to attend.

Of course, had Mr. Wickham seen fit to ignore Colonel Forster's restrictions on following Elizabeth and neglecting his duties, an unpleasant experience in the camp's stockade undoubtedly awaited him, which seemed to compel his compliance.

On the one occasion in which Elizabeth was in his proximity — if not directly in his company — he had feigned ignoring her, though she had felt his eyes surreptitiously watching her.

Mr. Denny, by contrast, was just as much in evidence as he had been in the past, but though he was still amiable and attentive when directly speaking with her, he was much more relaxed in both his manner and his vigilance. The one exception was the occasion in which she and Harriet had visited the camp and been in the presence of Wickham — in that situation, Denny had stayed close to the ladies and had spent much time conversing with Elizabeth while watching Wickham carefully. Elizabeth had had to endure more teasing from her friend as a result of this, for Denny's ardor was deemed by Harriet to have cooled.

But whereas the first few weeks in Brighton had been spent searching for any sign of Wickham following her, now Elizabeth had begun unconsciously searching for any sign of Mr. Darcy. While she did not have any reason to believe that Darcy's presence in Brighton was to be attributed to anything but what the man had said himself, this was one of those instances in which her head and heart were disconnected from one another. Intellectually, Elizabeth knew that Mr. Darcy had not decided to visit Brighton because of her; her heart — and perhaps her vanity — refused to believe it, and she wondered if he had actually learned of her presence and had purposefully sought her out.

But how could his affection for her not have cooled? She had refused him in a manner which could have left no doubt in his mind of the true state of her feelings for him. And though her opinions had been based on faulty assumptions and deliberate misinformation, the fact of the matter was that she *had* refused him . . . and vehemently so. No man — especially one of Mr. Darcy's stature and sense of personal pride — could possibly continue to seek her out given the history between them.

No, her initial impression had been correct; she could not help but imagine that Mr. Darcy could easily find a replacement for her in his heart. Other considerations would surely drive all transitory affection for her away, allowing him to move on to some other young lady more deserving by society's standards.

What she could not be certain of was the state of her own feelings for the man. The dislike that she had felt early in their acquaintance had evaporated as if it were nothing more than a faint aroma on a windy day. But though she had lost her previous dislike for him, still she did not precisely *like* him either. It would take more than one dance spent companionably to transform her opinion entirely. But the precise definition of her feelings eluded her, leaving her at a loss. For a young woman of Elizabeth's confidence and intelligence, it was not a welcome state of mind.

It was two days after she visited Blanche when Mr. Darcy once again unexpectedly entered into Elizabeth's life.

As promised, Blanche returned the visit to the rented townhouse, and the three ladies chatted amiably in the drawing room. Blanche had not been there for many moments before the sound of the door chimes was heard throughout the house, announcing another visitor. A minute or two later, the door opened, the visitor was announced, and Mr. Darcy strode into the room.

Though she was able to gather herself enough to stand and curtsey to Mr. Darcy, Elizabeth was unsettled. Mr. Darcy had come. He, a man who had more cause to avoid her than perhaps anyone of her acquaintance, had actually sought her out!

He bowed to the ladies' curtseys, greeting them amiably but with his characteristic taciturnity. Knowing that her newest friend had not been introduced to the gentleman, Elizabeth took on the office of making them acquainted with one another.

"Mr. Darcy, it appears that you have had fortunate timing indeed," said Elizabeth. "Please allow me to introduce my friend, Blanche Wade. Mrs. Wade, this is Mr. Fitzwilliam Darcy, whom I had the pleasure of meeting in Hertfordshire last autumn."

"Delighted, madam," said Mr. Darcy, bowing over Blanche's hand.

"The feeling is mutual, sir," said Blanche. "I had hoped I would meet you, as I have heard much of you."

Mr. Darcy raised an eyebrow. "Truly? I had no idea my fame had preceded me to such an extent."

"Elizabeth has told me a little of your time together in Hertfordshire and then Kent earlier this spring."

Faintly blushing, Mr. Darcy glanced at Elizabeth. "I hope the opinion of me that she gave was favorable."

"Indeed, I believe it was, Mr. Darcy," said Blanche with a smirk. "I have learned that though Elizabeth has a tendency to be very forthright with her appraisals of others, she is scrupulously fair. I dare say the picture she painted of you was one that you would have found pleasing. She seems to believe your opinions worth listening to."

"Come, now," said Elizabeth, her own cheeks coloring slightly to match Mr. Darcy's, "you shall give away all my secrets!"

Blanche looked at her and raised an eyebrow. "What is the matter, Elizabeth? Are you suggesting that Mr. Darcy's opinions would not match your own?"

"The opinions of two people can never be completely in harmony," replied Elizabeth, directing a warning glare at her friend and hoping that Mr. Darcy could not recognize it for what it was. "For instance, I suspect Mr. Darcy is much more interested in the running of his estate and the availability of sport than I am, and I doubt very much that he would care to hear all about my well-formed opinions on dresses and lace!"

Mr. Darcy tilted his head, and Elizabeth was not certain, but she believed there was a hint of amusement tugging at his eyes. "I am surprised to hear you professing such care for clothing. I seem to recall a time when your petticoat was covered in several inches of mud and you cared not a whit for its state."

The reminder of her walk from Longbourn to Netherfield to see her ill sister made Elizabeth avert her eyes in slight embarrassment, but Mr. Darcy's strangely humorous mood was apparently contagious, as Blanche cried out in response: "Ah, so the truth is now out in the open for all to see! Elizabeth, you cannot tell me that you have any special care for clothing, though you might pretend at times to feel otherwise. Perhaps you are more like Mr. Darcy than you realize!"

"Ah, do not be unkind," said Harriet, "for I dare say Elizabeth has at least a little of the fondness for clothing held by many of our sex. She always makes such a fine figure at assemblies, as I am certain you notice when watching the number of young men who wish to sweep her off onto the dance floor. Her clothing is never lacking, even if it is occasionally dusted with mud or dirt from her walks."

"Come!" cried Elizabeth. "I do not know how this conversation progressed from a discussion of Mr. Darcy to a discussion of me, but I think we should leave off the current subject! I am certain we have better things to talk about."

Mr. Darcy dipped his head slightly in acknowledgment of Elizabeth's request, though his slightly pursed lips made it appear as though he were inclined to argue. Then, slowly, he turned to Harriet, who had been somewhat quiet. "Mrs. Forster, are you enjoying your time in Brighton?"

Elizabeth nearly raised an eyebrow in surprise. Was Mr. Darcy being sociable?

"Certainly, Mr. Darcy," said Harriet. "But how could I not with Elizabeth here by my side?"

"How, indeed," murmured Mr. Darcy. He glanced at Elizabeth, and then he asked Harriet: "And your husband, Colonel Forster, is he well?"

"Yes, he is quite well, I thank you," said Harriet pleasantly. She paused, as if uncertain whether to speak, and then she continued: "I must say, Mr. Darcy, it was truly a surprise to see you at the assembly. I should not have taken you to be one to find delight in sea baths."

"Then perhaps I retain some mystery yet," said he. "Young ladies are not the only ones allowed their secrets."

"Well," said Blanche, "I should like to come to know you and your opinions much better, Mr. Darcy." She almost seemed to give Mr. Darcy a significant look before adding: "No man should be allowed to keep his secrets to himself for long."

"That sounds like a curious double-standard, madam," said Mr. Darcy, his brow furrowing slightly, though he did not appear to be displeased.

Elizabeth frowned, wondering what the look Blanche had given Mr. Darcy meant. It was the sort of look that seemed to have the primary purpose of communicating something that would only be understood by the giver and the receiver.

Elizabeth was thrown into further confusion when Mr. Darcy went on to say: "But be that as it may, I should like to see more evidence of your fine intelligence myself." He, too, almost appeared to attribute some special meaning to his words, as if he were conversing with Blanche on a different plane.

Elizabeth did not understand what was happening in the slightest. Blanche and Mr. Darcy had just met. How could they already be speaking in some sort of strange code? Though it was nothing new for Blanche to speak in a mysterious fashion, Mr. Darcy was not fond of socializing with new acquaintances, and as a result, he would have had no reason to engage in any sort of veiled conversation with someone who was barely more than a stranger to him. Of course, perhaps Elizabeth did not know him as well as she thought. The Mr. Darcy she had known in Hertfordshire was nowhere near as amiable as the one before her. Was he simply trying to change how he normally handled social situations for the better? And if so, why would he be so eager to do so? He was a great enigma to her, and she was not comforted by the fact that Blanche had suddenly become one to her as well.

As she stared at him, she wondered what exactly he had meant by "fine intelligence." It seemed such an odd thing to say.

"I do not know if I should call my intelligence 'fine,'" said Blanche slowly, "but I suspect that I know a thing or two that you do not, Mr. Darcy."

"I suspect every woman knows things a man does not," inserted Harriet, who did not appear to have seen what Elizabeth was seeing. The reason for *that* was likely because she was too busy looking at Elizabeth with a grin on her face, no doubt thinking of what she had been told about Mr. Darcy's proposal.

"Many men are scoundrels," said Blanche with much firmness, "so I think it would be beneficial for most women to have a greater awareness of the dangers in becoming too close to some of them. To be suitably wary, a woman should need to know things the man does not. Unfortunately, however, some women do not seem to take the threat seriously enough. Perhaps they believe no real harm will ultimately befall them."

"Men and women alike can fall prey to the whims of fortune hunters," said Elizabeth, who was trying and failing to gain some grasp of the conversation, "so I should think that men would need to have some secrets of their own."

"And I believe they do," said Harriet confidently. "Men and women both thrive on secrets, though they may dislike owning it. Gossip, after all, is so integral to our lives, and it should not be quite so pleasing were it not for the sense of untold secrets being revealed."

"Perhaps it is good for some secrets to be revealed," said Blanche in response. "Regardless, I know I should do everything in my power to help someone dear to me if that person were in trouble."

"And you are a great friend," said Elizabeth softly, wondering if the conversation was finally losing some of its hidden meaning — and if she had simply imagined that meaning to begin with.

Blanche gave her a fond smile. "Friends must watch out for one another, must they not?"

Elizabeth smiled in return and pleasantly turned the conversation to the other matters. At last, Mr. Darcy left, but not before Blanche said something to him in a low voice that Elizabeth could not hear. Then, he was on his way, and Elizabeth moved toward Blanche, frowning as she thought about the look she had just seen on Mr. Darcy's face.

"Blanche, what did you say to Mr. Darcy? His expression was

almost stern."

"Ah, I merely spoke some nonsense about his shoes which I suppose he did not find very amusing," said Blanche dismissively.

"His shoes?" said Elizabeth doubtfully.

"I did not notice his shoes," said Harriet. "I was too busy watching his face. My, he has changed from Hertfordshire, has he not, Elizabeth? There, I do not believe I ever saw a smile on his face! Here, however, he seemed to be approaching what I might call 'happy.'"

"He seemed amiable enough to me," said Blanche. "Do you like him, Elizabeth?"

"I do not quite know how I feel about the man," said Elizabeth cautiously. "He is usually not so agreeable as you saw him today. He is normally much more taciturn."

"Well, perhaps he has decided to shun taciturnity and embrace something more pleasant." Blanche smiled, and the three women talked for a few moments more before Blanche, too, left.

"This has certainly been an eventful morning!" cried Harriet. "And to think, the day has only just begun!"

"Yes," murmured Elizabeth. She was too busy thinking about Mr. Darcy's shoes—and how she did not believe they had been the subject of Blanche's comment to Mr. Darcy.

But whatever Blanche had truly said, Elizabeth would obviously not find out any time soon, so she had best move on to other thoughts and leave well enough alone.

Chapter X

*F*or the next few days, Elizabeth and Harriet spent time in their normal pursuits, and if Elizabeth's thoughts dwelt more on the gentleman from Derbyshire, it was also true that she was able to rein them in to some extent—she did not *constantly* think of Mr. Darcy, though sometimes she felt it a near thing.

Of the gentleman, they saw much, for since he was a well-known figure in English society, his good will was immediately sought after by those members of high standing in Brighton. And since Blanche was a member of such circles, by associating with her, Elizabeth was able to meet in company with Mr. Darcy as well.

And that was not all. The colonel, having made an acquaintance of Mr. Darcy in Hertfordshire, was eager to include him in the society of the regiment, which resulted in Mr. Darcy's receiving invitations to dinner at the Forster townhouse. Elizabeth learned through Harriet that Mr. Darcy and Colonel Forster had discovered that they shared a mutual connection—the colonel had been a good friend of Colonel Fitzwilliam's before the demands of rank had separated them. However, they still maintained a friendly correspondence with one another and considered themselves close friends. And as Mr. Darcy had seen his cousin recently in London, he was able to impart more current intelligence about Colonel Fitzwilliam's movements than

Colonel Forster currently possessed.

It was during a dinner at the Forsters' residence that Elizabeth saw Mr. Wickham again for the first time since Mr. Darcy's arrival, and though she still did not fear him, he continued to make her uneasy. Fortunately, he did not approach her, and when he was not engaged with speaking to someone else, he merely contented himself with watching her from across the room with a slight frown upon his face.

His countenance, however, changed dramatically when Mr. Darcy arrived for dinner. Elizabeth happened to be facing in his direction when the gentleman entered the room, and as Mr. Darcy moved directly to her side to greet her, he was immediately visible to Mr. Wickham as well. At the sight of the man he had used so ill, Wickham's face turned completely white, and he gulped down the drink he held in his hand in one swallow. However, his color heightened alarmingly when he realized that Darcy had stopped specifically to speak with Elizabeth, and a scowl remained painted on his face for the rest of the evening.

Mr. Darcy, however, did not spend long with Elizabeth—after exchanging a few pleasantries, he excused himself to greet his host. For a moment, Elizabeth was afraid that Mr. Wickham was about to break the colonel's decree. But then Mr. Denny approached to greet her, and her fears were allayed.

"Miss Bennet!" said he. "How do you do? I must say you look remarkably well this fine evening."

"I thank you, Mr. Denny," replied Elizabeth with pleasure. Even setting aside his assistance with regard to Mr. Wickham the previous few weeks, Elizabeth thought Mr. Denny was a delightful conversation partner.

Denny glanced about furtively, noting Wickham's presence, before he leaned forward and addressed her in a quiet voice: "I apologize for my tardiness. I am afraid I had a matter of regiment business to attend to before I arrived. Mr. Wickham has not imposed upon you in my absence, has he?"

Elizabeth glanced in the other man's direction, noting that while he was now speaking with another group of officers, his eyes frequently darted toward her. "No, indeed, Mr. Denny. He does not appear happy, but he has not approached me."

"Very good, indeed!" said Denny, moving back to a more respectful distance. "I would echo the colonel's suggestion, though—if he does come to speak to you, I should very much appreciate it if you would inform either the colonel or me. I *have* been tasked with your safety, after all."

Elizabeth laughed at the wink and the outrageously playful manner in which he addressed her, as though he were guarding a great secret which he would share with her alone.

"And I thank you for your protection, Mr. Denny," said she. "It makes me feel truly at ease to know that I have such a gallant young man looking out for my welfare."

"Excellent, Miss Bennet! Now, if you will excuse me, I see one of my fellow officers with whom I would very much like a word."

As he left, she shook her head and smiled to herself.

For the rest of the period before dinner, Elizabeth mingled with the other diners, enjoying herself and the society immensely. It was as dinner was approaching when Mr. Darcy once again approached and engaged her in conversation.

"Miss Bennet," said Mr. Darcy as they separated slightly from a group of several others with whom she had been conversing, "I do hope that your time since we last met has been spent agreeably."

"Indeed, it has, Mr. Darcy," replied Elizabeth. Though she perhaps did not realize it herself, her voice and manner were enthusiastic, and her behavior toward the man was quite different from that of the previous autumn—or even that of the spring when they had been together in Kent. "Harriet and I have continued our exploration of the city and have even gone sea bathing yet again. I cannot dream of calling any time in which I have been able to sea bathe anything but delightful!"

Mr. Darcy's responding smile was genuine and held a hint of tenderness, provoking a fluttering within Elizabeth's midsection. "Ah, so you enjoy sea bathing, do you?"

"I do very much. There is something so very relaxing and carefree about the pursuit, and I find that the sea water does agree with me very well indeed."

"So you sanction the activity, then. In that case, I should very much like to try it myself. I am sure it cannot be anything but delightful if you approve of it."

Elizabeth cocked her head to the side, even while a large smile bloomed on her face. "You put so much stock in my good opinion, do you?"

"I confess I do," was the prompt response. "You do not bestow your good opinion frivolously or to please the world. Therefore, I believe your judgment to be sound and trustworthy."

By this time, Elizabeth's cheeks were fairly burning. "I thank you for the compliment, Mr. Darcy."

"It is not unearned, Miss Bennet." Mr. Darcy's smile was friendly and his eyes kind as he regarded her with a gentle expression on his face. "As you well know, I abhor any kind of deception."

The reference to his words that night at Hunsford brought a laugh to Elizabeth's lips while simultaneously causing her to mentally sober at the thought of what had occurred. She could not repent of her refusal—she would do it again if she found herself in the same situation—but she could regret the manner in which the refusal had been delivered. To respond to his less than tactful proposal with contempt and derision did not, after all, make her performance any better than his.

Suddenly nervous, Elizabeth focused on her gloved hands, even as she sought desperately for the words of the apology which she suddenly knew she must make. Mr. Darcy, perhaps sensing her discomfort, did not speak or press her to respond—instead, he waited patiently, though what he was thinking, she could not say, as she was unable to peer up into his face. At length, she began thusly:

"Mr. Darcy, I did not think I would ever have the opportunity to speak with you thus, but I am thankful for your arrival in Brighton. It affords me the chance to express my regret for my behavior at Hunsford—what I said was unconscionably rude and uncalled for, and I apologize for it most fervently."

Her declaration finally made, Elizabeth found the courage to glance up at his face, and she was surprised to see an expression of utter compassion and regret directed back at her.

"I will accept your apology, Miss Bennet, if you will accept mine. Had I not provoked you to say what you said—indeed, if I had courted you openly as you deserved—I do not doubt you would never have been put in a position to respond with such acrimony. Neither of us behaved in a manner which was strictly above reproach, and I fear I own the greater share of the blame."

"Mr. Darcy—"

"Miss Bennet, I should prefer that we do not allow this to linger between us. I forgive you with all my heart and ask the same of you. I should prefer to begin anew, now that our regrets have been dealt with. Do you not agree that it would be best?"

There was something in Mr. Darcy's eyes which at once frightened her and filled her with a warmth the likes of which she had never before felt. He truly was a handsome man, and he was gazing at her with such earnest intensity that she could not help but respond in a like manner. Indeed, had she still been in the midst of her bitter feelings for the gentleman, she doubted she would have been capable of perpetuating her grudge and withholding her forgiveness. So she did the only thing she could do—she reciprocated his smile and agreed with his request.

"I do, Mr. Darcy, and I extend my own forgiveness in kind. In fact, I believe your proposal is very much in agreement with my own personal philosophy: think of the past only as it gives you pleasure."

"A very good thought indeed, Miss Bennet. In the matter of *our* past, I shall endeavor to follow your advice most particularly. Now, as I believe dinner is about to be served—and I believe our hostess would not mind should you prefer not to be seated according to rank—I should be very happy if you would agree to be my companion for dinner."

It appeared the man still possessed the ability to astonish her, though Elizabeth was rapidly becoming somewhat accustomed to the unforeseeable nature of his behavior. She had thought on the possibility of making her apologies to him at some point in the future, but she had deemed it unlikely that she would ever be in his company and able to do so.

Yet here he was, visiting the same city and partaking in the same society as she was, and rather than avoiding her, he was seeking her out, speaking to her more than he ever had before—and much more amiably!—and asking her, with the greatest of civility, to dine with him! Could his previous preference for her have survived the bitter recriminations she had leveled at him less than three months before? It defied all logic. Part of her wished to explain it as his desire to prove to her that he could be civil and agreeable in company, but Elizabeth could not be certain. Further study of his actions was in order before she would be able to come to any kind of conclusion.

"I shall be glad to, Mr. Darcy," replied Elizabeth at last, an uncharacteristically shy smile upon her face.

"Excellent!" said he. It was that moment when the company was called to dinner. Elizabeth grasped his proffered arm and allowed herself to be escorted into the dining room at his side. The situation seemed almost a dream. Why *was* Mr. Darcy escorting her to dinner?

After they were seated, the atmosphere between them continued to remain amiable. Elizabeth was not certain, but there appeared to be a spark of life in his eyes that she had not noticed before. As she spoke with him, they discussed what had transpired in their lives since they had been in each other's company in Kent. Their conversation remained pleasant, and despite the presence of Mr. Wickham, she was able to enjoy the evening. Denny was not even required to come to her rescue, as Darcy seemed intent on remaining by her side. Perhaps Wickham's face was even darker than usual when he glanced at her from the opposite end of the table, but he appeared to be attempting to keep his eyes away from her to some extent.

At the end of the evening, as she was readying herself for the night, she found her thoughts consumed by Mr. Darcy. She still was unable to completely fathom the reason for his attention to her, but she was glad for it. She found it to be immensely pleasing that they had been able to move past their disastrous argument in the parsonage. It was fortuitous indeed that she had come across Mr. Darcy in Brighton.

Elizabeth saw much of Mr. Darcy from that day forward. His renewed acquaintance with Colonel Forster was such that he would often arrive for a morning visit and spend some time in the colonel's study, and it soon became evident that both men were pleased with the acquaintance. As for his time with the ladies, Mr. Darcy took care to ensure that he did not interrupt them on their frequent outings to see the sights of Brighton. He would often ask in advance concerning their plans, and he would avoid visiting on days when he knew they would be out.

This consideration endeared him to Elizabeth all the more, for it showed that while he took pleasure in her company, he remained sensitive to her own desires and pleasures and had no intention of suspending them for his own selfish purposes.

Of Wickham, Elizabeth saw nothing. Whether he was now cowed by the colonel's blistering set-down, had decided that she was not worth the effort, or was simply biding his time, Elizabeth could not say, but she enjoyed the freedom his absence allowed her.

One morning perhaps two weeks after Mr. Darcy had first appeared in Brighton, he arrived to call on Elizabeth and Harriet during the normal morning visiting hours. The two young women had not planned any outings for that day, as they had determined that it was to be a day of rest—they had hardly stopped to take a breath during the previous week, and they were both looking forward to such a respite from the pace of their adventures.

When Mr. Darcy showed up that morning, however, Elizabeth was easily convinced to walk to a nearby park in his company. His invitation included Harriet as well, but she had simply laughed and claimed that she needed to go over the household accounts and that they should venture outside and enjoy one another's company.

They wandered to a nearby park, talking amiably to one another, but on no particular topic. Elizabeth was beginning to enjoy his company as she never had before, though at this early stage, she could not quite decipher the nature of her own feelings for the man. A chance comment about his sister and her studies in London caught Elizabeth's attention, and she asked after the girl.

"It sounds like your sister is well?"

"I thank you, yes," replied Mr. Darcy. "Georgiana is well indeed."

He seemed disinclined to speak any further, but Elizabeth, with Mr. Wickham's words concerning Miss Darcy ringing in her ears, wished to know more concerning the young woman of whom she had heard so much but knew so little.

"From Miss Bingley's raptures on the subject—not to mention Lady Catherine's own comments—I take it that she is a very accomplished musician."

"Yes, but primarily on the pianoforte," was Mr. Darcy's reply. "She has had some training on the harp, but she prefers the pianoforte. And though she sings very well indeed, she lacks confidence in her voice and prefers to play pieces which do not require her voice."

"I certainly understand that sentiment," said Elizabeth with a nod. "Personally, I am certain that my voice is far finer than my ability on the pianoforte, but as I cannot sing without such accompaniment, I must make do."

Mr. Darcy smiled. "No one admitted the privilege of hearing you can think anything wanting."

"Flattery, Mr. Darcy?" asked Elizabeth, recognizing his words from a night at Rosings Park.

"I am merely speaking the truth," replied he. "Though I can certainly flatter when necessary, I try to maintain the truth, and I cannot imagine that anyone could listen to your playing and singing with anything other than pleasure."

Blushing, Elizabeth looked down, uncertain how a discussion concerning his sister had instead turned to one about her instead. Gamely, she turned back to him, trying to move the conversation back to his sister.

"She is at Pemberley now?"

"In the company of her companion," affirmed Mr. Darcy. "In truth, she feels more comfortable at Pemberley. She has ever been of a shy and retiring disposition, and recent events have caused her to withdraw even more."

Immediately, Elizabeth apprehended what he was referring to. "The business with Mr. Wickham," said she softly.

Mr. Darcy said nothing in response, but he did give her a tight nod of acknowledgement.

"Is she much recovered, Mr. Darcy?"

A sigh met her question. Elizabeth thought to retract it as too much of an impertinence when Mr. Darcy looked down at her and smiled, though she had the sense that it was more of a tight smile than a genuine one.

"I believe that her new companion has been a great help in her recovery, but she still lacks confidence in herself. Fortunately, however, her melancholy has largely dissipated, and when she is in my company or the company of our extended family, she is cheerful and happy, much as she has ever been."

They walked in silence for several more minutes, and Elizabeth, though she was thinking about Miss Darcy, was able to appreciate the greenness of the grass beneath their feet and the bounty of majestic trees which towered over the city park through which they walked. Few people were in the park this day, so Elizabeth and Mr. Darcy largely had their privacy; she was particularly grateful for such due to the matter they had been discussing.

"Perhaps I could introduce her to you when next she is in town," said Darcy. "I believe that she would love to meet someone of your confidence and vivacity, and I am certain that you would be of great assistance to her."

By this time, Elizabeth was no longer astonished at this man's newfound civility, though he still did have the ability to surprise her. The fact that he wished to introduce her to his sister was somewhat of a surprise to her. That he felt that she could help his sister was also a little surprising, but given what she knew of Miss Darcy, she supposed it was not that much of a shock after all. A shy girl would almost certainly benefit from the friendship of another who was generally at ease in most social situations.

"I would like that very much," said Elizabeth in a quiet voice. "She sounds like a lovely young girl."

"Thank you," said Mr. Darcy, favoring her with an appreciative smile.

"I believe that your sister and I might understand one another quite well indeed," said Elizabeth suddenly.

Mr. Darcy looked at her, the question clearly written on his face, and Elizabeth felt her cheeks warm slightly in response. It would have been better if she had not addressed the matter of Mr. Darcy's mortal enemy, even obliquely. But now she had no choice but to respond to his unanswered question.

"We have both been taken in by Mr. Wickham," said Elizabeth. "I dare say your sister would benefit from the knowledge that another who was older and had more experience was also a victim of Mr. Wickham's lies."

Mr. Darcy was silent for a few moments, and though he did not appear to be displeased by her mention of Mr. Wickham, Elizabeth was unable to tell exactly what he was considering, as his mask was firmly in place.

"I was wondering . . ." He paused and Elizabeth knew that he was searching for the proper words to express whatever it was that he wanted to say.

"What I mean to say is . . . Well, I would like to know . . ."

"Please continue, Mr. Darcy," said Elizabeth, taking pity on him. "You may ask whatever you like, and I shall do my best to answer you."

Seemingly reassured by her words, Mr. Darcy smiled and said: "You just referenced the fact that you had been taken in by Mr. Wickham. I . . . I know it is perhaps not my place to ask, but I was wondering to what degree he imposed himself upon you."

It was a question which could perhaps be taken in a number of ways—some of them completely improper given the status of their relationship—but Elizabeth was certain she knew what Mr. Darcy was asking, and she resolved to ease his fear.

"Mr. Wickham preyed on my trust, Mr. Darcy. I believed his slanderous stories, much though I wish that it had not been the case. But this is *all* that I can place at his feet. In truth, I never had any strong feelings for him other than friendship and admiration for his amiable manners.

"You may not know this, but after you departed, Mr. Wickham began to pay particular attention to a young lady who had recently come into a sizeable inheritance. I can truthfully state that my disappointment was slight, and though I did not think ill of him—though perhaps I should have seen his tendency toward impropriety in his actions—I was able to accept his defection without any real disappointment."

Mr. Darcy's relief showed in his face, and he smiled at her. "In that case, I must say that you showed remarkable understanding. Most of Wickham's conquests do not realize that he is duping them until after he has left them to move on to another target. I commend you, Miss Bennet."

Elizabeth ducked her head in embarrassment. "I should not have listened to his tale of woe. I should have realized how improper his communications were when he made them so soon after our acquaintance began."

"Do not castigate yourself, Miss Bennet," said Mr. Darcy. He stopped and looked at her closely, his manner as serious as Elizabeth had ever seen. "Mr. Wickham has had many years to hone his craft, and among those whom he was able to fool completely can be numbered my own father, who remained ignorant to Wickham's true nature until his final breath."

"I shall try to remember that, Mr. Darcy," said Elizabeth, dipping her head.

The remainder of their time walking together was spent more in silence than in conversation. But it was a companionable silence rather than an awkward one. Elizabeth thought of what she had been told, and she decided that she would indeed love to become acquainted with Miss Darcy. She sounded like a sweet soul, much like Jane, and coming to know her would be no true hardship for Elizabeth.

Of course, this presupposed that Mr. Darcy still had some interest in her, a fact which Elizabeth had been unable to confirm by observation as of yet. That he still wished for her company was clear, but the extent to which he desired to see her was not.

Still, they did not need to be courting for her to meet his sister. She hoped he would eventually make good on his promise. Perhaps she could help further the recovery of the young woman's spirits.

Chapter XI

Though the city of Brighton was greatly entertaining, the prospect of doing something new was not unwelcome, and so it was that Elizabeth and Harriet were pleased to hear of Blanche's plans for a picnic in the countryside. Upon asking about the guests—which would include Elizabeth, Harriet, and Colonel Forster—Elizabeth and Harriet were told casually by Blanche: "Oh, there shall be a few officers there, a few more interesting residents of Brighton, and one or two others." They were not able to pry much more from her than that.

If there was one thing Blanche was skilled at doing, it was molding the emotions of others to her wishes, and she managed to induce Elizabeth and Harriet to experience considerable excitement about the delicacies that would be prepared and the surroundings which had been carefully chosen for their enjoyment. Elizabeth was particularly pleased at the thought of leaving the city for a short time to be surrounded by the beauty of nature. The sea was quite lovely, yet Elizabeth had a fondness for grass and trees which the city did not quite satiate. Though the picnic would not be intimate, as it appeared there would be quite a number of people present, it would still be an improvement on the crowded bustle of Brighton.

Yes, Elizabeth was truly looking forward to the venture. The morning of the picnic, however, she received a letter which surprised her exceedingly and made her briefly forget the event of which she had been thinking so frequently. It began:

My dearest Lizzy,

Perhaps I should start my letter by speaking of Papa and his library or Mama's nerves, but the latter appears to have almost disappeared for the time being — rather than being nervous, she is now quite excited. She has even ceased complaining about Brighton, which I am certain must shock you exceedingly. I dare say you shall be even more surprised at what I have to tell you, and so I shall hold back no longer: Mr. Bingley has returned to Hertfordshire.

When we heard the news that the house at Netherfield was being opened again, we dared scarcely believe the rumors. But they were true, and Mr. Bingley was hardly in Hertfordshire for long at all before he came to visit Longbourn! I was so stunned I could hardly speak at first. Oh, dearest Lizzy, I barely know what to think! I know I should be cautious, but I cannot help the happiness that has come over me. I had despaired of ever seeing him again, yet here he is! You do not think me silly, do you, Lizzy? I have such fears, I must confess, but I also have such hopes —

Elizabeth stopped reading and stared down at the letter in stunned silence, barely able to believe what was in front of her eyes. Mr. Bingley had returned to Hertfordshire! Did he intend to stay on a more permanent basis?

Her thoughts turned to Mr. Darcy and his strange question about whether her sisters were at home. Could it be that he had talked to Mr. Bingley and encouraged him to return to Hertfordshire? Though the words between Elizabeth and Darcy had been heated at the time of the disastrous marriage proposal, Elizabeth knew now that he had been acting with good intentions when he had separated Jane from Mr. Bingley, ruinous though that had been to Jane's happiness. Charlotte had been correct — Jane did not wear her heart out on her sleeve like many young women, so it was not utterly surprising that Mr. Darcy had believed her unaffected by Mr. Bingley. Was it possible that Darcy was trying to make amends in more ways than simply bringing himself and Elizabeth to a point in which they would speak to each other congenially?

Contemplating the matter made Elizabeth somewhat uneasy. If Mr. Bingley was returning for a reason other than to court Jane, then Jane was likely to have her heart broken a second time — and Jane's gentle nature might not survive a second heartbreak. Elizabeth wished suddenly that she could be at Longbourn with her sister. If only she could see the two of them together! Jane was too modest to give an opinion on this matter which could truly be trusted.

Knowing the time to depart for the picnic was approaching, Elizabeth turned her attention back to her letter. But though Jane had not finished speaking of the topic of Mr. Bingley—her raptures were such that several pages had not seemed to do them justice—she mentioned nothing more of substance regarding the details of his arrival. Elizabeth was left with nothing but speculation as to the reason why Mr. Bingley had returned.

The letter ended with some small news about their family—Lydia was as vexed at having to stay at Longbourn as ever, Kitty was said to be improving under their dear aunt's tutelage, Mary was making her own steps of improvement, and Mr. Bennet was ensconced in his library as usual. When she had completed reading the letter in full, Elizabeth read over some of the earlier passages once again, trying to divine a reason in between Jane's lines as to what had prompted Mr. Bingley's return. Unfortunately, there was no further information to be had. She would simply have to write to her sister and prompt her to share further details.

The time had come to depart for their outing, however, and Elizabeth, taking her bonnet, descended the stairs and soon found herself situated in the carriage and on her way to the much-anticipated picnic.

It was not many moments before Harriet noticed Elizabeth's distracted manner.

"Elizabeth, I hope all your family is well."

Blinking at Harriet for a moment, Elizabeth recalled that she had yet to share the contents of Jane's letter with her friend.

"Oh, Harriet, I am sorry. I must be a very poor companion, given my distraction."

"Not at all, Elizabeth. Was there something in Jane's letter to excite your concern?"

"No, indeed," said Elizabeth. "It is quite the opposite. In fact, Jane has astonished me exceedingly, and I am quite unable to deduce the meaning of her letter."

Harriet directed a mock glare at Elizabeth. "You are intriguing me, Elizabeth. If you do not stop your teasing and share your intelligence immediately, I shall be quite put out with you."

Laughing at her friend's affected glare, Elizabeth replied: "I have not the slightest intention of exciting your anger. It appears that Mr. Bingley has returned to the neighborhood."

This report was obviously as surprising to Harriet as it had been to Elizabeth herself. "Mr. Bingley? He has returned after all this time?"

"Indeed, according to Jane he has," said Elizabeth. "She could hardly give credit to the rumors when she first heard them, but it seems that he visited Longbourn almost as soon as he returned to Hertfordshire. Jane is beside herself with joy."

"I can well imagine." Harriet broke out into a wide smile. "That is truly wonderful news, Elizabeth! Poor Jane has suffered so since he went away."

Elizabeth, however, could not be so certain that the news was good. Though she knew Bingley to be an amiable man, a part of her remembered Jane's melancholy and lack of enthusiasm over the winter and feared what Mr. Bingley's intentions might be. When she voiced her concerns to Harriet, her friend was silent in thought for several moments before she finally responded.

"I understand your fear, Elizabeth, but I urge you to worry no more on the subject. I cannot fathom what kept Mr. Bingley away all these months, but both his return and the fact that he immediately called at Longbourn to renew his acquaintance speak to his intentions."

When Elizabeth still looked concerned, Harriet continued: "Indeed, you should believe me, Elizabeth. Though their relationship did not perhaps turn out the way everyone expected last autumn, Mr. Bingley is not the sort of man to simply play with a woman's affections and then abandon her. Indeed, showing favor to her a *second time* will only cement his purpose; I suspect he has acted in the manner he has in order to leave no doubt in the minds of anyone in the neighborhood. If he has not, then his actions are horribly misjudged, as his honor will be engaged."

Elizabeth could only nod and state her agreement with Harriet's assertions. Surely, she *knew* Mr. Bingley had retained his feelings for Jane by Mr. Darcy's testimony. He *was not* the type of man to engage a lady's feelings and then leave them—unless he was *induced to do so by his sisters and his friend!*

This, of course, brought out a whole new set of worries. Mr. Bingley had shown a remarkable lack of fortitude in allowing himself to be persuaded against courting Jane. Though Elizabeth could not be certain that Mr. Darcy had had anything to do with his return, Mr. Bingley's strength to resist his sisters' displeasure was uncertain. Mrs. Hurst might not make much of a fuss over the matter when she discovered that he had returned, but Caroline Bingley was another matter entirely.

Elizabeth even considered applying to Mr. Darcy for any knowledge he possessed on the matter, but she quickly discarded the notion. It would be an impertinence, she decided, and as she was slowly becoming better acquainted with the gentleman, she did not wish to offend him by making such a query. Besides, she had no real information at present—everything was mere conjecture on her part. She would wait for more information from Jane before she asked Mr. Darcy anything.

The companions rode in silence until they had arrived at the location where the picnic was to be held. There, the carriage stopped, and they were assisted down by Colonel Forster, who had arrived on horseback directly from the militia encampment.

Elizabeth looked around the area, immediately enchanted by the beauty of the location. Blanche had chosen for her outing a small meadow surrounded by copses of trees with great branches which waved in the wind. A small brook murmured in the distance while patches of wildflowers added color and a pleasant fragrance to the scene. In all, it was a beautiful locale and would not have been out of place near Elizabeth's home.

"I say," said Harriet to her husband and Elizabeth, "look over there at Blanche and Mr. Darcy. They make a handsome couple, do they not?"

Turning, Elizabeth peered in the direction Harriet had indicated. It was indeed Mr. Darcy and Blanche, and they stood close together, engaged in a very earnest conversation. Blanche in particular was very animated, waving her hands about in such a fashion that Elizabeth was almost surprised the woman managed to avoid hitting Mr. Darcy, for the two were standing in *very* close proximity, and Mr. Darcy was listening intently to what Blanche had to say.

Though Harriet's words were a little shocking to Elizabeth, she did not see anything untoward in the scene, and she turned her back to them and responded: "I believe it is indeed them, but do you not think you are putting the horse before the cart, Harriet?" She directed a mischievous smile at her friend and continued, "We have indulged in so much matchmaking discussion since arriving in Brighton that you seem intent upon pairing off all of our unattached acquaintances with someone else!"

"Oh, I meant nothing by it!" said Harriet, swatting at Elizabeth's shoulder playfully. "But you must own that there is some intrigue regarding Blanche's intentions. It would certainly be a fine match if she were to marry Mr. Darcy."

"Yes, it certainly would," said Colonel Forster in agreement, still regarding the pair.

Elizabeth made a noncommittal noise. She knew at the moment that there could be nothing between Mr. Darcy and Blanche — they had only known one another for a very short time, after all!

Out loud, she commented: "Mr. Darcy has probably been paired off with hundreds of high-class women ever since he entered society. I should think that it is very common for idle gossip to connect him with just about any eligible young woman, and I would not wish to add any unsubstantiated rumors to the mix."

"Elizabeth!" whispered Harriet in warning. "Mr. Darcy approaches."

Startled, Elizabeth turned to see Mr. Darcy coming toward her with the hint of a smile on his face. He greeted the three of them by name and then said: "It is a pleasure to see you again."

"It is a pleasure to see you as well," managed Elizabeth. She nearly stumbled over the words, and it was difficult to disguise her own consternation with herself. She had spoken with Mr. Darcy many a time, and she refused to be reduced to a stammering girl in his presence simply because she thought he might be interested in her friend!

"Mrs. Wade has certainly chosen a pleasant location for this event," said Mr. Darcy, his appreciative gaze taking in the beauty of the area.

"She does have a fine eye for her surroundings," replied Elizabeth, forcing herself to look at the scenery once more. "I imagine there are few in Brighton who are even half as skilled at organizing events as memorable as hers."

The woman they had been discussing soon began to approach them, having extracted herself from the company of a man who had accosted her once Mr. Darcy left her side.

"You are here at last!" cried Blanche. "I could not enjoy this outing until you arrived. You must know that I require your presence so that we may laugh together at the fopperies of my guests!"

"Come, Mrs. Wade," said Colonel Forster good-naturedly, "surely you do not truly intend to laugh at your guests!"

"What else is a gathering for if not to provide some enjoyment to its participants?" said Blanche with a smile. "Some of us happen to enjoy observing the foolishness of others more than simply conversing with them."

"Come, Blanche," said Elizabeth, trying to speak with a lightness she did not feel. "I thought we had discussed this before. You must not give away all of our secrets!"

Blanche waved a hand in the air dismissively. "I doubt Colonel Forster and Mr. Darcy see us as more than silly women with unusual occupations."

"You are unkind to us," said Mr. Darcy. "I can assure you that neither of us believes you to be merely silly women."

"Certainly not!" said Colonel Forster.

Blanche clapped her hands together. "Well! Now that we have established that we are *not* silly women, shall we all move forward to join the rest of the party? I believe you will find that I have collected a delightful assortment of personages who are certain to both entertain and amuse!"

They moved forward to mingle with the other guests as Blanche had suggested, and Elizabeth soon found that the situation at the picnic was one which confused her. Mr. Darcy was her nearly constant companion, paying her a significant amount of attention. Yet Elizabeth knew that Harriet had not been mistaken about the closeness of the conversation that had occurred between Darcy and Blanche. As a result, it seemed odd that he was being so attentive to *Elizabeth* rather than Blanche. Elizabeth simply could not understand it.

To make the picnic even more puzzling, Harriet seemed especially distracted. Several times when trying to speak with her friend, Elizabeth had been required to repeat what she had just said. Only Colonel Forster failed to arouse Elizabeth's curiosity—he remained as jovial as ever, speaking loudly but pleasantly, making various compliments or observations to his wife and her companion whenever he was nearby.

Other than those somewhat vexing items, the picnic was a great success. The opportunity to once again be out in nature, feeling the warm summer sun on her face and the wind in her hair, not to mention listening to the buzzing of insects and the songs of birds, was one which Elizabeth relished. She had not truly realized how much she had missed such experiences throughout her sojourn in Brighton, delightful though her time visiting Harriet had been.

Elizabeth even spent some few moments alone with only Mr. Darcy for an escort. The day being light and warm had induced her to take a few moments and walk out to the fringes of their picnic area along a small bubbling stream. Mr. Darcy had offered to accompany her when hearing of her desire, and they walked toward the stream with her arm linked with his. She stumbled briefly on a rock before they reached their destination, and his grip on her tightened as he kept her from falling.

She smiled as she steadied herself and looked up to remark on her clumsiness, only for her breath to catch her throat as she saw him gazing intently upon her.

His dark eyes were questing, searching, no doubt attempting to determine whether she was well or had twisted her ankle, and she hastened to say to him: "I thank you for your assistance, Mr. Darcy." She glanced at the stream and nodded. "This is a quaint area, is it not?"

"It is indeed, Miss Bennet. Mrs. Wade has chosen a pleasant location for the picnic, but I dare say the company she has chosen is much more commendable."

Elizabeth blushed, and after removing her arm from the crook of his, she stepped a few feet closer to the water, listening to the stream's persistent whispers. "I agree that the company is very pleasant," said she, "but I always have a fondness for the beauty of nature."

"Though I am prejudiced since it is my home, I believe Pemberley to be one of the fairest places in England. I am certain it would garner even your discriminating approval."

There was a slight teasing tone to Mr. Darcy's voice, and Elizabeth said warmly: "I believe you are right. Yet I find myself more curious to witness you at your home than I am to see the grounds themselves."

"And why is that, Miss Bennet?"

"I suspect that a man as reserved as you have proven yourself to be must feel much more comfortable when among surroundings with which you have been intimately familiar all your life."

"You are quite right, Miss Bennet. In my own home, I often feel I can face anything. I must own, however, that I still feel more at my ease when among familiar company. When my sister is home, I can benefit from conversation with her, yet when she is gone, the great halls of Pemberley can often feel quite empty."

Elizabeth was uncertain what to say to that; the remedy, of course, was for Mr. Darcy to take a wife, yet neither she nor he seemed inclined to say such outright.

Instead, they spent a few more minutes admiring the stream and enjoying each other's company before finally moving to return to be with the rest of the party.

It was late afternoon when the picnic finally began to break up. Blanche once again enjoyed her status as a premiere entertainer, accepting the thanks of her guests with true enjoyment, not to mention a modicum of smugness, no doubt due to her confidence in her own abilities to please.

The colonel had just said goodbye to his wife and Elizabeth, assisting them into the carriage for the journey back to the house, when Harriet caught Elizabeth's attention.

"Look, Elizabeth—Mr. Darcy and Blanche are in close conference once again."

Peering out the window of the carriage, Elizabeth saw that Harriet was quite correct—Blanche and Mr. Darcy *were* standing quite close to one another, and they appeared to be in an animated conversation once more. This time, however, Elizabeth noticed them both furtively glancing in the direction of the carriage, and once, she met Mr. Darcy's eyes for an instant.

She was unsure what this scene before her could mean. She had been able to dismiss the intimate conversation that had taken place between them when she arrived, but for it to happen a second time seemed far too coincidental. Was it possible that Mr. Darcy would begin to court Blanche?

It would not be an unusual match. Blanche's position in society was one of which to boast; Mr. Darcy certainly would do no harm to his reputation if he were to wed her, even if her style did seem a little too flamboyant for the proper Darcy. But certainly Blanche would make an entertaining companion for one as inclined to taciturnity as Mr. Darcy.

But as Elizabeth considered the idea, it brought a sickening feeling to her stomach. The thought that Mr. Darcy might have released his previous preference for her was enough to bring her a startling level of grief. She had come to enjoy the time she had spent in Brighton with him, as it had taught her what an excellent companion he could be. Yet if he took another woman as his wife, the friendship that had arisen between him and Elizabeth would surely dissipate. Though Blanche had become quite dear to her, Elizabeth was not certain she would be able to face her friend with the same amiability that she now possessed were Blanche to marry Mr. Darcy. Elizabeth's relationship with both Blanche and Mr. Darcy would change entirely, and she felt a pang of sadness at the mere idea.

"It certainly appears that they are becoming closer—and after such a short acquaintance, too!"

Though Harriet's words were somewhat cavalierly spoken, Elizabeth's stomach once again tightened at the suggestion.

Not wishing to alarm her friend or let any hint of her feelings escape—feelings which she did not understand herself!—Elizabeth attempted to be nonchalant.

"Perhaps you are correct. However, I find very little in their interactions which leads me to believe that they have formed an attachment. Perhaps they merely discuss a common acquaintance."

"Perhaps," was Harriet's only reply.

Elizabeth turned and regarded her friend as the coach set off. Harriet, while never talkative on Lydia's level, was not one to be silent or often distracted. Yet that day, she had appeared to have difficulty focusing her attention on anything for longer than a few moments. First, Mr. Darcy and Blanche had been acting strange, and now Harriet, the one Elizabeth had counted on to be sensible and dependable, was not acting like herself!

Elizabeth turned and stared out the window, wondering at the changes wrought overnight. Yet though Harriet was acting strangely now, Elizabeth knew she could trust her to eventually find her voice and say what was bothering her. The more unsettling situation was that involving Mr. Darcy and Blanche, for in truth, Elizabeth knew not what to think of them, particularly in regard to Darcy's behavior.

One question which plagued Elizabeth was: what did she herself want? She felt unsettled by what she perceived to be Mr. Darcy's attention to Blanche, yet she was not certain why it bothered her so much if he should develop an attachment with Blanche.

Did she wish for Mr. Darcy to once again pursue her? Though she attempted to objectively consider the matter, she found that she could not be certain. All she could state with a surety was the fact that the thought of him once again paying attention to her brought a warmth into her heart which she never would have associated with Mr. Darcy a few months before. But whether that was due to the pleasure of being admired or the thought that it was *Mr. Darcy* who admired her, she could not say.

The two friends continued in this attitude for more than half the journey home, Harriet peering out the carriage window at scenery which she did not appear to see and Elizabeth brooding on the difficulty of deciphering her own feelings.

At length, however, Harriet turned to Elizabeth with a great seriousness in her manner which was quite uncharacteristic of her.

"I suppose you are wondering why I have been acting so strangely," said Harriet. "You are far too perceptive to have missed my distraction."

"I own that I had noticed, Harriet," said Elizabeth. "Has something happened which has caused you concern? If so, please allow me to be of use to you as a friend—after all, was it not you who charged me to do the same only days ago?"

Harriet laughed and leaned forward to pat Elizabeth's knee. "Indeed, you did. Thank you, my friend, but the news I bear is not of a severe nature; in fact, it is quite the opposite."

Knowing her friend's propensity to tease her, Elizabeth directed an exasperated glare in her direction. "Well, what is it then? Do not sport with me, Harriet—please let me be privy to this great secret."

Giggling, Harriet puffed herself up very importantly, as though she were about to disclose some great and terrible secret, and she affixed Elizabeth with a conspiratorial gaze.

"Elizabeth, I believe I shall have to ask for your congratulations, for I am with child. I should have a little one sometime soon after Christmas."

"Harriet!" cried Elizabeth in surprise and joy, clasping her hands together. "This is wonderful news indeed, and you have my most heartfelt congratulations! But is it certain?"

"All the signs point to it, though I suppose I shall not know it to be fact until the baby actually moves. But short of that, I am certain as I can be."

Elizabeth shook her head in amazement. "My, what tidings to have kept to yourself! I should not wonder that you have been distracted. I should only wonder that you have been able to keep it to yourself for so long!"

Harriet beamed at her. "It has not been easy, Elizabeth! I can assure you of that! It has not been until the past day or two that my suspicions have progressed to near certainty. In truth, I had thought to keep it from you longer, as I do not wish it to be known yet, but I could not contain myself. You are my dear friend, and I want you to share with me in my joy."

Elizabeth placed her hands over her friend's. "That I do, dear Harriet. Why, Christmastime shall be such a special occasion for you this year. I suppose your husband is beside himself with joy?"

Her companion beamed. "He certainly is. I know it is difficult to tell, as my husband is always a jovial fellow, but there is a certain extra note of cheer to his voice and an added skip in his step."

"For a military man, that is impressive indeed," teased Elizabeth, "for I know they pride themselves on the regularity of their footsteps!"

Harriet chuckled, dipping her head. "Well, I do always know what to expect from my husband when we are dancing."

"Colonel Forster is certainly enamored with you, and I know you shall both be quite the doting parents." Elizabeth then turned a jesting grin on her friend and continued, "But if it is a girl, you must be very careful not to allow her to act as my youngest sister does!"

"Happy though my husband always is, he is still a military man, and as a result, he does believe in discipline," said Harriet. "I foresee no danger there!"

"Well, you shall have to allow your child's old maiden aunt to visit her from time to time," said Elizabeth lightly.

"Oh, Elizabeth!" said Harriet, shaking her head. "I know you shall be married and with child yourself before long. You are far too great a prize to be passed by. You must merely wait until the right man comes along—one who will fully appreciate you and your great heart."

Elizabeth, who had been distracted from thoughts of Mr. Darcy upon hearing Harriet's good news, suddenly found her mind filled with an image of the young gentleman speaking so intimately with Blanche, and she resolutely pushed that mental picture away. But though she commenced speaking in greater detail with Harriet about the future addition to the Forster family—this being a subject which caused Harriet to speak at great length without many pauses for comments from her companion—her thoughts were continually drawn back to Mr. Darcy and Blanche. Even Harriet, distracted though she had been at the picnic, had observed their close interactions. Elizabeth would be blind and stubborn not to acknowledge that there could potentially be something springing up between them. It worried her greatly, though she knew she should be happy at the thought of her friend finding a suitor who could bring her some measure of happiness. Yet despite all her efforts to think about the situation in a logical fashion, she could not help but feel somewhat betrayed; Blanche, after all, was very perceptive, and she must have noticed that Elizabeth had begun to find a great deal of pleasure in Mr. Darcy's company.

Certainly, Elizabeth and Mr. Darcy had put the troubles of their past behind them. At the picnic, they had engaged in very pleasant conversation. Their brief venture to the stream had been delightful, and Elizabeth was finding that she enjoyed nearly every moment spent with him.

But again, this situation between him and Blanche was troubling, in part because of the unusual way in which it was playing out. What had it meant when they had given such quick glances toward the carriage she and Harriet were in? Were they engaged in an illicit affair? Yet that was so difficult to believe! Mr. Darcy was nothing if not proper, and for him to endanger the reputation of a woman through improper activities was unheard of! While it *was* true that Blanche, as a widow, was afforded a certain amount of freedom in her behavior that Elizabeth, as a maiden, was not, Elizabeth knew that Mr. Darcy would never carry on in such a manner.

Well, whatever the reason for the closeness that had arisen between Mr. Darcy and Blanche, there was little to be done about it. All Elizabeth could truly do was observe how the relationship between the two progressed. She thought briefly of asking Blanche directly about what was happening, but she could already envision her friend dismissing the question and moving on to a different subject. Blanche sometimes took secrecy to extremes, and such an issue as this was one she would likely hide until she had an engagement to announce to the world. Elizabeth could rely only upon her own powers of observation; that was the only thing to be done.

She made a few comments relevant to what Harriet was saying and smiled at the happiness of her friend. For now, Elizabeth needed to concentrate not on her own troubles, but on Harriet's joy. There would be time enough to contemplate Mr. Darcy — and her confusing feelings for him — later.

The next day was Sunday, so they had no engagements after attending their church services and thus spent the day at home. The colonel was quickly made aware that Harriet had already informed Elizabeth of their good fortune.

"In that case, I am glad we shall not have to keep it from our houseguest any longer," was his response. "Indeed, I have been bursting to share the news with *someone* of our acquaintance."

"I am sure you have, sir," replied Elizabeth with an understanding smile.

"And though I still wish to shout it from the housetops, I think that having my wife's dear friend know of our happy news shall do very well for now."

Elizabeth laughed. "Indeed, it is truly a wonderful thing, sir. I am very pleased that you both consider me trustworthy enough to be privy to such dear information."

"You are a good girl, Miss Bennet. I am truly grateful you are here for my Harriet and wish you to know that you are always welcome to visit with us."

Elizabeth warmly assured him that she was quite happy to be in Brighton and would love the opportunity to meet with her dear Harriet again in the future, wherever she did reside.

"In fact, I hope that your children will consider me to be a favorite aunt. I would be happy to teach all of your dear children how to write their letters, walk country paths, and play their instruments very ill."

"But Elizabeth, your playing is delightful!" said Harriet with a laugh.

The colonel shook his head in amusement and asked: "And what is this talk of teaching *our* children? You shall be far too busy with your own for such pursuits. I should rather think that we shall encourage our children to be the best of friends as they grow."

"That presupposes that I shall find a man whom I can both love and respect—and such a wondrous specimen is so difficult to find."

"Nonsense!" cried the colonel. He tilted his head and said with a wink, "Speaking as a member of the sex you have so grievously disparaged, I must say that I know with a certainty that there is a man out there who can satisfy even someone as exacting in their standards as you. And I cannot but suppose that there are many men who are willing to please you, even to the point of reforming their characters entirely should they be required to do so."

"I am happy you think so kindly of me, though I might doubt my abilities to effect such miraculous reformations."

The colonel smiled at her affectionately. "As I have said, you are a good girl, Miss Bennet, and none of the praise is overstated. In fact, if I were not already so distractedly in love with my lovely wife, I might have fallen under your spell myself."

After giving an embarrassed laugh, Elizabeth attempted to affix the colonel with a stern glare. "If you persist in speaking in such a manner, you shall turn your wife into my most hated enemy, sir. I demand you cease immediately!"

"I assure you that I am completely confident of my husband's constancy," said Harriet with a chuckle. "And I second his claim—do not underestimate yourself, Elizabeth. One day, I am sure you shall make a spectacular match. Then we may have the pleasure of our children growing up together as we remain the best of friends."

There was not much Elizabeth could say without embarrassing herself further, so she thanked her friends for their kind words and informed them that she would be happy to continue their friendship for as long as they desired.

As that day progressed, Elizabeth witnessed the relaxed and contented meeting of minds between two people who were truly in love with one another. Though she had perhaps missed it previously, it was now quite evident that the colonel was even more solicitous of his wife than he had ever been before. Nothing was beyond his ability if it was to be done for Harriet, and she obviously enjoyed the attention and doted upon her husband in turn.

However, for one as independent as Harriet, being waited on hand and foot was not something she could withstand for long, and she was not hesitant to inform her husband that while she was with child, she was not an invalid, and she was thus completely capable of going about her daily routine in much the same manner as she always had.

The colonel, however, merely laughed gently at her protestations, claiming it the prerogative of all married men to spoil their wives in such situations. He lovingly informed her that the nature of his duties was such that he would not have nearly as much opportunity as he should like to wait on her, and he therefore requested she indulge him in his whimsy whenever possible.

Elizabeth merely smiled at their antics and did her best to remain as unobtrusive as she could, leaving the acknowledged lovers to their own devices. In the back of her mind, she hoped that her friends' words would be proven true and that she could expect a loving relationship of her own in the future.

The picture of Mr. Darcy's face as they danced the first night of his arrival in Brighton came into her mind, accompanied by the image of their walk soon after his arrival, and she immediately blushed at the thought. She looked at her friends surreptitiously, relieved to discover that they were far too involved with one another to notice her sudden surge of emotion. Her estimation of Mr. Darcy had certainly changed—especially since meeting him in Brighton—but Elizabeth was still not ready to consider him in such a manner, particularly in light of all the uncertainty about the precise nature of his relationship with Blanche.

That Sunday began a pattern for the next few days for the two friends. Though Elizabeth had thought to spend some quiet time at home in deference to Harriet's condition, her friend would have nothing of it and insisted that they continue their previous activities. She had not requested Elizabeth's companionship in Brighton for the purpose of gaining a nursemaid, she reasoned, and as she knew of Elizabeth's active and lively nature and shared in such an attitude to an extent, they would continue to see the sights of Brighton.

And so the two friends continued to pursue their previous activities, participating in the attractions of Brighton with all their old eagerness and energy. Harriet was indeed no invalid, and the two young women were able to enjoy themselves much as they had before.

On the Brighton social scene, Elizabeth found herself coming into contact with both the eager-to-please Mr. Denny and the much more confusing Mr. Darcy. Fortunately, though she saw Mr. Wickham somewhat frequently, she did not have any true contact with him, and enduring the occasional attentions of Denny was no hardship. When it came to Darcy, however, her feelings were utterly mixed.

The man remained very attentive to her, providing her with great companionship and conversation. She still marveled at how her opinion of him had changed so drastically, but she was more than willing to acknowledge the inaccuracy of her initial assessment of the man. Still, determining the exact nature of her feelings toward him was a difficult task. All she knew was that she was enjoying his attentions perhaps a little too much.

There was also a part of her mind that could not relinquish the unease she felt when considering the few guarded conversations that had taken place between Mr. Darcy and Blanche. Though they seemed inclined to have no further such conversations, she could not forget what had already occurred. Yet she told herself there must be nothing to concern her.

Matters were progressing quite positively with Elizabeth's family. Jane appeared to be spending many hours in the company of Mr. Bingley, and that brought Elizabeth no small amount of joy. Reading her sister's letters always served to bring her great cheer; though Elizabeth attempted to keep her thoughts away from Mr. Darcy when not in his company, she found her mind dwelling on him more and more frequently by the day, and as she feared she might have her growing hopes one day dashed, Jane's letters acted as a welcome relief from heavier contemplations.

Kitty appeared to be making great progress, and that filled Elizabeth with delight. The young girl's letters were brimming with energy as always, yet now that she had departed with the Gardiners for the North Country, there was a restraint to her letters that was quite heartening. No more did fripperies and redcoats take the main role in her communications. Rather, she expressed herself with more clarity than ever before, wrote of the locations they had toured with thoughtfulness, and even showed an occasional insight that surprised Elizabeth. Kitty had been removed from the restricting rein—and the somewhat ridiculous shadow—of Lydia, and she was blossoming in a way that Elizabeth could have scarcely dreamed of even several months before. Until Elizabeth saw Kitty in person, she would not know for certain whether the change was as great as had been reported — and as appeared to be evident in the improvement of Kitty's letters — but she was quite hopeful that it would be a permanent and welcome transformation.

When it came to Lydia, however, Elizabeth knew there was still quite a lot to be done before even the slightest hint of improvement might be seen. The silly girl refused to acknowledge the fact that Elizabeth was much better suited to traveling to Brighton with the Forsters than she was. Lydia's complaints about the injustice of the situation remained numerous, and Elizabeth despaired of ever seeing her reach a true maturity. Since Lydia was Mrs. Bennet's favorite daughter, she was allowed to run about as she pleased, even though such actions threatened to bring disgrace upon the whole family.

Elizabeth shuddered to think about what might have happened had it been Lydia acting as Harriet's companion. With the great number and variety of personages in Brighton — not to mention the heavy presence of redcoats — there was no end to the amount of mischief a reckless girl could wreak, even if she had a sensible woman such as Harriet to look after her.

Still, Elizabeth knew there was little she could do to curb Lydia's actions while in Brighton, so she ignored her sister's complaints and simply tried to enjoy the city's many amusements. She was in good company and in a pleasant place, so there was no reason for her to be unhappy, yet still she felt as if a cloud were persistently hanging over her, threatening to destroy her sunny day with a torrential downpour of cold and unwelcome rain.

It was during a visit to Blanche's house when an unexpected visitor was shown into the parlor. Truly, the shocks Elizabeth had endured since arriving in Brighton seemed to be unending!

The visit had started as a merry one, with the friends speaking animatedly of a troupe of performers who had recently arrived in Brighton and were receiving some positive reviews from the local papers. Elizabeth was in a marvelous mood, and her friends were both feeling somewhat playful that morning. To Elizabeth, it was almost as though she had gone back in time to her first acquaintance with Blanche, before the trouble with Wickham and the arrival of Mr. Darcy had caused a shadow to darken their friendship.

Fifteen minutes after their arrival, another visitor entered the parlor behind Blanche's butler, and Elizabeth rose to her feet in shock.

"Colonel Fitzwilliam!"

Smiling and seemingly unsurprised at Elizabeth's presence, the colonel grasped Elizabeth's hand affectionately and bowed over it.

"Miss Bennet! How fortunate to find you here. I am most delighted to renew our acquaintance!"

Though normally at home in any social situation, Elizabeth blushed and returned the greeting in as composed a manner as she possessed, though she suspected she appeared quite flustered to her friends.

What could Colonel Fitzwilliam possibly mean by calling on her while she was visiting her friend? Could the colonel—though he had assured her of the opposite—possess some lingering regard for her? First Mr. Darcy and now his cousin—would the shocks never cease?

However, knowing now was not the time to indulge such thoughts, Elizabeth recalled her social duties, and smiling at the colonel with slightly more composure, she turned and introduced him to her companions.

And in that she was astonished anew. Whereas Harriet smiled and announced how delighted she was to finally meet Colonel Fitzwilliam, Blanche merely laughed at her.

"Elizabeth, sometimes you can indeed be such a silly goose. I assure you that I am well acquainted with the colonel, and I have been this last twelve-month at least!"

Immediately understanding her mistake, Elizabeth nevertheless gathered herself and offered her apologies. And though the glint in Blanche's eye told Elizabeth that the other woman was *very well aware* of what she had thought, Blanche apparently decided for once not to embarrass her young friend.

"Colonel, I am delighted to see you once again," was Elizabeth's only reply.

"The feeling is mutual, I assure you," said the colonel in his easy manner. "I have met Mrs. Wade and Miss Bennet before, but I am not familiar with Mrs. Forster, though my reputation appears to have preceded me. I suppose your reprobate of a husband has seen fit to blacken my good name with stories of our time together as young officers?"

"Should you be afraid of his ability to tell tales?" was Harriet's playful reply.

"No more than *he* should be afraid of *my* ability, I assure you," replied the colonel with a wink.

"In that case, I am all ears, Colonel Fitzwilliam. I should love to hear how my husband comported himself as a young officer."

"And I shall be very glad to share some of his more dazzling exploits with you all," said the colonel somewhat smugly.

"But first," continued he, turning his attention toward Elizabeth, "I suspect Miss Bennet is wondering at my lack of surprise upon seeing her here today."

Elizabeth blushed but managed to return his smile. "I confess I was."

"It is no great mystery, I assure you. I dined with my cousin Darcy last night, and he informed me of your presence in Brighton. And as he had also mentioned your friendship with Mrs. Wade, it was no great shock to see you here this morning."

"Ah, that explains it, then," said Elizabeth. "And how did you find your cousin?"

"Very well, indeed," replied the colonel, his countenance taking on a mischievous glint. "In fact, I do not know that I have ever seen him as animated as he appears at present. The last time I saw him this happy was when we were all visiting Kent. You have some previous experience with him, Miss Bennet—would you not agree?"

The gleam in his eye told Elizabeth that the colonel was at the very least aware of Mr. Darcy's previous attraction to her. However, deciding that she would not take the bait, Elizabeth affected an ignorance of Mr. Darcy's moods and replied as nonchalantly as she was able:

"Perhaps the air in Kent is good for your cousin, then, if he appears to be in such great health to one of longstanding and intimate acquaintance. As for myself, while I cannot claim such a degree of familiarity, I have noticed no great difference in Mr. Darcy's demeanor, though perhaps he does appear a little more willing to mingle in company than I have often witnessed to be the case."

When the colonel's smile became almost predatory, Elizabeth once again spoke, hoping to change the subject to something less likely to cause her embarrassment.

"I believe Blanche mentioned that you were already acquainted? Do you come to Brighton often, sir?"

The colonel appeared as if he would much prefer to pursue the previous conversation, but he smiled and nodded in answer to her questions.

"Indeed, I do, madam. One of my primary duties is to oversee the preparedness of the militia companies stationed throughout the country. And as Brighton is a major encampment of militia companies in the south, I believe that I might find myself in residence here some two or three months out of the year.

"As for my acquaintance with Mrs. Wade, we met at an assembly here over a year ago, and I try to visit when I am in residence. She has the most interesting collection of foreign objects, and I love to see what she has managed to acquire during my absence."

"Well, you simply must see my newest acquisition!" cried Blanche. "It is just out in the hallway here. Elizabeth, Harriet—if you will please excuse us for a moment?"

Elizabeth watched as the pair moved out into the hallway so Blanche could show the colonel her most recent treasure. The colonel's boisterous voice and Blanche's excited tones could both still be clearly heard.

"My!" said Harriet. "What a surprise it is to see Colonel Fitzwilliam here! I am glad to have had the good fortune of meeting him at last."

"He is a kind man," said Elizabeth with a smile, recalling the many pleasant conversations she had had with him in Kent. "I was surprised to discover he was acquainted with Blanche, though I dare say his explanation makes sense. And besides, Blanche is a person of such importance on the Brighton social scene that I should not be surprised to learn she has met several others of our acquaintance."

"I suspect you are correct," said Harriet. "Yet how strange it is that we should see both Colonel Fitzwilliam and Mr. Darcy here!"

"It certainly is," murmured Elizabeth.

Both women turned as Colonel Fitzwilliam and Blanche returned to the parlor.

"Mrs. Wade has certainly outdone herself, has she not?" asked the colonel, shaking his head in wonder. "I doubt there is a home in all of England which could hope to compete with the collection of treasures she has amassed."

"Careful, Colonel Fitzwilliam," warned Blanche, "or you might inflate my vanity."

Elizabeth laughed. "Come now, Blanche. It is the place of men in our society to flatter women, is it not?"

"I should hope men were expected to do a little more than that," said the colonel with a smile.

"Certainly, you have other duties," said Elizabeth, "but none so important."

"You must tread carefully, Colonel Fitzwilliam," said Blanche, "for in a battle of wits against Elizabeth Bennet, there are few who would ever be able to come out unscathed."

Colonel Fitzwilliam smiled. "Then I shall concede defeat to Miss Bennet at once in the hope of saving face."

"A wise move, I should think," said Harriet. "You are indeed a military man."

"I do enjoy thinking of myself as such from time to time," said the colonel. "Yet perhaps it is my way of inflating my own male vanity."

"Surely a man with the rank of colonel is allowed a little vanity?" asked Blanche with an uplifted brow.

"I do not know if 'allowed' would be the correct term, but you will certainly find many a vain colonel!" said the man with a laugh.

The conversation continued in such a pleasant manner for a while before at last it was time to depart. As Elizabeth stepped into the carriage, she marveled again at the strange coincidence of running across both Colonel Fitzwilliam and Mr. Darcy in Brighton! There was also the surprising news that Harriet was with child. What other things were in store for Elizabeth during her stay in Brighton? Surely, there was nothing more that could be thrown at her!

Chapter XII

A few days later, Elizabeth again found herself in company. Unfortunately, however, some of the familiar faces she had come to enjoy seeing were not to be found. Mr. Darcy and Colonel Fitzwilliam were attending a dinner elsewhere, and Colonel Forster had been called to London on a matter of military business with his superiors. While Elizabeth had felt no misgivings even on the carriage ride to her destination, she now felt an extreme sense of discomfort that was almost paralyzing. As people were milling about in conversation, she somehow managed to find herself in a secluded corner, separated from Blanche due to the unfortunate circumstance of an officer calling the other woman's attention. It was then that Mr. Wickham — whom she had seen as soon as she had entered the room — began moving through the crowd toward Elizabeth with definite purpose.

Her eyes darted around, searching for escape, but she had no time to take more than a single hesitant step before Mr. Wickham was upon her.

"Miss Bennet," said he coldly.

She fixed her own face in an expressionless mask, determined not to let him see how uncomfortable she was in his presence. "Mr. Wickham."

If only Mr. Darcy or Colonel Fitzwilliam or even Mr. Denny had been nearby! She did not wish to view herself as a damsel in distress by any means, but just the presence of one of those men tended to be enough to make Mr. Wickham more wary and less inclined to accost her. Her own words and actions appeared only to make him angrier, yet she found it difficult to follow any conversation path that might appease him. She did not *wish* to appease him! She simply wished he would leave her alone permanently.

"You are not deceiving me," said he in a flat voice.

Despite her best efforts, surprise flickered through her mask. "I beg your pardon?"

"I said you are not deceiving me."

"Mr. Wickham, I am not aware of what you speak. Now, if you will please excuse me—"

As the man's anger grew, his countenance started to become perilously dark. "Do not play the part of the fool with me. You know of what I speak."

"I must insist that I do not, Mr. Wickham—"

He drew closer to her, his hands in white fists at his sides. "You are paying attention to that *despicable* Darcy just to make me angry."

"What?" blurted Elizabeth incredulously. What was Wickham talking about?

"I have seen the two of you talking together, as you know. But I must give you this warning—if you believe you will receive something from him in return for your attentions, you are wrong. Darcy will never be interested in the likes of you. He is much too proud to associate with a penniless nobody such as you for long. You have none of the things he desires above all—no great family connections, no wealth. I am surprised he has been willing to talk to you as frequently as he has. I suspect it has something do with his more base desires."

"And I suppose that the subject of base desires is one with which you are very well acquainted, are you not, Mr. Wickham?"

Her retort was an unqualified rudeness—and more than justified in this instance, she felt—and its effect on Mr. Wickham was immediate. Though she had known him to be angry already, it appeared that what she had seen before was only the surface of his emotions. As he flushed, his jaw tightened, and his eyes narrowed in complete fury. He was unable to speak for several moments as he visibly fought down his ire. And when at last he spoke, his voice was low and menacing.

"I thought you were a discerning and intelligent woman, Miss Bennet. I have always been completely honest and proper in my interactions with you, yet you repay me by listening to the worst sort of slander about me from a man who has done me great wrong."

"Honest? Proper?" said Elizabeth with a laugh, her manner insolent and sarcastic. "How proper is it to tell unsubstantiated stories to an acquaintance of only a few moments with the intent to defame another man? Even if you had known me for a full year and spoke nothing but the truth, your communications would have remained nothing more than sheer impertinence!"

Mr. Wickham had nothing to say in response to the charge; even he could not dispute the veracity of her statement.

"Now, I would very much like for you to completely drop the subject, Mr. Wickham," continued Elizabeth after a moment of silence. "The exact status of my relationship with Mr. Darcy is none of your concern. You are completely unconnected with me, Mr. Wickham, and I will thank you to cease to speak of it.

"Furthermore, given our frequent and animated disagreements, it has become very clear that the two of us can never be anything like friends again. I must insist you keep your distance. Do not importune me again."

After directing one last glare at the now stunned gentleman, Elizabeth raised her head high and stalked away from him.

The confrontation now a thing of the past, Elizabeth threw herself into the festivities of the evening, taking the opportunity to dance and speak with as many of her new Brighton acquaintances as she could. Perhaps her actions contained a hint of desperation, but she could not repine them, as they helped her forget the wretched man. This was made easier by the fact that she did not see Wickham for the rest of the evening. Perhaps he had taken his leave of the assembly after her words to him. She knew not, but she was profoundly grateful that she was not required to interact with the man any further.

But though she would have hoped that her confrontation had gone unnoticed, she had not counted on the hawk-like eyes of a certain acquaintance. She had taken a break from the activity to visit the refreshment table when Blanche approached her with a stern expression written upon her face.

"Elizabeth! I would speak to you for a moment."

However, Elizabeth, knowing what Blanche likely wished to discuss, was not in a mood to indulge her friend. Quite frankly, she was tired of this situation with Wickham, and she wished to enjoy her remaining time in Brighton without scoundrels or well-meaning friends intruding upon her consciousness. Therefore, her response to her friend's demand was not precisely polite.

"Of what, Blanche?

Blanche's eyes narrowed, and she took Elizabeth's arm and pulled her to an open balcony like a mother manhandling an errant child. "You know perfectly well of what I speak, Elizabeth. You continue to tell me that nothing is wrong, yet whenever Mr. Wickham has an opportunity, I find him openly accosting you and you responding in kind. What the blazes is happening between the two of you?"

"Absolutely nothing, Blanche," snapped Elizabeth.

"Do not obfuscate! This matter is becoming more severe, and I will not allow that man to hurt you, Elizabeth. Will you not confide in me?"

Angry though she was, Elizabeth could not help but be touched by her friend's obvious care and concern. She could feel the anger bleed from her, replaced by an affection for the older woman, who was, after all, merely concerned for her. But that did not change the fact that Elizabeth *knew* that Wickham was a coward at heart, and though he might attempt his little games to confuse and intimidate her, he would not hurt her in any way, especially not when she was under his commanding officer's protection. The man had far too much self-interest for something of that nature!

"Blanche, you need not worry. Mr. Wickham is eager for me to believe him to be the wronged party in the matter of his history with Mr. Darcy, and he seems to be confused that his pretty manners have not drawn me in as they have so many other young ladies. I am perfectly fine, particularly as I have so many ardent protectors looking out for my well-being."

Blanche, however, was not convinced, though her voice was far less demanding and more affectionate than it had been before.

"Elizabeth," said she with some compassion, "I believe that as you are intimately involved with the situation, you are not seeing clearly what is happening. Mr. Wickham is not simply acting as the injured party; he is actively attempting to terrorize you, and I am afraid that your independence and strength of personality are blinding you to what is potentially becoming a dangerous situation. Has not Mr. Wickham been reprimanded and told in no uncertain terms to leave you alone?"

Elizabeth allowed that he had indeed.

"Then why does he still do so—and when none of your usual protectors are present at that? Do you not see what is happening?"

"It is nothing, Blanche. He is too much of a coward to try to bring any real harm to me. Please, do not concern yourself in this matter."

"Elizabeth—"

"Truly, Blanche, I must insist there is nothing to concern yourself with."

Blanche sighed. She might have said more, but Elizabeth turned away slightly, signaling an end to the conversation. As she moved to speak to an acquaintance, however, she felt certain that Blanche's eyes remained steadily fixed upon her.

Still, she refused to pay Blanche any more heed at the moment. While the older woman might have convinced herself that Mr. Wickham was a definite danger to be feared and guarded against, Elizabeth felt he was nothing more than a small dog with a large bark and an ineffectual bite. To waste more of her time thinking about the man would be to give him power over her which he did not deserve. No matter how frequently he threatened her, she would continue to shun him, affording him only the slight attention that one might an annoying gnat.

That was her intention at least. But there was a small part of her which could not help recalling those times when he had been at his angriest. Should she be wrong about him—and he should turn out to be more of a rabid mongrel than a noisy lapdog—then he could certainly cause trouble indeed.

Still, he had made no moves thus far, and she was certain his cowardice would prevent him from ever moving beyond idle threats. She had witnessed his true colors, and there was nothing else to see.

The day after the unfortunate encounter with Mr. Wickham, Elizabeth had decided she must inform Colonel Forster of her most recent incident with Mr. Wickham. Though she still felt that the man was no real threat, the colonel's instructions had been most explicit, and she could not in good conscience neglect to speak with him about what had happened. Unfortunately, the colonel had not yet returned and was not expected back until the following day. Determining that she would inform him when he returned, she put the matter firmly from her mind, as she did not wish to allow her concern to ruin her time in Brighton any further.

Fortunately, there were various amusements to be had. That evening, after a day somewhat uncharacteristically spent at home, Elizabeth attended a concert with Blanche, Mr. Darcy, and Colonel Fitzwilliam. Harriet had declined to accompany them due to fatigue, and while Elizabeth had offered to stay with her to keep her company, Harriet insisted that Elizabeth go to the concert and enjoy herself. As

Harriet would not be gainsaid, Elizabeth conceded and prepared herself for the evening, anticipating an enjoyable night spent with her other companions.

The night did not proceed as she had expected, however. Before the concert began, Blanche and Mr. Darcy somehow managed to separate from the group—though of course, they could not go far—in order to speak privately with one another. From the way Blanche was positioned, Elizabeth could only see the animation of the woman's movements, not her face and the feelings behind them. As for Mr. Darcy, his expression appeared to be blank, so she could receive no indication of the content of their conversation from him. Whether that was by accident or design, Elizabeth was not certain.

Colonel Fitzwilliam—who was at Elizabeth's side—made some sort of comment, but she gave only a short and distracted response that might very well have been quite inappropriate. She was too engrossed in the deepness of her thoughts to wrench them away even for a brief time to concentrate on the mundane. She knew not what the pair could have been discussing, and it was perplexing in the extreme!

As the seconds went by, Elizabeth found her agitation increasing and becoming somewhat akin to irritation. She had thought there were to be no more secret trysts between Mr. Darcy and Blanche, yet once again she was finding the pair engaged in the most intimate of conversations.

It was especially frustrating since Blanche knew that Elizabeth had mixed feelings toward Mr. Darcy which still needed to be sorted through. It would have been courteous for Blanche to keep her distance from Mr. Darcy until Elizabeth had been given the time she needed.

The tumult of her thoughts was nearly giving her a headache, but the stress was not resolved when the objects of her attention pulled apart and returned to their forgotten companions. Mr. Darcy was immediately at Elizabeth's side, and Blanche moved toward Colonel Fitzwilliam to make some sort of remark about looking forward to finally hearing in person the acclaimed violinist of which everyone in town had been speaking. The colonel leaned toward her with a smile and made some sort of quiet comment that Elizabeth could not catch.

Her brow furrowing slightly, Elizabeth brought her eyes away and looked up into the concerned expression of Mr. Darcy.

"Are you well, Miss Bennet?" came his soft voice.

For a moment, she could do little other than blink stupidly at him. Those simple words had been spoken with a surprising tenderness much at odds with the privacy he had indulged in with Blanche mere moments before.

When she at last found her voice, she managed to assure him: "I am well, Mr. Darcy. Thank you."

His dark and intense eyes remained fixed on her for a few seconds before he nodded. "I am glad to hear it."

The concert began soon after that, affording Elizabeth the opportunity to examine her thoughts, which were a mire of confusion.

Mr. Darcy's attentions appeared to have returned to her. What was more, Blanche appeared to be enthralled with Colonel Fitzwilliam. It scarcely seemed possible that Blanche and Mr. Darcy could both be interested in two people at the same time.

Elizabeth knew that Blanche could on occasion be demanding, monopolizing a person for great lengths of time. It was not wholly inconceivable that Blanche would be able to force a man to speak with her. Yet Mr. Darcy was surely not the sort of man who would do something he did not want to, no matter who was involved.

Surely Elizabeth was being ridiculous. Blanche was not conspiring to capture the attention of half the men in Brighton. Yet hard feelings toward the woman were rising up in Elizabeth's heart nonetheless.

The evening passed much the same as any other evening in such company and at such a venue. The concert was indeed inspired, and the violinist of whom Blanche had spoken played delightfully.

Unfortunately for Elizabeth, she was unable to enjoy the performance nearly as much as she otherwise would have, so great was the perturbation and confusion of the circumstances. And these problems were only exacerbated throughout the course of the evening. Mr. Darcy's attentions were firmly upon Elizabeth, and though he occasionally shared a glance with Blanche, he made no further effort to distinguish her with his attention. On the contrary, Blanche's focus was firmly upon the colonel, who seemed to reciprocate the expression of interest, though he remained the same jovial and talented conversationalist he had been in Kent when speaking with any of his companions.

Elizabeth was uncertain what she should think of the situation. However, as the evening progressed, she began to feel much closer to the man at her side. Not only was he truly intelligent and well-mannered, but she could find no fault in either his opinions or his deference to her opinions. Now that she had a chance to know him, she found that he was rapidly fitting into the mold of what she thought a true suitor should be. Their tastes and judgments, far from being diametrically opposite as she had initially thought to be the case, were in fact aligned, leading her to believe that she had spurned a man who could truly make her happy in every way possible. How fortunate she was to have another chance with him, to show him she could be amiable and intelligent and not a shrew who would spurn his deeply felt sentiments!

Still, she wondered if she did truly have another chance. This situation and his discussions with Blanche were truly vexing her, and the more she thought of the matter, the more upset she became with Blanche and the less she wished to speak civilly with her. She knew she was not behaving properly, but she could not help herself. Instead, she took to avoiding any discussion with Blanche in the attempt to prevent herself from snapping at her. She truly *did* esteem Blanche greatly, after all, and she had no wish to cause offense. Perhaps she could gain control over her reactions if she were allowed a little time to reflect and come to terms with the situation.

The next morning, the situation with Mr. Wickham once again intruded upon Elizabeth's senses, but this time, it was the colonel who brought up the subject. Stern-faced and clearly agitated, Colonel Forster called her into his office in the middle of the morning, having returned from the encampment. Elizabeth was surprised, as she had not even known of his return, let alone the fact that he had visited his officers already.

The first words out of his mouth filled Elizabeth with consternation. "Miss Bennet, I understand that you have had another confrontation with Mr. Wickham."

Though astonished that he had learned what happened so quickly, Elizabeth was able to overcome her surprise and reply to him. "Yes, I did indeed speak with him. Two nights ago at a dinner I attended, Mr. Wickham approached me, and I was not able to immediately escape him. My apologies—had I known you had returned, I should have ensured that you were aware of it ere you went to the encampment."

Colonel Forster ducked his head in what seemed to be slight embarrassment. "So you did mean to inform me?"

"I did indeed," said Elizabeth. "While the thought of keeping it to myself did cross my mind, your instructions were most explicit, and I could not keep it from you in good conscience."

"Your independence sometimes does you a disservice, Miss Bennet," said Colonel Forster with a chuckle. "Knowing you as I do, I had thought that perhaps you intended to deal with the scoundrel yourself. I am relieved that my conjecture was incorrect."

Elizabeth smiled at him. "Thank you for your concern, Colonel Forster. Please be assured that I would never disregard your instructions in such a manner while I am under your roof. I respect your authority, both as master of this house and the commander of your regiment."

"I am glad to hear it, Miss Bennet," said the colonel with a smile. "And I assure you that his actions and threats are not a small matter, and I take them very seriously indeed. Wickham has once again ignored my instructions and broken the restrictions I placed upon him. I must have discipline in my regiment, and my officers will be held to high standards. If Wickham cannot obey my instructions in so simple a matter as this, then how can I trust him if we should ever be thrust into battle?"

"I can see indeed where this would be a problem, Colonel Forster," replied Elizabeth.

Smiling, Colonel Forster roused himself from where he reclined against the desk and approached her, crouching down on one knee beside the chair in which she sat. He gazed at her earnestly and with a touch of the affection she knew he possessed for her.

"Miss Bennet, I assure you that my words of admiration for your abilities and your courage were not made in jest, nor were they misplaced. I do indeed have the highest opinion of you, and I completely respect you and your competence. I am happy that you will allow me to be of use to you and to protect you from a man whom I am rapidly coming to consider a scoundrel of the first order. As I stated before, I am responsible for your well-being here in Brighton, and I assure you that I take my responsibility most earnestly."

"I thank you for your concern, Colonel Forster," replied Elizabeth with a measure of the fondness she felt for him.

The colonel dipped his head. "It is nothing less than you deserve, Miss Bennet. Now, I wish to assure you that I have discussed Wickham's behavior with him once again, and he shall have even less opportunity than he had before to impose himself upon you. If he should even give you so much as a glance, you must inform me as soon as possible. I am already very troubled by his behavior, and it shall not take more for me to decide to strip him of his military rank entirely. Discipline is very important in the militia, and I cannot retain a man who proves himself willing to constantly disobey my orders. I need only a little more from him before I can feel justified in taking such permanent steps."

"I do not believe I shall face any more difficulties with him," said Elizabeth. "You need not worry."

Colonel Forster stared solemnly at her for a few moments before smiling and accepting her words with a nod. "I hope you are correct, Miss Bennet. But though I have restricted his activities, please promise me you shall continue to be careful. That is extremely important—now more than ever before, I fear."

"That is an easy promise to make, Colonel Forster," said Elizabeth with a smile of her own. "I have no intention of seeking Mr. Wickham out and every intention of avoiding him. Besides, I have several protectors in Brighton. I am certain not a one of them would allow me to come to any harm."

She was not merely saying that in an attempt to lessen the man's feelings of worry and deflect his attention from her; rather, she believed it was true. Between Colonel Forster, Mr. Denny, Mr. Darcy, Mr. Woodston, and now—she suspected—Colonel Fitzwilliam, there was little cause for alarm. She merely had to take care when none were present, which was a rare occurrence. The most recent night when Mr. Wickham had approached her had been an unusual one. It was not likely to happen again. Moreover, she was certain that Colonel Forster—if he had not ordered them to do so before—would now have some of his men keeping a close eye on her when she was in company. There truly was nothing to be concerned about. Mr. Wickham would not find a second opportunity to speak with her alone.

Chapter XIII

When Mr. Darcy reserved a box at a production of *King Lear* and invited Elizabeth and the Forsters to accompany him, Elizabeth felt the activity to be an appropriate one. Despite her determination not to worry about Mr. Wickham and her attempts to forget the intimate interaction she had seen between Blanche and Mr. Darcy, she found her mood to be rather grim, so a Shakespearean tragedy fit especially well with her state of mind.

Perhaps the drama suited her mental state a little *too* well. Even before she had arrived at the theater, she could not help but think of Goneril and Regan's betrayal of their father and their sister Cordelia. Unfortunately, that in turn made her think of Blanche, who seemed in many ways like a sister to her. While Elizabeth knew in her heart that Blanche was doing nothing wrong, it was difficult not to feel somewhat betrayed by her actions, though it scarcely seemed even feasible that Blanche would want to leave her position as vaunted Brighton socialite by marrying Mr. Darcy and settling down into a quieter life at Pemberley.

Still, love could make people act in ways they would not normally, and the dramatic Blanche would likely be willing to make a grand gesture for the one with whom she deemed herself in love. Thinking about the possibility of losing Mr. Darcy forever—yes, Elizabeth could not help but own to herself that he had come to mean so much to her—was enough to bring a pang of sorrow to her heart. And every day that she spoke with him increased the strength of her feelings. The thought that Blanche might be experiencing the same sensations was painful, so Elizabeth pulled her mind away from its current course and tried to focus instead on the pleasure of her present company. It was good to be with Harriet and Colonel Forster, of course, but she saw them every day. Her mind was instead drawn to the other member of their party.

Mr. Darcy looked particularly well tonight. Though he was always impeccably dressed—and no woman could ever call him less than handsome—there was something about the darkness of his coat and the curl of his hair that made Elizabeth's breath catch in her throat and her heart pound a little faster than was its usual wont. His dark eyes—always so intense and perceptive—were especially enthralling tonight, and she found herself wishing she could stare into them forever.

And his manner was no less appealing. He saw with careful attention to her every comfort and every need, as if she were the most important person in the entire world.

They alighted from the carriage at the theater, the gentlemen preceding the ladies before handing them down. Her hand secured in the crook of Mr. Darcy's arm, Elizabeth followed the married couple into the theater, where she and Mr. Darcy almost immediately garnered some attention from the other attendees. It appeared that even here in Brighton on the opposite end of the kingdom from his usual haunts, Mr. Darcy's reputation—or perhaps the size of his pocketbook—had preceded him.

They stopped in the foyer and exchanged pleasant greetings with a few of the Forsters' acquaintances. If Blanche had been there, they would no doubt have been inundated with the attentions of friends and those wishing to curry favor, as the woman appeared to know just about everyone of consequence in Brighton.

Mr. Darcy, as was his wont, said little, yet Elizabeth could not help but recognize that he maintained a friendly countenance. It was clear to her that though this setting was not where he felt his best, he could be genial in the company of others if he strove to be. It was also clear that while just about everyone in attendance knew *of* him, he was acquainted with relatively few of them.

"Miss Bennet, are you quite comfortable?"

Startled out of her ruminations, Elizabeth looked up at her companion, noting his expression of affectionate interest.

"Yes, I am," replied she, instantly composing herself. "I thank you for asking, sir."

"I am glad to hear it," said he. "Shall we adjourn to the box? I believe the production is due to begin shortly."

"Of course, Mr. Darcy," said Elizabeth with a smile.

Mr. Darcy had a word with the colonel before escorting her to the upper gallery and the entrances to the boxes, and as they walked, he noted that the Forsters would be joining them momentarily.

They arrived at their destination, and Mr. Darcy gallantly took her to her seat. Elizabeth gazed out over the theater, noting the fineness of the box and the location, which provided an excellent view of the stage. Clapping her hands together with delight, Elizabeth turned to her companion.

"What an excellent vantage from which to view the play, Mr. Darcy! I thank you for the invitation this evening. I am looking forward to the night's entertainment most enthusiastically."

Giving her an indulgent smile, Mr. Darcy took his seat by her side. "Am I to infer that you have not witnessed the theater from a box before, Miss Bennet?"

"Your inference would be correct," said Elizabeth. "I have been to the theater a number of times—with my Aunt and Uncle Gardiner while visiting them in London—but we have never had the good fortune to secure a box. My uncle promised that he would make certain to do so when next I visit."

"And so he should," said Mr. Darcy pleasantly. "There is nothing quite like witnessing Shakespeare from the excellent vantage which a private balcony provides."

Elizabeth's eyebrow rose, and she looked at him archly. "Mr. Darcy, I have it on good authority that you are a man with vast resources at your disposal. I would have assumed that you maintain a box at the best theater house in London and, therefore, would always have witnessed the theater in comfort and privacy. How can you make any comparisons if you have never sat in the gallery?"

As intended, her jesting tone induced him to smile in response rather than take insult at her words. "I can assure you, Miss Bennet, that your supposition is true—I do have a box at the theater. However, I have had occasion to view productions from the gallery. Last year in particular, there was a time when I had promised the box to an acquaintance, but Georgiana insisted she must see the production that evening. As a result, we sat in the gallery and enjoyed ourselves immensely."

"Ah, then you do have the experience from which to form an

opinion," said Elizabeth with a bright smile. "I look forward to obtaining my own experience so I may judge for myself."

"In that case, we shall have to compare our experiences," said Mr. Darcy with a laugh.

Reaching into the pocket of his jacket, Mr. Darcy pulled out a small silver case and offered it to her, saying: "Miss Bennet, I would be pleased if you would use these for the performance this evening."

Elizabeth reached forward and grasped the small case with great care, and after an encouraging look from Mr. Darcy, she opened it. Inside was nested a small but exquisitely wrought set of theater glasses. They were fashioned of silver with golden highlights, and when Elizabeth put them to her eyes, she marveled at how clearly she could see the stage. It was truly a wonderful gesture for Mr. Darcy to think of her comfort and enjoyment in such a fashion, and Elizabeth smiled shyly at him, putting her pleasure and gratitude for the gift in her response.

"They are lovely, Mr. Darcy. I thank you for allowing me to use them this evening. I can tell that they are very important to you."

"They belonged to my mother," said Mr. Darcy. "While Georgiana uses them from time to time, they have largely gone untouched since my mother's death. Your delight in the setting and the coming performance are obvious, Miss Bennet; I can think of no one better to put them to the use for which they were intended."

Elizabeth only kept her countenance with great difficulty, knowing that his words were almost a declaration of his regard. She returned his look, fancying that she could see his heart in his eyes. Elizabeth was certain her returning gaze mirrored his in every particular.

The married couple joined them in the box a few moments later, and Elizabeth gathered her composure with some difficulty and welcomed them, noting that Mr. Darcy appeared to be as affected as she was. She directed another shy smile at him and then turned to Harriet, who had begun to praise the venue and the coming play. Caught up in her friend's good humor, Elizabeth joined in, and the four chatted for several moments until the curtain rose for the beginning of the performance.

Elizabeth had to acknowledge that Mr. Darcy was correct—watching the performance from this vantage was much finer than seeing it from below. There was so much more to be seen, and Elizabeth felt that it almost literally took her breath away.

Through it all, Mr. Darcy remained particularly attentive. Her every gasp or frown seemed to be enough to draw his attention, and once, when he saw that she realized he was looking at her, he favored her with a gentle and almost embarrassed smile that endeared him to her all the more.

The grimness she had been feeling in regard to the tragedy's atmosphere and her own dark thoughts dissipated. Mr. Darcy still held her in great esteem—there could be no doubt of that. And she . . . she could not deny to herself that she had strong feelings toward him as well.

She was not certain her feelings could be called love—but oh, they were approaching it! She could not deny it to herself.

What she had taken for rudeness she now knew to be shyness. Her negative impressions of him had been wrong, and he was illustrating that to her every time she saw him. Somehow, he had ingrained himself in her life.

How fortunate it was that he had come to Brighton! She still knew not why he had decided to visit the city, but she was eternally grateful that he had. He very well could have passed out of her life forever after leaving Hertfordshire, and she would not have realized what a great loss had befallen her.

Lifting the theater glasses to her eyes, she watched as the actor playing King Lear demonstrated the character's growing madness. Using the glasses made everything feel much more vivid and real, and she almost trembled at the thought that only Mr. Darcy's mother and sister had used them. Mr. Darcy's gesture—providing the theater glasses for her use—seemed to hold great significance. It was no proposal, certainly, but her acceptance of them, though it was only to borrow them, pointed toward the fact that there could be something substantial between them in the future.

She almost smiled at that thought. Somehow, "something substantial" did not appear to truly cover the magnitude of such things as marriage and love.

That was a sobering thought. Was she truly—*truly*—considering marriage to the man whom she had disdained not so long ago?

Her eyes moved to him, and upon noticing her attention, he gave a slight nod, almost seeming amused.

She returned her gaze once more to the play, suppressing a chuckle. Perhaps she was making just as much of a fool of herself over him as he was over her. Yet she felt nothing less than happy. Perhaps spending a lifetime with Mr. Darcy would be something indeed!

The next day found Elizabeth in a pleasant mood. The night at the theater had been enjoyable indeed, and she could not help but continue to reflect upon it. When Mr. Darcy had asked that she compare her experiences after the play had ended, she had told him that a box was certainly a superior way to view a performance, but that it had been much aided by the exquisite theater glasses he had brought for her use. He had seemed quite pleased to hear her express such sentiments, and he commented that perhaps she would find another opportunity soon to use the glasses.

Harriet and Colonel Forster also appeared to enjoy the performance; while they did not seem as inclined to compare notes in a literary sense as Elizabeth and Mr. Darcy were, they did have their own remarks to make on the quality of the performance and the costumes of the players. Everyone left the theater quite content, and Elizabeth even found herself wishing that the play had gone on a little longer.

When Elizabeth received a letter from Jane in the morning, she opened it with no particular expectations, just with her normal happiness at the sight of a communiqué from her dear sister. The letter's contents, however, were enough to surprise her and vanquish all thoughts of the previous night's pleasures.

In fact, she had to read the letter twice to be certain that she truly knew what was being imparted by it. Jane, whose penmanship was normally quite neat, had evidently been somewhat shaky with excitement when writing the letter, for it was certainly not penned with a steady hand.

Though Jane attempted to cover other subjects, it was obvious there was only one item truly on her mind: Mr. Bingley had proposed to her, and she had accepted.

As Elizabeth considered the situation, her surprise faded a little, for she knew Mr. Bingley could be somewhat impulsive. However, in truth, she could not help but be a little puzzled as to how such a thing had come about. Not long before, it had seemed as though Mr. Bingley had left Hertfordshire—and Jane—permanently. While that had obviously not been the case, it had seemed a reasonable conclusion at the time, and the sudden reversal of events was strange, to say the least.

She tried to push aside her confusion and focus instead on what was most important: Jane was to have a bright future ahead of her at Mr. Bingley's side. Furthermore, Mrs. Bennet would no longer need to fret about the notion of Mr. Collins taking over Longbourn, for Jane and Mr. Bingley—two of the kindest people Elizabeth had ever known— would never allow Jane's mother and sisters to be turned out into the streets to eke out a meager existence with what little funds they would have at their disposal.

It was thus in a happy state of mind that Elizabeth and Harriet visited Blanche that morning. Though it was difficult to refrain from sharing her intelligence with Harriet immediately, Elizabeth waited until she could tell both her friends at once. When they were finally sequestered in a drawing-room, Elizabeth imparted her news with an eagerness she had not felt in some time.

"Your sister and Mr. Bingley engaged!" cried Harriet. "What a surprise this is! Oh, but how glad I am for them! I know they shall be very happy together. They are both such kind people."

As Elizabeth looked at Blanche, she realized that the woman had not seemed surprised in the slightest upon hearing Elizabeth's news. In fact, Blanche had what Elizabeth would almost call a knowing smile on her face.

Oblivious to Elizabeth's scrutiny, Blanche said warmly: "I am certain they are."

Unable to contain her surprise, Elizabeth gaped at her friend. Blanche was speaking as though she actually *knew* something of Mr. Bingley and Jane. What could she possibly be about?

Upon noticing Elizabeth's expression, Blanche asked: "Does something trouble you, Elizabeth?"

Eyes narrowed, Elizabeth stared at her friend accusingly. "It appears almost as though you already know a fair amount about the principals involved with my announcement, yet I am quite certain you have never met either, and I have certainly not discussed Mr. Bingley much with you. What can you mean by it?"

If Elizabeth had not been watching Blanche closely, she might have missed the instant of consternation betrayed by the apprehensive look on her face. However, Blanche was quick, and she recovered immediately.

"Come now, Elizabeth, you have told me so much of your sister that I fancy I already know her quite well indeed. And as for Mr. Bingley, his closest friend resides here in Brighton."

"Mr. Darcy has told you of Mr. Bingley?"

"Of course. By all accounts, Mr. Bingley is a genial and pleasant man and is well liked by all whom he meets. He appears to be a perfect match for your sister."

Everything Blanche said was completely believable, but Elizabeth did not trust it; or perhaps it was more correct to say that Elizabeth did not think that Blanche had told her everything. For one thing, Blanche's words were a little too glib, as though she was were happy to find an excuse for what must have been a small blunder. She certainly had not meant to betray her knowledge of the situation; what was more, the way Blanche had spoken almost indicated a foreknowledge of the event.

The specter of Blanche's animated discussions with Mr. Darcy again reared its ugly head, and Elizabeth found herself wondering once more exactly what was happening between her friend and Mr. Darcy.

Elizabeth was distracted for the rest of the visit, her mind churning over the mystery. She felt quite disheartened and contributed little to the conversation, though she knew her friends were wondering what had caused her sudden withdrawal. Yet while she attempted to concentrate on their discussion, her mind often slipped back to unpleasant thoughts.

How had Blanche come into such an intimate knowledge of events of which Elizabeth had not even known herself? Elizabeth could not understand it!

As it turned out, though Elizabeth was not able to have her questions answered, she *was* able to obtain a greater understanding of exactly how her sister's engagement came about. That she obtained this intelligence soon after her visit with Blanche was a further blessing, as it distracted her from her sometimes dark thoughts.

The next day, Mr. Darcy, in the company of Colonel Fitzwilliam, stopped by the Forsters' townhouse for a short conversation with the colonel, after which he joined the ladies in the sitting room while the two military men prepared to depart for the encampment. As fate would have it, Harriet left the room soon after Mr. Darcy's arrival, claiming fatigue due to a long night in which the heat of the summer had prevented her from sleeping well. Though Elizabeth privately wondered whether her friend was trying to be sly and allow her to have time alone with Mr. Darcy, she was far too relieved to be afforded the opportunity to query Mr. Darcy in confidence to question her motives overmuch.

Their conversation was easy—effortless even. It was also a simple matter for Elizabeth to pretend that the uncertainty of the previous day had never occurred, for she and Mr. Darcy seemed as at ease in one another's company as they had been on the night of the theater. Knowing, however, that she wanted—needed—some answers from him, she brought up the fact that she had received a letter from Jane on the previous day.

"I hope your sister is well, Miss Bennet," was his simple reply.

"She is indeed, Mr. Darcy. I thank you."

She regarded him for a moment, wondering whether he would betray any knowledge of the current situation in Meryton. When he said nothing else, Elizabeth resolved to prompt him further.

"In truth, Jane's letter has astonished me exceedingly, Mr. Darcy," said she, watching him closely. When he made no reply, she continued. "Are you aware of the current situation in Hertfordshire?"

"I have not received a letter from Bingley for some time," was his response. "However, as he is not a diligent correspondent, that is hardly unusual."

"Then I suspect you shall receive one shortly, for Mr. Bingley has proposed to my sister, and she has accepted him."

An expression of delight appeared on Mr. Darcy's face. "Oh, well done, Bingley! I am truly happy to hear that, Miss Bennet, and I extend my most heartfelt congratulations to your sister and your family."

His smile widened, and he continued: "I suspect that you are correct and that I will receive a letter from him shortly, but I truly appreciate your intelligence, as it shall greatly assist me in translating his words."

"Is he truly that poor a correspondent?" asked Elizabeth with a laugh, curious in spite of her determination to discover the extent of Mr. Darcy's influence in the matter.

Mr. Darcy's mock shudder sent her into further peals of laughter. "I assure you, Miss Bennet, that anything you have heard is an understatement. I hardly know how he was able to graduate—I suspect he drove the professors at Cambridge to drink with his blots and his half-formed ideas."

Though Elizabeth was diverted by his playful depiction of his friend, she could not allow herself to become distracted from her purpose. She peered at him intently, all laughter forgotten.

"Mr. Darcy, perhaps it is not proper for me to make such a query, but I truly must know. What was your role in Mr. Bingley's return to Hertfordshire?"

Mr. Darcy looked at her for a few seconds, though she could not tell whether he were trying to discern the depths of her earnestness or gather his thoughts.

Finally, however, he responded: "I shall not deny that I played a small part, Miss Bennet, but I must insist that it *was* only a small part."

She looked at him expectantly, waiting for him to explain himself further.

Fortunately, he obliged her. "In order to mitigate the effects of my unfortunate interference in the matter between your sister and Bingley,

I confessed to my friend that I was mistaken in my estimation of your sister's feelings. I told him that her regard was actually far greater than I had thought based upon what I had seen of her behavior. As a modest man, Bingley had been willing to accept my opinion of your sister's feelings. Upon hearing me acknowledge my error, however, he resolved to take matters entirely into his own hands."

Mr. Darcy paused briefly before continuing. "While I confess he did ask my opinion, which I did not withhold from him, I believe he settled on a course of action almost immediately after I told him of my mistake. He was the one who decided he should return to Hertfordshire in order to court your sister and make amends. And of course, he was the one who recently proposed marriage to her." At this last statement, Mr. Darcy gave a wry smile. "My role was but slight, Miss Bennet, and meant to correct an error rather than place Bingley on a specific path. It was his esteem for your sister that led him back to her and not any pressure from me."

Elizabeth stared at Mr. Darcy, her eyebrows furrowed in thought. She suspected that his part in the matter was greater than he was saying; she also could not help but wonder precisely what the substance of the opinion that Mr. Darcy had given Mr. Bingley was. She knew Mr. Darcy was a proud man, and though Jane was the daughter of a gentleman, she had no dowry to speak of, and Mr. Bingley, whose relatively new wealth carried with it the stench of trade, would have been much better off marrying someone of higher social consequence.

Elizabeth thought back to the letter Mr. Darcy had written that described how he had helped separate Mr. Bingley and Jane. He had noted that Mr. Bingley was swayed only by a strong assurance of Jane's indifference. And she believed it. Mr. Bingley—with his kind and earnest heart and his eagerness to accept others into his company—could never have been swayed by an argument based solely on social class. It was only because of Mr. Bingley's modesty that Mr. Darcy was nearly successful in tearing Mr. Bingley and Jane apart permanently.

Now, however, Jane and Mr. Bingley would be together at last, and no one could tear them asunder; there was no sense in dwelling on the averted catastrophe. And perhaps what had happened would strengthen their marriage—Jane would learn to show her feelings so they could not be misunderstood, and Mr. Bingley would learn to trust his own judgment.

Unfortunately, Elizabeth was quiet for so long that Mr. Darcy appeared to be growing concerned. Upon seeing his expression and realizing that she had not said anything for an inordinate amount of time, she favored him with a gentle smile. "I am glad that you talked to your friend, Mr. Darcy. I truly believe that he and my sister will be very happy together."

"I believe you are correct," said he in agreement, the barely perceptible note of relief in his voice making her feel guilty for having been so lost in her thoughts. "If only we all could be so fortunate."

His gaze was steadily fixed on her as he spoke, and she was almost certain she could not be imagining the feeling of significance imbued in his last statement.

Yet she knew not how to respond, so she said simply: "One never knows what the future shall hold."

"No, indeed, Miss Bennet," murmured he, his gaze so strong now that she had to look away. "However, I firmly believe that we have the ability to make our own future. Much of what we decide today can affect us tomorrow and for the rest of our lives, regardless of the various unforeseeable events that we shall face. In some ways, our autonomy can be beneficial to our future happiness, but in other ways, it can be detrimental, as I have recently discovered to my sorrow. I hope that by changing those things which brought about this decline in my fortunes, I might reverse them and perhaps gain the happiness I have sought all my life."

Elizabeth's breath caught in her throat. She had never known Mr. Darcy to be particularly eloquent—intelligent, proper, discerning, yes, but never eloquent. But at that moment, it was as though his heart were speaking to hers.

Elizabeth longed to respond with equally tender words of her own, but she found her tongue stilled in her mouth, her emotions running the gamut between elation, confusion, and caution. Before she could say anything in response, Colonel Forster walked into the sitting room, his face lighting up into a jovial smile.

"Mr. Darcy!" cried he. "I am truly delighted to find you here, sir."

"Colonel Forster," replied Mr. Darcy, rising and bowing before his host.

The colonel peered about the room, and turning to Elizabeth, he said: "But Miss Bennet, where is my wife?"

Though the emotions of the morning still felt quite fresh, she took hold of herself enough to respond with some composure. "Harriet felt a little fatigued, so she sought some rest in her room."

"Ah, the little one is sapping some of her energy. It is to be expected, I suppose, though I wish I could do more for my dear wife than I am currently able."

Elizabeth laughed. "The only thing you could do more would be to carry her from place to place without regard for her own feet, sir!"

Colonel Forster laughed at her declaration. "Perhaps, Miss Bennet, but it would be the least I could do for my dear wife. Not that she would allow me such frivolities."

"Nor should she, sir," said Elizabeth in a tone of mock severity, once again prompting his laughter.

"Ah, Miss Bennet, I am truly fortunate to have you in residence; somehow, you brighten the room with your presence and induce all of our cares and concerns to flee from the force of your personality."

Elizabeth blushed, as she suspected was his intention, and the colonel grinned at her with some satisfaction.

However, he did not continue his teasing. Instead, he turned his attention to Mr. Darcy, who was regarding the scene with some amusement, and said: "It is extremely fortuitous that you have not yet left, sir, for I have one more matter about which I should like to ask your advice, and your cousin suggested I apply to you directly. May I prevail upon you for a moment of your time?"

"Of course," said Mr. Darcy with a bow. He then approached Elizabeth and grasped her hand, bestowing a lingering kiss on its back. "I shall bid you farewell then, Miss Bennet. I have truly enjoyed this opportunity to speak with you."

Rising, Elizabeth let her pleasure show through in her smile. "As have I, Mr. Darcy. I truly hope you find your happiness at the end of your search."

His answering smile was brilliant, and he bowed once before following the colonel from the room.

Elizabeth was thus left alone to think about what had occurred that morning and to become vexed over not being quick enough to respond to Mr. Darcy. Once again, her doubt over the state of their relationship had disappeared, to be replaced with the warm glow she had come to associate with the surety of his continued affections.

Chapter XIV

$\mathcal{T}$he next few days were quiet and calm, spent largely in the comfort of the Forsters' townhouse. Mr. Darcy had informed Elizabeth the day after their tête-a-tête that he was obliged to return to London on a matter of business, though he had taken great pains to assure her that he only expected to be away for a few days. She said farewell to him warmly, attempting to show him the true state of her affections, and he returned her sentiments in a like fashion.

But though one of her protectors was now absent from Brighton, it seemed as if his presence was not truly required. Elizabeth saw nothing of Mr. Wickham in the time Mr. Darcy was gone other than on one occasion in which the officers dined with the Forsters. The colonel had spoken with her before the event, informing her that while Mr. Wickham was under suspicion and out of favor, he had already been excluded from three dinners in a row. Colonel Forster pledged to her that if she desired, he would once again find something else to occupy Mr. Wickham, but he worried that too many more instances of exclusion would encourage accusations of favoritism.

Elizabeth assured him that she was fine and that he should not prohibit the man from attending dinners at the Forsters' townhouse on her account. After all, with Mr. Denny, Harriet, and the colonel himself in attendance, it was not as if Mr. Wickham could venture to do anything untoward. And her words were proven correct: while Mr. Wickham appeared sullen and uncommunicative—indeed, he hardly said a word to anyone the whole evening—he kept his distance from Elizabeth, preferring to brood by himself.

The day following Mr. Darcy's return, they had arranged an outing to once again go sea bathing.

And so it was that Elizabeth, the Forsters, Blanche, Mr. Darcy, and Colonel Fitzwilliam gathered together for a short time before forming two groups, male and female, and journeying the short distance to their separate beaches with the intention of gathering together once again after they had all had their sea baths.

The three women enjoyed their brief venture into the sea very much. Elizabeth found that the cool water did much to ease the tension that had recently been snaking through her shoulders, as if the salt were able to erase all her concerns pertaining to the motives of Mr. Darcy.

When the three women finished their sea baths and were ready to compare notes out on the beach, Blanche declared loudly: "Ah, there is nothing quite like a sea bath for both body and soul! It has done wonders to relieve the stresses brought on by the intensity of the social field."

Elizabeth smiled to herself and refrained from commenting on the fact that Blanche loved nearly everything involved in socializing with her peers.

Harriet expressed her own agreement: "My body is feeling much improved since my own dip into that healing saltwater. I dare say this was quite a splendid idea!"

"And you, Elizabeth?" asked Blanche. "Did it aid in banishing your own aches and pains?"

"Indeed, it did," said Elizabeth. "We truly are fortunate to have such an opportunity as this. Were it not for Harriet, I would not have experienced Brighton's attractions at all!"

"And were it not for you, Elizabeth, then Blanche and I would not be benefitting from your lively disposition," countered Harriet.

"I should have suffered the loss of Elizabeth most of all," declared Blanche, "for I should never have met her. Fortunately, however, we have not been handed such misfortune. We are allowed to enjoy each other's company and benefit from each other's knowledge and experiences."

"That *is* what friendship is about," said Harriet.

The three ladies, content with their companionship, then walked to meet back up with the men. The three gentlemen entreated the ladies for an account of their enjoyment before venturing to express their own contentment with the wondrous—and almost miraculous—effects of the saltwater.

Rather than dispersing and taking carriages to their separate residences, they decided to stretch their legs and enjoy a leisurely stroll to the Forsters' townhouse for a bit of refreshment. They somehow— Elizabeth knew not how exactly it happened—separated into couples. The Forsters walked together, of course; Blanche and Colonel Fitzwilliam, both talking in their characteristically lively voices, paired together; and Mr. Darcy took upon himself the task of escorting Elizabeth, who was quite confused with the present state of affairs. She still could not discern what—if anything—was taking place between Mr. Darcy and Blanche, and that lack of knowledge came back once more to vex her. Mr. Darcy's choice to walk by Elizabeth's side rather than Blanche's certainly did not clear up the mystery. Still, she resolved to enjoy herself while she could.

As they walked together under the bright and cheerful sun, Mr. Darcy was quiet for only a few minutes before at last he began to speak. "I am not much for trifles, Miss Bennet, but you will have to forgive me this once for my slight breach of propriety. Upon the ocean floor, I found a shell that caught my eye and brought you to mind. Ordinarily, I should not be so—so forward, but I took the shell into my possession primarily because I felt that you should have it. As an avid lover of nature, you are one, I believe, who would appreciate such an item despite its utter lack of intrinsic value." As he was speaking, he brought the object in question up into her sight and held it out for her to take. There had been something strangely awkward in his speech, and it made him all the more endearing.

Gently, Elizabeth took the shell from his hand—trying not to linger as she felt her fingertips gently brush his palm—and lifted it up so she could admire it properly. She smiled down at the shell with true enjoyment, her eyes tracing its intricate patterns and the twinkling colors reflecting from the light of the sun. But enjoyment was not all she felt. Inwardly, her heart was pounding. The gesture, though seemingly a small one, was touching, kind, thoughtful—she could not help but realize that it meant she had been on Mr. Darcy's mind while he had been luxuriating in the gentle touch of the sea. By giving her the shell, he hoped to please her; there was no other explanation for it. And that made her examine her feelings for the man—once so infuriating but now so alluring—yet again.

The thought that she might still be on his mind—despite the horrible things that had passed between them—only made her heart swell even greater. She could not deny to herself that she no longer looked at him as she once had. He did not seem to be a cold and proud statue that she wished to ridicule; rather, she viewed him as a warm and kind man whom she wished to know better. Mr. Darcy was indeed a thousand times more worthy of praise than Wickham. The appearance of goodness was not the same as the possession of it, and now Wickham and Darcy's outward appearances even seemed to be changing. While Wickham was becoming sullen, Darcy appeared to be allowing himself to become more agreeable to strangers. Elizabeth knew not whether it was due to her own influence or because Mr. Darcy was more comfortable among the people of Brighton than those of Hertfordshire, but she was glad for the change. And she knew that she, too, had undergone a transformation of sorts; she had been forced to examine her prejudices, both positive and negative, and the experience had taught her not to rely on first glances and quick judgments.

Elizabeth looked up, intending to thank her companion, but the words died in her throat. Though he was nervously watching her, his gaze also contained an almost indefinable quality which Elizabeth fancied was an abiding and enduring love, an affection which had survived despite all which had come between them. He had yet to confirm it by word, but by deed, it appeared to be well and truly decided upon.

Her feelings of resistance—if any indeed still existed—seemed to crumble. Could she still claim to be indifferent to this man?

No. The thought beggared her imagination. She was in love with him—there was no other explanation.

She glanced down at the shell once again, and gaining control over her emotions, she began to speak:

"Mr. Darcy, you speak of intrinsic value. I am afraid I must disagree with your assessment."

She met his eyes to see his puzzled expression reflected back at her.

"Truly, Mr. Darcy, what in this world can have more intrinsic value than a gift freely given, with nothing more than the anticipation of giving pleasure to the receiver?"

Mr. Darcy's soft smile illuminated his face. "Nothing, Miss Bennet. As usual, you are correct."

"And thus, I must tell you that your gift is exquisite and of far more worth than had it cost you a thousand pounds. I thank you, Mr. Darcy, not only for the gift, but also for thinking of me with such care and attention."

"I could hardly care for you in any other fashion, Miss Bennet," said Mr. Darcy. "You are truly an exceptional woman, and I dare say I have become a better man simply due to the privilege of having known you."

Elizabeth blushed and averted her gaze, taking some interest in her surroundings while she attempted to find a way to respond to the man's overt praise. She noticed that Colonel Forster and Harriet, who were at the front of the procession, had chosen to lead the group through a pleasant city park. Trees dotted the landscape, and the scent of crisp, freshly cut grass wafted through the air while the long ribbons of pathways meandered here and there through the foliage. It was a place which almost felt incongruous in the middle of a bustling city—a haven amidst the business of life. As a lover of nature, Elizabeth felt that the locale possessed a soothing quality which allowed her to once again regain her composure.

They had just passed beneath the outstretched boughs of a large yew when Mr. Darcy abruptly stopped and turned to face Elizabeth.

"Miss Bennet—"

But whatever he would have said was to remain a mystery forever.

"Be careful, young man."

Startled, Elizabeth peered around, espying an elderly lady sitting on a nearby bench and smiling at them with some amusement.

"I beg your pardon?" asked Mr. Darcy.

"The tree you stand under—that is the tree of lovers. They say when a young man and woman stand beneath it, they are certain to fall in love."

Blushing all over again, Elizabeth risked a glance at Mr. Darcy, only to find him peering at her with some amusement, though it was evident that the state of his cheeks was not dissimilar to her own. She lifted her eyebrow archly in challenge, wondering what he would say in response.

"And how long has this tree been known to induce undying love?"

Elizabeth stifled a giggle as the old lady responded:

"That particular tree has stood there for a great many years, young man, and it has long been known as a special place to all lovers. I, myself, became engaged to my husband beneath that very tree, so I will thank you not to make light of my words."

"I would not dream of doing so, madam," replied Mr. Darcy while inclining his head. "And since the particular location is sacred to all lovers . . ."

He trailed off, gazing at Elizabeth as he spoke, prompting her to look away from the intensity in his eyes.

"Darcy!" cried Colonel Fitzwilliam. "Is it true? Have you succumbed to the charms of a lady due to the influence of a *tree?*"

The Forsters, who had turned back to witness the spectacle, were all smiles, but Blanche's face was nigh unreadable as she scrutinized the pair. Colonel Fitzwilliam, however, was watching them closely, no doubt relishing the opportunity to make sport with his cousin.

"I had always thought it would require something particular to induce you from your solitary and inscrutable bachelor's state, but even I never imagined something of *this* nature."

The company laughed at the colonel's words, but Elizabeth felt a small frisson of disappointment flow through her. Though she could not be certain exactly what Mr. Darcy had been about, it was clear that there had been *something* there—or something on the verge of occurring. But the mood had been broken, and with it, Elizabeth felt an almost tangible loss.

"I assure you, cousin," replied Mr. Darcy evenly, "that I am fully capable of finding a woman who would induce me to give up my bachelor state without the assistance of a tree."

He turned and bowed again to the old lady. "However, when I do, I shall certainly keep this particularly fine specimen of a tree in mind as a place to formalize my engagement."

Elizabeth was almost certain her face was to be afflicted with a permanent rosy hue, for she felt that Mr. Darcy's last words, though spoken to the company at large, had been directed at her alone. She was given no time to think about it, however, as Mr. Darcy bade farewell to the lady, who was fairly grinning at him with delight, and offered his arm to Elizabeth. And though Elizabeth was of two minds about quitting the place—part of her was filled with embarrassment, though the greater part wished that she and Mr. Darcy had not been interrupted—she took his arm and allowed herself to be guided once again down the path.

The rest of the walk to the Forsters' townhouse was agreeable enough—indeed, it would have been difficult not to enjoy both the pleasant weather and the even pleasanter company—yet Elizabeth could not force her mind away from the remarkable incident which had just occurred. Even later, after Mr. Darcy, Colonel Fitzwilliam, and Blanche had departed from the Forster townhouse, Elizabeth found her thoughts consumed entirely by a contemplation of that so-called "tree of lovers" and Mr. Darcy's final words to the elderly lady. There was something portentous about the event, as if it pointed unwaveringly at the promise of things to come, and Elizabeth could scarcely quell her feelings of excitement. She could not wait to see what the future held, and it set her heart aflutter.

For the next few days, Elizabeth almost felt as if she were walking on air. Part of this could be attributed to the fact that there was no further evidence of any intimacy between Mr. Darcy and Blanche, and part of it was because of the confidence she now found in Mr. Darcy's attentions.

Indeed, Mr. Darcy was very much in evidence during those days. He called at the Forsters' townhouse every morning—sometimes in the company of Colonel Fitzwilliam, but more often alone—and Elizabeth was always happy to see him. She could not help but think that he took much pleasure in her company as well. His attentions seemed to be unmistakable—they walked outside together, discussed everything books to acquaintances to politics, shared dances at assemblies, and spent many a pleasant hour in various other pursuits of interest to both. In some ways, though Elizabeth still partook in many activities with Harriet, much of her time began to be gradually consumed by Mr. Darcy's attentions. And while she was worried that Harriet might feel neglected, her friend was Mr. Darcy's foremost champion, encouraging Elizabeth to spend as much time as she liked with the man.

But in the midst of her euphoria, she lost sight of the difficulties she had previously faced with a certain officer of the militia. This was a mistake she was forced to acknowledge to herself very quickly, for the next day, while she was mingling contentedly among the company at an assembly which Mr. Darcy, regrettably, was not attending, she found herself suddenly cornered by the irascible Mr. Wickham. Being forced into such contact with him was enough to dampen her mood, and the misfortune of the incident was even to go beyond that, which she soon discovered.

As Elizabeth stared at Mr. Wickham, unsure what was to come due to the utter unpredictability of the man, she could not help but reflect on how he appeared to grow angrier and angrier every time he saw her near Mr. Darcy. She did not wish to make it a habit to watch Wickham, yet the barely concealed rage he often displayed could not help but draw her notice despite. Even now, his face was a strange mixture of ire and arrogance and scorn, and Elizabeth might have been fascinated with how a man could mingle such emotions into one expression were she not so repulsed by Wickham's mere presence.

"Miss Bennet," snarled Mr. Wickham in a tone that was almost a growl. His hands were clenched at his sides as he stared unflinchingly at her. There was something unhinged to his bearing, as if he were a coiled snake about to strike.

"Mr. Wickham," returned she coolly, standing her ground as he stepped still closer to her. She forced herself to meet his gaze rather than attempt to look over his shoulder and plot an escape. Though the notion was tempting, she did not wish to give him the satisfaction of making her flee. He believed he had too much power over her as it was, and she did not want to contribute any further to that notion; she needed him to see her as an equal rather than as someone he could frighten into doing his bidding and believing his lies.

"Your two dear friends appear to be growing quite intimate," said he. He spoke quietly, with the low tones of a man imparting a secret, yet the look on his face had not changed. He was still a ball of barely restrained fury, and no honey he attempted to add to his voice could make its sound seem sweet to her ears.

"I beg your pardon?" asked she, not even bothering to hide her confusion.

"Darcy and your dear Mrs. Wade," specified he.

When she stared blankly at him, he said with a sneer: "Why, Miss Bennet, do not tell me you have not noticed how *close* they appear to be. They shall marry before long, and you shall be left bereft of your friend's company and that of Darcy's, such as it is. I am afraid your pathetic attempts to ensnare Darcy have all been for naught, *Miss Bennet.*" Her name was like an epithet on his lips. "He will do as he always intended, marrying a beautiful woman of status and fortune rather than a penniless nobody such as you. He has never seen you as more than a temporary plaything to amuse him until he found a proper wife, and I am only sorry that you should have ever believed otherwise."

Elizabeth felt her indignation rise at the audacity of Mr. Wickham, and she pinned him with her fiercest glare. How dare this pathetic excuse for a man speak in such a fashion! Mr. Darcy had more honor and integrity in him than Mr. Wickham could ever hope to attain. A true gentleman would never use a lady as a "plaything," as Wickham had so coarsely suggested, and Mr. Darcy was nothing if not a gentleman!

"You believe you have a superior understanding of people, Mr. Wickham, but you do not. Sadly, your rakish nature does not enable you to keep any friends so that you might study their behavior—and thus it is impossible for you to comprehend the minds of others who are not governed by selfishness and avarice."

Even while she was speaking scornfully to him, Elizabeth knew that it was not wise. She felt something was about to happen, and when it did, it happened so quickly that she had little time to prepare.

His hand shot out and grabbed her arm. His other arm raised to strike her. Elizabeth prepared herself for a blow, moving her hand up to block it.

A loud scream resounded, startling both Elizabeth and Mr. Wickham. They turned, almost as one, to find Blanche staring at them in horror. Elizabeth nearly melted in relief at the realization that she and Mr. Wickham were not alone, but she had no time to even contemplate her good fortune before Colonel Fitzwilliam came charging forward from a nearby group of people.

"Unhand the lady this instant, cur!" snapped Colonel Fitzwilliam.

Though Mr. Wickham must have recognized the air of unmistakable command in the colonel's voice, something stopped him from releasing Elizabeth immediately. He made no more threatening moves in her direction, but he glared at her for a moment before turning to face the approaching colonel.

"I see you have many protectors, Elizabeth," said Wickham with a sneer. "Perhaps far more than you deserve."

He let Elizabeth's arm go, but it did it in a rather violent fashion, shoving it downward and causing her to stumble slightly. "There, I have released the *lady*, Fitzwilliam." His contempt for her was evident in the way he almost spat the word. "Now, if you will excuse me, I believe I have had enough of this assembly."

"I think not, Wickham," growled the colonel. "You did not truly think that I would allow you to leave after your appalling behavior toward Miss Bennet, did you? You are a disgrace to the uniform you wear—indeed, you are a stain upon the human race, and you shall not go unpunished this time."

He leaned toward Wickham and in a low voice continued:

"You have finally given me the opportunity to repay you for the misery and heartache you have caused not only my family but also everyone upon whom you have ever imposed your miserable existence. Enjoy the harvest you will reap."

He turned away and signaled to two officers who were standing nearby. "Barnes! Jackson! Take the former lieutenant into custody and deliver him to his encampment. He is to be confined to quarters pending my discussion with his commanding officer." He turned and sneered at Mr. Wickham. "I imagine your freedom will be curtailed for some time, Wickham, given what I know of your general proclivities."

The two officers snapped their salutes, and after divesting Mr. Wickham of his saber, they each took hold of one of his shoulders and propelled him from the room. Mr. Wickham made no further comment, but his expression as he stared at Elizabeth was filled with such a poisonous rage that she was required to consciously restrain herself from shrinking away from him in fear. It appeared that she had finally provoked the true man to emerge, and he terrified her. Here was someone without scruples, a man who would hurt her for the simple fact that he could . . . and because she had dared to contradict his words. It was a sobering realization.

Colonel Fitzwilliam grasped her arm, breaking the flow of her swirling thoughts, and he gestured toward a nearby chair. "Miss Bennet, are you well?"

Though Elizabeth most certainly did *not* feel well, she gathered herself and indicated that she had not been physically harmed.

"I shall take care of Elizabeth, Colonel Fitzwilliam," said Blanche as she stepped forward to lead Elizabeth to her seat. "If you would be so kind, perhaps you would obtain some punch to calm her nerves."

The colonel bowed, and after favoring them with a significant glance, he departed on his errand.

Blanche peered at Elizabeth with some concern before she initiated the interrogation which Elizabeth had anticipated.

"Elizabeth, you are unharmed?"

When Elizabeth answered in the affirmative, Blanche directed a scathing look at her. "Do not favor me with the platitudes you directed at the dear colonel, Elizabeth, for I will not be taken in by them."

Elizabeth pressed her hands over her friend's. "I assure you that I am well, Blanche, for you stopped Mr. Wickham before he could do anything. I am perhaps a little shaken by the incident, but there is nothing wrong with me."

"And will you now acknowledge that Mr. Wickham is a danger to you?"

Sighing, Elizabeth nodded her head. "It appears as though you were correct in your estimation of him, Blanche. Though I always considered him to be a coward who would choose the path of least resistance, it appears the coward does indeed possess an impressive set of fangs. I assure you that I shall not take his ability to harm lightly again.

"And I thank you, Blanche, for your care and attention toward me," said Elizabeth, grasping her friend's hands. "I know not what would have happened had you not been there to interrupt him."

"You are welcome, Elizabeth," said Blanche with a great deal of affection. "I am very fond of you and would not wish for you to be harmed by that scoundrel. However, I think it best that we depart this assembly immediately. Not only will rumors be spreading due to the altercation, but I believe we must seek Colonel Forster's counsel—he must be made aware of what has happened forthwith."

Elizabeth agreed, noticing for the first time that there were many hushed conversations taking place all over the assembly room, not to mention several surreptitious glances in her direction. Feeling mortification welling within her, she accepted Colonel Fitzwilliam's promptly obtained punch and sipped it, her emotions settling.

Then, once a sufficient time for recovery had passed, she allowed her friends to escort her from the hall. She resolved to put Wickham from her mind for the rest of the day, though she feared such would be much easier said than done.

Chapter XV

Once they had returned to the Forsters' townhouse, Colonel Fitzwilliam immediately pulled Colonel Forster into his study to acquaint him with the events of the evening. Elizabeth was joined by Blanche and Harriet in the parlor, Harriet gasping at the tale of Mr. Wickham's perfidy while fussing over Elizabeth in an attempt to ensure her friend was well. Elizabeth was appreciative of the sentiment, but now that the confrontation had passed, she found herself irritated at being treated like an invalid and angry at Mr. Wickham's attempts to ruin her time in Brighton.

It was not much later when she was summoned to the study to recount her tale of what had occurred between herself and Mr. Wickham, and though she was embarrassed at the things which the man had said—especially regarding herself and Mr. Darcy!—she decided they required a full accounting and forced herself to tell them.

"Miss Bennet," said Colonel Fitzwilliam, kneeling by her side once she had finished her account, "while I cannot speak for the exact feelings of my cousin or the state of his relationship with Mrs. Wade, I *can* tell you that he thinks very highly of you. He would never behave in a manner such as Mr. Wickham has charged."

"I thank you for your kindness, Colonel Fitzwilliam," responded Elizabeth with a smile. "But I had already determined that much for myself. Mr. Wickham, I dare say, is almost incapable of telling the truth, especially when it relates to Mr. Darcy. Please do not concern yourself even for an instant that I believed his words to hold any truth."

Colonel Fitzwilliam smiled at her and nodded. "Very well, Miss Bennet. I thank you for your faith in my cousin."

"Miss Bennet," interjected Colonel Forster, "I can assure you that Mr. Wickham will not only lose his rank, but he shall also be held to account for his deeds. I suspect that a trip to the stockade and a potential court martial are in the offing for Wickham. If nothing else, Colonel Fitzwilliam and I will see him transferred to a regiment in the midst of the fighting against the tyrant before we allow him to importune you again. Now, I believe it may be best for you to retire, as you have had a trying evening."

Elizabeth nodded weakly. "I believe I shall. I must confess to being a little out of sorts." That certainly was an understatement. Simply remaining upright was taking an exorbitant amount of her concentration.

"I shall take care of Wickham," said Colonel Forster. "You need not worry about him any longer."

But in spite of the colonel's kind words, the next morning, Elizabeth could not help but indeed worry about Mr. Wickham. After having witnessed Mr. Wickham's utter cruelty, she felt quite shaken and almost fearful. She was fortunate that he had simply grasped her arm. It could easily have been much worse.

Elizabeth determined to visit Blanche in order to put her mind at ease, believing that seeing the ever-happy widow would improve her mood. Harriet was not feeling especially well, so Elizabeth, after some urging by Harriet to go out, went alone, though she was of course attended on the journey by Mr. Woodston.

She was shown inside Blanche's townhouse by a servant, and as she was escorted to the door of the sitting room, she saw Blanche and Mr. Darcy speaking within, standing much closer to each other than could be expected of mere acquaintances.

Elizabeth was announced by the servant before she entered the room, and upon hearing the servant's voice, Blanche and Mr. Darcy immediately ceased their conversation to turn toward her with kind smiles, though they seemed loath to discontinue their discussion.

Still, they greeted her pleasantly, acting as if they were pleased to see her, though she could not help but wonder if in reality they felt the opposite. Mr. Wickham's hate-filled words returned to her with the force of a raging tempest. Could he—despite his all-consuming malice—have actually been correct in his prediction that the pair would marry soon?

Elizabeth reined in her tumultuous feelings, pasting a smile on her face and engaging half-heartedly in the banter into which Blanche soon slipped. But when Mr. Darcy at last excused himself, leaving the two women alone, Elizabeth's emotions were close to overflowing, and she could not contain them much longer. It certainly did not help that Blanche's first subject of choice was Mr. Darcy . . . and that high praise for the man was on her lips.

"Mr. Darcy is quite the gentleman," said Blanche, looking at the door through which Mr. Darcy had disappeared. "His initial reticence to speak to those with whom he is not well acquainted can be difficult to surpass—and it is tempting to believe the effort not worth the reward—yet once you are able to penetrate that air of aloofness, you find that he is quite a kind and pleasant man more than worthy of knowing."

Elizabeth attempted to hold her tongue, not wanting to ruin things between her and her friend, yet she could not remain silent. The stresses she had been undergoing were not merely to be thrust away with the ease of brushing aside feathers. They needed to be released.

"Yes, Mr. Darcy is quite the gentleman," said Elizabeth in a voice that could not but be called caustic. "I suspect you have become very well acquainted with that fact over the past few weeks while speaking so intimately with him. I suspect you two shall be very happy together quite soon."

Blanche's face was filled with confusion, and her voice was no less so. "Of what do you speak, Elizabeth? Mr. Darcy and I?"

"I have seen the two of you talking quietly together," said Elizabeth in a fierce voice that held something of an accusatory undertone. "Do you deny it?"

"No," said the other woman, her brow furrowed. "I do not deny that we have spoken together frequently, Elizabeth, but—"

"Then what more is there for you to say?" interrupted Elizabeth. She knew she was not making much sense, but her head was too clouded for her to care. "What more is there for either of us to say?" She felt close to tears.

"We have been conversing together," said Blanche, "but that is not why—" She stopped speaking suddenly, as if she felt she had said too much.

"Then why, Blanche?" demanded Elizabeth. "Why have I seen you and Mr. Darcy so frequently caught up in close conversation with one another?"

"Because of you, Elizabeth!" cried Blanche in exasperation. "We have been speaking with each other because of you!"

"What?" was all Elizabeth could manage.

"We have been worried about you!" Blanche said with a sigh. "I had thought to keep this from you, but I see now that perhaps I should not have done so."

"What have you kept from me?" asked a puzzled Elizabeth.

"Mr. Darcy did not simply happen to come to Brighton while you were visiting Harriet; it was no mere coincidence. It began with Mr. Wickham. Though I had hoped it would not reach such a level as it has, I saw something about Mr. Wickham that concerned me enough that I was fearful for you. In order to learn what I would need to know about Mr. Wickham so that I might keep you safe from him, I wrote an express letter to Mr. Darcy. As we had never been introduced, it was terribly forward of me, yet I would not stand on formalities when it came to protecting a dear friend such as you. I needed information, and Mr. Darcy was the best source for such information, so I did not even hesitate."

Elizabeth felt as if her head was filled with a viscous liquid, and her thoughts seemed to move with the slowness of honey dripping from a beehive.

"You wrote to Mr. Darcy?" was all she was able to say.

"I did, Elizabeth," replied Blanche kindly. "It was perhaps the most impertinent thing I have ever done, though perhaps you may not credit it as such, having known me these past few months."

Her attempt at a jest brought a weak smile from Elizabeth, though she certainly did not feel up to laughing at that particular moment.

"In my letter," said Blanche, "I demanded outright that Mr. Darcy tell me what he knew about Mr. Wickham, and I shared my concerns with him regarding the man's behavior."

"And Mr. Darcy's response?"

"There was none—other than his arrival here. He did tell me he had never been so surprised at such an impertinence in his life, and though he suspected it was a machination with the intent to induce him to matrimony, he opened my letter rather than consigning it to the fire as he thought he ought. The contents, however, spurred him to action, provoking him to come here so he could take care of Mr. Wickham himself if necessary. I believe your Mr. Darcy thinks it his responsibility to handle Mr. Wickham due to their history together. In my opinion, he takes far too much on his shoulders."

Blanche's countenance became a little mischievous at this point. "He also told me that he would rather have expected such an impertinence from a certain lady from Hertfordshire, if it were to come from anyone."

Feeling her cheeks flaming, Elizabeth sighed and glanced down at her feet. "What must he think of me? To consider that *I* would be *expected* to behave in such a way!"

"Oh, I think quite the opposite, Elizabeth," said Blanche. She moved from the chair in which she was sitting and perched beside Elizabeth, grasping her in a close, comforting embrace.

"*Your* Mr. Darcy almost literally flew to Brighton at the first hint of any possible danger to you, and every time we have spoken, our conversations have centered around you, whether we were discussing the situation with Mr. Wickham or not. When he spoke those words to me, Elizabeth, he spoke them with the greatest of affection — and with a distant look in his eye. I do not believe you need to worry about catching your young man, Elizabeth, as I am convinced that he is already yours."

Elizabeth's blush deepened, but Blanche did not notice — either that, or she feigned ignorance to allow Elizabeth time to gain her composure. Regardless, Blanche's account was not yet complete.

"My initial intention was to show you whatever Mr. Darcy deigned to impart to me concerning Mr. Wickham in his returning letter, should any such missive be forthcoming. However, the man completely surprised me by traveling to Brighton himself posthaste. I decided then that there was no reason to tell you of my epistle to Mr. Darcy — he was now in Brighton, and I assumed he would exert some control over the situation."

"When did you write him?" blurted Elizabeth, finally finding her tongue.

"The day after Mr. Wickham accosted you at the assembly," said Blanche. "You treated the situation as though it was nothing more than an inconvenience, and I was concerned, for I felt that Mr. Wickham was much more dangerous than you would acknowledge."

"But Mr. Darcy arrived in Brighton only a few days later!" exclaimed Elizabeth.

Blanche's responding smirk was positively smug. "Yes, he did. He was in London at the time, and at the first hint of trouble for you — particularly involving Mr. Wickham — he dropped everything and immediately made his way to Brighton."

Feeling as though her face were about to burst from the blood rushing to her cheeks, Elizabeth swatted at Blanche playfully. "I must insist you desist in this teasing and complete your account!"

Laughing, Blanche pulled away from Elizabeth and once again resumed her tale:

"Initially, Mr. Darcy and I merely compared notes on Mr. Wickham. I shared with him my observations of his behavior in general—and toward you specifically—while Mr. Darcy shared with me some of his mutual history with the man."

At Elizabeth's questioning glance, Blanche clarified:

"I do not doubt he kept some of the man's misdeeds from me, Elizabeth, but I do know of the connection between the two men through their fathers, the debts Mr. Darcy has paid off in Mr. Wickham's stead—both at Lambton and at Cambridge—and the conditional living about which Mr. Wickham is so fond of claiming ill use.

"But the thing which was most concerning to me—and to Mr. Darcy, once I had shared with him my concerns—was Mr. Darcy's account of Mr. Wickham's propensity toward seduction. And while I did not believe you to be in danger of falling victim to the man's flattery and manners, I was worried about the depths to which Mr. Wickham was capable of descending. Though Mr. Darcy was adamant that he had never seen Mr. Wickham behave in a violent manner, he could not categorically state that the man would not pose such a threat to you, given his mood. I believe yesterday's events have justified my concerns."

"Indeed, they have," said Elizabeth quietly.

"I wish they had not, my friend," was Blanche's affectionate reply. "I would rather Mr. Wickham had simply left you alone rather than make your time here any less pleasant than it should be.

"As for the rest of my tale, there is not much more to tell. We continued to observe and protect as much as we were able, but when Mr. Wickham's mood continued to darken and he refused to desist, Mr. Darcy approached Colonel Forster and acquainted him with Wickham's deeds and character.

"In fact, Mr. Wickham was not even supposed to be at the assembly last night," said Blanche. "He had been confined to the encampment due to the information which Mr. Darcy had brought to light, but somehow he managed to give the sentries the slip. I would have expected a man such as Mr. Wickham to desert, given such an opportunity, but it seems his obsession with you overcame his sense of self-interest."

It was too much for Elizabeth to process—the situation with Mr. Wickham, the danger she was now feeling, and the lengths her friends had gone to in order to keep her safe . . . . However, the subject which most concerned her was that of Mr. Darcy. To think that Mr. Darcy, whom she had spurned and ridiculed when he had offered for her, might still harbor feelings for her as strong as they had been during his botched proposal in Kent!

"But if Mr. Darcy is so concerned about me, then why was he so reserved this morning?" asked Elizabeth. "Why did he not say more before leaving with hardly a word?"

Blanche gazed at her kindly, but with an upturned eyebrow. "I speak of all of these events regarding Mr. Wickham, and all you can think of is Mr. Darcy? Elizabeth, I believe you have revealed your feelings!"

Her face feeling as though it had become permanently red, Elizabeth nevertheless glared defiantly at her friend. Blanche only laughed in response.

"Oh, Elizabeth, can you not see?" declared she. "The man is besotted, and he is deathly afraid that you will reject him."

"He told you that?" asked Elizabeth with a gasp.

"Not in so many words, Elizabeth, but I have eyes to see and ears to hear."

Once more, Elizabeth felt herself pierced by Blanche's scrutiny.

"Elizabeth," said the woman, "I know that something has passed between you and Mr. Darcy, though neither of you have been explicit. Will you not share your burden with me?"

Elizabeth turned away from her friend, trying to gather her thoughts. After Blanche had proven herself to care so dearly that she would flout the strictures of propriety by writing to Mr. Darcy, whom she had never before met, how could Elizabeth refrain from sharing both the events of the past and the contents of her heart? It would be unfair to show such a disregard for Blanche's display of affection by not making a similarly grandiose move of sorts.

Elizabeth turned back with a slight smile. She had to own to herself that the idea of at last making Blanche acquainted with all of what had happened in Hertfordshire with Mr. Darcy was an attractive one. And so, she began to speak:

"I suppose it would be unkind of me to keep it from you any longer, Blanche, and in truth, I do not wish to. I already spoke to you of how Mr. Darcy told me some of the details about what had happened in Mr.

Wickham's past, though I did not give you the true reason as to why I was entrusted with such intelligence. In Hertfordshire, when Mr. Wickham first began telling me untruths about Mr. Darcy, I was so prejudiced against Mr. Darcy that I could afford him nothing but scorn, and I was in fact eager to hear someone else speak ill of him. And so, when Mr. Darcy—to my utter surprise—proposed marriage to me, I rejected him in the most appalling fashion imaginable, throwing those lies about Mr. Darcy's heartlessness in his face. With my hurt pride and my hasty impressions of his behavior, you will no doubt apprehend that I was certain that Wickham's lies could be nothing but factual."

Blanche was staring at her with a look of shock upon her face. "Mr. Darcy proposed to you, and you rejected him outright?"

"Not only rejected him but insulted him most abhorrently," said Elizabeth. "In fact, I told him he was the last man in the world whom I could ever be prevailed upon to marry. I believe he was as surprised by my rejection as I was by his proposal, and we both said some unkind things that it is best not to repeat."

"I can only imagine what you must have told him," murmured Blanche in amusement.

Trying to ignore her friend's amused words, Elizabeth continued. "The next morning, he gave me a letter in which he explained how very skewed Mr. Wickham's tales of his sorrows were, telling me to appeal to Colonel Fitzwilliam for a confirmation of his story. Mr. Darcy also acknowledged in his letter to having separated my sister and Mr. Bingley, which was something of which I had accused him while rejecting his proposal. He was quick to assure me in his missive, however, that he had believed himself to have done so for good reasons, including his belief that Jane was insensible to Mr. Bingley's affections." Elizabeth shook her head. "You can imagine how certain I was then that I would never see Mr. Darcy again—and would never be able to offer him an apology to ease the mortification I felt for the harsh words I had spoken to him. While I knew he was not without his faults, I was also aware that I had treated him most abominably. Imagine my surprise at finding him in Brighton, of all places! Upon first seeing him, I scarcely knew whether to run away and hide or fall at his feet and beg for forgiveness."

Blanche clasped her hands together and smiled brightly. "Well, Elizabeth, you need not worry about that any longer. After all, *now* you can see that this disastrous proposal of which you spoke did not have a detrimental effect on his feelings for you! Of his desire to protect you, there can certainly be no doubt, and of the strength of his feelings, well,

I have no doubt of that either."

Elizabeth again turned a light shade of pink. "And yet I have doubted those very feelings of his for some time. There has been a part of me that believed—that feared—he was smitten with you . . . and you with him. And I have treated you somewhat poorly at times as a result."

"Ah, Elizabeth," cried Blanche, "if only you had known I was in fact quite smitten with another gentleman!"

Elizabeth raised an eyebrow and gave her friend an entreating expression. "Another gentleman, Blanche? Come! You must tell me of whom you speak!"

"Perhaps I have said too much," said Blanche coyly, turning away.

"Nonsense, Blanche!" cried Elizabeth, pulling on her friend's arm so she could see her face. "I have bared my heart to you, and now it is time for you to do the same!"

"Very well," said Blanche with a laugh. "I would not wish to treat you unfairly."

"I should hope not! It would be most rude of you to do so."

Blanche smiled, and an almost dreamy look came over her face. "In fact, I find myself quite taken with one of the officers."

"Who, Blanche?" asked Elizabeth with no small amount of eagerness. But the image of one man immediately filled her head as she considered the available officers, and she ventured: "Could it be Colonel Fitzwilliam?"

Blanche's resultant blush was all the answer Elizabeth needed.

"Ah, Blanche! Dear Colonel Fitzwilliam! I should have known him to be just the playful sort to catch your eye!" And they had been speaking with each other quite frequently. If only Elizabeth had been more attentive to what had truly been happening with her friend, she might have realized the connection between Colonel Fitzwilliam and Blanche earlier!

"I suppose I have not been very observant lately," said Elizabeth, feeling embarrassed. "I have neglected to notice many things around me."

"I believe you have a very good excuse for your inattention, Elizabeth," said Blanche with some warmth.

Elizabeth regarded her friend slyly. "Well, that is at an end. Shall I be wishing you joy very soon, do you think?"

"Elizabeth!" exclaimed Blanche, swatting her lightly on the arm. "I believe you may be putting the cart before the horse!"

"Can you deny it? Blanche the besotted—it shall be all over

Brighton by sunset. The most eligible lady in Brighton society has been caught—and by the son of an earl, no less! Blanche, you shall be even more of a sensation than you already are!"

Inducing Blanche to blush was no small feat, yet Elizabeth had accomplished it. She allowed herself a small smirk of triumph, even as her friend huffed and glared at her, folding her arms across her chest in mock disapproval. It was only fair to pay Blanche back for all the times she had made Elizabeth blush.

"You know, Blanche," said Elizabeth, "if you should marry the colonel and I should marry Mr. Darcy, then we shall be related by marriage and be able to continue our acquaintance with no difficulties at all."

Smiling fondly, Blanche grasped Elizabeth's hands. "I dare say we shall be able to continue our friendship anyway, Elizabeth. I have grown very fond of your company and would not wish to sever our acquaintance."

"Then we shall simply have to remain friends."

"Indeed, we shall."

That evening, Elizabeth found herself once more in the company of Mr. Darcy. Upon arriving back at the townhouse, Harriet immediately drew Elizabeth aside and informed her of the events of the morning.

According to Harriet, Mr. Darcy had arrived not long after she left, and he had immediately been closeted with the colonel for some time before they left together. However, they had not left without Colonel Forster informing his wife that the officers of the regiment would be coming to dinner and that Mr. Darcy would be joining them. He also informed her that Mr. Wickham would *not* be one of them, as his actions against Elizabeth were being investigated and he had been confined to quarters under guard until the investigation was complete.

After explaining some of what had happened at Blanche's house— but leaving out Blanche's feelings for Colonel Fitzwilliam and the misunderstanding pertaining to her perception of the relationship between Blanche and Mr. Darcy—Elizabeth retired to her room, feeling the need for rest. She never would have acknowledged it out loud, but Harriet's dancing eyes and her less than subtle suggestions about the focus of Mr. Darcy's interest were large factors in her decision to withdraw for a time. There was simply too much to take in, and Elizabeth thought that reflection was the best way to work everything out in her own mind.

She felt much more like herself by the time she left her room to descend to the sitting room for dinner that evening. And while she did not possess all the answers she sought, she understood one very important fact—she was in love with Fitzwilliam Darcy, and should he ever deign to favor her with his attention again, her response this time would be a most emphatic "Yes!"

It was almost time for dinner when the man himself arrived. Elizabeth was speaking with Lieutenant Denny, but once Mr. Darcy entered the room, he commanded all of her attention. Denny, perhaps understanding what was happening, excused himself with a smile— which Elizabeth hardly noticed—and allowed Darcy to approach her unimpeded.

The man made his way to her side, his eyes never leaving hers, and Elizabeth could not help but read the determination shining in their depths. He stopped in front of her and, grasping her hand, bent low to press his lips to its back.

"Good evening, Miss Bennet," said he, and though his tone was outwardly confident, she thought she detected a hint of nervousness in his manner.

"Mr. Darcy," replied Elizabeth, allowing all the warmth she felt toward him to shine through her smile.

"May I say how utterly entrancing you look tonight?"

Elizabeth blushed. "I have not done anything special with my appearance tonight, Mr. Darcy."

"I am aware of that," was his even reply. "I must own that I find you captivating regardless of how much effort you have put into your appearance."

"Thank you," said Elizabeth, knowing there was no other way to respond to such a statement.

"However, before I continue to compliment you and provoke your most fetching blushes," said he with a grin, "I must take the time to apologize to you most fervently."

"Apologize, sir?" asked Elizabeth in confusion.

"Yes, indeed. I fear that my departure this morning at Mrs. Wade's house was most precipitous and somewhat rude. I can only say in my defense that I was most concerned over something Mrs. Wade had related to me, and I was anxious to ensure the matter had been addressed appropriately."

"Was this news perhaps relating to what happened between myself and Mr. Wickham last night?"

"It was," replied Mr. Darcy. "I assure you, Miss Bennet, that I shall not allow that libertine to importune you any further. Colonel Forster knows all of the particulars of my transactions with Mr. Wickham, which will certainly be weighed when it comes time to pronounce judgment upon him for his misdeeds. If nothing else, I shall see him in debtors' prison, as I still hold the receipts for his debts in Cambridge and Lambton, though I do not doubt we shall find more in Meryton."

"I thank you for your care and attention, Mr. Darcy," replied Elizabeth. "I did not find your farewell this morning to be anything lacking, and even had I felt it was, Blanche explained the matter to me in its entirety."

Mr. Darcy started. "In its entirety?"

"Indeed," said Elizabeth. "And I find that I am quite speechless — your attention to my safety quite takes my breath away, though I fear Blanche did not fare so well against my ill humor."

Appearing perplexed, Mr. Darcy said: "Ill humor?"

"Yes. You see, after having observed you and Blanche speaking together privately so many times, I was under the impression that you were becoming close to her and that you were on the verge of . . . courting her."

Had the conversation been slightly less serious, Elizabeth might have laughed at the sight of Mr. Darcy's eyes bulging out of his head.

"No, Miss Bennet," managed he at last, though his voice betrayed the slightest tremor. "I do not view Mrs. Wade in such a way. I am afraid that my heart fully belongs to another young lady."

She knew she should have been blushing, but this time, Elizabeth, now feeling comfortable with *his* feelings and attentions, merely gazed at him expectantly. She would not be so foolish as to throw away *this* chance at happiness.

"Miss Bennet," continued Mr. Darcy at length, "I wonder if I might call upon you tomorrow morning?"

"Mr. Darcy, I assure you that your presence would be most welcome at any time convenient."

"I am glad to hear that," said he softly.

As he continued to stare at her, Elizabeth gazed back at him, finding herself at a loss for words, something which really had become a more frequent occurrence when she was in the presence of Mr. Darcy.

Finally, however, she told him with no small amount of warmth: "Mr. Darcy, I am most grateful for everything you have done to assist me in this unfortunate situation with Mr. Wickham." It was an understatement; she felt beyond grateful now that she knew just how far Mr. Darcy had been willing to go to make certain she was safe. The fact that he had left off everything and come to Brighton — and that he had stayed for so long to ensure her continued safety—helped prove that actions could speak much louder than words. And his actions also reassured her that the harsh words they had exchanged were now in the past. She doubted either of them could ever truly forget what they had said to one another, but perhaps that was for the best.

They had both learned a lesson from that heated and disastrous encounter in which he had proffered a poor proposal and she had rejected it with all the venom she could muster. As a result, she had learned much about him, and he had learned about the poor impression he had made on her. Both of them had been forced to reexamine their behavior and opinions, and she believed they were both the better for it. It would have been too painful to acknowledge such a thing at the time, but she now believed it was the truth. She dared not ask Mr. Darcy his opinion on the subject for fear of embarrassing them both, but she suspected it would be in line with hers. While she and Mr. Darcy were of different temperaments, their perspectives seemed to be in harmony when it came to important matters.

"Miss Bennet," said he, cutting into her thoughts, "you need not thank me for whatever it is I have tried to do for you. I shall always be glad to provide you any assistance within my capacity. And should something ever be beyond my capacity, I shall nonetheless strive to aid you by going to all possible lengths to accomplish what needs to be done."

Elizabeth's breath caught in her throat, and she found herself wanting to reach out to touch him. "Mr. Darcy—"

"Miss Bennet," interrupted he, giving her an earnest look, "there is nothing I should not attempt to do for you in order to ensure your continued safety and happiness. If ever anything should come to pass with which you find you require assistance, you need only to come to me and ask for my help. You must not hesitate. Please, never hesitate."

Elizabeth gave him a warm and appreciative smile, allowing herself the pleasure of studying his dark eyes and striking features. He truly was a handsome man, but her appreciation of his appearance was enhanced by her appreciation for the man himself. After all, he had just declared he would do anything for her, and knowing that warmed her heart and filled her with courage. With Mr. Darcy by her side, she felt she could triumph over anything. And considering the words he had spoken to her this day, she wondered if they would be by each other's sides for the rest of their lives. It was a pleasant thought, and it caused a shiver to crawl down her spine.

"Your concern means more to me than you can ever know," said she, clasping her hands together and staring down at them. She felt there was so much to be said still, but she knew not how to go about it.

What she did know, however, was that with Wickham restrained, she had only to look forward to the future. And it was looking as if it would turn out to be very bright indeed. She was filled with anticipation, and she was eager to see Mr. Darcy the next day. While her time in Brighton had not unfolded the way she had expected, she would not trade it for ten such trips.

"I am happy to hear it," said Mr. Darcy, speaking so quietly she was not certain he intended for her to hear what he had said.

So she simply smiled to herself and endeavored to let the evening continue just as pleasantly as it had been these past few minutes. Seeing as she spent most of the evening in Mr. Darcy's company, it was not a difficult thing to accomplish.

Chapter XVI

*L*ater that night, Elizabeth went to sleep with a smile on her face. Her dreams were quite blissful and filled with images of Mr. Darcy and his intense stare.

Such serenity did not last, however. She awoke suddenly when she was wrested from her bed.

She moved her head around wildly, trying to determine what was happening. Then a gag was thrust in her mouth by someone from behind her and quickly tied in place.

She struggled to free herself from the strong arms that held her. Her assailant had lit only a sole candle on the other side of the room to abet his attack, so it was difficult to make out her surroundings.

She tried to throw her elbows backward to force her attacker to let go, but her arms were quickly pinned behind her back. She tried to twist and to kick, but to no avail. She was helpless.

She felt warm breath against her ear and shuddered.

A voice whispered: "You are coming with me, Miss Bennet."

Elizabeth froze upon hearing the sibilant hiss of Wickham's voice in her ear. Suddenly, the situation became all the more frightening — she could smell the rancid odor of his breath and feel his rough hands against her wrists as he tried to keep her still. Thoughts concerning how she had dismissed the idea that he was a threat flashed through her mind. He was still the worst of cowards—his actions against a young woman such as herself were proof—but he had clearly shown that he was more dangerous than she had thought.

Feeling the desperation of her situation, Elizabeth mustered all of the strength in her body, throwing her legs out, trying to connect with something hard enough that the noise would wake someone in the house. She threw her head back, hoping to catch him in his face, break his nose, or cause some other damage which would relax his iron grip. The gag in her mouth stifled her cries to little more than muffled squeals. Desperation made her strong, but it was not enough.

Pain exploded in the back of her head as she felt Wickham's fist make contact with her. With her vision muddled, she fell awkwardly, and her elbow impacted with the hard and unyielding wood of the floor. She weakly scrabbled about, trying to rip off the gag, clamber away, and escape all at once, but he was too quick for her.

She was stopped by the look of his eyes staring into hers, inches from her face. Her breath caught as she witnessed the almost wild look in them, the image of madness evident in their depths. This man would kill her if she were not careful. She wanted desperately to remove the gag, yet she knew deep within her heart that he would see to it that she never breathed again were she to do so.

"*Miss* Bennet," rasped Wickham, his voice coldly implacable, "you should remember that I am a desperate man with little to lose. Had it not been for you and your bewitching ways and pert opinions, I would have been long gone from this place ere now, but to my detriment, something always kept me back. It was you—you and your damnable belief in that arrogant bastard. I somehow could not convince myself to leave you be, much though I wished to do so."

He grasped her bedding from behind her, and pulling it toward him, he began to tear it as quietly as he could while he continued to speak to her.

"Darcy, with his debt receipts and his tales to Forster of my *misbehavior*, has given me no choice but to flee this place. But he has not beaten me. I know of no better way to repay him for his interference in my life than to take you with me.

"I have seen how he looks at you, Elizabeth," continued he, even as he began binding her ankles with the strips he had torn from the blanket. "And I am well aware of what that look entails. The loss of you will be my final revenge against him—one from which he will never recover."

A spark of Elizabeth's spirit rose up again, and she glared at him.

He laughed at her. "Oh, you thought I was being truthful when I told you I thought he would never make you an offer? It suited me to see your confusion and sow some discord between the two of you. I would never want Darcy to be happy, now, would I?"

Wickham stopped and gazed at her, malevolent glee almost radiating from his repugnant leer. "It seems that you, Miss Elizabeth Bennet, have managed to do what no one else has done. You have pierced the cold and disdainful mask of the master of Pemberley."

He began tearing a few more strips from Elizabeth's bedding. "To be honest, I did not think he had it in him—he always seemed coldly reserved and incapable of passion. However, I cannot fault him for his taste in women. It is the one thing we have in common, after all; even I believe you *are* rather delectable."

He stopped what he was doing and reached out to run his finger along Elizabeth's jaw. She slapped his hand away and glared at him, her wrath enflamed into an even greater fury.

He sneered at her, the look self-satisfied and utterly loathsome, and then he pulled her hands roughly together and bound them as tight as he could. After he checked to make certain that the bindings were firmly fixed and would not come undone, he once more looked in her eyes and smirked.

"You should be quiet now, Elizabeth, and accept what is to come. *I* am in control of the situation, and your fate will be what I decide it to be. If you cooperate with me, you might emerge from this alive.

"Stay here *quietly*—if you make even the slightest sound, I will snap your neck. I suspect you know that already. After all the trouble I went to picking the front door's lock, neither of us would want our journey together to end so soon, now, would we? Now, I will return after I have obtained a dress and bonnet from your closet for you, and then we shall depart. We would not wish anyone along our path to think I had abducted you from your bed, would we? Instead, I believe we shall make them think you are my doxy. Yes, that would certainly be acceptable."

He turned his back and entered her closet. Elizabeth, using the brief time he was absent, tested her bonds, finding them as tight and as unyielding as Wickham seemed to think they were. Tears pricked the corners of her eyes, but she held them back. She refused to cry over her predicament. She must hold out hope that she could escape from the criminal—her life and prospects were so much brighter now than they had been only a few days ago. Mr. Darcy would surely rescue her somehow!

It was only a few moments before Wickham returned, a dress thrown haphazardly over his right arm. "You can change into this once we have left this place," said he, grinning all the while.

He bent over and picked her up, throwing her over his shoulder as he prepared to depart.

"Remember, Elizabeth, not a sound. You may prevent me from escaping, but you shall be dead ere you are rescued."

Cowed to silence, Elizabeth remained still as Wickham carried her down the stairs and through the hallways of the house. He stopped several times, listening intently to the night sounds of the house, before he finally made his way out the door and toward the small stable attached to the side of the house. There, he set her down and began saddling a horse. He had finished the task and turned back to Elizabeth when a voice rang out through the darkness, causing her heart to leap into her throat with hope.

"Miss Bennet! What the devil is happening?"

Despite the difficulty of moving while bound, Elizabeth managed to twist her body in an attempt to glimpse the bearer of the voice. A man was standing in the stable entryway, the pale light of the moon casting his long shadow onto the stable floor, making him seem almost like a monster of the night. At another time, the sudden appearance of such a form at this late hour might have terrified Elizabeth. At this time, however, it filled her with relief. Someone had come to rescue her.

Wickham froze. He stared at the other man with an expression that somehow managed to convey both frustrated anger and genuine surprise. "Denny," growled he under his breath, "you should not have come."

"I had to come, Wickham. Considering all your recent behavior, I could not but be suspicious of what you would do, even if you *had* been assigned a guard. I found poor Richardson—I am only thankful you did not kill him. What object did you use to hit him?"

"What does the jailer's fate signify so long as the falsely imprisoned is released?" replied Wickham in a low voice. He had taken a few steps toward Mr. Denny, glaring at him dangerously, as if he might strike him down with a mere look.

"Falsely imprisoned!" cried the other man, stepping forward. "Look at you, Wickham! You are doing the very thing we feared. Do not make your fate any worse. You must free Miss Bennet and return with me to the camp before you dig yourself a deeper grave."

"I am afraid I cannot do that, Denny."

"Then I shall have to force you myself," said Mr. Denny firmly.

Elizabeth was unsure whether Mr. Denny had heard the threatening and almost mad undertone of Wickham's words, and with foreboding stirring her gut and helplessness squeezing her heart, she turned her eyes to her captor with dread. If she had not been so tightly bound, she could have attempted to rise and escape. As it was, however, there was nothing she could do. Even if she managed to stand, any attempt to hobble away would likely end up with her back on the ground. Casting her eyes about for a sharp implement revealed nothing of any use to her.

Wickham turned his head to the side, his eyes sliding from Denny to the saddle of the horse he was intending to steal — and to the musket he had strapped to the pommel a few minutes before.

Wickham leaped the few feet toward the brown horse, fumbling to get the musket loose. Mr. Denny rushed toward him. The two men struggled to gain control of the weapon, both grasping it tightly and trying to wrench it away from the saddle. Denny let go of it with one hand and punched Wickham in the face. Wickham took a few steps backward, his hands losing their grip on the musket, one of them coming up to touch a lip that was likely bleeding.

Denny released the weapon and flung himself at Wickham. Elizabeth scrambled to get out of the way as they tumbled to the ground. Though she succeeded, she fell onto her side, and it was a struggle to sit back upright as she watched with fear and the slightest trickle of hope as the two men remained locked in their brutal combat.

At another time, the two men might have been evenly matched. But Wickham was filled with the desperation of a man fighting for his life, and for every blow Denny landed, Wickham landed two more. Yet Denny showed no signs of giving up.

The two men rolled around in the stable, flailing arms and legs embroiled in a vicious fight. And then Mr. Denny had his hands around Wickham's throat, and Elizabeth's breath caught as she dared hope that Denny might prevail.

Wickham struggled to push away Denny's hands. Slowly, the hands from his throat lifted, forced upward by his grip on Denny's arms. Wickham's gaze flicked to the wall of the stable, where a shovel rested. So quick he was almost a blur, Wickham shoved Denny off him, jumped to his feet, and grabbed the shovel. Then, like a viper striking, he leaped at Denny.

Denny, who was trying to rise, managed one loud cry of surprise before the sickly noise sounded that signified the blade of the shovel connecting with his head. Elizabeth did not see it; she had turned her head in horror, knowing how this would end.

She did not have to look to know that Wickham had hit Denny repeatedly. And she did not have to see blood glistening on the shovel to know that Mr. Denny was now dead. She closed her eyes tightly, barely able to believe what had just occurred.

Cursing under his breath at the noise made by Mr. Denny, Wickham hauled Elizabeth to her feet. She opened her eyes and looked on him in accusation—*He was once your friend!* she wanted to cry out—but he ignored her, too caught up in a rush to flee the stable before someone in the attached townhouse raised an alarm. He showed no remorse at Denny's death, only frustration that the man's final cry might lead to his capture.

And then Wickham placed his hands on her hips as he moved his head beside hers. She felt sickened by his touch and his closeness.

"I shall not tolerate any attempts to foil my plans," whispered he in her ear. There was no doubting the madness in his voice this time. "And I do not need Richardson's musket to kill. You will do well to remember that, Elizabeth, should you start to entertain any foolish thoughts of escape."

Quickly, Wickham turned away from her, and after one last check of the horse and its accoutrements, he dragged her up with hasty roughness and settled her on the back of the horse. It was then that he stopped and peered at her, a half frown upon his face.

"I can see that if I keep you gagged and bound, someone may well notice it and interfere with our escape. We would not wish for that to happen, now, would we?"

He smirked at her when she glared in response to his words, and then he produced a knife. He sawed through the bonds on her feet before stowing it away in his boot again. Finally, he removed the gag from her mouth.

"Now I shall be pleased to hear your pretty voice and the sound of your delightful conversation throughout our journey, though I believe you understand why I would wish to leave your hands bound."

Elizabeth did not deign to make him a response, but it appeared that Wickham did not require one. He scrambled up behind her, and then, clucking to the horse, he urged it forward at a fast walk, taking care to make as little noise as possible.

"Remember, Elizabeth," whispered he in her ear, "should you attempt to call attention to us in order to effect your rescue, you shall be dead long before any such help can be brought to bear. Your sole chance of survival is through my mercy. I suggest you do nothing to try my patience."

Elizabeth was careful to give no reaction to the man's words. She knew that she was completely in his power and that she had best do what he said for the moment. Perhaps there would be an opportunity later to escape from his vile clutches. Regardless, she would by no means permit him the least iota of victory which was in her power to deny. Refusing to answer him was a small and insignificant matter, but to her it signaled her continuing defiance and her determination to break free.

As they rode away, however, Elizabeth listened desperately for any sound that they had been discovered. But the night remained stubbornly silent, and no lights appeared in the windows of any of the townhouses. It appeared as if Wickham would make good his escape; it would surely be morning before her disappearance was discovered.

But she knew that Mr. Darcy would never stand for this. He would come after her — she knew it! And then Wickham would finally pay for his crimes.

Thus began a long journey which felt interminable in its length and vastly uncomfortable in its execution; it was most certainly not helped by the fact that it was taken unwillingly and in the most insupportable company imaginable.

After clearing the immediate vicinity of Colonel Forster's townhouse, Wickham urged his horse into a fast trot, likely attempting to put as much distance between himself and his superior's vengeance as he could. Elizabeth maintained some hope that someone — anyone — would witness their awkward and suspicious journey through the city, but in this wish, she was to be disappointed. Since Brighton was a large city, its denizens could be found going about their business at all hours of the day and night. However, though Elizabeth and Wickham's path crossed that of many others during their journey through the city streets, they were mostly ignored, and those people who did take notice of them were put off by Wickham's contrived greetings and rude comments concerning what precisely he was doing with a young woman on a horse in the middle of the night.

Only once did Elizabeth's hope truly begin to rise that they might be discovered by someone who could assist her. They were nearing the edge of the city when in the distance she espied several of the distinctive red coats of the militia. However, before she could even begin to become excited at the thought, Wickham saw them and directed the horse onto another street, bypassing the soldiers completely.

"We shall certainly not be caught with such ease, my little doxy," said he with a sly laugh.

Again, Elizabeth did not deign to respond to his vile comments. She merely continued to search the night for anything which could be of some help in her predicament.

They left the city soon afterward, and Wickham urged the horse on to a faster pace. With the press of people left behind and the distance flying past at the speed of a quick canter, Elizabeth felt the rogue's tension relax, and he began to laugh at the ease of his escape.

"I always *was* more quick-witted than Darcy!" crowed he. And though Elizabeth, situated in front of him as she was, could not see his face, she could sense the feral smile on his face and the madness in his eyes as if they were physical entities. "Darcy and his ever-proper behavior and his slow and methodical way of thinking—he cannot hope to measure up to me! My quick wits and ability to improvise have allowed me to make my way successfully in the world in spite of his incessant meddling. Once again, I have snatched that which is most precious from under his fool nose!"

He continued to speak in such manner for several moments, many of his words repeated, others seemingly random or incomprehensible. Elizabeth was not certain of what the man was capable, but it seemed as if his grip on sanity was weakening, and she was rapidly coming to the conclusion that she would have to escape to save herself.

They rode on through the night, and Elizabeth found herself dozing a little. True sleep was almost impossible due to the uncomfortable position in which she rode in front of Wickham, however, and she felt her joints becoming stiff and sore due to her limited ability to move. Furthermore, the bonds were cutting into her skin, chafing at her wrists. It was truly a miserable night.

At length, as the sun's rays began to rise over the horizon, Wickham directed the horse toward a small copse of trees off to the side of the road, where he dismounted. He immediately grasped Elizabeth by the waist and set her on the ground. Elizabeth lay there, the wonderful feeling of being off the horse contending with the weariness of bone and mind which encompassed her. She doubted she could move if she tried.

Wickham did not allow her to rest, however. "Come now, Elizabeth—I had thought you were made of sterner stuff than this. You have only spent a few hours on a horse, after all."

He unfastened the bonds around her wrists and set the bundle he had taken from her boudoir the previous night in front of her. "Now, make haste and dress yourself—we have much more distance to travel this day."

Rubbing her wrists and wincing at the pain, Elizabeth stood awkwardly, grasping the bundle and opening it to find one of her dresses balled up inside. Though Wickham had thought to take a pair of her stockings, none of the other items she would have deemed necessary were inside. She would simply have to make do.

As expected, the scoundrel did not even have the decency to turn his back as she changed. Wickham smirked at her and kept watch, and though she took care to cover herself as best she could, she could not help but feel dirty because of the man's leering stare. It was made even worse by the fact that her fatigue made it difficult for her to move.

"Now, we shall continue," said he once Elizabeth was dressed to the best of her ability. "I shall not bind you for the duration of our journey—that would appear suspicious, would it not?" He laughed at his own words. "But remember not to do anything to draw attention to yourself. The consequences would be most . . . severe."

Elizabeth's gaze desperately took in the surrounding area. She might have enjoyed the sight of the trees in different circumstances, but right now, they seemed oppressive. Despite Wickham's threat, she could not help but contemplate escape. Even facing other challenges—such as getting a message to Mr. Darcy and Colonel Forster or even wandering in the woods lost—would be preferable to continuing in the power of such a treacherous snake. Without thinking, she took a step to the side.

Wickham sprung forward in a heartbeat. His fingers dug into her arms like talons.

She struggled, yet her efforts were to no avail, as Wickham was a very strong man. She had not actually intended to free herself when she took that foolish step, but she certainly did not want to make it any easier for Wickham to treat her in such a loathsome manner. She had more wits than he had brawn, but they could not help her in that moment.

He pulled her sharply to his chest, holding her arms in the air so high that she was forced to stand on her toes, and he placed his head beside her ear, letting his hot and putrid breath wash over her before he spoke. "If you escape me, Elizabeth, then you shall simply face the wolves by yourself. I doubt you could charm *them* into submission as you do so many others."

Elizabeth sincerely doubted there were any wolves lurking about in this copse of trees, but she nonetheless snapped back at him, infuriated at his closeness and her helplessness. "I would much prefer to take my chances with wolves than a viper such as you. At least there would be a chance that a wolf might have a small shred of humanity hidden within his bosom. You, I fear, can no longer claim even that."

Wickham gave a bark of laughter, and though Elizabeth could not see him well due to his firm hold on her, she thought for a moment that he seemed very much the wolf. He released her roughly, pushing her back a few feet as he unclenched his hands from her arms, leaving red marks behind on her flesh.

The corner of his mouth lifted upward in a sneer as he regarded her with a gaze filled with both calculation and amusement. "Not all wolves walk on four feet, Elizabeth. Should you manage to escape me, you might find that an unattended woman will come across far worse than what you now face. You should be glad I am here to protect you." He laughed again, but this time it was more chilling, as if somehow it were utterly devoid of anything human.

Then, leisurely and almost absentmindedly, Wickham reached an arm out and caressed the musket strapped on the poor beast that had been consigned to carry two riders over who knew how many miles. If Elizabeth had been a better horsewoman, she could have leaped upon the creature and tried to race away from here. But with the bulk of her dress to hinder her—and the recognition that Wickham would be able to catch up to her before she had brought the horse to a full gallop—it seemed a foolish thing to contemplate.

Elizabeth knew she would not prevail in this instance. She did not believe herself capable of firing the musket, even should she succeed in wresting it away from the man, and if she ran—which was more tempting than the idea of trying to escape on the horse or attempting to use the weapon—she suspected Wickham would simply take his musket and fire upon her to prevent her from escaping. Her suspicions about his willingness to use the musket were only further heightened when he said: "And I promise you, Elizabeth, I shall do anything to keep you from returning to *Darcy*. After all, I must ruin his life as thoroughly as he ruined mine."

Elizabeth refrained from pointing out that Wickham had in fact ruined his own life through his actions. She knew there would be no encouraging the man to listen to reason. He was far beyond that.

He stepped forward and rubbed his arms along hers lightly, and she slapped them away, putting every ounce of the fury she felt into a glare. "Keep your hands off me," said she in a low voice.

Wickham smirked at her, but his voice was smooth and calm, which only made Elizabeth feel even warier. "I only intended to assist you in mounting the horse, my dear Elizabeth. And must I remind you that you are, without a doubt, utterly at my mercy? Should you wish matters to remain amiable between us, I suggest you do as I say. So long as you do not try to escape or draw attention to yourself or do anything else similarly foolish, I shall not put any bonds on you, but I must insist that you do not try my patience with foolish attempts to return to your precious Darcy."

Elizabeth did not give him the satisfaction of any response at all; rather, she merely gazed at him with contempt. There truly was no knowing what Wickham would do to her should she try and fail to save herself. She would merely have to be on the lookout for a chance to escape in which there was less chance of being caught . . . or hope that either Mr. Darcy or Colonel Forster would manage to catch up to her. The disappearance of both Elizabeth and Wickham at the same time could not be taken as a coincidence by any man with even half his wits about him. Surely Colonel Forster's men were hunting for both of them! And the longer Elizabeth stayed on the road, the greater the chance that she would be rescued. She was no expert about traveling by horse, but she knew that long distances would tire the beast quickly since it was carrying two passengers. And even if he had the funds, Wickham likely would not be foolish enough to acquire a horse specifically for her, knowing that she would attempt escape in a heartbeat given such an opportunity.

"Now," said Wickham, "if you have finished contemplating your erstwhile paramour, we should leave this place. We have quite a distance yet to travel."

Scowling, Elizabeth knelt and wrapped her nightgown in the bundle. "Mr. Darcy is *not* my paramour," ground out she as she worked. She did not mention that she wished for nothing more than to see Mr. Darcy riding up the road to rescue her, nor did she mention that, given the choice, she would now accept with pleasure the proposals and assurances with which Mr. Darcy had favored her in Kent not so many months ago.

"Perhaps not," said Wickham with a sneer, "but I assure you that he was ready to make you an offer. I never would have believed it had I not seen it with my own eyes—that Fitzwilliam Darcy should be captured by a dowerless country girl is beyond belief. I salute you, Elizabeth, for doing what others could not."

Elizabeth said nothing in response. She held her meager possessions to her body and suffered the rogue's hands on her person as he lifted her onto the horse and then scrambled up behind her. They set out immediately, the horse beneath them moving at a brisk pace. Elizabeth, however, could not help but glance in the direction they had come as they approached the road, silently willing Mr. Darcy to appear to rescue her.

Chapter XXVII

$\mathcal{T}$he ensuing three days were difficult and painful for Elizabeth. Wickham set a quick pace—or as quick as he was able, given the fact that his horse carried two riders—and allowed little time for rest or recuperation. They generally stopped early in the afternoon for a few hours of fitful rest and then arose after dark to continue their journey. It was obvious to Elizabeth that her captor wished to avoid questions, not to mention leave as little trail to follow as possible—hence their travel at night—but his occasional worried looks in the direction from which they had come spoke to his concern for the possibility of pursuit.

Whenever feasible, he avoided contact with other travelers, taking the horse into the concealment of whatever trees or brush was available, especially at night. During the daylight hours, such concealment was generally not possible. As a result, he would ignore the looks they received as they traveled, though he would often jest with the bawdier sort which could be found on the road. These jests did not endear him to Elizabeth any further, of course, as they were crude and insulting.

The worst parts of the ride, however, were the constant gait of the horse and the bone-deep weariness which spread through Elizabeth's person as the journey progressed. Her lower extremities suffered in particular due to the jolting gait of the horse. She was not accustomed to the constant pounding of many hours of constant riding. Elizabeth had never been a horsewoman, and though she was not precisely inexperienced, she had always preferred to use her own legs rather than substitute them with some great animal whose actions she could not predict and could only marginally control. Even further, the riding she had done in the past had always been sidesaddle. Wickham, however, forced her to ride astride the horse in front of him, as it gave him greater control over the horse and lessened the possibility of her falling during a moment of inattention. Privately, Elizabeth was aware of the fact that he almost certainly felt that it gave him greater control *over her*, but she would not deign to speak out loud about such a matter. She did not miss his leers at her stocking-clad legs which were open to his gaze due to the way her skirts bunched up. Feeling that modesty was really a secondary concern at this point, she ignored it to focus on other matters.

As a point in fact, Elizabeth did her best to speak as little to the man as possible. Though there was nothing she could do to escape Wickham, she could ignore him and make no response to his words.

It was not as if he seemed to require her response, in any case. In fact, Wickham spoke almost incessantly, the words he imparted at times sounding bitter at the hand that life—and the dastardly Mr. Darcy—had dealt him and at other times sounding exultant at his perceived victory over his hated foe. His rambling discourse was so disjointed and random that Elizabeth quickly came to the conclusion that he was coming to believe his own stories of Mr. Darcy's perfidy and was, as a result, treading further down the path toward madness.

Unfortunately, Wickham's loosening grip on reality had not made him stupid. If anything, he was sharper and more focused than Elizabeth had ever known him to be, and he kept a close watch on her, denying her any opportunity to escape. She wondered if he ever slept; despite her fatigue, she did not manage to sleep much during their journey, as she was too uncomfortable, too heartsick, and too unaccustomed to the hardness of the earth for that. But even when she did manage to sleep a little, every time she opened her eyes, he was awake, watching her. And though he said nothing further about his attraction to her, his words concerning the similarity of his and Mr. Darcy's tastes rang through her ears, and she shuddered at the glint in his eye which bespoke thoughts and feelings upon which she had no wish to dwell.

The journey continued in such a manner for three full days until finally, after the horse crested a hill, a sprawling city lay before them, the sea sparkling off in the distance. Though the sight of the ocean was beautiful, Elizabeth felt only a sense of foreboding — the time in which she must make her escape was growing short indeed. She did not know what Wickham intended, but his single-minded focus on making it to Bristol and his stated intention of making certain that she never saw Mr. Darcy again seemed to hint at his intention to board a ship — undoubtedly with her in tow.

"There it is, Elizabeth," crowed Wickham in her ear. "Bristol. Our destiny awaits, my dear. Let us not tarry."

Elizabeth's mouth was filled with a bitter taste that matched her bitter feelings, and her heart felt heavier than the heaviest stone. They had finally reached the city that was Wickham's goal, and Mr. Darcy had not come racing up behind them on a brilliant steed to free her from her captor. She did not know what precisely awaited her, but she knew that Wickham had all but accomplished what he had set out to do. Unless she could find an opening to escape, there was nothing more to be done. The chances of Mr. Darcy catching up with her now were slim, if they even existed.

In her despair, she could not help but ask Wickham: "Why are you doing this?" Perhaps it was a foolish thing to attempt to understand the reasons for a madman's behavior, but she felt she had to say something, lest she burst into tears which she knew could only cause him pleasure.

Upon hearing her question, Wickham let out a bark of laughter that was followed by a low chuckle. "The wealthy always believe themselves to be so untouchable. Tragedies, catastrophes, failures — these are not to happen to them; they are above such things, beyond them. They think nothing of trampling on those not so fortunate as they, those not born with a trail of gold behind them. The world, they believe, is theirs to manipulate, mold, crush, torment, tease. But they are not untouchable. They can be shown — *should* be shown — that what they believe is theirs can be taken away without warning. Their wealth cannot always protect them." Wickham's rambling tone suddenly became soft and intense. "Tell me, Elizabeth — why do you prefer Darcy to me?"

"The reason I prefer Mr. Darcy to you has nothing to do with the size of his pocketbook," said she in a voice that she managed to keep relatively level despite her anger. "Mr. Darcy is a gentleman; you, however, have proven yourself to be a scoundrel who deserves nothing more than to be sorely punished for his ill treatment of others. By continuing with this ill-begotten abduction, you are doing nothing but digging a deeper grave in which to lay yourself. You would do well to release me and flee far away from here before the authorities put their hands on you."

"Oh, I intend to go far away from here, Elizabeth," said he in a tone that made her suppress the urge to shiver. "But I intend to take you with me. We must, after all, prove to Darcy that he is not above the world. The world can reach out and take things from him, just as he takes things from the world."

"The only one who has taken anything from anyone is you, Wickham!" cried she. "You have rejected the kindnesses bestowed upon you by others in favor of living a life of depravity! Do not blame others for your misfortunes; you have brought them upon yourself."

He shook his head and spoke to her in a gentle, condescending tone, much like one might use with a small child. "Oh, Elizabeth. You are so naïve. You have been blinded by Darcy's riches, just as so many before you have. What you view as captivity by me is actually a rescue. I am removing you from the clutches of that man. A cold one such as he could never make a warm-blooded woman such as yourself happy."

Elizabeth narrowed her eyes, bristling. "I am certain that *you* could not have any understanding of what could make me happy. You are not trying to save me, Wickham. You are merely trying to obtain your revenge on Mr. Darcy. We both know that I am nothing more than a convenient means for you to do so. Do not pretend otherwise. The only man from whom I need to be saved is *you*."

"A man can have many designs in mind, my dear," returned he in that sweet tone he took upon himself on occasion, as if he forgot at times that he had kidnapped her—and that she utterly despised him. "Just because I wish to prove to Darcy that he is not all-powerful does not mean that I do not also wish to save one as lovely and lively as yourself from a monster such as him."

Elizabeth wanted to say more, but she kept her mouth closed. No matter what she said, Wickham would never listen to reason. If anything, speaking only seemed to heighten his madness and make him rail even more against the perceived injustices he had suffered.

"Yes, a beautiful future is almost within our reach. We must merely find the proper people in order to make our dreams come true."

The "proper people," Elizabeth suspected, could only be those who sold passage on a ship. Wickham intended to take her far away from here—and once they boarded a ship, Elizabeth could not see how Mr. Darcy would have any chance of reaching them. Time had run out. She had wished so desperately that Mr. Darcy would arrive, but that had been asking for a miracle.

Still, she could not help but lower her head and let out one last desperate plea, hoping that there might be some shred of humanity left in Wickham which might make him feel even the smallest bit of remorse for what he had done: "Please, sir, let me go. I have done nothing to you."

"Sometimes, the sins of others must come down on our own heads," whispered he in her ear. And then he pushed the horse forward, and the last of her hopes disappeared as she drew nearer to the cold and merciless sea.

The matter of procuring passage aboard a ship was almost anticlimactic after all that Elizabeth had suffered. As Wickham was not known in Bristol—so he told her, with an exceedingly smug expression—he guided the horse through the town with an arrogance and conceit which Elizabeth would once have attributed to another man entirely. So confident was he of his security that even the presence of a company of redcoats passing them in the street did nothing to rein in his smugness. Though Elizabeth's heart leaped in her chest at the thought that she might possibly be able to effect her own rescue, Wickham merely chuckled and held her all the more firmly when he felt her tense. His warning was clear, and though Elizabeth had often prided herself in the thought that any attempt to intimidate her brought out her courage, she was forced to give way to his threat. After all, it would do her no good if he was hung for her murder after she was dead.

Making a quick tour of the local drinking establishments, Wickham negotiated their passage on a merchant vessel which was scheduled to depart a few scant hours hence. It was most disquieting to Elizabeth to learn that the vessel was bound for the port of Baltimore in the former colonies, far from any influence of the British Empire.

The captain of the ship appeared pleased that his final cabin had been let for the journey across the ocean mere hours before its departure; his glee upon counting the money Wickham deposited in his hand was almost disgusting in its depraved greed. And though she had pleaded with her eyes, peering at him beseechingly with every ounce of piteousness she had in her power to convey, he remained insensible to her plight. Either that, or he felt it did not signify as long as he received his coin.

"You injure me, Elizabeth," said Wickham with a laugh when she questioned him about his possessing sufficient funds to purchase the cabin. "Denny might have turned out to be a false friend in the end, but his generous surrender of his purse has bought us the means by which we may begin our new life.

"Of course, it is not merely Denny's largesse to which we are indebted," said he while lifting Elizabeth once again into the saddle and hoisting himself up behind her. "I made certain that as many of my erstwhile friends in the militia as I could arrange contributed to our available funds."

He laughed, a most unpleasant sound, before he continued. "You should be grateful, Elizabeth. We have resources enough to begin a satisfying new life once we arrive at our destination. I may even be persuaded to allow you to share in that life, as long as you temper your impertinence."

"I doubt any such funds will remain for the duration of the crossing," spat Elizabeth. "I have no doubt that your ability to gamble it all away shall leave you penniless long ere you reach the shores of the New World."

"In that case, you had best hope that I find some other means of supporting us," hissed Wickham. "There are very few professions into which a gentlewoman such as you may enter to support herself, and the colonies are not nearly as civilized as Mother England. You would do well to remember this."

Elizabeth did not deign to respond, aware that trying his patience by arguing with him was not improving her situation in any way.

Wickham spent the last few hours before the ship was to depart divesting himself of all those possessions which he would not be able to take with them. His primary negotiation was the exchange of the horse that had faithfully carried them for a pouch full of coins which he shook with some glee, bragging over the funds he possessed which would enable him to make his fortune in the new land.

When the time came to embark, Elizabeth, who by now was almost petrified with fear at the thought of being forced to leave with this man, decided she would finally attempt to flee, rationalizing that he would not jeopardize his imminent freedom by doing anything overt to her at that late moment.

She bolted, dodging a group of sailors. For a brief moment, she thought she would make it. Then the back of her dress was grabbed, and she was jerked backward.

Wickham twisted her around and smirked at her, shaking his head in amusement. Then, catching her hands and forcing them to her side, he hoisted her up over his shoulder and swaggered onto the ship.

Elizabeth pounded her fists against his back in impotent fury as he carried her, but it was all to no avail. Even the sailors laughed and pointed, shouting bawdy comments at the libertine, which he returned with a grin and a few choice pronouncements of his own.

"You must realize that you have lost, Elizabeth," whispered Wickham in her ear as the crew was making ready to sail. "I have escaped with the one woman who could turn the head of the *great Fitzwilliam Darcy*. I have beaten him and caused him a loss from which he will never recover."

Wickham grew silent for a moment as he savored his victory; then he continued in a contemplative tone of voice. "In fact, I no longer require your presence at all. Perhaps it would be better if I simply cast you over the side during the voyage. Then it will be impossible for him to know what has happened to you, which will make his suffering all the more acute."

Elizabeth gasped. She knew he would do it, even with all the people nearby on the boat. She began struggling against him, even as the ship began to move away from the dock, fighting desperately to make him relinquish his grip. Yet her struggling was for naught, as his arms were unyielding. She fought as a wild woman would, putting every iota of effort into escaping from his grasp, but he only held on even more tightly than before.

It was in the midst of her struggles that she heard a voice crying her name—one which she had been praying to hear since her ordeal had begun.

"Elizabeth!"

She turned, her heart pounding in her throat as she gazed upon Mr. Darcy standing at the pier like some majestic hero in a story, staring at her and promising simply by his presence that everything would be well. It took her a moment before she could truly believe what her eyes were showing her, so certain had she been that there could be no escape from the dire future awaiting her.

"Mr. Darcy!" shouted she after she had assured herself that he was indeed real, feeling as if she might cry out of sheer joy. Yet despite his presence—despite the rescue that it promised—there was one difficulty she had to surmount. How was she to pass from the moving ship to Mr. Darcy? The captain would obviously not stop it for her.

Mr. Darcy had her answer. But it was not one that she was thrilled to hear. "Jump, Elizabeth!"

Without any thought for the consequences, Elizabeth acted. Feeling her captor's grip slacken ever so slightly—most likely due to the surprise of finally seeing Mr. Darcy appear—she twisted herself violently and wrenched herself free. Desperation gave her strength, and she swiveled around to face Wickham, only to bring her knee up and slam it into his most sensitive spot as hard as she was able. He let out a cry of pain, nearly crumpling to the ground in agony. Freed from his odious grasp, she took a deep breath and flung herself off the ship.

The recognition of sheer cold hit her first as the water engulfed her. After that came the terrifying realization that her dress was causing her to sink despite her efforts to swim toward the surface. Her skirts tangled in her legs, rendering them almost useless in her attempts to move upward.

But she had only to face a few moments of panic before she was in someone's arms and being raised toward the surface. Even as she gasped for air and tried to blink the water out of her eyes, she did not have to see her savior to know that it was Mr. Darcy.

With what was likely a considerable amount of effort, he pulled her up to the pier and helped her stand despite the weight of her sopping wet dress. With no regard to how it might look or how others might perceive them, they came together in an embrace that was filled with relief and joy, their joint trembling not entirely due to the coldness of the water. After lightly touching his forehead to hers in a sort of verification that they were together again, Mr. Darcy brought his mouth up to her ear and whispered in a trembling voice: "Elizabeth, I am so glad you are alive. I feared I might be too late. I feared what he might do to you."

Elizabeth blinked back moisture that might have been either tears or water droplets streaming down her face from her wet hair. She knew not which and did not care. She whispered back what she felt must be the truest statement of her life: "I am so happy to see you, Mr. Darcy." Words seemed insufficient to express how she felt.

Yet despite her joy, she could not help but look back at the ship where the villainous Wickham stood, glowering at her with all the hate that a man could possess, enraged that his efforts had come to naught. Though he was intruding even now on such a wonderful moment with the malice that he exuded, her consolation was that she would never see him again. He had not won after all. She was with Mr. Darcy once more, and Wickham was bound on a ship for America. The only thing that could make this moment any better would be if she and Mr. Darcy had been dry and warm. But in the greater scheme of things, that was a minor inconvenience. She was in Mr. Darcy's arms, and if there were people staring, well, then let them stare. At that moment, she cared not a whit. Everything would be well. She kept repeating that in her head, barely able to believe it.

"Elizabeth," murmured Mr. Darcy into her hair, perhaps even unaware that he was speaking at all. But the sound of his voice brought a smile to her face.

"I am well, Mr. Darcy," assured she. And truly, she was.

Chapter XVIII

*L*ater that same day, Elizabeth found herself in the sitting room of a nearby inn, though if she were to be asked, she could not state exactly how she had arrived there. Whether it was simply the relief of finally being rescued or the hopelessness and fear of the most recent days which made her insensible, she could not say. Looking back on the day, she could only state with a certainty that she was left with mere flashes of memory, much akin to seeing the landscape at night due to the illumination of a lightning strike.

In those flashes that she could recall, Mr. Darcy, strong and tall and so very real, was prominent. However, she could also remember other flashes, such as her brief greeting with Colonel Fitzwilliam, who had accompanied Mr. Darcy on his mad rush to find her; the interior of a hired carriage, which had been procured to carry them to the inn; and the sensation of warmth imparted by a bath, which had been drawn to clean and refresh her after her ordeal.

Now, sitting alone in the room adjacent to what would be her bedchamber for the night, Elizabeth reveled in the feeling of being safe and knowing that Wickham had been defeated by the combination of her courage and Mr. Darcy's persistence and love. And though she briefly pondered how the British authorities would proceed to make Wickham pay for his deeds, she realized that she did not care whether he was ever apprehended. He was out of her life forever, and that was what truly mattered.

What she could not account for was how exactly Mr. Darcy had been able to track her location. While it was relatively simple to make the connection between the death of Mr. Denny and the disappearance of Elizabeth and Wickham, how had Mr. Darcy known where to go?

There was another concern that was more pressing, yet she attempted to push it away as best as she could. She knew not what would become of her reputation—an unmarried woman traveling with an unmarried young man could very well be seen as ruined, no matter what the circumstances were—but even more important than the state of her reputation was the way in which Mr. Darcy might react to the idea of an alliance with her. Still, at the moment, she wanted to focus on the fact that she had escaped a wretched fate.

She had been thus engaged with her thoughts for some time when the door opened and in stepped Mr. Darcy and his cousin. Elizabeth felt a brief and irrational desire to leap from the chair in which she sat into Mr. Darcy's arms, longing once more to feel their strength and ensure herself of her safety. Instead, however, she rose to her feet and curtseyed, greeting the pair with reasonable decorum, if not perfect composure.

The two men approached, and Mr. Darcy bowed and, taking her hand, bestowed a tender kiss upon it, sending a shiver up Elizabeth's spine at the sensations it engendered.

"Miss Bennet," said Mr. Darcy, "I cannot tell you how good it is to find you well."

"And I am very grateful to be in your company again, Mr. Darcy," replied Elizabeth quietly. "I had quite despaired of ever seeing you or your cousin again, though I hoped and prayed and watched for any sign of you."

"I dare say you acquitted yourself admirably, Miss Bennet," said Colonel Fitzwilliam as he greeted her. "I shall never forget the look on his face as you struck him and then made your escape."

Elizabeth laughed and sat back down in her chair. "I would like to have seen it myself, though I must own that I was rather preoccupied at the time. But I fear I shall not be able to sleep tonight unless you account for your success in tracking us."

"All in due time," said the colonel with aplomb.

"What my rather jovial cousin is trying to say, Miss Bennet," interjected Mr. Darcy, "is that we would appreciate any information you can give us about what happened after your abduction and about

Wickham's destination."

"Indeed," said his cousin. "The British military cannot afford to allow curs such as Wickham to behave in such a fashion and escape punishment. Colonel Forster will undoubtedly wish to know what has become of his officer, and the high command will pursue him and return him to justice, if at all possible."

Agreeing, Elizabeth recounted the events of the past week, making sure to inform them exactly what Wickham's plans had been regarding her and telling them of his threat to throw her over the side of the ship to ensure Mr. Darcy never saw her again. The tension in Mr. Darcy's jaw as she recounted the tale spoke to the fate which would await Wickham should his path ever cross Mr. Darcy's again.

Finally, when Elizabeth had finished her story and disclosed what she knew of Wickham's final destination, Colonel Fitzwilliam and Mr. Darcy exchanged a look, after which the colonel stood to take his leave.

"Miss Bennet," said he, "I shall go directly to the local commanders and impart what I know of Wickham so that he may be pursued forthwith. I must say that I do not know of any other lady who would have acquitted herself so well in the face of such tribulations. You are a singular young woman, and I count myself fortunate to have made your acquaintance."

He then bowed and took his leave, stating that he would return in time to take supper with them.

Once he had left, the air almost seemed to become thicker. Elizabeth was grateful to Mr. Darcy for following her all this distance, but she was also nervous. It was not as if she had ever been in love before, and she was finding the experience both exhilarating and frightening at the same time. The situation might have become awkward had Mr. Darcy not taken the initiative to open the conversation.

"Miss Bennet, I believe I know the answer to my question—certainly, your good mood indicates only one answer to be possible—but I must ask it nonetheless. Before I do, however, I must assure you that your response will in no way change my opinion of you, nor shall it change my feelings and intentions toward you."

"Mr. Darcy—"

"Please, Miss Bennet, I must know—did Wickham . . . harm you?" There was a fire in the man's eyes which indicated he would pursue Wickham to America should she provide any answer other than the one he hoped for.

She gave him a gentle smile, her heart swelling with love. She knew the question was asking something deeper, and she truly was fortunate that she was able to give him the response he desired. "Apart from such things as restraining me and lifting me up on his horse, Wickham did nothing which would cause you concern." She met his gaze and held it, trying to impart deeper meaning to her words.

At length, he let out a relieved sigh. "Miss Bennet, I am glad to hear that. Now, I suppose that you have many questions of your own which you would like to be answered. Perhaps we should begin to address those deficiencies before the conversation moves on to other subjects."

"I would appreciate that very much, Mr. Darcy," said Elizabeth with a smile.

"I suppose you would like to commence with how we managed to find you?"

"That would be an ideal place to start," agreed Elizabeth. She could not even begin to fathom how they had managed it.

"I am afraid precious time was lost in the beginning. While a faint cry was heard at the Forsters' townhouse and awakened a few of the occupants, there was some confusion before Mr. Denny was discovered."

Elizabeth closed her eyes briefly. "He was trying to save me. He was a good man." He had been trying so hard to save her, but he had failed to save himself. She would never have suspected Wickham capable of murder before that terrible night. Had she suspected it, perhaps there might have been something she could have done differently, though she knew not what. She only knew that a good man had died.

"His outcry *did* save your life," said Mr. Darcy gently. "While it took a little while for Colonel Forster to confirm that Wickham had killed Denny—and it took a little more time for Mrs. Forster to realize that you had not come to investigate the commotion like the other occupants of the house—his cry did, in the end, assist me in being able to reach you before it was too late. When you were discovered to be missing, I was alerted, and after making some plans, we set off to find you. Colonel Forster took a company of men, including my cousin Fitzwilliam, and they made inquiries. Since a man carrying a woman on horseback attracts some attention, mention of you was found. The authorities had been alerted, which Colonel Forster and I discovered while searching for evidence of where you had gone."

"Had Wickham told someone where he was going?" She could not recall an instance where something such as that could have happened, but she was already trying to block those days with the reprehensible man out of her mind.

Mr. Darcy shook his head. "No. While it did take me some time, after gathering enough information, I was able to guess that Wickham was trying to flee to America. With travel in Brighton to the Atlantic being restricted due to its proximity to France, he had to go elsewhere to find a ship to take him on such short notice. Perhaps more importantly, he never would have been able to flee on a ship leaving Brighton, as we would have caught up to him long ere he would have been able to board. Bristol was his only hope."

"And I suppose my extra weight slowed his horse's progress considerably," mused Elizabeth. Would that his horse had been completely lame!

Mr. Darcy nodded, but his face had darkened. "While I was more fortunate in being able to switch horses and travel more swiftly, I still was nearly too late to rescue you."

"But you were *not* too late," said Elizabeth with no small amount of firmness. "You faced odds that would have been insurmountable for any other man."

"If I had failed, I should not have forgiven myself." His voice was so quiet that she almost could not make out his words.

"But you did not fail. So let us not speak of that." She was alive. There was no need to think of what might have been. But what was to happen next? An abduction by one such as Wickham was no small matter. Even now that she had been rescued, there were other things to consider.

Mr. Darcy must have sensed the line of her thoughts, for he said: "Perhaps you are wondering of your reputation and where you are to go next? You need not worry, Miss Bennet, for Colonel Forster is a wise and far-sighted man."

Elizabeth raised her eyebrows in surprise. There were many kind terms she would have used to describe Colonel Forster, but "wise" was certainly not one which would have made her list. "Whatever do you mean, Mr. Darcy?"

"He was able to think more clearly than I at the beginning. I am afraid I was too distraught to make such plans as he did. He proceeded rather optimistically with the belief that you would be found unharmed and that Wickham would be brought to justice. In particular, he hoped that you would be found by him, Colonel Fitzwilliam, or me, that we might ensure your reputation was protected. He informed his men that Wickham killed Denny because Denny discovered he was trying to desert the militia. Furthermore, he told them that Wickham might be traveling with a brown-haired woman. He knew that any redcoats who found you could be sworn to secrecy if necessary. Before Colonel Forster left, he and his wife created the illusion that you were confined to bed due to illness. It served as an explanation for why you were not appearing at any public events."

"But surely the servants—"

"They are loyal to the Forsters and to you for your kindnesses. I am sure Colonel Forster will buy the silence of any who might be reluctant."

"The money—"

"It is no concern of yours," said Mr. Darcy firmly. "Colonel Forster is no poor man, and you are his wife's dear friend. You need pay no heed to that."

Elizabeth stared at him for a moment before frowning to herself. "I fear you are taking too little credit for this plan and your own actions, but so be it. Is there anything else you have not told me of which I should be aware?"

Mr. Darcy gave her a small smile. "I could not in good conscience keep your disappearance from your father. I sent a private letter advising him to travel to Brighton. I informed him that you had been taken by Wickham and that an illusion of illness was being maintained in order to preserve your reputation. We have sent news of your recovery to him in Brighton. That is where we shall go next—after you are able to have a full night's rest, of course."

Elizabeth shook her head, amazed at the thought that these men had put into her rescue. She truly was fortunate.

"I hope that I have not worried Papa too terribly," said Elizabeth.

"I should think, Miss Bennet, that your father will be overjoyed to see you safely returned to him; any worry which resulted will be quickly forgotten."

"I dare say it shall," said Elizabeth. "But I have always been his favorite, and though he is well aware of my penchant for engaging in mischief—mostly when I was a young girl—I do not believe he would ever have expected for *me* to take part in such an adventure. I shall never hear the end of it now that I am safely found."

Mr. Darcy laughed at her cheeky portrayal of the situation before he returned his attention to her with an almost rueful smile. "I must confess that . . . events," his cheeks reddened somewhat at this point, "did not allow me to spend much time with your father last fall. After your rather droll way of speaking of him, I am anticipating the opportunity to become better acquainted with him."

Knowing he was speaking of his behavior the previous fall, Elizabeth would not allow him to castigate himself on what she now knew to be completely understandable distraction.

"My father is certainly not dull," said Elizabeth, attempting to inject a note of levity into her voice. "I believe, in fact, that you share some common character traits and enjoy similar interests. You should speak to him of your love of books, for nothing will provoke his approbation more quickly than the informed opinion of a fellow book lover."

Though the words were spoken mostly in jest, Elizabeth immediately felt her cheeks burn. Certainly, Mr. Darcy had followed her all the way to Bristol in order to rescue her from the clutches of his most hated enemy, and she believed that his affections remained unchanged from the spring. However, to be so forward in recommending a more intimate relationship with her father when he had yet to come to the point was not entirely proper. She did not wish him to feel obligated, after all, regardless of her own wishes and hopes on the subject.

The rosiness of her cheeks only deepened when she dared to look up at him and witnessed his smoldering gaze, which bored into her with an intensity that made her feel breathless. She found herself unable to glance up at him again, and her heart fluttered at the thought that he was about to once again make his declaration.

In this, however, she was to be disappointed. He was silent for several moments, and while she regained her composure, she remained a trifle disappointed. When he at last found his voice again, their conversation turned to more general topics, never approaching the personal grounds into which they had unthinkingly wandered.

At length, the colonel returned, and they adjourned to the private dining room which the gentlemen had engaged for their use. The food was good and conversation lively, yet Elizabeth could not shake the sense of discontent which lingered.

It was not until after dinner when she was finally able to shed some light on Mr. Darcy's diffidence. Colonel Fitzwilliam had retired to his room, leaving his cousin to walk Elizabeth to her bedchamber. Mr. Darcy was largely silent on their short journey to her door, only speaking when they had arrived. The words he spoke, however, completely erased any worries she had felt for his silence.

"Miss Bennet, I should w-wish . . ." stammered he, clearly looking for the proper words. "That is—I know that this is perhaps not the proper time . . ."

He paused yet again, searching for what to say. After a brief moment, a hint of the confident Mr. Darcy that she had come to know emerged. He almost visibly straightened his shoulders and gazed at her unabashedly.

"What I mean to say is that I very much wish to continue our discussion once you have been safely returned to the Forsters' townhouse in Brighton. There is something which I have very much wanted to ask you, and I should be very grateful if you would grant me some few moments of your time when we are both more at our leisure."

His declaration filled her with the warmth of assurance that her regard was still returned in full measure. She gave him to know — almost coherently! — of her perfect willingness to accede to such a request, the sure knowledge of which prompted the most brilliant smile she had ever witnessed upon his face.

They parted soon afterward, both happy with the final resolution of the evening, if not with the fact that they were required to part at all.

The journey back to Brighton was tedious, as such journeys tended to be when anticipating the reunion with loved ones at the end. Elizabeth traveled in a hired carriage while the colonel and Mr. Darcy rode alongside on their stallions. They made the journey in easy stages, and Elizabeth was satisfied with the looks and gestures which passed between her and Mr. Darcy.

At the journey's end, Elizabeth was subjected to the rather unique experience of being smuggled into her friend's house. Colonel Forster, it turned out, had already been informed of Mr. Darcy's discovery of Wickham's trail, and knowing he would not have arrived in time to do any good, he had returned to Brighton to attend to his duties and maintain the illusion that Elizabeth was struck down by some illness.

They arrived at the outskirts of Brighton late in the evening, as Mr. Darcy had designed, after the sun had set and the stars had begun twinkling in the sky. Donning a rather large bonnet to obscure her face, Elizabeth disembarked from the carriage in a narrow lane and was then bustled into the Forster townhouse via the servants' entrance, and from thence, she was taken straight to her room.

She had no sooner entered than she was engulfed by her father's strong arms. Though she knew the Forsters and Mr. Darcy were watching, she returned the embrace fiercely.

"Ah, my dearest child," said her father with far more emotion than was his wont, "I am so grateful for your safe return."

"And I am very happy to be here, Papa."

"I dare say your dear friends have done quite well for themselves in bringing you back safely," said Mr. Bennet. "More than once have I doubted the probability of their success, but never have I been happier to be mistaken."

"I am sorry to have caused you worry, Papa. But what of my mother and sisters?"

"Like the society here, they believe you are ill. Certainly, your mother could not have been trusted with the truth, as you and I both know," said Mr. Bennet.

Elizabeth winced at the insult to her mother, but her father continued, drawing her attention once more: "Upon receiving Mr. Darcy's letter, I announced to the family that you were sick and that I wished to visit you. Lydia pleaded to go—wanting to visit redcoats, no doubt, but claiming the utmost concern for you, her dear, dear sister—and her mother supported her, but I told them both I would not have Lydia finding trouble in Brighton, which she no doubt would have done. Even Jane wanted to come, but I knew not what to expect, so even she was not allowed to accompany me."

While Elizabeth was not thrilled that her father was speaking of somewhat private matters in front of others, it was still a relief to hear that her sisters were doing well. "Papa, I am sorry you had to journey so far—"

"Nonsense," said Mr. Bennet with a resolute firmness. "Even a book-lover such as I must leave his safe haven occasionally. But I am certain Mrs. Forster has tired of my presence—I am certain that I have badgered her mercilessly these past few days for any scrap of information concerning you. She will, no doubt, find it a relief to be rid of me at last."

"That is not true," protested Harriet with utmost sincerity. "Both Blanche and I were glad to have a kindred soul with whom to share our concerns."

"Well," said Mr. Bennet, "enough of this! We are glad to have you back, dear child, but we must now plan your recovery. We must make it convincing, lest we cause anyone suspicion. I must confess that I am not utterly heartbroken at the thought of spending a small amount of time by the sea."

And make it convincing, they did. Elizabeth was by no means a skilled actress, but she believed she comported herself very well when it came to crafting an illusion of recovery from an illness. Walking slowly, feigning weakness—these things were not so difficult to pretend as one might think. The only problem with them was that they took a little time and no small amount of patience for one who was accustomed to a robust constitution and frequent walks out of doors.

So it was that Elizabeth at last found herself able to go out on a walk to breathe in some fresh air and stretch her legs, accompanied by the Forsters, Mr. Bennet, Blanche, Colonel Fitzwilliam, and, of course, Mr. Darcy.

Before long, Mr. Darcy and Elizabeth were walking ahead of the others, gaining some distance so they could partake in private conversation. Elizabeth scarcely paid attention to where they were going, as she was too caught up in contemplation of the many turns her life had taken in so short a time. Yet though she was sorting through her thoughts, still there was a part of her that took great enjoyment in a walk . . . and the presence of the man at her side.

Though their other companions were talking quietly behind them, she and Mr. Darcy said little. She thought perhaps he, too, had much to think on, and so it was with some surprise that she realized his seemingly aimless steps had actually led them to the city park they had visited some time before.

As they entered the park, Elizabeth allowed herself a moment to pause and breathe in the fresh smell of grass and gaze upon the great trees surrounding them. Mr. Darcy waited patiently for her, a hint of a smile on his face.

And then Elizabeth moved forward again, resisting the urge to run among the trees and laugh. This haven amid the city bustle served to soothe her and cleanse her soul of the horror brought on by that wretched journey with Wickham. She was glad they were not simply walking along city streets; Mr. Darcy knew of her love for nature, and he must have brought her here because of it. She was full of joy — Wickham was gone forever, and her life was hers again.

Before long, they came upon a large familiar yew, and Elizabeth broke away from Mr. Darcy to step toward it. She touched its bark lightly, smiling, and turned back to her companion. "Mr. Darcy, this is the tree the woman called —" She broke off suddenly, wide-eyed and barely able to keep herself from uttering: "Oh."

"'The tree of lovers,'" finished Mr. Darcy, staring at her with a nervous intensity.

Elizabeth found that she could not hold his eyes, for the force of his stare left her feeling rather weak and breathless. With her gaze fixed firmly upon the ground, she felt — rather than saw — him approaching, though she did see his boots draw near.

"Elizabeth," she heard him breathe, his voice almost caressing her name.

Gathering all her courage, Elizabeth risked a glance up at him, only to be immediately lost in the depths of his eyes. She turned away from the tree and leaned back against it, allowing Mr. Darcy to lean on the tree himself, one arm braced against the trunk beside her head as he looked at her, an unmistakable tenderness evident in his manner. He was close enough that she could almost feel his breath on her skin, though far enough that there could not be any breach of propriety.

"Elizabeth," said he, somewhat forcefully, "you must allow me to tell you how ardently I admire and love you."

A giggle escaped from Elizabeth's lips, and at Mr. Darcy's answering smile, she allowed herself to laugh delightedly, the gentleman soon joining her. The tension thus broken, Elizabeth allowed herself to gaze up into his well-loved face, and between her fits of giggles, she was able to reply:

"But Mr. Darcy, you have forgotten to impart how you have overcome your struggles."

"I assure you, Miss Bennet," said Mr. Darcy with a shake of his head, "that there have been no such struggles. Even the merest whisper of doubt has long since fled. There is no question that you are the only woman to whom I would ever wish say these words.

"The fact of the matter," continued he with an impish smile, "is that those words are very proper for the beginning of a proposal, but the words I followed them up with last time were abhorrent, and I should like the opportunity to improve upon them."

Elizabeth smiled and reached up to touch his cheek gently. "I do not believe that you are a man given to flowery speeches, Mr. Darcy, but I am more than happy to allow you the opportunity to improve upon your previous endeavor. The benefits of practice are, after all, not to be overestimated."

Grasping her hand, Mr. Darcy gently kissed her palm before he brought their joined hands down to their sides.

"I thank you for your magnanimous gesture, my lady," said Mr. Darcy. "I believe that you are correct. I am *not* a man who is inclined to extravagant words, and I am *definitely* a man who has often found himself tongue-tied in the presence of the woman he loves.

"In this instance, however, I find myself completely at ease, knowing exactly what I wish to say. I have found myself to be utterly in your power these past months, and I find the experience to be exhilarating and excruciating all at once. Your beauty and generosity are to be admired, as are your innate ability to put others at ease, your unfeigned interest in the concerns of those around you, and your ability to inspire those with whom you come in contact. You are everything I am not, Miss Bennet—friendly and gregarious, kind and generous, witty and learned—and I would be a much better man if I were to be so fortunate as to convince you to grace my life with your constant presence."

He looked into her eyes with his typical intensity. "Would you do me the honor of sharing the rest of my life with me? Will you marry me, Miss Bennet?"

"I am afraid I must disagree with at least part of your assertions, Mr. Darcy," answered Elizabeth. Mr. Darcy's eyebrow rose in response, and though his manner still suggested a modicum of nervous energy, he appeared to be in no doubt of her response, ironically much like the first time he had proposed. This time, however, he was justified in being confident of her response, as she had given him enough indication of her feelings that he should know exactly how she would answer him.

"In what way?" queried Mr. Darcy.

"When you said that I am kind and generous where you are not. Not every man would race at breakneck speed halfway across England to save a foolish woman who had already rejected him."

"This man would," was his response. His lip quirked upward, and he added: "Though I would never venture as to call you foolish."

"Well, I am very glad you are such a man," said Elizabeth with a smile. "I accept your proposal without reservation and affirm to you that my feelings match yours in every respect. I would be honored to be your wife."

A brilliant smile came over his face, and he once again brought her hand up to gently caress it with a kiss. Elizabeth sighed, wondering that after all the misunderstanding, after all the hardship wrought by their words and actions, after the manipulation and interference of a rogue of the worst sort—after all that, they could still arrive at this happy resolution. There must indeed be a deity looking out for them; no other explanation existed which would allow them to overcome all that had been set in their path.

They stayed by the tree for several more minutes, cherishing this time, indelibly etching this moment in their memories. And though Elizabeth would never remember the endearments they spoke or the words they exchanged, her feelings would always be kept preserved within her heart.

At length, however, the world intruded, and they made to depart, both wondering where their companions had gone. It was with the utmost surprise that after they turned from the tree and proceeded a short distance away, they found a bench along the side of the path occupied by Mr. Bennet. He was holding a book, but it looked as if he were not truly paying attention to it, which was an oddity in itself. The expression on his face as they approached was gentle and happy, though it contained a hint of melancholy which he could not hide. He rose from his seat and, closing his book, peered at Elizabeth with some expectation.

"Papa," said Elizabeth as they approached. She disengaged her hand from Mr. Darcy's arm and threw her arms around her father's neck, hugging him close.

"Ah, Elizabeth, my dear," said he, fondly returning her embrace, "it appears you have a story to tell your old father." After they separated, he bowed to Mr. Darcy before turning his attention back to his daughter. "And it also appears that I shall be losing you soon, Elizabeth. Let us walk—you can tell me about it on the way back to the Forsters' townhouse, where, I suspect, your young man will wish to have a word with me."

Elizabeth scarcely knew what to say. How could she begin to describe all that had happened in Brighton, much less in front of the man around whom her life now gravitated? Obviously, things had changed quite drastically between them since Hertfordshire. Her father must have realized that many days ago, what with Mr. Darcy playing such a pivotal role in rescuing her from Wickham. There could be no hiding the importance of his assistance in bringing her back intact.

Mr. Bennet must have sensed her hesitation, for he said: "I suspect there shall be time enough for stories later. I suppose the short of it is that you have seen much of each other in Brighton?"

Elizabeth glanced at Mr. Darcy, who apparently intended to keep his silence. "In fact, I am the reason he came to Brighton in the first place."

That seemed to surprise Mr. Bennet, who paused briefly to peer at her. "Are you indeed? I was under the impression that—ah—the situation between the two of you was not an especially congenial one."

"Much has changed since Hertfordshire," said Elizabeth, glancing at Mr. Darcy. Her cheeks colored faintly at the thought of some of the things she had said to—and about—him. Even now, when her happiness was all but assured, she found it difficult to think about that part of their past. It might have helped lead them to where they were presently, but she was still not proud of it.

"Well, Lizzy," said Mr. Bennet, "since you do not seem inclined to tell your poor father much, I suppose I shall have to be content with what I do know for now. Maybe another time will find you more willing to talk with me — a time when you do not feel the need to blush whenever you speak of your suitor. Perhaps you are nothing but a foolish girl after all." This last was spoken in jest, with the utmost affection.

"Oh, Papa!" said Elizabeth, shaking her head with a smile.

"I can assure you, Mr. Bennet, your daughter is anything but foolish." Mr. Darcy had spoken up at last.

Mr. Bennet regarded him for a moment as they walked. "Yes, I suppose she is not. She has certainly chosen a good protector. But has she chosen a wise one? I suppose that is something I must determine. Tell me, Mr. Darcy — I should like to hear your opinion on a few subjects dear to my heart."

As Elizabeth walked and listened to her father converse with Mr. Darcy — ever reticent, but this time trying to fight his natural taciturnity with a sort of nervous desire to please, which she found quite endearing — she felt her heart swelling once more with joy. The two men who were dearest to her could carry on a conversation that was intelligent and unstilted. It boded quite well for her future happiness.

Chapter XIX

efore Mr. Bennet spoke in private with Mr. Darcy, he insisted on talking to Elizabeth herself. He claimed he wanted to speak about her sisters, but Elizabeth felt Mr. Darcy was no more convinced of that reason than she was.

Indeed, Mr. Bennet did not even say a word about her sisters. What he first said was: "Now, I think I know what your answer is—though I must say that the idea is still somewhat of a surprise to me, knowing as I do your previous opinion of the man—but I must be straightforward and ask. I can do no less for my favorite daughter. Lizzy, are you certain you wish to marry him?"

"I am, Papa," declared Elizabeth. "I truly am." She had never been so certain of anything in her life. She could no longer imagine a life without Mr. Darcy. His heart and hers now beat as one. They balanced each other perfectly, complementing each other like two halves of the same whole.

"Then you love him . . . and respect him? I know you could not live happily with anything else."

"Yes, Papa. I do. I love him, I respect him—he is the one I wish to marry."

"Well, though I do not believe I could deny a man such as him anything, you shall be glad to hear you have my blessing. But I must make the young man himself sweat a little, you must understand. It is a time-honored tradition, after all, and I dare not go against tradition."

Elizabeth threw her arms around her father and pressed her head into his chest. "Thank you, Papa."

He chuckled as he returned her embrace, showing no less love, though much more restraint, and then he pushed her away gently. "Yes, yes. Now, go and fetch your beloved suitor. If we get this over with quickly, I might be able to read a few chapters of my book before the next meal."

Elizabeth fought her grin and went to Mr. Darcy. "Papa wishes to see you," said she in as solemn a tone as she could manage.

Her expression gave him some alarm, though he tried to hide it, and she took pity on him and allowed him to see the hint of a grin. He shook his head at her—she knew he would have to grow accustomed to the playfulness of Elizabeth Bennet, and she would enjoy every moment of it—and then left her, but not before reaching out to take her hand and give it a gentle squeeze.

As she watched him go, she could still feel the ghost of his fingers on her hand. The smile broke out in earnest.

She had to wait for some time, but Mr. Darcy finally exited the room. Of course, Mr. Bennet gave his blessing. But while Mr. Darcy refused to speak of what exactly his soon-to-be father-in-law had told him—or asked him—Elizabeth thought he looked a little haggard, as if he had been exposed to some intense questioning.

Applying to her father for the details was met with no more success—it seemed the men had decided to keep what passed between them in strict confidence. And while Elizabeth was naturally curious, she soon desisted in her attempts to learn, knowing it was not truly important.

Her engagement was soon officially acknowledged to all of her friends and acquaintances, and Elizabeth found herself the recipient of warm congratulations, not to mention a certain amount of smug satisfaction. Of the latter variety, Blanche and Harriet were especially vocal in their approval, Blanche in particular claiming that she had long suspected that Elizabeth was not as indifferent—or as averse—to Mr. Darcy as she had initially stated. Elizabeth had shaken her head and laughed gaily at such assertions; they were so like Blanche after all.

The next few days were spent forwarding the illusion of Elizabeth's recovery, though by this time she was able to partake in more of her favorite activities. She attended several events, always in the company of her newly betrothed and her ever-watchful father. It was a carefree time, idyllic and happy, and Elizabeth was content in her situation and in the attentions of her beloved.

It did not escape her attention, however, just what an object of curiosity and envy she had become in Brighton society — the curiosity no doubt due to the fact that she, a country girl from Hertfordshire, had managed to catch the elusive Mr. Darcy, and the envy due to her good fortune. Elizabeth had been so caught up in her enjoyment and the newness of Mr. Darcy's overt attentions that the dark looks which she had received before she became engaged had gone largely unnoticed. Now, she was well aware of the way many other young ladies regarded her with no small amount of jealousy. She was not to be intimidated or made unhappy, however, and she met every situation with fortitude and good humor. Fortunately, those who were truly upset were very small in number and kept their own counsel.

As must eventually be the case with all things, her time at Brighton was coming to a close, and soon enough, talk began turning toward their departure and return to their homes. Elizabeth had decided not to write to Longbourn with her news, though she was anxious to inform Jane in particular of her happiness and changed status. Her former dislike of Mr. Darcy had been acknowledged throughout the neighborhood, and she felt his image in that society was so low that nothing less than a personal testament to her changed feelings and his innate goodness would do.

Mr. Darcy, however, proposed a detour to their journey north, suggesting they call on Lady Catherine at Rosings to announce their engagement. To say that Elizabeth was unexcited by the prospect of such a scheme was a rather large understatement.

"I feel that I must," insisted Mr. Darcy as they discussed the proposal, Elizabeth's father looking on with some curiosity and amusement. "I believe that you are well aware of my aunt's . . . ambitions regarding my future felicity."

"She is likely to be very disappointed, is she not?" asked Elizabeth.

Mr. Darcy allowed it to be so. "She has always been thus, and she is not accustomed to allowing anything contrary to her designs. I have tried to tell her over the years that I had no intention of marrying my cousin, but she would hear nothing of it, insisting that I — nay, both my cousin and I — would come to her way of thinking and do our duties."

"A veritable love triangle, Mr. Darcy," said Mr. Bennet with a chortle. "With such dramas to be played out in life, why bother with novels?"

By now, Mr. Darcy was well aware of the sardonic view of the world possessed by Elizabeth's father, and he smiled in response. "I assure you, Mr. Bennet, that no such triangle exists. Elizabeth is the only woman in the world whom I have ever loved."

His words were spoken with such affection and good humor that Elizabeth found herself blushing, even as she returned his smile.

"I am very happy to hear that, Mr. Darcy," said Mr. Bennet. "However, I must own that I am concerned with precisely how the grand lady will react—and specifically with what she might say to Elizabeth."

"I am not afraid of Lady Catherine, Papa," assured Elizabeth.

"And your indomitable spirit impressed my aunt, I believe," said Mr. Darcy. "But she will not be sanguine about this, and I agree with your father. However, I know that should my aunt learn that I was in Brighton, became engaged here—to a woman with whom she was acquainted, no less!—and bypassed her completely on the way back to London and Hertfordshire, she would be offended, and her reaction would be much more severe. Perhaps I could call on my aunt while you visit Mrs. Collins at the parsonage?"

"That will not do, Mr. Darcy," was Elizabeth's firm response. "I will not hide away as if I have done something wrong. We will face her together."

"Your courage is one of the many reasons I care for you so very dearly, Elizabeth," said Mr. Darcy as he gazed at her with devotion and love. "But as we are now to be wed, I would ask that you address me in a more familiar manner. My sister calls me 'William,' and I should be very pleased if you would do the same."

Elizabeth smiled shyly and nodded her head. "I would be most happy to do so, William."

"Well, it seems as though we are for Rosings," said Mr. Bennet, breaking the spell between the two young lovers. "And I for one am greatly anticipating making her ladyship's acquaintance."

Elizabeth shook her head at her father's words, knowing that he was anticipating the amusement he would feel when witnessing the follies which Lady Catherine would no doubt betray when braved in her lair. But there was no alternative, not if Elizabeth wished to remain on good terms with her future husband's relations. Still, knowing her ladyship's temperament as she did, Elizabeth could not look on the approaching meeting with anything but dread. Lady Catherine would protest the match, she knew; it was merely a question of how she would choose to do so, and to what lengths she would go in order to have her own way.

For her fiancé's sake, however, Elizabeth spoke lightly of the upcoming event. If she had done otherwise and made the depth of her misgivings known, he might very well have attempted to bar her from visiting Rosings to make the announcement with him, and she felt it was necessary for her to be at his side, supporting him despite any unpleasantness which would ensue. It was her duty as his companion and future wife.

But that did not mean she had to like it.

There were a few matters to attend to before making the journey to Kent and then Hertfordshire, and one of those was a parting with Blanche. Since Elizabeth had discussed certain aspects of Lady Catherine de Bourgh's personality and had mentioned the impending visit to Rosings, Blanche seemed to view what was to come with a measure of amusement not unlike that expressed by Mr. Bennet.

"I am certain she shall not detest you forever, Elizabeth," said Blanche teasingly after Elizabeth had explained the reason for stopping in Kent and her reservations concerning it. "You will be her nephew's wife, and even should she become angry, she shall likely deem it necessary to continue her attempts to interfere in his life. She shall not be able to do that if she refuses to speak with you. Unfortunately from what you have told me of the great lady, you might wish it."

"Perhaps the meeting will actually be a congenial one—" Elizabeth began, but Blanche's laughter cut her off.

"Come now, Elizabeth! We both know you are a better judge of character than that!"

"I suppose I must then consider alternatives. Perhaps I shall pack you in my trunk! Then you and my father can tend to her ladyship while Mr. Darcy and I visit Charlotte. I am certain the three of you could talk quite calmly over tea. There must be at least one book you have all read."

Blanche shook her head, chuckling lightly. "I am afraid I am a little more discriminating in choosing those with whom I shall sit down to tea. However, I believe you are more than capable of withstanding her ladyship yourself. You are far more likely than I am to have read one of the same books as Lady Catherine, for I have not dedicated myself to reading as you have."

"Well, regardless of what is to come, I do know one thing. I shall miss you, Blanche. You have been such a dear friend to me—far kinder than I deserve. I am fortunate to have met you."

"Not so fortunate as *I* am to have met *you*, Elizabeth—you deserve all the kindness I have to give! But this is not goodbye forever. I fully intend to be there on your wedding day. After all, I must see your mother flitting about and frantically handling wedding preparations. I have heard much about her, but I have yet to meet her!"

Elizabeth smiled. "Well, if you intend to come to my wedding, then I am certain you shall see her in all her anxious glory. Truth be told, I am somewhat nervous about seeing her myself. There is little that can send her whirling about quite so much as the prospect of having one of her daughters married off to some well-to-do gentleman."

"Well, I think her excitement shall be more than justified in this instance. You have chosen a worthy man to let into your heart, Elizabeth Bennet. Just do not forget your friends in the excitement of your wedded bliss."

Elizabeth clasped the other woman's hands with her own. "Never, Blanche! After all, I am more than capable of handling a pen."

"Perhaps you should bring one to your meeting with Lady Catherine. You might have need of something sharp to defend yourself."

"Now, Blanche, surely it shall not be as bad as all that." In truth, Elizabeth was uncertain how the announcement of her engagement to Mr. Darcy would be received. She knew only that it would not be dull.

"You never know. But surely someone as officious as Lady Catherine shall always have one at hand—perhaps you can grab hers!"

Elizabeth laughed and shook her head. "I shall not be wielding any of Lady Catherine's pens as weapons, Blanche!"

"See if you shall say the same thing when she is squawking in your ear!"

"I would brave a thousand Lady Catherines for Mr. Darcy's sake!" proclaimed Elizabeth.

"Well, you are a far better person than I am; I believe that one would be my quota."

"If you intend to marry Colonel Fitzwilliam, then I am afraid your quota might be filled! With Mr. Darcy getting married, Lady Catherine may be searching for another man to marry her daughter. Colonel Fitzwilliam could be her next target!"

Blanche shuddered. "I certainly hope not! I do not possess quite as much patience as you do, Elizabeth. I fear I might say something I would later regret."

"No, you are skilled in handling society of all sorts. I am certain you would deal with her with your usual aplomb."

"But I choose which society to handle," noted Blanche, "and I would never choose hers."

"Well, let us both hope it never comes to that!"

"Indeed!" agreed Blanche. "I suspect I now have a new item to add to my prayers."

Elizabeth simply laughed.

They spoke a little longer before they had to part, but they did so with smiles and repetitious confirmations of how they would indeed see each other again.

As for Elizabeth's farewell with Harriet, well, it was much less lighthearted — neither she nor her friend spared the other the sight of tears — and her other partings were also met with sorrow. She had truly enjoyed her time in Brighton and would miss it very dearly.

It was, therefore, with regret that Elizabeth entered the carriage after her teary goodbye with Harriet, departing for the much unanticipated meeting with the formidable Lady Catherine de Bourgh.

The journey was undertaken in an easy manner, as there was no need for them to arrive home with any particular haste. The road to Rosings would consume the better part of a full day, and Mr. Darcy recommended that they take rooms at a traveling inn to the south of Rosings; it would be best, he said, to visit her the next morning before they continued on to London and Hertfordshire. Though it obviously pained him to acknowledge any expected incivility on the part of his relation, he was certain that Lady Catherine's hospitality would not be extended once she learned of the nature of their errand. Though Mr. Bennet raised the possibility of her annoyance in knowing that they had not visited the night before, Mr. Darcy felt it was prudent that they proceed as he had previously suggested, and he pointed out that if they started late in the day, then they could truthfully state that they had stopped when travel had begun to become hazardous due to the darkness. Mr. Bennet chuckled at this slight obfuscation, and Mr. Darcy had the grace to blush. Elizabeth merely smiled and indicated her assent, knowing Mr. Darcy had planned carefully. Though she was aware of his feelings about disguise, she could not fault him and would not tease him for his indulgence in this one instance.

The journey was a relatively pleasant one, as the weather was fine and the company agreeable. Initially, upon entering the carriage, Elizabeth had taken her seat next to her father as propriety demanded, allowing her betrothed to sit across from them. Her father, however, must have noted their longing looks, for when they entered the carriage after their first rest stop, he guided her into the carriage and ensured she sat on the opposite side from him. When Mr. Darcy entered after them, Mr. Bennet looked pointedly at the seat next to Elizabeth and said:

"Would you not much rather sit next to my lively daughter, Mr. Darcy? It would be vastly more agreeable than sitting next to your future father-in-law, I am sure."

Mr. Darcy surveyed the situation for the briefest of moments before he took a seat beside Elizabeth, apparently deciding that a rather mild breach of propriety was well worth the reward of being able to converse quietly with Elizabeth.

Mr. Bennet looked on with satisfaction, saying, "It shall be our secret. Now, if you would be so good as to confine your lovers' speech to low murmurings, I shall enjoy my excellent book."

Elizabeth and Mr. Darcy needed no further encouragement, and in this pleasurable manner, they passed the time it took to travel to the inn, where they disembarked for the night.

The next morning, they took a leisurely breakfast and then departed for Rosings. The inn in which they had spent the night was no more than an hour from the great lady's estate, and all too soon, they had arrived before the entrance to Rosings.

They were expected, as Mr. Darcy had sent a note that morning announcing their arrival, and they were swiftly ushered into the formal parlor to wait upon Lady Catherine and her daughter. The moment they entered, Elizabeth felt the weight of Lady Catherine's curiosity bear down on her, and though Anne de Bourgh was the same frail and quiet thing that she had been months before, she also regarded them with an expression of inquisitiveness, the likes of which Elizabeth had never witnessed upon her face.

"Welcome, nephew," said Lady Catherine. "I was most surprised to receive your message this morning, not to mention to hear of your . . . singular choice in traveling companions. Why, I had not even known that you were in the area!"

"Good morning, Lady Catherine, Anne," said Mr. Darcy, bowing to his relations. "I believe that you are both acquainted with Miss Elizabeth Bennet. I would like to present her father, Mr. Henry Bennet. Mr. Bennet, this is my aunt, Lady Catherine de Bourgh, and this is my cousin, Miss Anne de Bourgh. Lady Catherine is my mother's sister."

Mr. Bennet bowed to the ladies. "I am delighted to make your acquaintance, madam," said he to Lady Catherine with a broad smile. "I have heard much about you, both from my daughter and from your parson, Mr. Collins. I assure you that none of Mr. Collins's effusions have been exaggerated."

"Indeed," replied Lady Catherine with some indifference before she turned her attention back to Mr. Darcy. "You have still not answered my question, Darcy. Have you been long in the area, and if so, why have you not visited before?"

"I have spent this last month complete in Brighton, Lady Catherine."

"In Brighton!" cried Lady Catherine. "I suppose you visited there for the sea bathing, though I do not know what could have kept you for so long—Brighton is nothing compared to London, after all. I know nothing so invigorating as sea bathing, and I suppose there are few who could appreciate its benefits so much as myself. Anne would have appreciated it in a similar manner, of course, had her health permitted her participation in the activity."

"Indeed, sea bathing is a most wondrous pursuit," said Mr. Darcy, "but I did not spend an excessive amount of time in the channel. I assure you that I was most agreeably engaged in many other pursuits."

The soft smile he directed at Elizabeth as he said this caused her to blush slightly, but she gamely returned his smile and refused to allow herself to be embarrassed.

Lady Catherine, unfortunately, did not miss the look which passed between them, and her brow furrowed with suspicion.

"And why were *you* in Brighton, Miss Bennet?"

"I was staying with my friend, Harriet Forster, who is wife to the colonel of the militia regiment which was recently quartered in Meryton."

"And there you had the good fortune to once again be noticed by my nephew?"

"Indeed, I did," said Elizabeth, ignoring the churlishness of Lady Catherine's inquisition.

"You cannot imagine my surprise when I arrived in Brighton to see Mr. Darcy again, Lady Catherine," interjected Mr. Bennet. "Though I had known that they had visited Kent at the same time in the spring, I had not realized that their acquaintance was so extensive. I believe that my daughter has not been as open with her old Papa as she once was."

It was clear by her ladyship's expression that she was not at all pleased with the direction in which this discussion appeared to be going. Mr. Darcy, however, was not about to let her launch into her displeasure without first making his announcement.

"I assure you, Lady Catherine," said he, neatly interrupting her before she could speak, "that it was it was *my* good fortune to renew my acquaintance with Miss Bennet. In fact, I have some very happy news to announce—Miss Bennet has done me the very great honor of accepting my proposal. We are to be married."

Had Elizabeth not witnessed it, she was not certain she could have imagined the unhealthy purple hue which spread over Lady Catherine's face. But though her ladyship had instantly descended into a rage of apoplectic proportions, no words issued from her mouth.

Surprisingly, it was Miss de Bourgh who responded first. She stood and approached Elizabeth and Mr. Darcy, and then she leaned over to kiss her cousin on the cheek.

"Congratulations, Fitzwilliam," said she. "I am very happy for you, and I am sure that Miss Bennet will make you an excellent wife."

Turning to Elizabeth, she sat on her other side and grasped her hand. "I am very happy for you, Miss Bennet, though I own that I must question your judgment. Taking on my dour cousin and his antisocial moods is quite the undertaking. Are you certain you are up to the challenge?"

Though Elizabeth was astonished at this side of Anne de Bourgh, which she had never before seen, she recovered quickly and replied: "I have determined I shall have to laugh him from his taciturnity, Miss de Bourgh. I dearly love to laugh, and I will have to ensure my companion laughs as well."

"Good girl," said Miss de Bourgh in response, directing a smirk at Mr. Darcy.

"I assure you that I shall have no hesitation in indulging my wife in anything she shall desire, whether it be a laugh or the entirety of my holdings," said Mr. Darcy.

Elizabeth began to smile fondly at Mr. Darcy, but it was at this point that Lady Catherine finally found her voice, and it quickly became evident that her ladyship was not about to relinquish her dream of uniting Rosings and Pemberley without a fight.

"Anne! Darcy! What is this nonsense? You both know very well that you are betrothed to each other, and no pretentious, fortune-hunting country upstart shall come between you!"

Lady Catherine's outburst was met with a mixed chorus of responses. From her daughter, it was a mortified "Mother!"; from Mr. Bennet, it was an offended, "Madam!"; and from Mr. Darcy, it was a disgusted "Aunt!" Only Elizabeth did not immediately cry out, though it was not for a lack of desire. Instead, she gazed steadily at the woman, containing her own feelings of offense and anger with what she thought to be an admirable measure of self-control. Certainly, she would have enjoyed immediately lashing out at the woman. Lady Catherine deserved to be put in her place—and to discover that not everyone would fawn over her as Mr. Collins did.

Yet Elizabeth had known from the beginning that this would not be a pleasant scene, and she did not want to worsen it by saying things she would regret later. It was important to Mr. Darcy to maintain good relations with his aunt—though one would think he might enjoy the thought of being severed from the meddling woman forever!—and so it was important to Elizabeth, too, though only grudgingly. Even though she did desire to say several less than polite things to Lady Catherine, she would maintain a semblance of civility for as long as possible. She would try to prevent the woman from goading her.

Elizabeth did not wait long to speak, knowing someone else would soon step in once the shock of Lady Catherine's openness—and outright rudeness—had worn off. She began: "Lady Catherine, I can assure you that I am no fortune-hunter—"

"I have seen her kind before, nephew," interrupted the great lady, an expression on her face such as one might wear when standing near a foul-smelling animal. "Women of her sort seek out compassionate men—such as yourself—with great estates and fortunes in an attempt to rise in the world. Men are simply a conquest and game to them, trophies to be won for the sake of improving their images and allowing them to attain a higher level of society to which they have no claim. They have no concern for the men themselves—just what their stations in life can bring to them."

"Lady Catherine," said Mr. Bennet, a slight edge to his voice that was far removed from his usual tone of sardonic amusement, "I can assure you that my Elizabeth is not concerned about the size of your nephew's pocketbook. You and I have been in the same room together for less than ten minutes, and I have already taken my measure of you. I can tell you with all sincerity that my daughter has more—"

"What my father means to say," interrupted Elizabeth, knowing Mr. Bennet was about to begin dispensing insults of his own, which would then lead this conversation even faster into acrimony than it was already going, "is that I have more love in my heart for Mr. Darcy than any other man in the world. I care for him on an emotional and intellectual level, not a material one, and I have no desire to influence others' opinions of me simply through marrying one such as he. The idea of doing so is simply abhorrent to me."

"Ha!" cried Lady Catherine. "I suspect you scarcely know what love is, child, and I sincerely doubt you are as insensible of how others view your situation as you claim. Furthermore, you do not understand that there are far greater issues than love for integral members of high society such as my nephew to take into account. As I have told you before, it was the dear wish of his mother and mine that he and my daughter marry and unite the two great estates of Pemberley and Rosings. We planned the union while they were both in their cradles, and it shall come to pass. A man of my nephew's station cannot marry one of inferior birth such as yourself, so you need not attempt to exercise your arts and allurements any longer!"

Elizabeth's resolution to restrain her tongue and her temper was forgotten. "Need I remind you, your ladyship, that my father is a gentleman? You appear to have forgotten that fact in your focus on what you have decided is best for Mr. Darcy rather than what he believes is best for himself!"

Mr. Darcy, who had made motions as if to speak more than once, finally managed to say something: "Lady Catherine, I did not bring my future wife here so that she could be insulted. I brought her here because I abhor disguises and evasions. I will not allow her to suffer such abuse."

"Surely, nephew," said Lady Catherine, "you understand that a woman such as this could only bring dishonor to your name! You deserve a wife of much higher stature. You were meant to wed my daughter. A union between the two of you shall bring honor to you both, as is necessary for a marriage. *She* is of your station, not this presumptuous wealth-chasing girl! I tell you, nephew, it is only proper!"

"What is proper is that I marry the woman I choose," said Mr. Darcy coldly. "Need I remind you that the decision of whom to wed remains in the hand of the man who makes the proposal? You have made your wishes clear. I believe I have stated mine."

"Your wishes!" Lady Catherine's words were almost screeched out in her growing anger and frustration. "What of your duty, Darcy, not only to the family, but to Anne and to me as your closest relations? What of the wishes of your late mother? She would most certainly be disappointed if she were alive today to witness the folly of your dalliance with one who is so wholly unsuited to taking her place as mistress of the Darcy estates!"

"I must protest these attacks against my *betrothed* and ask that you cease them forthwith," said Mr. Darcy, his own anger beginning to show through his impressive control. "My mother never spoke to *me* of an agreement concerning Anne and me, and *we* have certainly never desired it either.

"And as for my duty, I see that my primary duty must always be to myself and my estates, and though Miss Bennet is not the daughter of an earl, she is the woman I love and will be an excellent mistress of Pemberley, I am sure."

"So you are prepared to endure the scorn of society for this fortuneless girl?"

"I would endure the scorn of society and more for the woman I love!"

"And surely you exaggerate, Lady Catherine," interrupted Elizabeth. She would not allow her betrothed to bear the sole burden of refuting his aunt's claims, and she felt an urgent desire to stand with him. "Mr. Darcy is a gentleman, not a duke, and the inequality you persist in espousing simply does not exist."

"No, he is not a duke, but he *is* grandson to an earl," said Lady Catherine sharply. "Can your own mother offer you the same lineage?"

"You know very well that she cannot," said Elizabeth evenly.

"Of course she cannot, and your demeanor, your manner of speaking, the very way you carry yourself — why, everything about you confirms the fact of your inferior birth. Mark my words, Darcy," continued she, turning back to her nephew, "if you continue along this path, you will set yourself up for censure. You will be despised by the world and will degrade your noble lineage irrevocably."

"Really, Lady Catherine," said Mr. Bennet, "I believe that Mr. Collins's effusions and flattery have induced you to believe his drivel."

"I have nothing to say to you, Mr. Bennet," replied Lady Catherine with a sniff of disdain. "You should know better than to encourage your daughter to quit the sphere in which she was raised. I am well aware of your family's situation and the manner in which you seek to raise your fortunes through marriage. I tell you that I will not have it!"

"I would ask you not to speak to my future father-in-law in such a manner, Lady Catherine," said Mr. Darcy, his voice now as cold as ice. "If you must blame someone, then blame me, for it was I who pursued Miss Bennet, it was I who proposed marriage to her, and it was I who brought her here to introduce her as my betrothed to my relations out of a courtesy to you. And hear me well, Aunt — it *is* a courtesy to you as sister to my mother. I will not have Miss Bennet abused by you or anyone else."

"My brother the earl!" cried Lady Catherine. "*He* will support me in this! He will force you to bend your stiff neck and give up this girl."

"You place an excessive level of confidence in the ability of *anyone* to move me from my purpose," said Mr. Darcy. Elizabeth quickly saw his implacable expression and knew what it meant, having seen it many times herself. She put her hand on his arm in wordless support, thrilled that he was the kind of man who would not only be an ideal husband, but an ideal protector as well.

Mr. Darcy glanced at her with a smile and put his free hand atop hers before turning his attention back to his aunt. "Lady Catherine, I would ask that you cease your attempts to influence me and intimidate my betrothed. Those of my true friends will support me as they always have. Why should I care about the rest of the world?"

Throwing her hands up in the air, Lady Catherine turned her formidable stare on Elizabeth.

"What will it take, Miss Bennet?"

Nonplussed by the seeming non sequitur, Elizabeth frowned. "I have not the pleasure of understanding you, Lady Catherine."

"I wish to know what it will take for you to break this ridiculous engagement," snapped the great lady in response. "As it has not been announced, it may be put aside with little difficulty. I shall provide you with whatever you require in order to ensure this travesty never takes place."

"Mother!" cried Anne. "I demand that you cease these slanderous attacks on Miss Bennet before you drive my cousin from our lives forever!"

"You believe I can be *bought?*" asked Elizabeth, scarcely able to believe the audacity of the woman. She had known her ladyship to be capable of much, but this was almost beyond comprehension. "You may find it difficult to believe, but I can assure you that Mr. Darcy's love has proven priceless to me—"

"All women of your kind have a price," said Lady Catherine, scorn more than evident in her voice. "You need only name yours, and I shall gladly pay it to maintain the purity of my nephew's line."

"You presume too much," said Mr. Darcy darkly, the expression on his face powerful enough to cow a raging lion. "I refuse to remain here any longer. Your insults have gone too far, and as I have said, I will not allow my future wife to suffer such abuse. Not even if you were the queen of England—which you assuredly are not—would I remain here a moment longer. My feet shall not grace your doorstep again until you have offered an apology to the three of us. Come, Elizabeth, Mr. Bennet."

As Elizabeth and her father—neither knowing precisely what to say—moved to follow Mr. Darcy, Lady Catherine screeched after them in a voice filled with desperation: "Nephew, you cannot do this! Miss Bennet, you cannot support him in this travesty! Simply name your price, and I will pay it instantly! Surely your sisters could do with higher dowries, could they not?"

Though the woman followed them a short distance, continuing to plead in a similarly ridiculous fashion, she did not follow them out to the carriage, for which Elizabeth was grateful. Likely, her ladyship merely wanted to preserve some small shred of dignity, but no matter the reason, Elizabeth was grateful. While it was doubtful that Lady Catherine would stay away forever—the woman's desire to dictate the lives of others would certainly not allow that—Elizabeth could not help but find solace in the thought that it would be some time before the domineering woman would be able to swallow her pride long enough to actually offer an apology.

It was not long before the three travelers were well on their way in the journey to Hertfordshire, and though Elizabeth had hoped to make a visit to her good friend Charlotte at the Hunsford parsonage, she refrained from making the suggestion, in large part because it would mean seeing Mr. Collins, which was not something she was certain any of them would be able to do with equanimity.

Though the travel was somewhat exhausting after what they had endured, when they came to the Gardiners' home, where they would be staying for the night, Elizabeth was glad to see people she loved so dearly and was doubly thankful that the Gardiners had returned from their travels in the North Country. She was soon inundated with questions from her aunt, and while she had to promise the Gardiners to secrecy—it would not do to have Mrs. Bennet discover they had learned the joyous news before she had—Elizabeth was glad to tell them of her engagement with Mr. Darcy. Fortunately, her aunt knew she was tired from the journey, so it was not long before Elizabeth was able to retire and allow her mind some much-needed rest.

The next day brought more travel, of course, but when at last she stepped out of the carriage to look at Longbourn, she gave Mr. Darcy a smile that was truly content. He gave her an answering smile that buoyed her emotions even further. Despite all the Wickhams and Lady Catherines of the world, she had a blessed future before her. Nothing could tarnish her happiness. She and Mr. Darcy would face the world together, and it had already been proven that they would be able to face anything.

She soon met an onslaught of information and queries from her sisters and mother, and it was not long before the truth of the engagement came out. Then she had to handle the effusions of her mother, which was much easier for her to do than it was for Mr. Darcy, who she was certain would never enjoy being in the same room with Mrs. Bennet. It was all as she expected, except for one part of some sorrow in the middle of the chaotic happiness when Kitty asked about Mr. Denny.

A bit puzzled, Elizabeth nonetheless was compelled to reveal the man's unfortunate fate, only to be confused even further when Kitty suddenly began to weep. After a few minutes of consoling her sister with the aid of dear Jane, Elizabeth succeeded in inducing Kitty to speak.

"We were writing to each other," said Kitty in between her sobs. "We have been doing so in secret ever since the militia left Brighton."

"Kitty!" said Elizabeth in surprise. "You were not secretly engaged, were you? Why would you write to him?" She glanced at her mother, who was across the room, speaking to Mr. Darcy of her excitement concerning the impending wedding, much to the discomfort of his ears and the fraying of his mood. Elizabeth was only thankful that Mrs. Bennet would not be privy to this discussion with Kitty. Lydia would not be either, for that matter, as she had stalked from the room a few minutes before, upset at the amount of attention Elizabeth was receiving.

"We were careful to make sure no one found out," said Kitty. "Oh, that Mr. Wickham should have killed him! I suspected him of ill, but not something so terrible as that!"

"What do you mean?" asked Jane with a frown.

"Denny expressed his concern about Mr. Wickham to me," said Kitty. "Lizzy, Denny heard Wickham say something derogatory about you, and that made him wary. Then when he saw Wickham's horrid behavior, he felt he needed to try to protect you, for my sake and your sake. But he never thought Wickham would truly hurt you, and he assured me he would keep you from harm."

"Were you writing to him on your trip with the Gardiners?" asked Elizabeth.

"No, it stopped when I left with them. But I meant to resume our correspondence when I returned the week before—oh, if I had only realized just how dangerous Wickham was! Dear, dear Denny! Oh, Lizzy, we loved each other!" And then Kitty's tears began anew.

While not convinced that Kitty truly knew what love was, Elizabeth tried to comfort her, and in this, she was assisted once more by Jane, who would obviously need to learn more about what had happened to

Elizabeth when a better opportunity presented itself. Poor Mr. Denny's death truly was the worst thing to have come out of Elizabeth's trip to Brighton, and she would never forget his sacrifice.

But though Elizabeth was and always would be grateful for what Mr. Denny had done, the matter of her sister's impropriety must be addressed. Elizabeth, with Jane's help, spent some time explaining exactly how Kitty was acting improperly and what the consequences could be. Though the girl had made strides in improving herself, it was obvious that no one had ever sat her down and explained such things to her in detail. Needless to say, it was a much subdued Kitty who emerged from that discussion, determined to do better and make her sisters proud. Mr. Denny's death would always be with her, but she was now determined to find someone in her future—someone who would cherish her as her elder sisters' fiancés cherished them.

When Mr. Bingley came to call, Elizabeth was able to witness the loving relationship between her dear sister and the young gentleman, and soon, any concerns she might have had concerning his constancy were allayed. His eyes were filled with Jane, and there was no need for alarm there.

Elizabeth was then able to contentedly sit with her betrothed and enjoy the attentions she received. Though the other Bennets were all of disparate personalities and could sometimes be somewhat improper, they were her family, and she loved them. And the fact that Mr. Darcy was taking the opportunity to become better acquainted with them without any of his former reserve in evidence was merely the final blessing on a wonderful day. Surely, theirs would be a happy marriage, though with two such strong personalities as hers and Mr. Darcy's, it would certainly not be completely smooth. But she was not Jane—she would welcome a little turbulence in her life from time to time.

It was there in the family parlor that she finally felt that all was right with the world.

Chapter XX

$\mathcal{H}$appy was the day when Elizabeth finally made her way to the nearby church and her destiny by the side of the man she loved. The road had been long and arduous, but there was so much promise at the end of it that she could not help but feel it had been worth it.

Years later, the experiences of that summer would be discussed and laughed over, and the time spent in Brighton remembered with fondness and appreciation. For Elizabeth, it was where she had finally acknowledged Mr. Darcy's worth and discovered the feelings of her heart. For her husband, it was where the bitterness of the past had been put to rest and his love for her had finally been requited.

As for the others — both villains and heroes alike — their stories were different, and their experiences led them down various paths, but for the most part, their endings were no less happy than that of the Darcys.

Kitty, though it was many months before she was able to think of Mr. Denny with anything but sadness, was able to recover from her loss. With her sisters' assistance, her improvement was great, and she was introduced to London society the same year as her new sister Georgiana Darcy, and both made it through that first season unscathed. Georgiana eventually made a splendid match with a duke who loved her more than her dowry, and Kitty received her own marriage proposal within a week of Georgiana's. While Kitty's new husband was not of the consequence of Georgiana's, he was a landowner with some fortune, and it was hailed as a wonderful match. The two sisters by marriage remained close to one another throughout the rest of their lives, both in the proximity of their husbands' estates and in the bond they forged in those years before they were married.

By contrast, Lydia, ever the youngest and brashest of the Bennet sisters, never truly grew out of her wild years as her elder sister did. She continued to be loud and obnoxious, demanding attention and behaving with little propriety. It was a minor scandal when she suddenly left Longbourn in the middle of the night and eloped with a ship's captain she had met some months earlier in London. They sailed to the Americas soon after their marriage, and he made something of a name for himself there by questionable means. They did eventually settle in the former colonies, and Lydia never saw her sisters again. And while the elder sisters did feel a certain regret over the estrangement of their youngest sister, it was perhaps in the best interests of all that contact between them was severed.

Mary, ever studious and morally upright, finally met and married a man who was the parson of Kympton near the Darcy estate, and she settled within a few miles of her elder sister. Her improvement had also made her easier to associate with, much like her younger sister, though she was known as a most pious parson's wife. In this and with her many children, she was truly content.

As for Jane, she and Bingley soon gave up the lease to Netherfield and settled in Lincolnshire on an estate which Mr. Bingley finally purchased. Netherfield was a good property, but they found quickly that it was far too close to Longbourn and that if they allowed it, Mrs. Bennet would be mistress of the house rather than her daughter. In Lincolnshire, they found their true home, and though it was further away from the Darcys than either would have wished it to be, it was still near enough that they were able to visit frequently.

And what of the villains? Wickham made good his escape to America, and though agents were dispatched immediately and stepped foot in the new world within a few days of his own arrival, his trail soon grew cold, and no other trace of him was ever found. It was not known for certain what happened to him, but it was suspected that as soon as he had disembarked—with the purses of some of the men on the ship for good measure—he had immediately purchased passage heading west and had disappeared into the vast expanse of the western wilderness. Whether he changed his behavior and became a good citizen with a good life or retained his ways and eventually his luck ran out was never known. However, he never darkened the shores of his home country again.

Lady Catherine severed contact with her nephew and his "disgraceful paramour," and for a time, all congress between them ceased. This, however, did not stop her daughter Anne from attending their wedding and visiting them at Pemberley the next summer. Anne turned out to be far more resilient and impervious to her mother's ways than anyone could have anticipated, and it was soon evident that she had never had any intention of marrying her cousin. It was through Anne's reports that a reconciliation with Lady Catherine was effected, as her ladyship's curiosity concerning her new niece's conduct finally won out, and she made overtures to heal the breach. Elizabeth eventually learned to tolerate her officiousness and overlook her snobbery, though not until the lady was in perfect understanding of the fact that she *could not* browbeat Mrs. Darcy into doing as she wanted.

As for Elizabeth's good friends, their endings were good indeed. Life for Harriet went as expected. She had a beautiful baby girl—whom she named after Elizabeth—and later went on to have even more children. She and Colonel Forster were quite content with their brood, and Elizabeth loved any opportunity she was given to visit with them. Blanche's life, on the other hand, was not quite so predictable, and after she and Colonel Fitzwilliam eloped, they both delighted in confounding his relations—namely, Lady Catherine—and mystifying the upper social spheres of England. Many different circles spoke of their parties, and Blanche maintained her fascination with unique pieces of art. If anything, the passing of years seemed to increase her desire to push acceptable boundaries, and she always had a willing correspondent—and occasionally, a co-conspirator of ideas—in Elizabeth. They were, after all, relations by marriage, and it was only right that relations communicate frequently. At least, so they told their husbands anytime they sent off yet another lengthy letter.

Elizabeth and Mr. Darcy happily had their own brood of children, and Elizabeth named one of her sons after Mr. Denny, grateful for all the young man had tried to do for her.

Marriage did not tame Elizabeth's wit or imagination, and she knew her husband preferred it that way. After all, someone needed to make certain he maintained a more pleasant countenance than that he had first shown in Hertfordshire. She delighted in finding ways to make him smile, and while they had their share of disagreements, they always felt blessed due to the life they had been given together.

Everyone has their share of regrets, and for Elizabeth, it was no different. But she knew she would always be eternally grateful for her decision to travel to Brighton. Mr. Darcy seemed to feel the same way, for every year he suggested they visit once more, and every year, they went. Pemberley was her new home, but Brighton always seemed to be a second home to her. And the Darcy children, as they grew, seemed to feel the same way.

The End.

FOR READERS WHO LIKED *A SUMMER IN BRIGHTON*

ACTING ON FAITH Though Mr. Darcy has no assurances of Elizabeth Bennet's regard after she rejects his proposal, he moves forward in his quest to secure her hand. Unfortunately, neither Caroline Bingley nor Elizabeth's childhood friend Samuel Lucas will make it easy for him.

OPEN YOUR EYES Elizabeth Bennet is forced to reevaluate her opinion of Mr. Darcy when Mr. Wickham contradicts his own words. In the course of her dealings with the two men, she realizes that first impressions can sometimes be deceiving.

WAITING FOR AN ECHO, VOLUME I, WORDS IN THE DARKNESS When Mr. Darcy comes to Hertfordshire to decide between two prospective brides, he has no idea that his eye will be caught by someone so much lower in consequence than him as Elizabeth Bennet.

WAITING FOR AN ECHO, VOLUME II, ECHOES AT DAWN When Elizabeth travels to Kent, she meets Mr. Darcy's prospective brides and faces the consequences of two tragic events. Can her feelings for Mr. Darcy conquer the machinations of a former love interest?

**For more details, visit
http://rowlandandeye.com/**

Coming Spring 2015
from One Good Sonnet Publishing:

A Bevy of Suitors
A Pride and Prejudice Variation

When a chance remark from Mr. Darcy causes Mr. Bingley to rethink which Bennet daughter he wishes to pursue, Elizabeth Bennet finds herself the focus on Mr. Bingley's attentions. Jane encourages her sister to allow herself to determine her feelings for the man, yet Elizabeth finds her eye caught by the more reserved Mr. Darcy. But these are not the only suitors for Elizabeth's hand, as Mr. Wickham and Mr. Collins also prove themselves determined to draw her attention. Though Elizabeth would never have imagined she would be the focus of such attention, she finds herself forced to choose from among her bevy of suitors . . . .

About the Authors

Jann Rowland

Jann Rowland was born in Regina, Saskatchewan, Canada. He enjoys reading and sports, and he even dabbles a little in music, taking pleasure in singing and playing the piano.

Though Jann did not start writing until his mid-twenties, writing has grown from a hobby to an all-consuming passion. His interest in Jane Austen stems from his university days when he took a class in which *Pride and Prejudice* was required reading.

He now lives in Calgary, Alberta with his three children and his wife of almost twenty years.

Lelia Eye

Lelia Eye was born in Harrison, Arkansas. She loves reading and misses the days when she was able to be a part of the community theater group in Harrison.

Lelia has enjoyed writing since she won a short story contest in the sixth grade, and she graduated from the University of Central Arkansas with a Master's degree in English. It was while she was obtaining her undergraduate degree at Hendrix College that she took a Jane Austen class which sparked her interest in *Pride and Prejudice*.

She now lives in Conway, Arkansas, with an adorable toddler, her husband, three dogs, and two cats.

Their blog may be found at
rowlandandeye.com

Made in the USA
Las Vegas, NV
07 January 2025

15996286R00148